The Kangaroo Hunters

Or, Adventures In The Bush

by

Anne Bowman

Double 9
BOOKS

The Kangaroo Hunters
Or, Adventures In The Bush
by Anne Bowman

ISBN: 978-93-62763-71-6

Published by

DOUBLE 9 BOOKS

2/13-B, Ansari Road
Daryaganj, New Delhi – 110002
info@double9books.com
www.double9books.com
Tel. 011-40042856

ABOUT THE AUTHOR

Anne Bowman is an accomplished author known for her masterpiece "The Kangaroo Hunters: Or, Adventures In The Bush." Set against the backdrop of the Australian outback, Bowman's novel immerses readers in a thrilling tale of adventure, survival, and exploration. Through vivid storytelling and richly drawn characters, she captures the essence of life in the bush, weaving a narrative that is both captivating and immersive. "The Kangaroo Hunters" follows the journey of a group of intrepid hunters as they navigate the challenges of the wilderness, encountering danger, camaraderie, and the beauty of the natural world along the way. With meticulous attention to detail and a deep understanding of the Australian landscape, Bowman transports readers to a time and place where every twist and turn of the adventure unfolds with breathtaking intensity. Filled with excitement, suspense, and moments of quiet reflection, "The Kangaroo Hunters" is a testament to Bowman's skill as a storyteller and her ability to transport readers to distant lands through the power of her words.

CONTENTS

PREFACE

The rapid spread of education creates a continual demand for new books, of a character to gratify the taste of the young, and at the same time to satisfy the scruples of their instructors. The restless, inquiring spirit of youth craves, from its first development, food for the imagination, and even the simplest nursery rhymes owe their principal charm to their wonderful improbability. To these succeed the ever-interesting tales of Fairies and Enchanters; and the ardent boy only forsakes Ali Baba and Sindbad for the familiar and lifelike fictions of "Robinson Crusoe," and the hundred pleasant tales on the "Robinson Crusoe" model which have succeeded that popular romance.

It is the nature of man to soar above the common prose of every-day life in his recreations; from the weary school-boy, who relieves his mind, after arithmetical calculations and pages of syntax, by fanciful adventures amidst scenes of novelty and peril, and returns to his labors refreshed, to the over-tasked man of study or science, who wades through his days and nights of toil, cheered by the prospect of a holiday of voyaging or travelling over new scenes.

This spirit of inquiry has usually the happiest influence on the character of the young and old, and leads them—

"To know
The works of God, thereby to glorify
The great Work-Master."

In this belief, we are encouraged to continue to supply the young with books which do not profess to be true, though they are composed of truths. They are doubtless romantic, but cannot mislead the judgment or corrupt the taste; their aim being to describe the marvellous works of creation, and to lead the devout mind to say with the divine poet,—

"Great are thy works, Jehovah, infinite
Thy power; what thought can measure thee, or tongue
Relate thee?"

A. B.

Richmond, *October*, 1858.

CHAPTER I

"I am a selfish creature, O'Brien," said Mr. Mayburn, the rector of Wendon, to his invalid friend. "I cannot forbear from coming once more to annoy you with my lamentations, and to ask your counsel, for I am most unhappy. Every object I behold, every word I hear, recalls to my mind my bereavement. I cannot remain in this place after the loss of my beloved wife. She was the moving power of my household. It was she, in fact, who was the pastor and director of the parish, the skilful tutor of her children, the guide and the guardian of her weak and erring husband. Alone, I am unfit for my responsible office; I shudder over the conviction that I am faithless to my vows; I know, O'Brien, that I do not fulfil my duty."

"There is an easy remedy for your distress, my good friend," answered Captain O'Brien; "my advice is, do your duty, and be comforted."

"It is physically impossible, O'Brien," said the mourner. "My nerves are shattered; my health is completely destroyed. I shrink from communion with society; and though I exert myself to give my boys their daily lessons, I would afterwards gladly enclose myself in my study, and live amongst my books."

"No doubt you would," replied O'Brien; "but God did not send us into this world to vegetate in solitude, and bring forth no fruit. Act, Mayburn, I beseech you, man; power comes with action, you know well; and whatever man has done, may be done. Work! work! is the counsel of the worn-out dying soldier to him who has yet the labors of life spread before him."

"But you have no idea how feeble my bodily powers are," groaned the rector.

"I can form a very tolerable idea of your strength," said the captain; "for the last time I was out I saw you plunged up to the knees in the green marsh, regardless of a cold north-east March wind."

"I remember the day well," answered Mr. Mayburn, with animation, "for I was fortunate enough to obtain the eggs of the crested grebe in the marsh. You will not have forgotten that the preceding summer I got a fine specimen of the bird."

"Very well," said his friend; "now, if you were able thus to toil and to endure to save the eggs of a bird, you may surely exert yourself still more to save the soul of a Christian. Go more among your poor; talk to them, help them with your knowledge, and teach them to live happily and die happily. I am not without experience in such work, Mayburn; as long as I was able, I had a little flock of my own; and in secular matters at any rate, was a sort of parish priest among my soldiers. I felt an interest in the history and in the daily life of every man in my company, and was never more at home than in the nooks and corners where my poor fellows dwelt. It was this pleasant and profitable work that Mrs. Mayburn ably accomplished for you, and I see Margaret is treading in her steps; go with her, Mayburn, support her in her virtuous course, and you will discover that life has still its pleasures for you."

"Not here! not here! my dear O'Brien," answered Mr. Mayburn. "Sometimes I determine to relinquish this parish, and accept one of smaller population, where the responsibility would be less; at other moments I am prompted to adopt an entirely opposite course, and to make up for my past wasted life by devoting my remaining days to missionary labors in distant lands, where I might be more stimulated to exertion, in the necessity of action. Give me your advice, O'Brien, on which of these two plans to decide. On the one hand, I have the temptation offered me to exchange for a small living on the north-eastern coast, where I should meet with many ornithological novelties; on the other hand, I know I have still sufficient interest among my old friends to obtain the appointment to some mission in the colonies. I should prefer Northern India or South Australia, both affording rich fields to the naturalist."

"A matter of secondary consideration," said O'Brien, smiling. "But wait a month or two, my good friend; we must not decide hastily on such an important step; and before that time has elapsed, you will have fulfilled the last pious offices for me. Do not be agitated, Mayburn. I know that I am dying; these old wounds have slowly, but successfully, undermined the fortress; it cannot hold out long. But be comforted; I am resigned and calm, nay, I am happy, for I know in whom I trust. Now, Mayburn, to you and to your sweet daughter I must bequeath my wild, half-taught boy. Give him all the book-lore he can be made to imbibe; above all, Mayburn, make him a Christian. To Margaret I intrust his physical education. I should wish him to be fitted to perform such work in this world as it may please God to call him to. I am thankful that I must leave him poor, as he will thus be exempt from the grand temptation, and forced into healthy action. May God direct his labors to the best and wisest end."

The words of his dying friend had for some time a salutary influence over the amiable but vacillating Mayburn. With remorse and shame he looked on his own discontent, and with a brief gleam of energy he turned to the duties of his office; but long habits of self-indulgence in literary pursuits and literary ease were not to be suddenly overcome; and when the grave closed over his faithful friend and wise counsellor, O'Brien, he soon shrunk back into morbid, solitary musings, and gradually sunk into his accustomed indolence. But a waking of remorse induced him to write to his old college friend, the Bishop of − −, to pray that he might be allowed to resign his living, and be appointed to some distant mission.

Mr. Mayburn, though upright in principle and amiable in disposition, was yet unfitted, from his deficiency in firmness, for the responsibilities of his office; but his constitutional timidity and indolence had escaped notice during the lifetime of his valuable and energetic wife, who had directed his actions and concealed his feeble nature. But it was the will of God that she should be suddenly called from him; and, stunned with his loss, he abandoned himself to sorrow and inaction. The death of his valuable friend and counsellor, Captain O'Brien, cut away the last prop of the feeble man, who was now alternately sunk in useless grief or haunted with the horrors of neglected duties.

Pious and eloquent, his people declared he was an angel in the church; but in their humble dwellings his visits, like those of angels, "were short and far between." In his family, it was his pleasure to communicate to his children the rich treasures of learning that he possessed; but the lessons of life, the useful preparation for the battle of the world, he had not the skill or the energy to teach.

His daughter, now sixteen years of age, had been ably instructed by her excellent mother, and possessed good sense and prudence beyond her years. Arthur, the eldest son, one year younger, had benefited by his mother's advice and example equally with his sister, whom he resembled in disposition. His brother Hugh, not yet thirteen years old, was too young to have profited much by instruction, and was more volatile than Margaret and Arthur. But the children were all frank, true, and conscientious; and had yet escaped the temptations and perils of the world.

Gerald, the orphan son of the faithful and attached friend of Mr. Mayburn, Captain O'Brien, was the most weighty charge of his timid guardian; though but twelve years old, he was bold, independent, and forever in mischief; and hourly did Mr. Mayburn groan under his responsibility, for he had solemnly promised to fulfil the duties of a father to the boy, and he trembled to contemplate his incapacity for the office.

"Margaret," said he to his daughter, "I request that you or Jenny will never lose sight of that boy after he leaves my study. I am continually distracted by the dread that he should pull down the old church tower when he is climbing to take the nests of the harmless daws, or that he should have his eyes pecked out by the peacocks at Moore Park, when he is pulling the feathers from their tails."

"Do you not think, papa," answered Margaret, "that you are partly responsible for his mischievous follies? You have imbued him with your ornithological tastes."

"He has no taste, Margaret," replied her father hastily. "He has no judgment in the science. He has never learned to distinguish the *Corvidæ* from the *Columbidæ*; nor could he at this moment tell you to which family the jackdaw he makes war with belongs. He is negligent himself, and, moreover, he allures my son Hugh from his serious studies, to join him in rash and dangerous enterprises. He is totally deficient in the qualities of application and perseverance. I have a dim recollection, Margaret, of a childish hymn, written by the pious Dr. Watts, who was no great poet, but was really an observer of the habits of the animal creation. This hymn alludes prettily to the industry of the bee, and if you could prevail on Gerald to commit it to memory, it might suggest reflections on his own deficiencies."

"Papa," said Margaret laughing, "Gerald could repeat 'How doth the little busy bee,' when he was four years old, and I do not think that a repetition of it now would make any serious impression on him."

"He has no taste for the higher range of poetry," said his distressed guardian; "and has too much levity to seek knowledge in the direct paths. What would you think of giving him to learn an unpretending poem by Mrs. Barbauld, which describes the feathered tribes with tolerable accuracy. It commences,

'Say, who the various nations can declare,
That plough, with busy wing, the peopled air!'"

"Gerald is not lazy, papa, he is only thoughtless," said Margaret. "Let us hope that a few years will bring him more wisdom; then he will learn to admire Homer, and to distinguish birds like his good guardian."

Mr. Mayburn sighed. "But what shall I do with the boy," he said, "when my duties summon me to distant lands? I am bewildered with doubts of the future. Will it be right, Margaret, to remove you and my promising boys from country, society, and home, perhaps even from civilization?"

"No, no, papa, you are not fitted for a missionary to savages," answered Margaret, "you must choose some more suitable employment. And if you are bent on quitting England, surely you cannot suppose, whatever may be your destination, that we should consent to be separated from you."

"God forbid that it should be so!" exclaimed the father. "But I cannot but feel, my child, that I have been selfish and negligent. Give me some consolation—tell me that you think I may yet do some good in a strange land. I am persuaded that I shall be better able to exert myself among complete heathens than I am among these cold, dull, professed Christians."

"If you feel this conviction, papa," said Margaret, "it is sufficient. When we earnestly desire to do right, God always provides us with work. We must all try to aid you. And Gerald is now our brother, papa; he must accompany us in our wanderings. The boys anticipate with great delight the pleasures of a sea-voyage, and I myself, though I regret to leave my poor people, enjoy the idea of looking on the wonders of the world."

"Then, Margaret," added Mr. Mayburn, "I must trust you and Jenny to watch that giddy boy, Gerald. Warn him of the dangers that surround him. I should never survive if he were to fall overboard. I promised O'Brien much; but, alas! I have done little."

Margaret engaged to use all needful watchfulness, though, she assured her father, Arthur would care for the young boys; and being now convinced that her father's resolution to leave England was earnest and unchangeable, the young girl, assisted by Jenny Wilson, the old nurse, set about the serious preparations for this important change; and when a mission to a remote part of India was proposed to Mr. Mayburn, he found the whole of his family as ready as he was himself to enter into this new and hazardous undertaking.

"I looked for nothing better, Miss Marget, my darling," said nurse Jenny; "and my poor mistress, lying on her death-bed, saw it all plainly. Says she to me, 'Nurse,' says she, 'your good master will never settle after I'm gone. He'll be for shifting from this place; but mind this, nurse, you'll stick to my childer.' And then and there I said I would never leave ye; 'specially you, Miss Marget; where you go, I must go, and I hope God will spare me to nurse childer of yours. Though where you are to meet with a suiting match I cannot see, if master will choose to go and live among black savages."

"Not so bad as that, nurse," said Margaret, smiling. "I trust that our lot may be cast on a more civilized spot, where we may find many of our own countrymen living among the benighted people we are sent to teach; and even they, though ignorant and degraded, are not absolutely savage, neither are they blacks, my dear nurse."

"Well, my child, you know best," answered Jenny. "But there's a sore task laid out for you, that will have all the work to do. Not but what master is a grand hand at preaching, and can talk wonderful, nows and thens, to poor folks; but he cannot get round them as you can. He never seems to be talking to them as it were face to face, but all like preaching to them out of his pulpit; and somehow he never gets nigh hand to them. But it's God will, and, please Him, we must all do our best; we shall be missed here; and oh, Miss Marget, what will come of poor Ruth Martin? and we promising to take the lass next month, and make a good servant of her. Here's Jack, too; just out of his time, a fair good workman, and a steady lad, and none but you and master to look up to, poor orphans."

"Do not be distressed, nurse," replied Margaret, "I have thought of all my scholars; I have prepared a list of those I wish papa especially to recommend to his successor; and perhaps Mrs. Newton will take Ruth on trial."

"She won't do it, Miss Marget," answered Jenny. "I tried her before, and she flounces, and flames, and says all sorts of ill words again the lass, as how she's flappy and ragged, and knows nothing; and when I asked her what she could expect from childer as was found crying over their poor father and mother lying dead under a hedge; she said outright, she should expect they would turn out vagabonds, like them they belonged to. Yes, she said that; after you had given the poor things schooling for six years."

It was not the least of Margaret Mayburn's pangs, on leaving Wendon, that she must be compelled to abandon the poor children of the parish, whom she had long taught and cared for; and she sighed over the incapacity of the rough orphan girl that she now set out with her faithful nurse to visit.

Ruth and Jack Martin had been found one cold morning of winter in a lane leading to the village of Wendon, sitting by the side of the hedge, weeping over the dead bodies of their parents, who had perished from famine and fever, exposed to the storm of the previous night. The children were conveyed to the workhouse, and from their story, and further inquiries, it was made out that their mother had left a tribe of gipsies to marry a railway *navvy*, as the children called their father. He was a reckless, drunken profligate; and after losing his arm from an accident which originated in his own carelessness, was dismissed from his employment, and driven to wander a homeless vagrant. The children said they had lived by begging, and had often been nearly starved; but their mother would never let them steal or tell a lie, and she had often cried when their father came to their lodging very drunk, speaking very bad words, and holding out silver money, which their mother would not touch.

But at last he was seized with a bad fever on the road, and, houseless and penniless, they crept under a haystack; from thence the children were sent to the road-side to beg from passengers, or to seek some farmhouse, where charity might bestow on them a little milk or a few crusts of bread; but the poor wife sickened of the same disease which was carrying off her husband, and in their desperation the wretched sufferers dragged themselves to the road which led to the village, in hopes of reaching it, and finding shelter and aid. But it was too late. In the midst of the beating snow, and in the darkness of a winter's night, the man sank down and died. The wretched woman cast herself down beside him, and, overcome by sorrow and long suffering, did not survive to see the morning light.

The sympathy created by this melancholy event procured many warm friends for the orphans. They were fed and clothed, sent to school, and carefully instructed in that pure religion of which they had formerly had but vague notions. Jack, the boy, who was about eleven years of age when they were orphaned, was a thoughtful, industrious lad; for three years he made useful progress at school, and in the last three years, under a good master, he had become a skilful carpenter. Ruth, who was two years younger than her brother, had inferior abilities; she was rough, boisterous, and careless; and was ever the dunce of the school, till at length the schoolmistress begged she might be put to something else, for she declared she made "no hand at learning." She was then placed with an old woman, who daily complained that "the lass was of no use; she was willing enough; but if she was set to wash the cups, she broke them; and she could not even stir the fire but she would poke it out." At fifteen years old, Ruth was a strong, active girl, extremely good-natured, true, and honest, fondly attached to her brother, and devoted to her kind friends at the rectory; yet, certainly, Ruth was no favorite with the wives of the neighboring farmers, who unanimously agreed that she must have "two left hands," she was so awkward in all her undertakings. Under these untoward circumstances, it had been arranged that Ruth should undergo an apprenticeship in the rectory establishment, to fit her for household service. This event was looked forward to by the girl with great delight, and it was with much regret that Margaret set out to announce to her their plan of leaving Wendon, which must necessarily extinguish her hopes of preferment.

There was still another who would deeply feel their loss; and Margaret was accompanied by her brothers, who were anxious to see their untiring assistant, Jack. It was he who gave his useful aid to them in the construction of bows, bats, leaping-bars, and all the wooden appliances of school-boy sports; and above all the people of the village, the boys murmured most that they must part with Jack.

They found the industrious lad busily engaged in making a new crutch for Nanny, the old woman with whom the orphans lived. "You see, Master Hugh," said he, "poor Ruth happened to throw down Nanny's crutch, and then the careless lass fell over it, and snapped it. I reckon it had been a bit of bad wood; but this is a nice seasoned stick I've had laid by these two years for another purpose, and it comes in nicely; for Nanny was cross, and poor Ruth was sadly put about, and this will set all straight."

At this moment, Ruth, who had been sent out to milk Nanny's cow, entered in woful plight. She had neglected to tie Brindle's legs properly, and the animal, irritated by the teasing bark of an ill-taught little dog, had struggled to extricate itself, kicked Ruth into the mud, and the milk-pail after her, and then run off, pursued by its tormentor; and the girl returned with her dress torn and dirty, and her milk-pail empty. Nanny scolded, Jack shook his head, Margaret gently remonstrated with her for her carelessness, and, worst cut of all, the young gentlemen laughed at her. Then Ruth fairly sat down and cried.

"Well, Nanny," said Margaret, "you must look over Ruth's fault this time, for we have some sad news for you all. We are going to leave Wendon."

Jack threw down his work, and Ruth, forgetting her own vexation, held up her hands, crying out, "Not without me, please, Miss Marget. You promised to try and make me good for something; please do, Miss Marget, and I'll pray God to make me of some use to you."

"But, Ruth," said Hugh, "we are going far away from here, across the wide sea, and among people who neither talk, nor look, nor live as we do."

"How many legs have they, Master Hugh?" asked the awe-struck girl.

"Only two legs, and one head, Ruth," answered he, laughing; "and we feel pretty sure that they will not eat us; but, for all that, I am afraid they are a little bit savage, if they be roused."

"Will you be so kind as to tell me, Mr. Arthur," said Jack, "where you may be going really."

Arthur then explained to Jack the plans of Mr. Mayburn, and assured him they all felt a pang at leaving Wendon; and especially they regretted the parting from the children they had themselves assisted to teach.

"Then let us go with you," cried Ruth vehemently.

"Cannot we both work and wait on you? If I stay here I shall be sure to turn out a bad lass. Jack, honey, we'll not be left behind, we will run after Miss Marget and Mr. Arthur."

Jack was thoughtful and silent, while Margaret said to the weeping girl,—"If we had only been removing to any part of England, Ruth, we would have taken you with us, if it had been possible; but we dare not propose such an addition to the family in a long voyage, which will cost a large sum of money for each of us; besides this, we are going to a country where your services, my poor girl, would be useless; for all the servants employed in cooking, house-work, and washing, are men, who bear the labor, in such a hot climate, better than women could."

"If you please, Miss Margaret," said Jack, eagerly, "I have thought of something. Will you be kind enough to tell me the name of the ship you are to go in, and I will get my master to write me out a good testimonial, and then I will seek the captain, to offer to work for my passage and for that of poor Ruth, if you will agree to try her; for you see, Miss Margaret, we must never be parted. And when once we're landed, please God, we'll take care to follow you wherever you may go."

Margaret was deeply affected by the attachment of the orphans; and though she felt the charge of Ruth would be a burden, she promised to consult her father about the plan, and the brother and sister were left in a state of great anxiety and doubt.

As they walked home, Margaret and Arthur talked of Jack's project till they satisfied themselves it was really feasible; and Arthur believed that, once landed in India, the lad might obtain sufficient employment to enable him to support himself and his sister.

"Oh, Jack will be a capital fellow to take with us," said Hugh. "I know papa will consent, for he could always trust Jack to find the birds' nests, and bring away the right eggs, as well as if he had gone himself. Then he is such an ingenious, clever fellow, just the man to be cast away on a desolate island."

"I trust we shall never have occasion to test his talents under such extreme circumstances," said Arthur; "but, if we can manage it, I should really like Jack to form a part of our establishment. As to that luckless wench, Ruth, I should decidedly object to her, if we could be cruel enough to separate them, which seems impossible. But I shall always be haunted with the idea that she may contrive, somehow, to run the ship upon a rock."

"Oh! do let us take Ruth, Meggie," exclaimed Gerald; "it will be such fun. Isn't she a real Irish girl, all wrong words and unlucky blunders. Won't she get into some wonderful scrapes, Hugh?"

"With you to help her, Pat Wronghead," replied Hugh. "But mind, Meggie, she is to go. Papa will say what you choose him to say; and I will cajole nurse out of her consent."

And serious as the charge was likely to become, it was at length agreed that Jack and Ruth should be included in the party with the Mayburns; and the girl was immediately transferred to the rectory, to undergo a short course of drilling previous to the momentous undertaking.

CHAPTER II

Finally the successor of Mr. Mayburn arrived, was initiated in his office, introduced to his new parishioners, and had promised to supply, as well as he was able, the loss which the mourning poor must sustain in the departure of the charitable family. Mr. Mayburn's old friend, the Bishop of — —, himself accompanied the family to London, directed them in the mode of fitting out for the voyage, and for their new residence, and supplied them with letters of instruction as well as of introduction before he left them. Some weeks of delay followed, and several disappointments; but at length they were induced to embark, with nurse Wilson, Ruth, and Jack, on board the *Amoor*, a good sailing vessel bound to Melbourne, with many passengers; and from thence to Calcutta, with cattle and merchandise; Captain Barton, who commanded the ship, being an old acquaintance of Mr. Mayburn. Established in a large and commodious cabin, Margaret begged that nurse would keep Ruth always with them, for the girl was distracted with the strange objects around her.

"Sit ye down, lass, and hem that apron," said Jenny, in a tone of authority. "Truly, Miss Margaret, I wouldn't go through the last week again to be Queen Victoria herself, God bless her; and all owing to that unlucky lass. Jack is a decent lad, and it's unknown what a help he was about getting the things here safe; but all the folks in London seemed of one mind that *she* was fitter for a ' sylum than for a creditable gentleman's family. It's no good blubbering about it now, girl; just see and mind what you are about, for there's no police here to look after you."

"Did the police really get hold of her, nurse?" asked Gerald. "What fun!"

"I never took her out for a walk, Master O'Brien," answered Jenny, "but they had their eye on her; they marked her at once as one that needed watching—a simpleton! Why, it was no later than yesterday morning when she worked on me, fool-body as I was, to go with her to see St. Paul's; and what did she do then but start from my arm and run right across a street thronged with cabs, and wagons, and omnibuses. I just shut my eyes and screamed, for I never thought to see her again living; and there was such a hallooing among coachmen and cabmen, and such screaming of women, as was never heard. How they got all them horses to stop is just a miracle; but when I looked again, there was a lot of police holding horses' heads, and one man was hauling Ruth right across; and he had his trouble, for when she heard all that hullabaloo, she was for turning back to me through the thick of it. Oh! Miss Marget, wasn't I shamed out of my life when they fetched her back to me at last, and one fine fellow said I had better lead my daughter in a string."

Ruth giggled hysterically at the recital of her adventure, and when Margaret said to her gravely,—"You behaved very improperly, Ruth, why did you leave your kind friend, Mrs. Wilson?"

"Please Miss Marget," sobbed the girl; "it was a window full of bonnie babbies."

"She's just a babby herself, Miss Marget," said Jenny, wrathfully. "It was a fine toyshop she saw, and she had no more sense but run among carriages to it. She's hardly safe shut up here; see if she doesn't tumble into the sea some of these days."

But when Ruth's curiosity and astonishment had somewhat subsided, the quiet and firm government of Margaret, and the watchful care of Jack, had great power over her; though still the wild boys Hugh and Gerald sometimes tempted her to pry into forbidden places, or to join them in some mischievous frolic.

The greater part of the accommodation of the *Amoor* was given up to a gentleman of good birth and property, who was emigrating to Australia. He had obtained a grant of an immense tract of land in the very midst of the country, further north than the steps of the colonists had yet reached. To this remote district he was taking his mother, his young sister, and a younger brother who had studied medicine; and besides these, a number of male and female servants, carpenters, smiths, builders, drainers, shepherds, and various workmen likely to be useful in a new colony. These men were accompanied by their wives and children, forming a considerable clan, all depending on their worthy and energetic chieftain. The vast amount of goods brought out by all these emigrants, much that was useless, as must ever be the case, among the useful, had heavily laden the vessel.

The Mayburns and Deverells were drawn together as much by kindred taste as by inevitable circumstances, and they soon became as true friends as if they had been intimately acquainted for years. Edward Deverell, with promptness and practical knowledge, managed the affairs and smoothed the difficulties of the Mayburns; while Mr. Mayburn instructed the ignorant, and, at the desire of the captain, a right-minded man, daily read the morning and evening services publicly—a most beneficial practice, producing order and decorum, and implanting in the minds of the young the seeds of future blessing.

"How truly I should rejoice, dear Margaret," said Deverell, "if we could induce your excellent father to join our expedition. I would then undertake to build a church; and might hope for a blessing on my new colony, if the foundation were so happily laid. The climate is declared to be exceedingly salubrious, much more likely to suit you all than the unhealthy air of India. It would be an inestimable advantage to my dear sister Emma; she has never known the care and tenderness of a sister; she needs a more cheerful companion than her good mother, who has delicate health; and you, Margaret Mayburn, are the model I should wish her to imitate."

"I need a sister quite as much," answered Margaret, "to soften my rough points, and your gentle, gay little Emma charms and interests me; but, alas! papa has accepted a duty which he must not relinquish without a trial to fulfil it. I regret that it should be in such a locality for the sake of my brothers."

"You are right, my dear friend," replied he; "observe how happily they are now engaged. Arthur has looked over the dried plants, and he is now dissecting rabbits with my brother. Hugh and your ingenious Jack are at work with my carpenters, making models of broad-wheeled travelling-wagons and canoes for the rivers. Even the mischievous urchin O'Brien is out of danger when he is engaged with my grooms and herdsmen, in attendance on my valuable horses and cattle. What can these ardent boys find to interest and amuse them in the arid and enfeebling plains of India?"

Margaret knew that if her father heard these arguments, they would certainly agitate him, and might even shake his determination to proceed in the undertaking, which she and Arthur were of opinion he was bound to complete. She therefore begged Deverell to use no further persuasions; but she promised him, that if the Indian mission was beyond the physical or mental strength of her father, she would try to induce him to return to Melbourne, and from thence they would endeavor to make their way to the station of Mr. Deverell, who had promised to leave directions for their progress with his banker at Melbourne, which he proposed to make his mart for business.

It was truly the fact, that in pleasant employment no one found the long voyage tedious. Jack was especially charmed with his increase of knowledge. "You see, sir," said he to Arthur, "I was qualified to make a four-post bedstead, or a chest of drawers, as well as the best of these chaps;

but they tell me them sort of things isn't much needed in them forrin parts. But what they've brought along with them is quite another thing: frames for wooden houses, ready to nail up in no time; mills and threshing machines; great, broad-felloed wagons for their rough roads, and boats of all makes. Just look, Mr. Arthur, I've made bits of models of all them things, you see. We can't say but they may turn up useful some day."

Even Ruth the unlucky lost her cognomen, and became popular among the emigrant women; for when kept quietly at regular employment, she could be steady and useful; it was only when she was hurried, or thrown upon her own responsibility, that she lost her head, and blundered into mischief. She nursed the babes tenderly and carefully, helped the poor women to wash their clothes, and for the first time in her life began to believe she might be of some use in the world. Gerald, who always insisted on it that Ruth was not half so bad as she was represented, assured Jenny that all the girl's errors arose from improper management. "You do not appreciate her talents justly, nurse," said he. "She is quite a genius, and ought to have been Irish, only she was born in England. You have wronged poor Ruth; you see she has never drowned a *babby* yet."

"Well, Master O'Brien, wait a bit, we're not through our voyage yet," said Jenny, oracularly.

"The Ides of March are not gone, she would say," said Hugh.

"I didn't mean to say no such thing, Master Hugh," replied she; "you're so sharp with one. I'm not so daft, but I know March is gone, and May-day ought to be at hand; not that we can see any signs of it, neither leaves nor flowers here, and I cannot see days get any longer. How is it, Master Arthur? Is it because we're atop of the water?"

Arthur endeavored to make Jenny comprehend the natural consequences of their position, now within the tropics, and daily drawing nearer to the equator; but he only succeeded in agitating the mind of the old woman, without enlightening her.

"God help us!" she exclaimed. "Nigher and nigher to the sun! It's downright temptation and wickedness, my dears; and my thought is, one ought to stay where it has pleased Him to plant us. And think ye, Master Arthur, we shall all turn black, like them niggers we saw in London streets."

"No; certainly not, nurse," answered Arthur. "It requires hundreds of years, under a tropical sun, to change the color of Europeans. Besides, the negroes, although we are all children of Adam, are of a distinct race from us. We are certainly not, like the thick-lipped negroes, the descendants of Ham."

"Likely he had been the plainest of Noah's family," said Jenny, "for beauty runs in the blood, that I'll stand to," continued the attached nurse, looking round with complacency on her handsome young nurslings.

To the young voyagers there was an indescribable charm in the novelties which the sea and the air offered to them in the tropical region they had now entered. Now for the first time they beheld the flying-fish rise sparkling from the waves, to descend as quickly; escaping for a short time from its enemies in the waves to expose itself to the voracious tribes of the air, who are ready to dart upon it. And sometimes the elegant little Stormy Petrel, with its slender long legs, seemed to walk the waters, like the fervent St. Peter, from whom it derives its name.

"But is not this bird believed to be the harbinger of storms?" asked Margaret of her father, as he watched with delight the graceful creature he had so often desired to behold.

"Such is the belief of the sailors," answered he, "who have added the ill-omened epithet to its name. It is true that the approach, or the presence, of a gale, has no terror to this intrepid bird, the smallest of the web-footed tribe. It ascends the mountainous wave, and skims along the deep hollows, treading the water, supported by its expanded wings, in search of the food which the troubled sea casts on the surface:

'Up and down! up and down!
From the base of the wave to the billow's crown,
Amidst the flashing and feathery foam,
The Stormy Petrel finds a home,'

as a poet who is a true lover of nature has written. Yet it is not always the harbinger or the companion of the storm, for even in the calmest weather it follows a vessel, to feed on the offal thrown overboard, as fearless and familiar in the presence of man as the pert sparrow of London."

"Here, papa!" cried Hugh, "here is a new creature to add to your collection. I know him at once,—the huge Albatross."

With the admiration of a naturalist, Mr. Mayburn looked on the gigantic bird, continuing its solemn majestic flight untiringly for hours after the ship, its keen eye ever on the watch for any floating substance which was thrown from the vessel, and then swooping heavily down to snatch the prize voraciously, and circling round the ship, again to resume its place at the wake.

"I see now," said he, "why Coleridge wrote,—

'The Albatross did follow,
And every day, for food or play.
Came to the mariner's hollo!'

But the poet mistook the habits of the bird entirely when he added, that 'on mast or shroud it perched.' The difficulty of expanding its wing of five joints, so immensely long, would impede its rising from the mast of a ship; it scrambles along the waves before it can rise above them; and it has been well said, 'The albatross is the mere creature of the wind, and has no more power over itself than a paper kite or an air balloon. It is all wing, and has no muscle to raise itself with, and must wait for a wind before it can get under sail.'"

The family were assembled on deck in the close of the evening, after the fervid heat of an equatorial sun, and they beheld with enjoyment the wonders of the deep; but the old nurse seemed disturbed and awe-struck.

"Every thing seems turned topsy-turvy here," said she. "Days far hotter nor ever I mind them, and May-day not come; fishes with wings, flying as if they were birds, and birds walking atop of the water, as if it were dry land. It's unnatural, Miss Marget, and no good can come on it, I say."

"Ah! if you were but going with us, Mrs. Wilson," said Charles Deverell; "then I would engage you should see wonders. You should see beasts hopping about like birds, and wearing pockets to carry their young ones in; black swans and white eagles; cuckoos that cry in the night, and owls that scream by day; pretty little birds that cannot sing, and bees that never sting. There the trees shed their bark instead of their leaves, and the cherries grow with the stone outside."

"Now, just hold your tongue, Mr. Charles," answered nurse, angrily. "Your brother would scorn to talk such talk; but you're no better than Master Gerald, trying to come over an old body with your fairy stories."

"It is quite true, Mrs. Wilson," said Emma Deverell, "and I wish you were all going with us into this land of enchantments. Then, Margaret, dear Margaret, how happy we should be. You should be queen, and we all your attendant sylphs, and

      'Merry it would be in fairy-land,
      Where the fairy birds were singing.'"

"Merry for you, little wild goose," said her brother Edward; "but Charles has told you the fairy birds do not sing; and our sylph-life will be one of hard labor for many months before we make our fairy-land and court lit to receive our queen. Then we must try and lure her to us. How shall we contrive it, Emma?"

Margaret smiled and shook her head. "Too bright a dream," said she, "to be safely indulged in. But you must tell us all you propose to do, and we will watch your progress in fancy."

"Oh, do tell us all about it, Edward," said Hugh. "But, first of all, make a dot upon my map, that we may know where you are when we come to seek you."

"Very prudent, Hugh," answered Edward, "though I doubt the accuracy of my dot on this small map; but I suppose I shall not be more than a hundred miles wrong, and that is nothing in the wilds of Australia."

"But I see you will be close on this great river that falls into the Darling," said Hugh; "so if we only follow up the rivers, we must find you."

"You would not find that so easy a task as it seems, my boy," replied Edward. "Neither are we, as you suppose, close on that river, but fifty miles from it; but we have a charming little river laid down on our plan, which we must coax and pet in the rainy season, that it may provide us with water in the drought."

"You have a most extensive tract," said Arthur, looking on the plan.

"Oh, yes," said Charles, "we propose, you know, to build a castle for ourselves, and a town for our vassals."

"There lies my castle," said Edward, pointing to some large packages which contained the frame of his future abode. "As for the town, I am not without hopes to see it rise some time, and do honor to its name."

"Deverell, I conclude?" observed Arthur.

"So my mother wishes the station to be called," replied he; "but my own 'modest mansion,' I should wish to name Daisy Grange."

"I never understood that the daisy was indigenous in Australia," said Mr. Mayburn.

"Certainly it is not, sir," answered Edward; "but we have fortunately brought out a number of roots of this dear home flower, and will try to domesticate them in our new country; though I fear they will be apt to forget their native simplicity, and learn to flaunt in colors."

"I know why you wish to call your house Daisy Grange, Edward," said Emma, nodding sagaciously at Margaret, and the general laughter showed the little girl had surmised correctly.

"A very pretty and delicate compliment," said Mr. Mayburn: "our own glorious Chaucer speaks of the daisy as—

'La belle marguerite,
O commendable flower, and most in minde;'

and the noble Margaret of Valois, a Christian and a scholar, had the daisy, or *marguerite*, worn in honor of her name, and is herself remembered as the 'Marguerite of Marguerites'."

And thus they amused themselves till, without storm or delay, they had crossed the equator, and entered the South Sea, when a new source of enjoyment was opened to Mr. Mayburn, who had long desired to view the constellations of the south; and favorable weather enabled them to study astronomy every night. Never for a moment did the voyage seem tedious in the cheerful society of the happy families, and all things concurred to render it agreeable. The provisions were excellent, fresh meat and bread, with milk in abundance, prevented them from suffering from change of diet; and constant employment made the moments fly. In the morning the young Mayburns, with Emma Deverell, read with Mr. Mayburn, and studied Hindostanee; and in the evening they walked on deck, listening to the pleasant anecdotes told by Edward Deverell, who had been a great traveller. Then they had music, and occasionally dancing; and if sometimes a light gale tossed the vessel, or swept the dinner from the table, the *contretemps* caused mirth rather than wailing. Mr. Mayburn himself, busily engaged in teaching, lecturing, or in writing and delivering simple sermons to the poor emigrants, recovered his cheerfulness, and once more began to confide in himself.

And so, in good time, they reached the Cape, and Jenny discovered that now, "when May-day was turned," it was far colder than any May-day in England, and put on her warm shawl to land with her young charge to see the town, and to look after that "feckless Ruth." It was a great pleasure to the ardent young people to set their feet on the shores of Africa, to see the vessels of many nations crowding the harbor, and the people of many countries thronging the busy streets, to make excursions to the mountains and vine-covered hills around, and to collect the botanical treasures of a new and fertile region. Mr. Deverell was more usefully engaged with his herdsmen and shepherds, in completing his stock of cattle and sheep, and in making other purchases for his great undertaking; and thus many days were spent pleasantly and profitably.

Once more embarked, a shade of melancholy was perceptible—among the young especially—as they daily approached nearer to the shores where they must be separated; for the two families, so kindred in taste and disposition, had become truly attached during their long voyage; and notwithstanding the pleasant prospect of new scenes and pursuits, they were less cheerful every day. Even Edward Deverell, with his mind crowded with plans for clearing, draining, cultivating, sheep-shearing, and tallow-melting, felt deep regret at the prospect of separation from the lively, intelligent boys, and their amiable and sensible sister; and Margaret herself, usually so composed and contented, sighed to think she must lose the valuable counsel of Edward, the friendly protection of his mild invalid mother, and the warm affection of the sprightly Emma; and every evening, as they walked on deck, they indulged hopes, and sketched plans of meeting again.

After they had entered the Indian Ocean, they had no longer the favorable and pleasant breezes they had so long enjoyed, and while Hugh and Gerald were anxiously looking out for pirates, and talking of Malays, of prahus, and of kreeses, the sailors were watching the signs of the sky, wrestling with contrary winds, and guarding against sudden gales.

"How vexatious," said Hugh, "to be drifted about every way but the right way, and to have all this noise and splashing and dashing, and yet nothing to come of it. Now if we had a grand regular storm, and a shipwreck, and were all cast away on an uninhabited island, it would be an adventure; there would be some life in that."

"More likely there would be death in it," said Margaret. "Do not be so presumptuous, unthinking boy!"

"I should enjoy the thing amazingly myself, Margaret," said Gerald; "so don't you look grave about it. Or what would you think, Hugh, if a great fleet of prahus were to surround us and try to board us, while we, armed and ready for them, were to pour our shots into them, and put the rogues to flight. But first we would take care to capture the fierce pirate captain, and take possession of all his treasures. Then wouldn't we enter Melbourne in triumph, and have the robber hauled up to the gallows."

"Pirates do not usually carry their treasures about in their prahus," said Arthur; "nor do I think it is at all desirable that we should encounter a piratical fleet. Where are your guns to pour down destruction on the foe, Master Gerald?"

"Oh, murther!" cried the wild boy, "wasn't I forgetting the guns! Now, what for did we come in a merchantman, as quiet and dull as a quaker? Well, well, Arty, we have plenty of brave fellows, and our own rifles and pistols, besides knives and dirks. We should defend ourselves like Britons, I'll be bound."

But the next day there was no cause to complain of dulness, for a real gale came on, and all was confusion. The wind roared, the waves rose tremendously, the ship rolled fearfully in a heavy sea, and before night the maintop-gallant was carried away. Then sail was reduced; but louder and stronger grew the tempest amid the darkness of night. Mast after mast was rent away, and the crippled vessel continued to drift helplessly for twenty-four hours, when the violence of the gale began to abate. Signals of distress were made, but long in vain. At length a vessel appeared in sight, and distinguishing their signals, made up to them. It was bound to Melbourne, which was now within a few days' sail, and, with as much kindness as difficulty, the stranger succeeded in taking the disabled *Amoor* in tow, and bringing her into port in safety.

CHAPTER III

Weary, distressed, and suffering, the passengers on the *Amoor* gladly landed on the busy wharf, and were conveyed to Melbourne, where Mr. Mayburn and his daughter, Mrs. Deverell and Emma, were settled in a handsome hotel; but Mr. Deverell and his people, with the young Mayburns, remained at the port to land the cargo and inspect the damage done by the storm. It was soon ascertained that the loss must be considerable—a number of sheep and cattle, besides a valuable horse, had been swept into the sea; and all that had been saved were in bad condition; but it was to be hoped a short rest at Melbourne might restore these, and fit them for their long journey into the interior. Then Deverell had to search for experienced drovers to guide and assist his own men; and finally, he undertook to inquire for the first vessel to Calcutta that could accommodate Mr. Mayburn and his family, as some months must elapse before the disabled *Amoor* could be prepared to resume the voyage.

The girls looked out from the windows of the hotel with admiration at the broad and peopled streets, the handsome churches, and the European aspect of a town on the spot which, but a few years before, had been a lonely wilderness; but the pious Mr. Mayburn called them away to unite with him in thanksgiving for this their first experience of the progress of divine and social knowledge, even into the farthest regions of the earth.

"The spirit which has clothed the desert with the blessings of peace and abundance," said he, "and has planted the gospel of life in a newly-discovered world, will by God's blessing spread onwards like a fertilizing river till the word of the Lord be accomplished; for the blessed day draweth nigh when the scattered people of God shall be gathered into one fold, and the great shepherd shall say, 'Well done.'"

"God speed the day, dear papa," said Margaret. "But we must not be mere watchers; we must all be workers. Wherever we go, we shall find an untilled field, and we must all put our shoulders to the plough."

"You are right, my child," replied he, with a sigh; for though ever willing to fulfil the duty lying before him, Mr. Mayburn wanted resolution to seek out the hard work of the fervent missionary of Christianity. Evening brought to them the fatigued young men with satisfactory news. A vessel, the *Golden Fairy*, which had landed a party of gold-diggers from England, was going forward to Calcutta with sheep and merchandise. The captain, very glad to obtain passengers, readily agreed to accommodate Mr. Mayburn's family; he was to sail in three days, so no time must be lost in making preparations.

"As to my own affairs," added Edward Deverell, "I have succeeded in finding quarters for all my live-stock. The cattle, horses, pigs, and sheep were certainly somewhat unruly; but the women and children ten times more troublesome. Such an amount of bundles, bags, baskets, cradles, and cats as they have brought! How we have housed them all is a miracle; and how we are to get them up the country is a puzzling problem. Finally, I have bought a train of wagons, and engaged two gentlemen as guides, who are her majesty's prisoners, released on *parole*; in fact, two ticket-of-leave convicts."

A scream from Emma, and a groan from her mother, followed this information.

"Surely you have not been so rash, Edward," said Mrs. Deverell. "Let us make our way rather with our own people only. Consider the contamination of such society for our poor virtuous followers. Besides, it is but too probable we may be robbed and murdered by such wretches."

"It is an inevitable evil, mother," answered Edward, "for we cannot attempt the journey without guidance. These men have behaved well since their transportation; they are brothers—poachers—who, like many in their situation, have erred rather through ignorance and weakness than depravity. At least, such is the report of the overlooker who recommended them. They have been out before in the interior with squatters, and know the valleys of the Murray and the Darling, beyond which our ultra-frontier tract is spread. I have been to the Colonial Office, and have obtained the necessary forms for taking possession of fifty thousand acres of *waste land*, as it is called, for a long lease of years. And now, mother, we are, according to the legalized and elegant form, *squatters*."

"*Colonists*, my son; I cannot bear the strange, uncouth word *squatters*," said Mrs. Deverell.

"Nevertheless, mamma," said Edward, laughing, "it is official language. We may call ourselves, if we choose, landed gentry; but the world of Australia will rank us only as part of the *squattocracy*."

"Am I a squatter?" asked little Emma, in dismay; and great was the mirth of her favorite friends, Hugh and Gerald, when Emma was pronounced to be legally a squatter.

Early next morning the two convict guides were admitted to receive their final directions from Mr. Deverell, and were regarded with some uneasiness and much curiosity. One was a rough country lad, dressed in a fustian suit and a fur cap, rude in manner, but of pleasing, open countenance: the other, who was older, had a shabby-genteel appearance; he had discarded his convict's habit, and had expended the earnest-money received from Mr. Deverell in an old suit of black clothes, and a very bad English hat, which he had placed on his head in a jaunty style.

"Please to show me your district by map, sir," said he, bowing at the same time in a very conceited manner to the ladies. "You must look to me, *cartee blank*, sir; for you see, sir, my brother is not intelligible; he has not had the blessing of eddication."

"And your education, my friend," said Edward Deverell, "has not been a blessing to you, I fear. Have you not rather turned it to evil?"

"Quite the *contrairy*, sir," said the man. "I look forrard to its helping me up-hill in this free country. Why, sir, a man born anunder an hedge may top over quality and ride in his carriage here, if he can only come round his parts of speech rightly. But Davy will stick where he is, for he never could tell an X from an *anpassy*."

"It's all true," said the rough rustic, "I'se no scholar like Bill, master, but I'se do my best for ye, and glad to get out from amang yon rogues. It's hard for a lad to be sorted with such company for just sniggling a hare."

"*Ensnaring*, David," said his brother, pompously; "*sniggling* is colloquial."

"Sniggling, you know, Bill," answered David, "our lads call it in t' north country; and little harm is there in't I say, that they should send a poor lad amang thieves and cut-throats. But, please God, I'se out of their way, and it will be mony a day afore I come nigh them again."

"You seem a simple, though ignorant youth," said Mr. Mayburn, "and I cannot understand how it happened you were so severely punished for poaching; though doubtless it is an offence against the law."

Bill laughed contemptuously as he replied for his brother,—"You see, sir, Davy was always a fool, or we need not both have been expostulated to this place. Our master always called him David Simple, and sure enough, if it had not been for his downright idiosyncrasy, we might have got clear off; but nothing would serve him but to show fight."

"Now, just be quiet, Bill, man," said David; "it was for thee I stood out. You'se hear all, master; I'se tell t' truth. Bill had his gun, and brought down a few birds, and I were knocking a few rabbits over, and it chanced to be a moonshiny night, when out pops a keeper, and fells Bill down with a club; and I heard him shout out to me, as how his arm was broken. That aggravated me bitter, and up I ran, and leathered t' fellow well with my stick. Then Bill got up and ran off, but I was fain to stop, and give t' keeper a hiding; but he roared out so loud that two more chaps came up, and first took me, and then went off after Bill. When they got to our lodging, he made as how he knew nought about it, but they found birds and his gun underneath t' bed; and there was his arm all black and blue, but not broken, as he said. So off they carried us to prison, and Bill wanted me to say as how he that were with me were Jack Kay, an auld poacher; but I couldn't swear away a man's *charackter*, and t' keeper took his oath Bill wanted to shut him, and I were no better; so they sent us both over t' water. It's a thousand pities for Bill, for he's a scholar, cute as he is about sniggling."

David was the favorite of the family, who did not admire the flowery language and cunning look of *cute* Bill; but among a horde of lawless men, Edward Deverell congratulated himself that he had been fortunate enough to obtain two men less depraved than might have been expected.

It was with a sinking heart, oppressed with strange forebodings, that Margaret looked on the large, dark, dirty and gloomy ship honored by the inappropriate name of the *Golden Fairy*. She grieved for the separation from the new friends that the whole family had learned to love so well, and she shrunk from the prospect of unknown difficulties and dangers, when all decision and responsibility would be thrown upon her, from the helpless character of her beloved but irresolute parent. During the first voyage, the powerful and energetic character of Edward Deverell had swayed the judgment of Mr. Mayburn; but in future, Margaret felt she could only look to her young brother Arthur for aid.

"Yet have I not a greater aid?" she repeated to herself. "Forgive me, my heavenly Father! Thou art my friend and my counsellor! Let me ever turn to Thee in my trials, and I must be in safety." And thus, with a heart ever recognizing the presence and relying on the love of a watchful God, Margaret Mayburn walked on her way steadily and fearlessly.

The parting of the two families was very painful, yet they cheered themselves with the hope so unquenchable in the young. They talked confidently of their future meeting, the boys traced over and over again on the map the route they proposed to take to Daisy Grange; and, but for Margaret's firmness, even Mr. Mayburn, at the last moment, would have relinquished his hopes of spreading the gospel in the East, to follow the new colonists into the dreary untrodden deserts.

There was an appearance of neglect and disorder in the *Golden Fairy* that was repugnant to the taste of the Mayburns, after being accustomed to the trim, orderly arrangements of the *Amoor*; Edward Deverell pointed out to Captain Markham several necessary changes which must be made for the comfort of passengers who paid him so handsomely, and was annoyed to perceive that his suggestions were received slightingly and almost contemptuously. He himself procured more conveniences for the cabin of his friends, and he besought Margaret and Arthur to be firm and determined with Markham, who seemed careless, and, he suspected, addicted to drinking. Now, when too late, he regretted that he had not induced the family to remain at Melbourne for the sailing of the mail packet; but Arthur had been anxious for his father to hasten to his mission, lest his vacillating nature should lead him to relinquish it. Besides which, the throng of gold-diggers made the cost of living at Melbourne a serious consideration.

Finally, with tears and sorrowful hearts, the friends took leave of each other, with the remote chance that favorable circumstances might bring them together again; and it was not till the fair sunny shores of Australia had faded from their sight, that the voyagers retired to their cabin to endeavor to resign themselves to their changed circumstances.

The want of order in their new home was particularly trying to the scarcely-reclaimed Ruth. She had learned to be useful among the emigrant women in the neatly-ordered *Amoor*; but she soon relapsed into her usual heedless habits, amidst the scattered packages and general confusion in the *Golden Fairy*. She stumbled over boxes which were not stowed in their proper places, she was thrown down by some terrified sheep that had escaped from its pen, she trod to death some rambling chicken that had found its way into the cabins, or she destroyed the cups and plates by officiously spreading the table in the midst of a gale, though she had been warned of the consequences.

"Margaret," said Mr. Mayburn, who had been uneasily watching the girl's unlucky movements, "I am of opinion that poor Ruth should be subjected to some restraint I observe that the inevitable result of her undertakings is destruction. She is a curious study; nor can I solve the mystery why she should always do wrong when she designs to do right I am alarmed, Margaret; I eat my food in terror, lest she should have poured laudanum into the curry, or scattered arsenic over the pudding."

"Have no fear, papa," answered Margaret. "Ruth is never intrusted with culinary preparations: the cook is too cross to allow her to touch any of his dishes, nor has she the means of procuring any of those dreaded poisons. I do not fear that she will harm any one but herself with her heedlessness;

but, poor girl, she is covered with bruises and cuts from falls. Nor is she entirely to blame, for the cabins are filled up with packages which Arthur says ought to be stowed in the hold. We must, however, make up our minds to be inconvenienced for the short time I trust we shall be shut up in this prison."

"That I could do, my child," answered he; "but I fear Markham is not a man of understanding to depend on in emergency. This is a sea of perils, of storms and pirates. What would become of us if any of these dangers assailed us? Arthur, you look disturbed; you think with me, that Markham is unfit for his situation."

"Truly, papa, I have some doubts of him," replied Arthur. "I think he must be an experienced sailor, for he has made this voyage many times; and I should not have lost confidence in him, if I had not actually seen him intoxicated. And I fear he is utterly unprincipled, for he wanted us to join him in his nightly revels. Now, Margaret, if a storm should come on in the night, I feel assured that he would be incapable of giving orders."

"And a pretty set of queer-looking boys he has fished up at Melbourne," said Gerald, "to man the ugly ship. Hugh and I have marked our men, and haven't they *rogue* written on their black brows!"

"But, Gerald, is it not somewhat unkind to form so hasty a judgment?" said Margaret. "These sailors are strangers; why do you class them as rogues?"

"Because, Meggie," said Hugh, "Gerald saw with his own eyes a lot of fellows in their yellow convict dress brought up for Markham to choose a crew from, for all his own men had deserted to go to the diggings. And we both agree that he must have picked out the most villanous-looking of the lot. Now, just come up with us, Meggie, and take a look at the fellows, and you shall hear what Jack says."

Margaret went on deck with her brothers, to walk round the disorderly place; and, under the pretext of examining the various parts of the ship, she carefully marked the faces of the men she encountered, and could not deny that they were not only coarse and bold, but that most of them had the fierce, sinister, lowering expression which usually distinguishes the convict. She stopped to speak to Jack, who was busily engaged finishing a model he had begun at Melbourne, of one of the light-hung, commodious, broad-wheeled travelling wagons Mr. Deverell had bought at that place.

"I could easily make one for you, Miss Margaret," said Jack, "if it were needed; but they tell me you'll want no wheeled-carriages yonder. More's the pity. I wish master had been persuaded to stay with Mr. Deverell. I don't half like this, for, oh! Miss Margaret," added he, looking around, "we've got among a bad lot."

"What have we to fear, Jack?" asked she, pale with fear.

"Don't be down-hearted, miss," said the lad; "but I doubt we may have awkward work; for when Captain Markham is in his cups, everybody's master. But please God to send us fair winds, we shall soon get through the voyage."

"We must pray for His help, Jack," said Margaret; "and let us avoid these men as much as possible. You, Jack, as well as my brothers, must remain below; better endure confinement than encounter wickedness."

"And please, Miss Margaret," continued Jack, "would you ask Mrs. Wilson to mind and keep Ruth close; for these saucy fellows amuse themselves with sending her on some foolish errand, and getting her into mischief. I near had a fight with that big brute, the mate, for pitching her over a hencoop; but Wilkins, that little sharp fellow at the masthead, got me away."

Margaret and Arthur had many long and serious conversations on their uncomfortable position, particularly when their voyage was retarded by the contrary winds of that uncertain sea. Then the family secluded themselves in the two crowded cabins appropriated to their use, and endeavored, by prayer and regulation of the mind, to prepare themselves for the dangers into which such an ill-ruled vessel might be hurried.

After a day of great vexation, occasioned by the carelessness of Ruth, who had, by some mischievous device of the sailors, let all the poultry loose, and had been compelled by the violent captain to hunt them up from every corner of the vessel, the girl had been summoned before Margaret and Jenny, to be rebuked for her thoughtless conduct. She wept, and promised to improve, and was sent to her berth, Nurse declaring that she had made up her mind never to lose sight of her all the next day. Then, after meeting for prayers in Mr. Mayburn's cabin, they returned, to seek such repose as their close, uncomfortable berths afforded.

It might have been two or three hours after this, when Margaret awoke with a strange feeling of oppression and fear, which she vainly attempted to shake off. At length, she called out from her berth, "Nurse, are you awake? Will you go on deck with me for a few minutes? I long for the refreshment of the night air, for the cabin is more suffocating than usual to-night. Surely a storm must be at hand, for the air is positively scorching."

Jenny yawned and murmured, till at length, becoming aware of the request of her young mistress, she scrambled from her awkward berth; but no sooner was she on her feet, than, thoroughly awakened, she exclaimed, "God have mercy on us! for there must be something on fire. I smell and feel it must be so!"

Margaret sprang up, trembling in every limb, but firm in heart, to rush through the door that separated the cabins, and arouse her father and brothers. Jenny, in the mean time, opened the outer door, and then the smell of burning wood was plainly perceptible. While Mr. Mayburn and his sons hastily got ready, Margaret proceeded to the cabin of Capt. Markham, and knocked loudly in her fright, crying out almost unconsciously as she knocked, "Fire! fire!"

"Who calls fire?" cried Markham, with a bitter oath. "Who dares to say that?" and his head appeared from the cabin door. His voice was husky and broken, and Margaret feared he was intoxicated and might not comprehend her, as she rapidly narrated her observations and her fears. Deep and horrible were the curses of the wicked man, as he staggered forward, screaming and yelling for the watch. That there was any watch in this disorderly establishment, Margaret doubted. She hurried back to her father; and they were soon alarmed by the sounds of dreadful curses, the trampling of many feet, the ringing of bells, and the cries of the disturbed and terrified sheep. Arthur and Hugh were sent up to ascertain the fact of danger, and they found the lazy crew effectually roused to action; lanterns were flying about in different directions; and at length the fatal cry was heard, "Fire in the after-hold!"

CHAPTER IV

Then the harsh voice of Markham was heard pouring out orders, loud, but almost inarticulate with rage and drunkenness; while, regardless of his awful situation, with fearful blasphemy he imprecated curses on the negligence which had caused the accident, and on the tardiness of action among his insubordinate crew. At length the fire-engine was got to work; lengths of leather hose were stretched down to the burning hold; buckets were rapidly passed from hand to hand; and the splashing of water was followed by the hissing of the flames.

The four young men joined the sailors and worked manfully at the engine or with buckets, while Mr. Mayburn, alternately trembling, weeping, and despairing, and then, in earnest prayer, regaining his firmness and resignation, occupied the care and attention of Margaret almost entirely. Jenny, with practical good sense, was collecting the most valuable part of their property.

"If we be not burnt to death first, Miss Marget," she said; "Jack tells me we shall be took off in boats, God help us! so it's time to be making ready. Come, lass!" to Ruth, "and tie this bag. What ails ye, you simpleton? What are you staring round in that fashion for?"

Ruth was gazing about with a wild expression of terror in her eyes, and, unmindful of the injunctions of Mrs. Wilson, she suddenly threw down the bag, and fell on her knees before Mr. Mayburn, crying out, "Ah, master, will they hang me? I didn't think it would burn us all alive! I couldn't find it again, try all I would."

"Unfortunate girl," said Mr. Mayburn, "have you lost your senses, or what have you done? Speak the truth."

"I will tell truth, master," sobbed the girl. "It was when I were lating up them bonnie chickens as had got out, and big Peter tied a rope across in yon passage for me to tummel ower, and I rolled down t' ladder into that big, dark place where they keep great bales and barrels, and all manners of things; my lantern was broken and my candle was lost. I got mysel' gathered up, and I groped about for t' candle, but I couldn't find it, and I got sadly flayed in that dark hole, so I climbed up and said nought to nobody; but, oh, master, I couldn't get to sleep, for it came into my head, may be my candle might have set some of them bundles in a low, and we might all be burned in our beds, and me not saying a word alike, for fear."

"God forgive you, Ruth," said her master. "Pray for mercy; and if it please Him to save us in this fearful hour of peril, never forget the misery and destruction your carelessness has caused."

The penitent and affrighted girl shook in every limb, and Margaret kindly soothed and prayed with her till she calmed her agitation. Then the young and thoughtful daughter said, —

"Papa, we must not remain inclosed in this suffocating cabin. Let us go on deck, and if no other hope remains, we will demand a boat, that we may escape from a horrible death."

"Lead the way, my child," said Mr. Mayburn, "and I will follow you, as I ever do; for I feel utterly helpless alone."

They proceeded to the deck, followed by Jenny and Ruth loaded with packages; and when they reached the scene of terror and confusion, they were embarrassed among piles of boxes, barrels, and bales, which were continually drawn up from below, the bales which were blazing being immediately thrown overboard.

By the light of the torches, Margaret discovered among the throng her young brothers, busily employed in hauling ropes and carrying buckets; they were heated with exertion and blackened with smoke. O'Brien had even got his hair singed with the flames. Still untired, they would have continued their efforts, but all seemed ineffectual, from the total want of subordination and unanimity among the sailors. Mr. Mayburn walked up to Captain Markham, who stood aloof from the rest, in a perfect state of frenzy, from fear, anger, and intoxication. He continued to shout aloud contradictory and absurd orders, which were utterly unheeded by the lawless crew; each man doing what he chose, and nothing being done effectually.

"The fire is certainly progressing, Captain Markham," said Mr. Mayburn. "Let me entreat you to issue orders for some means of providing for the safety of so many human beings all unfit for death. We, who are your passengers, demand the means of escape."

With a fearful oath, the wretch said his passengers might care for themselves; he had enough to do to save his ship; and save it he would, if it cost him half the crew.

"I'll pitch the dogs into the fire," said he, "if they do not soon extinguish it; and not a man shall leave the *Golden Fairy* living."

"There's not many will do that," cried the audacious mate, "if they do not look sharp. The fire has just reached the tallow hogsheads, man, and where will your ship be then? Come along, lads, we can do no more; so let every fellow lay his hands on what he likes best, and lower the boats now or never."

The call was readily responded to, in spite of the threats of the infuriated captain; and though the flames were now heard roaring below, and were even visible in some parts, the after-deck was still uninjured; and from thence the boats were lowered. Arthur and Jack went up to the men to request that a boat, or at all events seats in one of the boats, might be given to their party, who would be willing to reward the men for any trouble they occasioned. The insolent mate, who seemed to have assumed the command of the rest, laughed at the request.

"Charity begins at home!" cried he. "We have no places to spare. Come on, my lads! lower the biscuit and the brandy casks. I'll manage the strong box. Out of my way, gentry. If you say another word we'll pitch you all into the sea—men and women."

"There's no hope of our getting a boat to ourselves, Mr. Arthur," said Jack, "for they 're all afloat now, and they'll soon have them off; so I would say, if you'd help a bit, we should set about getting up a raft as fast as we can—here are plenty of spare spars about."

When Markham saw the men preparing to forsake the vessel, he became more furious than ever, and seizing the mate by the collar, he swore he would have him put in irons. But his attempts were useless against the powerful villain, who flung him on one side like a noxious reptile; and the rest of the remorseless wretches, to rid themselves at once of the opposition of the violent drunkard, hurled him down into the flames, which were already bursting through the crevices of the deck.

"I can't stand that," cried Wilkins, one of the sailors, coming up to Jack; "I'se not the chap to turn my back on my comrades; but I've never committed wilful murder, and I'll just cut away from a gang of such deep-dyed rogues, and join ye, my honest fellow. Come, I'se ready to lend a hand."

A helping hand was truly desirable in their extremity of distress; but Mr. Mayburn shrank from the fierce, rough aspect of the convict sailor, and besought Arthur, in a low tone, to reject any association with crime and infamy.

"Be satisfied, my dear father," answered he, "I will do nothing unadvisedly; but if this man shrinks from evil and turns to good, how shall we excuse ourselves if we force him back to destruction? Besides, it is now too late; see, the first boat has already deserted the ship."

With loud cheers, the most daring of the crew headed by the mate, rowed off in the long boat, and were soon lost in the darkness that shrouded all except the fearful space around the burning ship. The second boat followed, the hardened men turning a deaf ear to the entreaties of the passengers whom they had abandoned on the wreck. They refused even to aid them in lowering their hastily-constructed and unsafe raft, but laughed and sneered at the rude workmanship.

But the flames, fed by the hogsheads of tallow in the hold, now blazed up through the cabin windows, and bursting through the decks, ran along with fatal rapidity, momentarily threatening the distressed family with a dreadful fate. It was now that the cool prudence and skill of their faithful friend Jack rescued them. His observing eye had noted the means adopted by the sailors; he had tools and appliances; he arranged and divided the labor, of which even the women had their share; and the rude raft was at length successfully lowered. A few necessaries were hastily thrown upon it, including a cask of biscuit and one of water, which Wilkins at great hazard had obtained; he had also brought up a small barrel of rum, but Arthur peremptorily refused to take it, and, to end all discussion, flung it into the sea, and firmly told Wilkins, he would rather leave him to perish on the burning ship, than carry him away with such a temptation to evil.

The man grumbled unavailingly, but at last returned to his duty. Nothing more could be secured, except a few ropes, and spars, with some tools to repair the raft. Then a spare sail was cast over the stowage, and, one after another, Mr. Mayburn and the trembling women were let down; the active boys quickly followed. Jack and Wilkins were the last to descend from their perilous position, where they had been so surrounded by the flames, now crawling up the masts, that Margaret dreaded every moment they should fall victims; but they happily alighted on the lumbering raft in safety. Then oars were taken up, and no time was lost in pushing off as far as possible from the ill-fated *Golden Fairy*; nor did they pause even to look round till they were at a safe distance, when they stood off for a few minutes to contemplate the splendid and frightful spectacle.

Wilkins now confessed to them that there were some barrels of gunpowder concealed in the vessel, which the reckless sailors had smuggled from Melbourne for their own purposes; for it had been their fixed intention, at a favorable opportunity, to murder the captain and passengers, or land them on some desert island; and to take possession of the ship for piratical enterprises in the Indian Ocean. The knowledge that this powder was in the ship had hastened their flight from the certain consequences, and Wilkins was surprised that the catastrophe had been so long averted. But now, as they watched the blackened ribs of the vessel, through which the intense flame glowed, while clouds of smoke, myriads of sparks, and burning flakes, rose from the wreck, a loud explosion almost deafened them; another and another succeeded; then blazed up a mass of flame, which seemed to rise to the very clouds for a few minutes, followed by utter darkness and silence.

"May God, in his infinite mercy, still preserve the weak creatures he has so miraculously delivered," said Mr. Mayburn, devoutly. "We were face to face with death, and never, my children, can the crackling, roaring sound of that fierce and unconquerable conflagration fade from my recollection. We had not the consolation of the martyrs who suffered for the faith, and who could look on the flames as the brief path to eternal glory. We were summoned in the midst of life's cares and frailties, unwillingly, fearfully, to be dragged to doom; and He spared us, that we might better prepare to appear before His tribunal. Blessed forever be His holy name!"

Solemnly and earnestly rose the Amen from the rescued. Even the hardened convict lowered his voice as he said, with levity, to Jack, "That was a canny bit prayer; will 'it help us ony, think ye?"

"Yes, Wilkins," said Jack, "I do believe that God never fails to help them who pray to Him. And some day, my man, you will be glad to believe it too."

Wilkins said no more, but he often remembered the new, strange words he had heard poured out amidst that horror of darkness.

"Now, Captain Arthur," cried out Hugh, "please to say where we are, and whither we are to go?"

"I wish I could determine where we are," answered Arthur; "but we have been so tossed about for the last two days, that I have no idea of our position. Certainly we are out of our regular course."

"If Bully Dan were right," said Wilkins, "we ought to be now a good bit north of Swan River, and among islands and reefs puzzling enough at noonday; and in this black darkness it's odd that we ever see land again. If any on ye had thought of an anchor, we might have laid off till day."

There was nothing but patience and resignation for the voyagers. The sea was less agitated than it had been during the day, and they drifted steadily over the waves; but in what direction they could not determine; for such was the confusion of their embarkation, and such the darkness that enveloped them, that no one could pronounce from what point the wind was blowing.

"What is that fluttering sound I hear?" asked Mr. Mayburn, in a voice of alarm.

A moment's silence followed, then every one distinctly heard the fluttering. At length Ruth said, "Oh! if you please, master, it was only me. I couldn't bide that they should be burned alive, bonnie things; it were not their fault! It's them bits of chickens as I were hunting up when all this bad work were done—God forgive me!—and I gathered them into a basket; and if ye please, Miss Marget, dinnot let them be eaten, they're so bonnie."

Margaret readily granted the noisy little prisoners their life, and applauded the humanity of Ruth, whose struggles to keep her restless charge in order created some mirth, and diverted them for a time from the contemplation of their own troubles.

But another sound was now heard above the monotonous rumbling of the unquiet ocean. It was surely, they thought, a human cry! It was again repeated; and Wilkins said very coolly, "It'll be some of our chaps. Like enough they'll have capsized yon big crazy boat. They'd a keg of brandy to fight about; and I'll be bound they'd never settle as long as there were a drop left in't."

"Can we not show them a light?" said Mr. Mayburn: "that was a cry of distress, and humanity calls on us to aid them."

"There's no room here for any more hands," muttered Wilkins. "Drunken rogues! they'd kick these few shaking clogs to bits in no time: and then where are we?"

"Nevertheless, Margaret, we must do our duty. Arthur, what do you say?" asked Mr. Mayburn anxiously.

A loud and dismal scream, at no great distance, decided the question without further discussion. Gerald produced a match-box; and though the wind had got up rather boisterously, they succeeded in lighting and displaying a long splinter of wood. Then a voice was heard to cry, "Help! help!" and Wilkins, with a suppressed curse, said, "It's that desp'rate rogue, Black Peter, and no mistake. Better let him drown, I tell ye, comrades; but I've heared 'em say, water won't haud him. They're all alike bad dogs to let loose among us; they've guns and powder, and they're up to ony sort of bloody work."

Mr. Mayburn groaned at this speech, and said, "What shall we do, Arthur?—we are wholly defenceless against those bad men."

"Don't you think of that, sir," said O'Brien; "Hugh and I looked after that. We brought off a pair of first-rate rifles, with lots of powder and shot. We are the boys to manage the defences. We left the nautical matters to our captain, Arthur; Jack sought up the spars and hammers, and such matters; and Margaret did the commissariat. Division of labor, you see, sir—all regular."

"I did not think your giddy brain could have arranged so well," said Mr. Mayburn: "I am ashamed to say I have not been so thoughtful."

"No, no, papa," said Hugh; "Gerald is taking more credit than is due to us. It was Margaret who arranged what each should do, and allowed us to add to our duties as we chose; in consequence of which, you see, Gerald and I thought of destroying life, and Ruth of preserving it."

While thus talking, the young rowers had been endeavoring laboriously to force the heavy raft, against the wind, towards the spot from whence the cries seemed to proceed. The darkness was so intense that it was in vain the eye sought to penetrate it; but the cry, still heard at intervals, seemed to approach nearer, probably directed by the light. Still it was not without an involuntary shudder, and a half-uttered shriek, that they felt and saw a hand grasp the raft, and heard a hoarse voice demand help. This was immediately given; Arthur and Jack, with much difficulty, drew upon the raft the almost lifeless form of a tall, powerful man, who lay gasping many minutes before he was able to reply to the anxious inquiries of his preservers if any of his companions yet survived.

"Every rogue among 'em gone to his reckoning," said he, with a diabolical laugh. "A good riddance! If we'd only saved the gold and the brandy! But hand me a sup of something, good folks."

"We have nothing but water," said Arthur gravely.

The man made a wry face, and said, "I've had more nor enough of that. Well, then, what are ye bound after in this queer craft? It'll not stand much weather, I take it. And," with an oath, "Wilkins, man, how came you to drop in among these saints?"

Wilkins gave the man a fiery glance, as he answered, "It were a bit safer to-night among saints nor amang sinners, it's like; and I guess ye were thinking so a bit sin' yersel'."

"Never heed that that's gone, man," said the careless villain: "I'm in as good a place as they are now."

"Ay, Peter," said Wilkins, "it's all true as how neither fire nor water will touch thee. We'se see what thou was born to."

"Keep a civil tongue in thy head," replied Peter, "for thou and me must chum together, and see what we can pick up."

"What was the cause of your accident, unhappy man?" said Mr. Mayburn, coming up to him.

"None so unhappy now," answered the surly fellow; "better off nor I have been for a few years past, if it were not for want of brandy. I'se free and idle, and can have plenty of grub, I reckon," looking at the casks; "so I'se do now. We might have kept together; but, ye see, we began ower soon with our brandy, and had only one drinking-cup among us, and everybody wanted it first; and so we chaps got to words, and then to hard hits, and then out came our knives. We were badly crowded; and, somehow, in our scrimmage, we all fell atop of one another, and capsized our boat, and away we all went down. Then, when we came up, such cursing and yelling never was heard on earth or sea, and, dark as it was, none could catch hold on aught to save him. It was soon settled, however; for all our chaps were over far gone in drink to help themselves, and they went down, shouting out, one after another. I had the luck to catch hold of the brandy-keg, and I took care to keep hold; but I could not stop it from leaking, and it vexed me sore that so much good liquor should be made into salt-water grog, and no time to get a sup. I shouted as loud as I could, and let myself float, till I got sight of your signal, and then I thought there was a bit of a chance; so I managed to swim a few strokes, keeping one hand on my barrel; but I made little way, if the sea and the wind hadn't brought me right up to you. When my barrel bumped again the raft, I lost hold, and I hardly know how it was I clutched the spars; but here I be snug and safe in harbor."

"Thank God for your preservation, reckless man," said Mr. Mayburn. "He, who is all mercy to His sinful creatures, has granted you a respite, that you may learn to know and serve Him. Cast not away the precious boon, but in this awful hour, turn to Him, repent, and pray."

The good man kneeled down beside the reprobate, and offered up an earnest prayer for the wretched sinner, who was sound asleep before Mr. Mayburn had concluded; and it was with a sigh he turned from the man, sorrowful, but not hopeless.

CHAPTER V

As the morning light dawned on the distressed voyagers, they became aware of their perilous situation. Around them lay the wide restless ocean, now agitated by a south-west wind, which drove them onward, washed and drenched by the waves, which threatened destruction to their frail vessel, in the midst of which the little knot of united friends were now gathered, their unwelcome guest still lying asleep apart from them. As soon as the light permitted him, Jack began steadily and carefully to repair and strengthen the raft. The spare spars he now lashed round to form a sort of gunwale, to protect them from the spray; and after taking out a supply of biscuit for use, he nailed over the whole of the packages the large sail they had brought away, to steady and preserve them from any injury from the waves.

The man they had rescued from death now awoke, and joined the rest: he was a tall, powerful, savage-looking man, still wearing the convict uniform, so offensive to the taste of the civilized; and his manners were rude and insolent.

"Have you no better prog than this poor stuff?" said he, as his portion of biscuit and cup of water were offered to him. "The Queen allows us better rations nor this, after your grand laws have made us out to be rogues."

"You fare as we do," answered Arthur, mildly. "As long as we have biscuit, you are welcome to share it. We make no distinctions in our common distress."

"You were a pack of fools," said the man, "not to bring away something worth freightage, when you had space enough. Had you sense to fetch a compass?"

"We had no opportunity to secure chart or compass," replied Arthur. "Besides, we were too thankful for the means God gave us to save our lives, to have many thoughts or cares about where we should go. We are in His hands, and I trust, by his mercy, may reach some safe harbor."

"It's as well to tell you beforehand," said the sailor, "that you'd better not get it into your heads that you are going to give me up to hard labor and irons again. Wherever I set my foot on land I mean to be my own master, and the first among you that peaches on me shall rue it." Here the man drew from his breast a brace of pistols, and added,—"You see I managed to keep my barkers safe. What would you say, man, to a ball right through your ugly head?"—and he presented the muzzle of the pistol to Wilkins, who shrank behind Arthur.

"You must mean that threat for a jest, Peter," said Arthur, in a tone of displeasure. "If you are in earnest, I can only remind you that we also have arms. I am commander here, and the first man on the raft that shows any signs of insubordination, I shall certainly shoot dead."

Peter stared scornfully and vindictively at Arthur, but seeing his unmoved countenance, he turned off with a sort of laugh, and withdrew to the stern of the raft.

"What a capital fellow Arty is, Hugh!" whispered Gerald. "See how he has cowed that huge bully. Are we not proud of our captain?"

Towards noon the heat of the sun became excessive, and was most distressing to the voyagers exposed to its beams; Margaret and her father especially suffered from it, till Jack contrived an ingenious canopy for them by raising some spars, over which he spread the boat-cloaks, which the boys had fortunately worn to protect them from the flames in the burning ship. As evening came on, the wind increased alarmingly, and they looked round anxiously to obtain some idea of their position, till at last Wilkins pointed out some hazy dots on the wide ocean desert, which he pronounced to be small islands.

"O Arthur," said Margaret, "if it be possible, let us land on an island; I long to feel my feet on firm ground. Have you any idea what islands these are?"

"I ken'em," said Wilkins, "and can tell ye they're all alike quite dissolute."

"Then I pray, Arthur," said Mr. Mayburn, "that we may avoid them. We had better continue to float on the solitude of the ocean, than seek the haunts of the wicked."

The boys laughed; they understood better than their father the peculiarities of Wilkins's language, and Arthur said,—"I have read, papa, that these north-western islands of Australia are generally small, barren, and uninhabited. If we could safely land on one of them, it would be desirable, that we might rest and improve our raft before we sought the mainland; but I fear they will be difficult of approach, from the coral reefs that surround them."

"Which I long to behold, Arthur," said Mr. Mayburn; "and I beseech you to endeavor to reach one of these reefs. I have ever desired to look upon the work of those toiling, wonderful insects; minute agents of the Omniscient for mighty purposes, laboring incessantly to carry out the plans of creative wisdom.

'As the kings of the cloud-crowned pyramid
Their noteless bones in oblivion hid,
They slumber unmarked 'mid the desolate main,
While the wonder and pride of their works remain.'"

Wilkins stared at the enthusiastic naturalist, and, turning to Arthur, said, "Does he want us to land among them reefs, think ye? A bonnie clash we should have with this log float. If we'd had a few of them bark boats as them black fellows has up country, we might have made a shift; but, ye see," indicating the fair sex by a finger pointed towards them, "they'd make no hand of swimming among breakers."

"Indeed, they would not," answered Arthur; "we must contrive some safer method for them, Wilkins. But if we could, by using our oars, draw near to these isles, I should like to inspect them."

"Ye cannot suspect 'em, sir," answered Wilkins, "without ye were right atop on 'em. Why, they're all dry and bare, and clear of aught but a few birds but I'se willing to use an oar, if ye'd like to see 'em."

It was hard work rowing that heavy raft, and the ungrateful Peter refused to assist, but sat apart, smoking cigars, of which, it appeared, he had contrived to bring a box about his person; still before night they had approached within a mile of a rocky island. Then the sudden darkness of a tropical region surprised them, and compelled them to wait for day, uneasy at the dangerous proximity of the coast, towards which, Wilkins pointed out, a current seemed to be urging them.

"We must have all hands at work, captain," said he, "to keep off them ugly rocks. Come, Peter, man, take up an oar."

"Not I," said the savage, "I'se take a snooze; and when we're drifted a bit nigher hand, rouse me up, and I'll make a swim to shore. I've no mind for another capsize."

It was a service of toil and danger, and the active young men plied the oars vigorously for hours, trusting they were standing safely off the dangerous reefs, till at last, worn out with fatigue, one after another they dropped asleep.

Jack and Wilkins held out till a pale light showed them breakers close at hand, and they felt the current carrying them into the danger. It was a moment of deep anxiety. "See," said Wilkins, "yon uncovered reef—let's try to get a bit nigher to it; then we'll knot a rope to our raft, and I'll swim off and find a way to moor it. If three on us were atop on yon reef we might haul up t' rest on 'em."

All the youths were now roused, and anxious to share this service of peril, for all could swim: but Wilkins was strong, and the most experienced; so while he tied one end of the rope round him, Arthur and Jack secured the other end to the raft, and then they continued to hold off against the current as they watched the bold swimmer till they saw him standing safely on the dry reef. In five minutes more they felt, by the strain, that the rope was fast to the rock. Then Arthur went off with a second rope, secured from danger by having the first to hold by if necessary. When he reached Will, he found the reef was broader and safer than he had dared to hope, while beyond it the water was not more than a foot deep to a shingly beach.

"If we had 'em all here, ye see," said Wilkins, "they could easy wade out."

"Then what shall we do, Wilkins? what is our next step?" asked Arthur.

"We must get more hands," answered he. "And here's a canny opening, clear of breakers; we'll try to bring her in here."

Then, after he had, with sailor's skill, secured the ropes to two huge fragments of rock, he continued,—"Now, let's be off again, and see how we can manage it. If we could get that big lubberly Black Peter to lend a hand, he's a powerful chap at a tug."

"Then he shall work or starve," said Arthur, firmly.

"That's the text, captain; stick to that," said Wilkins, as they plunged into the water again.

Their return to the raft was easier than they had expected, for the tide was ebbing, and already some of the rocks were bare which an hour before had been covered with breakers; besides, the stretched ropes afforded a rest for the hands when they needed it. Arthur explained his plan to his friends on the raft, and called on all hands to aid in propelling or hauling the raft towards the smooth opening in the reef.

"You must assist in hauling the ropes," said Arthur to Peter.

The man swore violently that he would never submit to be ordered by a boy.

"I have the management of the party," answered Arthur, "and all are willing to obey me except you. Take your choice: if you refuse to share the work, most assuredly you shall not share the rations."

The wretch darted a furious glance at Arthur, and put his hand into his breast; but observing the little band had their eyes on him, he muttered with a sneer, "A parcel of fools!" and plunged after Wilkins and Arthur to the reef, to tug at the ropes.

The raft had drifted among scattered rocks, and there was much difficulty in preventing it from being dashed against them; but those left upon it used long poles to push off from these dangers, while the men on the reef continued to haul the ropes, in hopes of drawing the raft to the opening they wished it to enter, belaying the rope anew as they gained a few yards. Slowly and painfully the work progressed; sometimes they snatched a moment for food and rest; sometimes the faint-hearted threw down an oar or pole, as a strong wave cast them back, after they hoped they had made some way.

At length, wedged between two reefs that ran out to sea, they found they could make no further progress, though there was yet a hundred yards of deep water between the raft and the dry rocks to which the ropes were attached.

When Arthur saw this, he called out, "Haul taught and belay the ropes; and now, how shall we convey the weak to the shore, Wilkins?"

"Bad job!" growled he. "We might swim out and trail 'em after us; but likely they'd be flayed."

"Halloo! Arthur," called out Hugh, "come over and see what we are about."

When Arthur had reached the raft, he saw that Jack, with the help of the boys, had lashed together three or four light spars to form a sort of *catamaran*, large enough for one person to sit upon. To each end of this they had attached a long rope, with one end of which Jack proposed to swim to the reef of refuge, ready to draw over in this float, one at a time, those who were unable to swim; and he engaged, if the voyager only kept quiet, there would be no danger; and though the raft was now firmly fixed, it was probable it would be dashed to pieces at high-water, so no time must be lost to make the trial, that the lading as well as the passengers might be saved; and Jack set off with the rope round him.

Now the question was, who would venture on this frail float the first? The water looked dark and deep, and all shrunk back. At length it was arranged that they should test the safety of it by first sending over a part of the freightage of the raft, as less valuable than human life. Still, these slender necessaries were precious to them, and they firmly lashed a part of the packages to the float, and anxiously launched and watched the light raft until they saw it safely drawn to the reef and unladed by Jack. It was then hauled back, and Margaret, to encourage her father, ventured next, her brothers having lashed her firmly down, and charged her to be calm and motionless.

After her safe arrival, Mr. Mayburn gained courage to follow her, and was succeeded by Nurse Wilson. Ruth begged to carry her basket of fowls; but was not permitted, which was fortunate for the chickens, for the terrified and restless girl, attempting to change her position, capsized the frail bark; but Wilkins and Arthur swam out to her assistance, and soon righted it, and, half-dead with fright and the salt water she had swallowed, she was turned over to Jenny, and the young men returned to the raft to assist at the removal of the most valuable part of the cargo—the provisions, guns, and ammunition.

In the mean time Peter had roused himself to take a trip to the raft, and when Arthur and Wilkins reached it, they found the ferocious man holding Hugh by the throat, and threatening to shoot him if he did not give up one of the guns, which the boy held in the case firmly grasped in his hand, while Gerald was releasing the other gun from the covering, that he might defend Hugh, and protect the powder and shot, which he guarded behind him.

As soon as Wilkins and Arthur stepped out on the raft, the savage relinquished his grasp of the boy; but called out in an insolent manner, "Give me one of the guns, and my share of the powder and shot you brought off. They are as much mine as yours, and I claim my right."

"You are mistaken, Peter," said Arthur; "the guns are our own private property. The powder is not legally yours or ours; but the necessity of the occasion caused us gladly to save it from destruction; at some future day we may be able to account for it to the owners. In the mean time, I choose to keep possession of such a dangerous material; nor will I allow you to commit deeds of violence. We have saved your life, and supplied you with food. If your nature does not prompt you to be thankful, at least be neutral; do not return evil for good."

The man did not answer, but there was a dogged look of ferocity in his eyes, that plainly spoke his feelings; and Wilkins whispered to Arthur, as they were tying on the packages,—

"Would you mind our twisting a rope round his arms and legs, and giving him a shove overboard? he's dangerous."

"No, Wilkins," answered Arthur. "Let the man live; we have no right to be his executioners, though I believe he deserves death. If we all reach land safely, we must watch and guard against him; and, above all, Wilkins, do you take care that he does not tempt you back to evil courses."

"We'se see," answered the man, "I'se not to reckon on; but I fancy I'd as lief take service with ye, as turn rogue again, with a cut-throat dog like him."

Arthur earnestly hoped that they might be able to reclaim this good-natured but ignorant man. He conversed kindly with him, as they carefully and successfully managed the transit of the whole lading, including Ruth's chickens; and then, Wilkins taking the charge of the two young boys as they swam to the reef, Arthur remained a few minutes to cut away the ropes, which were too valuable to be abandoned, after which he signified to the apparently careless Peter that he must look to his own safety.

"I see all that," said the man in a surly tone; "depend on't, I shall not stay here; you haven't got rid of me yet. So mind your own business, young fellow, and I'll mind mine."

Arthur left him and soon rejoined his friend; and Peter, drawing his knife and severing the cords that had lashed together the spars of the raft, he allowed them to float, and grasping one piece to support himself, he swam to the dry reef.

The tide having now left the beach uncovered as far as this reef, the family went forward to the lofty cliffs which rose from the narrow shingly strand, and immediately began to remove their property to a secure place above high-water mark.

"We may surely find a better spot for a night's encampment than this," said the indefatigable Arthur, when, resting from his labors, he looked up at the rocky heights. "There appears to be a belt of trees further north, that might possibly afford more shelter. Can you walk as far, papa?"

"I cannot exert myself more, my son," answered Mr. Mayburn. "Let us remain here; in this delicious climate, from what I have read, the night will produce no noxious vapor to harm us. Let us therefore offer our evening prayer to God, and rest calmly under the canopy of His skies, after this day of trial and toil."

The word of the father was the law of his children; and after they had made a sort of tent of the poles and sail from the raft, under which the boat-cloaks were spread, they joined in prayer and lay down to rest; but still apprehensive of the evil disposition of Peter, each took an hour of watching to guard the packages till daylight. The brilliant light of a tropical sun disclosed to the thoughtful castaways a smooth sea but a barren coast, and they looked round in vain for the means of subsistence or escape. They saw Peter at some distance, dragging out of reach of the tide the timbers of the raft, which had been thrown upon the beach.

"I am glad he is so usefully employed," observed Mr. Mayburn. "I trust he feels ashamed of his ingratitude, and means to build us a hut with these planks."

"Not he," replied Wilkins; "I ken him better nor that. He'd never fash to pick up them spars; but he wants 'em to use for his own purposes. But let him be, let him be. Chaps like him is always twining a rope for their own necks."

"Then, Wilkins," answered Margaret, "we ought not to 'let him be;' we ought to try and induce him to undertake some happier and more profitable undertaking; do, Arthur, speak to the man."

Arthur and Jack walked down to the beach, while Ruth made a fire and boiled some water from the casks, to make tea, a supply of which, and a considerable quantity of sugar, being among the provisions they had saved.

"Come, Peter," said Arthur, "you will need some breakfast, and such as we have, we offer to you. What are you going to do with these spars?"

"They are my property, by the laws of wrecking," grumbled the man, "so keep your mouth shut about them. I'll come to your breakfast, if I can get nought better nor your poor stuff."

Finding all their approaches to intimacy with this sullen creature repelled, they returned to the tent, where they found nurse in a state of great anger with Ruth the unlucky, who had literally *walked into* the China breakfast service, which the considerate Jenny had herself brought away from the ship, guarded on the wreck, and had just spread out on a clean napkin on the beach, when the girl being sent to summon Mr. Arthur, had rushed through the midst of the crockery, of which only the teapot and two cups escaped destruction. It was not in the nature of an Irish boy to be serious at such an accident, and O'Brien had laughed so provokingly, that Jenny was roused almost to distraction.

"A vagabond lass, as she is!" she exclaimed. "I blame myself, Miss Marget; I knew what was in her, and I ought to have seen to have had her shut up in one of them Union prison-houses. Nothing's safe where she comes; and see now, we may just drink tea, sup and sup round."

"And we may be thankful we have tea, nurse," said Margaret. "And see, here is a tin cup we used for the water, may do duty instead of our pretty Staffordshire ware."

"And we may meet with a china-shop before long, nurse," said Hugh. "We are not so very far from the great Empire."

"Well, Master Hugh," replied nurse, "I don't pretend to know where we may be; but there's little signs of shops or houses round us.— —If that doesn't beat all!" exclaimed she, as Peter took up the cup of tea she had prepared for her master, drank it scalding hot at once, and then coolly sat down, drew out his knife and began to open and swallow oysters, with which he had filled his cap.

"Shares!" cried Wilkins, good-humoredly, holding out his hand.

"Seek them for yourself," said the churl, continuing his repast; on which Wilkins, calling on O'Brien to follow him, took his biscuit, and set out to search along the rocks. Margaret felt alarmed to see Gerald accompany this man; but Arthur assured her he believed Wilkins might be trusted.

In a short time Gerald came running up to them, and throwing down a cap filled with oysters, he cried out, "Give us a rope, Jack! we have got a turtle, and turned him on his back, that he may not get back to the water; but he is such a monstrous fellow that I don't know how we shall get him dragged all the way to this place."

"Then our best plan will be to go to him," answered Arthur; "we have no temptation to remain in this barren spot; and you seem to have found a land of plenty; therefore I propose we should march at once."

Each took up some burthen to carry, leaving the casks and heavy packages for the present, and moved forward to encamp in a new spot.

CHAPTER VI

After walking about a quarter of a mile towards the north, they reached a nook, surrounded by mangrove-trees, which, like the banyan-tree, formed bowers propped by pillars of successive trunks and stems, and interwoven with roots and branches. At the part nearest to the sea, the lower branches were without leaves, and had been evidently laid bare by the visits of the sea. These branches were now at low tide uncovered, and clustered with oysters. The mangrove-wood, spreading up the steep cliff, was backed by some loftier trees; and it appeared as if an impenetrable barricade was formed by nature to forbid approach to the interior.

A niche formed by the up-rooting of some aged tree, of which few remnants remained, offered a shady retreat, much more attractive than their late exposed encampment. Then Jenny was shown the enormous turtle lying on its back, waiting for execution, the innumerable oysters clinging to the mangroves, the crabs crawling on the uncovered rocks, and the clouds of sea-birds sailing overhead or sitting stupidly on the rocks fishing; and, charmed with the promise of plenty, she said:

"We may do a bit here, Miss Marget, while this fine weather lasts, if we can light on any fresh water. Birds and fish may serve us well enough."

"Where all those tall green trees grow," said Arthur, pointing to the heights, "there must be water to be found; and, in the mean time, we have a large cask, which we must bring up if we make an encampment here."

"I have brought the kettle full," said Jenny, "and a bag of biscuits too. We might have got more here, but nought would serve Ruth but hug them weary chickens with her."

"They will die, shut up in that basket, Ruth," said Gerald. "Come, Hugh, while Jack and Wilkins are killing that poor turtle, let us make a poultry-coop under the roots of the mangrove."

"Above high-water mark, remember, Gerald," said Arthur.

"Oh, botheration! Arty," answered he; "and you fancy I can't make a hencoop without a blunder; but you shall see."

The boys selected a space among the arched roots, out of reach of the tide, and interwove the sides with branches, making a snug and airy dwelling for the fowls, which rejoiced in their emancipation from the basket; and the tropical shades were startled with the novel sound of the crowing of a cock.

In the mean time, Jack and Wilkins had killed the turtle, cut the flesh into pieces, and cleaned the strong back shell, which they proposed should be useful; and, after a fire had been made, a portion of the turtle was cooked in its recent habitation, to the wonder and delight of Jenny, who was in despair for cooking-vessels. Then the rest of the meat was placed under the trees, in the most shady situation, and scattered over with the portion of salt they could spare from the small store they had brought; but, in that sultry climate, they feared they should not be able to preserve it more than one day.

"We could easily knock down a few of those boobies, if you would like them, nurse," said Hugh.

"Certainly not, Hugh," said his father; "with the abundance of food we possess, it would be merciless to destroy more life; and I am able to study the form and habits of the sluggish bird as conveniently while it is seated on that rock as if it lay dead on the beach."

The mosquitoes were so numerous among the trees in their new resting-place, that Mr. Mayburn, who suffered remarkably from the attacks of insects, was greatly distressed; and Margaret said to her brothers:

"It will be impossible for papa to remain among these mosquito-haunted trees; we must either try to penetrate further into the island, or we must return to the bare and quiet rocky strand we have quitted. At all events, we must have the sail brought to make a tent."

It was finally decided that after their dinner they would, for one night at least, return to their landing-place; and the turtle being cooked as well as turtle could be cooked under such adverse circumstances, with Nurse Wilson as *chef de cuisine*, they sat down to enjoy it. Knives and forks they possessed; plates they had not; but the shells of some of the large oysters tolerably well supplied the want. After they had dined, sultry as it was, they were glad to resume their burdens, and flee from the venomous mosquitoes which followed them for some distance; but, unwilling to forsake the trees, their tormentors abandoned them when they reached the bare cliffs.

A cry of dismay from Hugh and Gerald, who had preceded the rest, announced some vexatious catastrophe, and hurried them forward to see with bitter mortification the disappearance of the casks and the various packages they had left on the spot where they landed.

"I mistrusted that rogue," exclaimed Wilkins, "specially when he didn't turn up to his dinner. He's a deep un, and no mistake."

The boys went to the sea, now flowing over the reefs, and saw that the spars of the broken-up raft, which had been thrown on shore, were also gone. It was plain the artful villain had constructed another raft, and set out on it, carrying off their provisions, one of the guns, and the powder and shot.

"And worst of all," said Jack, "my tool-chest, and my axe, which he borrowed from me this morning."

"More fool you to lend it to him," said Wilkins, furiously enraged. "It seems to me as how roguery thrives better nor aught, say what ye will otherwise."

"Do not speak so foolishly, Wilkins," said Margaret. "Wickedness can never thrive, even on this earth. This bad man has probably run into greater distress than he has left, with the added torment of a bad conscience. It is only when we walk in truth and honesty that we can hope for the protection of God."

"Where can the fellow mean to steer to?" asked Hugh.

"With a light raft," answered Arthur, "he may perhaps work round to the east of the island, if it be an island, and from thence he probably hopes to reach the mainland. We have sustained a heavy loss from his knavery; but we shall sleep sounder to-night from the knowledge that he is not near us."

After a good night's rest, they arose to look round them and consider what was the best course in their destitute situation. Mr. Mayburn was dejected, Margaret was anxious, but the boys were full of hope and energy.

"Hugh and Gerald," said Arthur, "I call on you to listen seriously to me. It is all very well to hunt turtles, and I do not object to your knocking down a few boobies, for we must have the means of supporting life; but we have a great object in view at present. We must ascertain where we are, and what step we are next to take. We cannot yet be sure that this is, as we suspect, an island."

"It seems a desolate spot," said Margaret, shuddering.

"Worse than Robinson Crusoe's island, Meggie," said Hugh, "for we have not even the goats. Not a four-footed animal have I set eyes on yet, and the bipeds are few and ugly."

"I wish we may not find some bipeds," said Arthur, "that are more offensive than the gulls and boobies."

"Oh, botheration!" said Gerald. "Sure you won't mean the savages, Arty. What jolly fun if we had an invasion! Wouldn't we drub them like British heroes as we are?"

"And pray, most valiant knight of Ireland," answered Arthur, "where are your weapons of warfare?"

"Oh, murder! what a blunderer I am!" replied the boy; "I had forgotten the state of our armory. Let us consider. We have one rifle, with a small amount of ammunition, one bowie-knife, two penknives, one capital stick-knife, the table-knives, and——has anybody else any dangerous weapons?"

"I have a silver fruit-knife and a pair of scissors," said Margaret.

"Quite useless," replied he. "Now, nurse, turn out your pockets."

Jenny produced a housewife, containing needles, thread, and scissors, thimble, a nutmeg-grater, a cork-screw, and the half-dozen useful forks. Jack, always prudent, still retained in his pockets a large clasp-knife, a hammer, and a few nails. Mr. Mayburn had a small microscope, forceps, a case of delicate instruments of surgery, some blotting-paper, and a sketching-book and pencils; all of which were regarded with contempt by the warrior Gerald.

"Well," said he, "we must just set to work to make bows and arrows, pikes and clubs. Those trees we saw yesterday will supply us with materials."

"We will trouble you, then," said Arthur, "to take your axe and cut down a tree."

"There you are caught again, Pat," said Hugh. "Another blunder! Poor unhappy fellows we are; destitute of means, we can neither fight nor run away, if this be an island we have been thrown on."

"That brings us to the point again," said Arthur. "That is the thing necessary to be known; so, without further delay, we three will set out and make a careful inspection of the coast. We will leave Wilkins and Jack to guard the encampment; I will carry the rifle and the few charges we have left, but I trust I may not be called on to use them, for I should grudge them exceedingly."

"Shed no blood, I beseech you, my son," said Mr. Mayburn. "We are intruders; do not let us become invaders. If we can obtain immunity for ourselves, let us be satisfied. Even if we should be attacked, we have no right to retaliate, but should rather take to flight."

"But, dear papa," answered Hugh, "we cannot fly without wings. We are at bay here, and must fight or fall. But, depend on it, we shall be cautious, with Arthur the prudent to lead us; and remember, this is only an exploring and foraging expedition."

The bold little party then set out towards the mangrove-wood, through which, with much toil and many windings, they forced their way, and gained more open ground. They crossed the bed of a river, which was now, however, but a series of muddy pools, from which, though anxious to have a draught of fresh water, they felt no inclination to drink. Beyond this spot some low bare sandhills rose, which they crossed, and thence to a steep eminence. They climbed up this, and found themselves among vast piles of rocky fragments mixed with tall wiry grass.

They looked round; all was silence and desolation, the barren chaotic scenery being varied only by the tall bare trunks of a species of acacia, which here and there broke the monotony of the prospect; and now the boys felt convinced that they were placed on a truly desert island.

Still they moved forwards, though depressed and silent, over the dismal wilderness; till at length they were cheered by the sight of vegetation, and hailed with pleasure some tall trees. Arthur recognized the cabbage-palm, the slender stem sixty feet in height, with the round tuft of edible leaves at the summit. Hugh would willingly have tried to climb the tree to procure the leaves, but his brother persuaded him to defer the exploit till a more favorable opportunity, and pointed out to him a fringe of the graceful casuarina, which promised the blessing of water. They made up to it, and found it bordered a broad and glittering lake, in the clear waters of which they distinguished multitudes of large fish, while on the banks the noisy water-fowl were building their nests. The edge of the lake was stuck over with fresh-water mussels; and but for the flies and mosquitoes which haunted the trees, this spot appeared a terrestrial paradise compared with the dreary bay they had left.

"This is the place for our camp and fortress," said Hugh; "let us bring up our rear-guard at once. We shall have the lake for our water-tank, and its feathered and finny inhabitants for our rations."

"And these winged monsters for our besieging foes," added Gerald, striking a mosquito from his nose.

"It is a pleasant and tempting situation, certainly," said Arthur; "and we might select a spot sufficiently distant from the water to avoid these bloodthirsty insects. But we must be certain that we shall have no neighbors more dangerous than the mosquitoes. We had better explore to the coast."

Hugh and Gerald had contrived to knock down two pairs of ducks, which they slung across their shoulders, and marched forward towards more fertile plains, where high grass and low bushes spread a verdant covering over the soil, till they reached a thick wood, sloping downwards, through which they penetrated, and found themselves on a narrow strand, similar to that on which they had landed.

A rocky promontory ran out to the sea at a little distance; the broken, rugged, rocky sides were clothed with brushwood, and a lofty headland jutted out at the summit. Their further progress would have been cut off had it been quite high water; but the tide was still low enough to permit them, with some care, to turn round the promontory, and gain a broader strand, which was strewed with huge fragments of rock, amongst which they saw, with great astonishment, the wreck of a large vessel lying. The hull was divided; the forecastle-deck was in one place, and at a distance lay part of the quarter-deck.

At first the boys were struck speechless with this unexpected sight; then they began to climb over the rocks to reach the wreck, and Gerald breathlessly asked: "Will we find any of them alive?"

"Alive, man!" exclaimed Hugh. "You may see at once this is no recent affair; look at this chain, the sea must have washed over it some hundreds of times, for it is covered with rust."

The sea was even now breaking over the scattered rocks, making the approach to the wreck at once difficult and dangerous; but the boys made out that the vessel must have been first thrown on the rocks, and afterwards broken up by the sea. It now remained a melancholy spectacle; timbers, decks, masts, and yards, scattered or piled in confused heaps, apparently untouched by man for weeks or months. The upper parts of the stern and hull as far forward as the mizen chains were entire, lying on the stern-frames; but no bodies were found, and the boats being missing, Arthur suggested that the crew must have got off, carrying with them the useful articles they might need; for little could be seen except the mere timbers, except that where the marks of an axe were found on the mizen-mast, the axe itself, though much rusted, was lying near, and gladly seized by the boys.

"Margaret will become alarmed," said Arthur, "if we delay our return; but to-morrow we must examine this wreck more closely. Much has doubtless been carried off by the boats or the waves; but even the yards and chains may be useful to us."

"I wish we could find any thing to eat," sighed Gerald.

"Depend on it, Gerald," said Hugh, "the greedy sea will have devoured the provisions. I cannot even see an empty cask which might be useful. But, halloo! captain, our retreat is cut off; the sea is washing the headland, and we may be glad to use the old hull as an ark now."

"I think we may be able to turn the next point," said Arthur, pointing to another jutting rock of the indented coast which stood out about a hundred yards in the opposite direction, and where a sort of shelf a few feet from the water afforded an unsafe pass. "Be quick, boys; we must beat the waves if we would escape before next tide."

Away the daring boys darted among the windings and over the barriers of broken rock, till they reached the second promontory, and with the waves dashing close below them, rounded it, coming out on an almost impassable narrow hem of encumbered beach, which stretched before them for several hundred yards. Crawling close to the cliffs, they found at length the strand grew broad and level, and they sprang forward to enjoy more freedom, when they were suddenly startled by the sight of the shell of a turtle, which they could not but suspect the hand of man had removed from the back of the rightful proprietor.

They looked intently on it, then Arthur said, "This shell has undoubtedly been roughly cut from the animal. The important question is, who cut it?"

"Perhaps the crew of the wrecked vessel," suggested Hugh.

"It may have been so," answered Arthur, somewhat relieved.

Then O'Brien shouldered the large shell, and they moved forward thoughtfully for a few minutes; till a dark spot at some distance from the water attracted the attention of Arthur; they hastened towards it, and saw to their great consternation, not only the traces of a recent fire, but the naked footmarks of men, the head of a turtle still bloody, a long wooden spear, plainly hardened by fire, and an instrument which Arthur recognized from description to be a throwing-stick for the spear, as it had a hook at one end which fitted a notch at the heel of the spear, which the holders were thus enabled to project with great force.

"We must carry away these curious arms," said Hugh.

"Certainly not, I think," replied Arthur. "In the first place, we have no right to take them, since they have been left here in good faith, as we might have left our spades in our own grounds at home; and next we should thus place ourselves in the position of invaders and marauders, and incur the enmity of dangerous foes. We had better obliterate all traces of our visit, and, like prudent fellows, retreat quietly."

"Run away! Arthur," exclaimed O'Brien. "You may as well speak plainly. And won't Margaret think us a set of poltroons?"

"We will talk of that as we retreat," said Arthur, laughing; "but we must carefully examine the way we came, that we may leave no footsteps."

As it happened, the vivacity and restless curiosity of the boys had induced them to keep close to the cliffs, leaping from rock to rock, peeping into crannies for nests, so that no traces were left, except where the tide would soon wash them away, and Arthur resolved now to ascend the cliffs at once, instead of going round the island, to escape any risking of meeting the savages. He calculated that they had reached a part of the shore nearly opposite to that on which they had first landed; and by directly crossing the island, which he felt could not be more than three miles over, they might safely and speedily rejoin their friends.

"I do not think it probable," he said, "that this barren island has any permanent inhabitants. The people who have left their traces on the coast may come over from some more productive soil, solely to catch the turtles."

"Do you think they came from the mainland?" asked Hugh; "I fancied from the heights of the east cliffs, I could make out a gray line, which was doubtless Australia."

"I scarcely can fancy," answered Arthur, "that a people whom we have seen described as so deficient in intelligence should be able to construct canoes to come such a distance. It is more likely they are inhabitants of one of the hundred dangerous islands of this sea. It will be prudent, at all events, to avoid them if we can."

As they rapidly made their way directly across the island, O'Brien wished there had been a boat left on the wreck, and Hugh said, "Couldn't we build a boat, Arthur? Jack is up to any work of that sort."

"We have not tools or time, Hugh," answered Arthur. "Only consider how long it would take, even if we had the means, to complete a boat to be useful to us. No; at present we must content ourselves to make the best of our situation; and as I do not think the savages have found the bay of the wrecked vessel, I shall propose that we move our encampment into that snug nook."

"What capital fun," cried Gerald. "We will bring them off directly."

"Softly, good youth!" said Arthur. "We must hold a council on such an important matter. But see Jack perched on yon tall tree, to watch for us and give notice; and here comes Meggie to meet us and hear the news."

CHAPTER VII

"Get all into marching order, Meggie," said Hugh. "We have found out a better site for a settlement than our present encampment, and Gerald and I mean to build a shealing."

"And not a mangrove or a mosquito to be seen near it," added Gerald; "nothing but a ship at anchor."

"A ship!" exclaimed Margaret, in astonishment. "What does the wild boy mean, Arthur?"

"You will only see the remains of a ship, Meggie," answered Arthur; "and though you may think the scene of a shipwreck a melancholy spot to select, yet it seems a convenient, sheltered cove, and a desirable retreat for a short time, till we arrange our plans for the future."

When they arrived at the encampment, and the adventures of the day had been told, Jack heard with especial interest the account of the wrecked vessel; and as he examined the rusty axe, he planned great undertakings with the aid of his new tool; while Jenny looked with much satisfaction on the ducks, which she declared were "more Christian meat than them slimy, fat turtles;" and Ruth, smoothing the beautiful plumage with her hands, and thinking, with foreboding dread, of the fate of her favorites, said—

"Bonnie things! what a sham' to kill 'em."

"And see what papa and I have found," said Margaret, producing a basket half-filled with the eggs of the turtle, while Jenny served up to them some roasted in the ashes, which the hungry ramblers thought delicious.

Then a consultation was held on the project of removal. Margaret shrunk from any risk of meeting with the savage islanders; but Arthur considered they should be safer from any encounter with them in the secluded nook they had discovered, which was guarded by coral reefs, dangerous even to such light canoes as these people usually had, and hidden by the jutting promontories, than they should be to remain in their present exposed encampment, or even in the more fertile regions of the interior.

Mr. Mayburn had some shadowy fancies of civilizing and converting the whole horde at once; but Arthur argued that the time was not favorable for the undertaking, and that they must try to establish themselves in a more independent position before they indulged any hopes of reclaiming a large body of heathens.

"Besides, papa," added he, "we must look forward to some plan of leaving this dull and desolate island, and we may have an opportunity of signalling some passing sail if we establish ourselves on the beach."

"Ye'll not see mony ships amang yon reefs," said Wilkins, "barring they're drove there in a gale, and then, as ye've seen, there's poor chance of they're getting off again."

"But we might build a boat with the remains of the wreck," suggested Jack.

"There's some sense in that," answered the man; "but when ye've gotten your boat fettled up, what port would ye be making for?"

"I am pledged to go to India, Wilkins," said Mr. Mayburn.

"Pledged to a fiddlestick," replied he, with contempt. "Think ye now ye can sail to Indy in a crazy bit boat like what we chaps can put together. Ye'll have to make right across for t' mainland; and mind what I tell ye: I'se stick to ye, and work for ye, and fight for ye, but ye're not to be 'liv'ring me up at Sydney yonder to be shackled and drove like a nigger slave."

"I fear, Wilkins," answered Arthur, "there is little probability of our reaching Sydney; but we are all too grateful for the services of a faithful adherent, to think of returning evil for them; and you may be satisfied we shall continue to protect you to the utmost of our power. And, my dear father, you must no longer distress yourself with the idea of fulfilling your appointment in India. We shall be reported lost in the *Golden Fairy*, and the mission will be filled up. You must resign yourself to accept any safe refuge that is accessible, and wait for happier circumstances."

"In the mean time, papa," said Margaret, "God will surely provide us with work. And till we have more extended opportunities our own hearts require our labor. We must not neglect our duty at home."

"I thank you, my child," answered he, "for reminding me of my wasted hours. It is indeed full time that I should resume the active duties of my profession. I have a weighty responsibility. Do you not think that I should begin at once, by recalling my boys to their daily studies?"

O'Brien looked piteously at Hugh, who laughed at his mournful countenance, and Margaret replied,

"The boys are not idle, papa. They are studying in the great book of Nature. Every hour shows to them some new wonder of creation, and raises their thoughts to the mighty Creator. Every sight and sound develops a new idea; and all you are called on to do, papa, is to watch and to water."

"That is all I am fit to do," answered he. "I want the energy and firmness that you possess—a blessed boon from God. The deep sorrow that ever haunts me is, that my life has been spent in vain purposes, never accomplished."

"My dear, conscientious father," said Margaret, "be comforted; I trust the hour may yet come when you will have a field for your pious labors: till then, have no remorse in following your simple and blameless amusements. I have no merit in my duties of attending, governing, and lecturing these wild boys. I love the office; I was certainly not born for any sphere more elevated. But you, papa, whose sole enjoyment is to sit in an easy-chair before a table laden with books and a cabinet filled with eggs and wings, were wrenched violently from your nature when you were doomed to pass days in forcing these unwilling boys to learn the rules of syntax, or the crabbed mysteries of Euclid. We are shaken from our proprieties here; you cannot teach Latin or work out problems without books; so you must take your ease, and consider this the long vacation."

"You are the girl for knowing a few things, Meggie!" said O'Brien, admiringly. "Be sure, sir, Hugh and I will work to any amount to help you in your ornithology and oology, if you will spare us the philology a bit. There's no running about with a conjugation in one's mouth."

"And as Arthur has demonstrated his problem on the best position for the encampment," said Hugh, "I conclude we had better move at once. No occasion to send forward notice about well-aired beds."

"And no occasion, Hugh Harebrain," said Arthur, "to be overtaken by darkness on our journey. Let us be deliberate. Jenny must roast the ducks for our breakfast in the morning, Jack must collect his valuable work-tools, Ruth must again imprison those luckless chickens, and then we must all have a night's rest. It will be time enough to set out in the morning, and we must take care to start before the sun blazes out in all its fervor."

All obeyed orders; and, with the first ray of light, the whole camp was alive. It was very important this time that nothing should be left behind. Peter had relieved them from the charge of biscuit and water, which he had carried off with the tool-chest and gun; but there was still a little tea and sugar, which was carefully preserved. The sail-cloth was rolled up; even the oars used for tent-poles were taken; and, after morning prayers, they set out slowly along the beach, and through the mazy, ascending woods, till they reached the table-land of the rocky isle. They crossed it this time at the head of the lake which they had discovered the preceding day, and found this part of the island still more fertile and lovely than any they had yet seen. Mr. Mayburn was in ecstasy; he stopped continually to point out some new and beautiful grass, some bright nameless flower, or some strange tree; while the notes, harsh, musical, or merry, of thousands of birds, filled him with amazement and delight.

"From this moment, my boys," said he, "I release you from the severe studies which, Margaret truly observes, are unfitted to our circumstances and the relaxing climate. I merely require from you to obtain me specimens—single specimens only—of the eggs and nests of these birds; and, if it were not cruel, I should long to possess some of these rare creatures in all their beauty."

"I fear, papa," observed Margaret, "that you have no means of preserving birds; therefore it would be useless to take them."

"You are right, Margaret," he answered. "I will be content with a nest and an egg of each species."

"Would you mind about having the nest and egg of that fellow, sir?" asked O'Brien, pointing to a majestic black swan sailing on the lake.

"*Rara avis!*" exclaimed he; then added, with a sigh, "no, no, Gerald, we have no means. The animal is weighty, therefore the nest must be large, and not of a portable nature. I relinquish the precious possession. But let us linger on the borders of the lake, to examine its wild charms. Would that I had saved my botanical library, that I might have made out the species of these broad flags and thick bamboos!"

"These round reeds will make capital arrows," said Hugh, cutting down a bundle of them; "and I doubt not but some of them would be elastic enough for the bows. We may surely, with all our learning, succeed better in making them than untaught savages. Then we may bring down our birds noiselessly, and defy the thievish tricks of Black Peter."

"But first, Hugh," said O'Brien, "we must have a trial with some of these big fellows in the lake," pointing to some large perch-shaped fish.

Jack sharpened some of the reeds to a point, and the boys were soon plunging about in the clear bright lake, pursuing and striking the fish; and after fifty vain attempts, they succeeded at length in spearing two, which, though young, were of large size, and Arthur concluded they must be the river cod (*Grystes Peelii*), so much praised by Australian travellers. Then, regardless of wet garments, which the hot sun soon dried, the boys triumphantly proceeded on with their spoil. Jack, in the mean time, had struck off from the edge of the lake a cluster of fresh-water mussels of various sizes, and emptied them, to serve for spoons and drinking-cups.

Thence they moved forward, anxious now to seek some shelter from the increasing heat of the day, and gladly entered the wood, from which, with some difficulties in the descent, they reached the wreck-encumbered bay. All were at once attracted to the side of the vessel; Jack, especially, examined it with intense interest, considering its future service to him. Margaret and her father were moved to tears, as they contemplated the shattered fabric, and thought on the brave but probably unprepared men who might have been hurried into eternity before the final catastrophe.

While Hugh and Gerald climbed the sides to explore the interior of the wreck, Arthur observed that some of the timbers had been carried away by the tide even since the previous day, and he consulted with Jack about the possibility of breaking up and endeavoring to save such parts as might be useful to themselves; and in order to lose no time they grasped a loosened plank, to draw it away beyond the reach of the tide. No sooner had they removed it, than a large cask rolled from the opening, which they concluded led into the hold. The cask broke open with the fall, and a number of potatoes ran out. Every hand was quickly summoned to collect and save the valuable contents; the cask was righted and carefully removed up the beach, and it was great amusement to the boys to pursue the straggling potatoes, and save them from being swept away by the next tide.

"I say, O'Brien, my boy, I wonder your Irish nose did not scent the *pratees* yesterday," said Hugh.

"Now isn't it luck, Arty," said Gerald. "Will we plant some? and then we shall never want as long as we stay here."

Margaret looked alarmed at the plan of planting potatoes for future provision; but Arthur replied, he hoped they should be able to leave the island before the potatoes were exhausted; nevertheless, he approved of the provident project of Gerald, and promised to seek a favorable spot to plant some, for the benefit of future visitors to this unproductive island.

"But do not be afraid, nurse," added he, "to boil us a large *shell* of potatoes to-day; we have abundance; and in our scarcity of bread, we could not have found a more valuable prize."

Ruth had been in the wood to seek for a convenient place for a hencoop, and now rushed out with torn garments, exclaiming, —"Oh! Miss Marget, come and see what a bonnie beck there is."

A *beck*, or stream of water, was, indeed, a valuable discovery; and, conducted by Ruth, Arthur and Jack forced their way through entangled roots and brushwood, till they reached a narrow rivulet of clear water, probably flowing from the lake by some unseen channel beneath the grassy region they had crossed; and after trickling down the rocks, it again disappeared in the sand and shingles of the beach.

"This is but a slender supply, Jack," said Arthur; "I fear it might fail us in a drought."

"We must dig a tank, Mr. Arthur," he answered; "that is, if we can raise a spade."

Jack considered for a few minutes. He was not to be checked by apparent difficulties in his undertakings. "What do you think, Mr. Arthur, of one of those big oyster or mussel shells? I could tie one to a stick with some of these stringy fibres of creeping plants; or, better far, there's a tree up above, that seems to have a bark you might ravel out into strings; and there's another tree, with a stiff, regular sort of gum, as good as glue, oozing out of it. Now, with all these, I'll be bound to make a spade or two that will turn up this light soil fast enough."

"Then the sooner we set about it the better, Jack," answered Arthur. "We cannot do better than remain in this spot, if we meet with no disturbance, until we can make some canoe or raft to take us off; and it is absolutely necessary to secure a supply of water. Let us go and choose our shells."

But when they returned to the beach, they found Mr. Mayburn so much overcome by the scorching heat of the sun, that their first care was to get up a tent or shelter of some kind for him. They selected a deep niche in the cliff, where the rocks formed a complete angle, and having procured from the wreck some suitable spars, they fixed them in the crevices of the rocks, to form the rafters of the roof, which they covered with the long grass which grew above the cliffs. The sail was thrown over the front, as a curtain, and they were thus provided with a shady and convenient apartment.

At low tide, Hugh and Gerald amused themselves with searching for nests in the extremity of the promontory, and finding an opening, they had penetrated into a spacious cave, the mouth of which would be covered at high-water; but as it shelved upwards to a considerable distance in the rocks, the back part was safe and dry.

"Just think, Hugh, my boy," said O'Brien, "what a fortress this would be for us if we were invaded. One man could defend the entrance with the gun, even at low-water; and how we should defy the rogues when the tide was up."

"But it would be horribly dismal, Gerald," answered Hugh. "We could never bear to live in it long; and, you know, we need no sleeping-rooms or houses to cover us in this fine climate; so we will leave it uninhabited, at least in peaceful times. But we will show it to Arthur, and ask him if it would not make a good storehouse."

Arthur congratulated the boys on their discovery, and the timid father was highly gratified at the thoughts of such a secure retreat; after he had satisfactorily ascertained that it could always be accessible at low-water, and never dangerous at the highest tide; and Margaret proposed that the cookery should be accomplished within the cave, that the smoke might not attract the observation of the dreaded natives. So Jenny established her kitchen here, and prepared an excellent dinner of fish, and potatoes boiled in the shells of the turtle, while Margaret kept watch for the returning tide, though Jenny said, "It's all little use, Miss Marget; it has to be, I feel. Ruth's sartain to be catched and fastened up in this eerie place."

Jack made a careful inspection of the remains of the vessel, and from the stern cabin, which was still uninjured, he drew out, with the help of the boys, a rough bench and a table,—useful acquisitions; and still better, a good-sized empty cask, which had contained brandy, and was now conveniently employed as a water-cask. Then, after a long survey of the state of the timbers, Jack announced that, with the help of Wilkins's strong arm, and Arthur's judgment and perseverance, he would undertake to build a sort of boat.

Wilkins shrugged up his shoulders at the prospect of hard work under a burning sun, and said, "Why, one had as lief be working in irons down yonder; where one was safe of full rations, and bacca, and rum into t' bargain."

"And ruin to body and soul, you may add, unhappy man," said Mr. Mayburn. "Be not discontented that the mercy of God has rescued you from evil, and cast you among true friends, who ask you to do no more than they do themselves; to fare simply, and to work. You were not placed in this world to live like the beasts, who eat, and drink, and perish for ever. Your life is here but the beginning of eternity; the hour of death is close at hand to all, when those who have done evil shall receive their punishment, and those who have listened to God shall find a blessed home in a new and glorious world."

Wilkins never replied to any of Mr. Mayburn's *preachings*, as he called these admonitions; but he scoffed less than formerly, and Margaret observed that his manners were somewhat softened; and she daily prayed to God that they might be permitted to aid in reclaiming, at least, one sinful soul.

The next day Jack succeeded in binding two large shells to stout handles, and fixing them with gum; then, while he left them to harden, he set to work to clean the rusty axe with sand and stones, and at length rendered it serviceable. He was thus enabled to break up the wreck, and to select such timber as would be useful for his projected undertaking; he extracted all the large nails that were uninjured, and after many days' labor, had accumulated materials to begin his great work.

But the first employment of the youths was to be digging the well; they went every morning to the lake to procure fish, birds, or eggs, for the provision of the day, and then returned to assist in digging, the spades being now available, as the gum had become as hard as the shell. After they had sunk the tank sufficiently deep, they lined it with flat stones; and saw with great satisfaction, that they need never be without a supply of fresh water, if they remained at this cove.

Some time passed, and they saw no more traces of visitors to the island, and they ventured to ramble to some distance along the beach, bringing in occasionally a turtle, or a basket of turtles' eggs, to vary their diet. They also used daily a small quantity of potatoes, but they were economical with these valuable roots, of which they hoped to raise a crop in the island, and, should they ever reach it, on the main land as well.

After the tank was completed, Jack selected a spot conveniently near high-water mark, and seriously set about boat-building. He had carefully examined the boats during their voyages, and while in the *Amoor* he made many inquiries of the obliging ship-carpenter; but though bold and sanguine in all his enterprises, he did sometimes feel that he had undertaken a stupendous task.

The planks that would best have suited his purpose were more or less injured by the sea; he had no means of forming iron bolts or screws, yet the indefatigable youth persevered; but the month of August, the early spring of that climate, was advanced before the boat assumed a form of promise. It was then caulked with matted cordage found in the vessel, and with gum, of which they had abundance. Now, though rough and clumsy, Jack declared it "looked like work;" and after two pair of oars had been made with little difficulty, to the great delight of the young workmen, a day was fixed for launching the boat.

CHAPTER VIII

It was necessary to carry the boat fairly out to deep water, to test its perfect security; but the reefs were impassable before the cove, and they were aware they should be compelled to row to some distance within them till they found an opening. A roller, left in the wreck, enabled them at high-water to run out the boat, and Wilkins and Arthur volunteered to make the first trial in it. Jack was detained on shore, where he was always usefully employed, and the two boys were considered too wild to be risked in the first trip—an arrangement which they would gladly have rebelled against.

The anxious watchers stood on shore to mark the boat first float on the water, and then the strokes of the oars, which carried it round the promontory at the south out of their sight. Then Jack and the two boys ascended through the wood to the heights, and crossed the cape, to watch the further progress of the precious vessel. But what was their consternation to see no traces of it. They hurried down to the beach beyond the promontory, and gazed wildly around, uttering cries of distraction. A few minutes of horror succeeded: then they saw the heads of the two swimmers, who appeared to be struggling violently against the receding waves.

The two boys would have plunged at once into the water; but Jack, in a tone of authority, commanded them to remain still, and throwing off his own light frock, he rapidly cut a long branch of mangrove, and swam out, holding it out towards Arthur, who seemed nearly exhausted, and who eagerly clutched the branch as soon as it was within his reach. Then Jack turned round, and swimming with one hand, drew the almost senseless Arthur, still firmly grasping the branch, after him into shallow water, where Hugh was waiting to receive him. Still fresh and unfearing, Jack set out again towards Wilkins, who had grasped an oar and was supporting himself with it, when, just as he saw his friend coming up to aid him, he either dropped the oar from exhaustion, or some unseen rock dashed it from his hand, and he immediately disappeared.

A great cry rose from the boys on the beach; but the minute after, he rose again, lying on his back, and apparently insensible. This enabled Jack to approach him with greater safety, and catching hold of his long hair, he drew the senseless body of the poor man towards the shore. But Hugh perceived Jack could not long hold out, and throwing off his clothes, he struck out to meet him, compelled him to relinquish the charge of Wilkins; and thus they were all enabled at length to reach the shore. But all were greatly exhausted, and Wilkins was apparently dead when they drew him on the beach.

O'Brien hastened through the woods, and by cries and signals brought Margaret and Jenny to their assistance, by whose prudent care and applications the poor man was restored to consciousness. No sooner was he recovered, than, trembling excessively, he looked wildly round, and said,—

"Good Lord! it is a terrible thing to die in one's sins!"

"How glad I am to hear you say these words, Wilkins!" said Margaret; "and now let all our words and thoughts be thanks to Him who has given you time to turn from these sins, and lead a new life. Pray to Him openly. We are all your friends, and we will join you;" and kneeling down by the side of the convict, Margaret offered up a simple and short thanksgiving for the two men happily rescued from death, and a prayer for continued mercy for their souls. For the first time the lips of Wilkins moved in prayer, and he audibly uttered "Amen."

In order to remove the anxiety of Mr. Mayburn, they returned to the encampment as soon as the exhausted swimmers were able to walk. Then Arthur related to his friends that as soon as they had got the boat into deep water, they suspected there was something wrong about her, and were endeavoring to make to shore, when she whirled round and was swamped in a moment, and the labor of weeks and the hopes of escape were at once lost.

The whole party were greatly dejected; but Jack, who was at first deeply mortified, was the first to shake off his chagrin, and to declare boldly that he would make another experiment. "We have plenty of materials quite handy," said he; "and it cannot be so far to the coast of the main land. If you will let me try again, sir, I feel quite certain I could make two bark canoes that would take us all, and, if we were once fairly over the reefs, could be paddled across without danger."

"My good boy," said Mr. Mayburn, "I am but an indifferent judge of nautical affairs; but you must allow your first adventure has been signally discouraging. Nevertheless, I admire that perseverance which must in the end subdue obstacles and command success, and I do not object to your continuing your experiments; but I would advise you to try your next boat on the lake, where, in case of accidents, no fatal consequences need be feared."

"I will make a canoe at once," answered he; "but I will risk no lives. I will paddle it across to the mainland myself, and then return to convince you of its security. This time I have no fears, provided we do not overload our vessels. I will set out to seek a tree immediately."

"You will eat your dinner first, my man," said nurse; "and if you had a bit of sleep after your swimming, before you set off to cut down trees, there would be more sense in it. Here's some good roast duck for you; a grand dinner it might have been if we had only had sage and onions."

Jack found Jenny was right. He was not equal to a long walk after his exertions and vexations; so he sat down to eat his roast duck, and then set about making models of canoes, prahus, and catamarans, from the recollection of what he had seen or read of. But next morning, leaving Wilkins, who was much bruised, and still weak, and subdued by mental and bodily suffering, in the care of Margaret and her father, the young men set out to explore the island for a tree of proper height and girth to make use of for their first attempt at a canoe.

"After all, Mr. Arthur," said Jack, "if this should fail, we could try catamarans. That would be easy enough, and we have mangroves close at hand that would answer exactly for making them. But then I have my doubts if the master, or Miss Margaret, could be brought round to trust themselves on such bits of floats for a voyage that far. Here's a grand tree! Now, if we can only peel it clean, it will set us up."

It was a tall fine tree of the *Eucalyptus* or gum species, with a thick rough bark, which seemed as if it might be easily removed. Arthur began by making a deep incision round the trunk at the bottom, and also in a perpendicular line as high as he could reach. By standing on a fragment of rock, he was able to carry it up to the height of twelve feet, and to finish it by another circular incision. Hugh and Gerald stood at the foot of the tree to receive the bark, which, when gently raised from the trunk, was easily separated, and let down in one piece without any injury, to the great delight of the boys. Jack was anxious to have it transported to the cove immediately; but the boys wished to take a peep at their first landing-place before their return, and they all turned their steps in that direction. Hugh and Gerald had distanced the two elder youths, who had not reached the cliffs, when they saw the two boys returning in haste, with dismay on their faces.

"Oh! Arthur," cried Gerald, "such a vexation! We are in for a battle, and we have no arms! The savages are ready for us on the beach."

"But we are not ready for them," replied Arthur, "and must therefore keep out of sight. Do you two hasten homewards with the bark, while Jack and I reconnoitre."

Then cautiously creeping along to the edge of the cliffs, they looked down on the narrow strand below, and saw a number of the dark natives gathered round some object close to the water, which seemed to have excited their curiosity. Jack, with a muttered exclamation of vexation, recognized this to be his unfortunate boat which had doubtless drifted on shore here.

"Oh! Mr. Arthur," whispered the lad, in great agitation; "as sure as you are living, I see that rogue, black Peter, that got all my tools, among the savages; depend on it he has brought them here to seek for us."

"To seek for the remainder of our property, I suspect, Jack," replied Arthur. "They are probably not very anxious to encounter our fire-arms; and we should be no prize to them, even if they could capture us. But we had best decamp now, as we are quite unarmed, and it might be dangerous to be detected; and, Jack, we must set to work directly. I am anxious now to get away as soon as possible, for these fellows will be constantly in our way on this small isle."

They withdrew with the same caution with which they had approached, and then hurried to overtake the boys, who were moving slowly along, carrying the bark; and with the additional hands they soon brought it safely into harbor, to the admiration of Mr. Mayburn, who was, however, greatly distressed to hear of another visit of the savages. Then, as they measured and arranged the work, they discussed with wonder the appearance of black Peter among the natives, and the cause of his disturbing their quiet seclusion.

"Peter's in his reet place amang 'om," said Wilkins, "and it's time for us to be off when he shows his black, ugly face. As sure as we're here, master, if he cannot 'tice me off to join his crew, and start bush-ranging, he'll take my life. He's a reg'lar black-hearted un for a bit of vengeance."

"But, surely, Wilkins," said Margaret, "there can be no fear that you, who have now learnt to know good from evil—you, who have seen the wickedness of your past life, should ever go back to such sin."

"Why, ye see, miss," answered the man, "it's little that such as ye know, what a queer tempting a chap feels for a free, roving life. Why! half of our biggest rogues *did* know good from evil; and what of that? They liked evil better nor good. I reckon there's a bad spirit as is always tugging at a fellow's heart."

"You are right, Wilkins," replied Mr. Mayburn. "It is the power of the Prince of Darkness that you feel in your heart, dragging you to the pit of perdition. But if you pray to God, my poor man, he will send you strength to resist the evil one."

Wilkins groaned, and his friends felt true pity for the unfortunate man, who was sensible of his own weakness; and while all deeply regretted that the infamous Peter had chosen to pursue them, they resolved continually to watch and pray for the complete reformation of Wilkins. Neither could the family feel in safety while they believed the savages remained on the island; it was therefore arranged that Arthur and Jack—the most prudent heads—should return to the cliffs above the landing-place of these unpleasant visitors, to watch their proceedings, and endeavor, if possible, to discover their plans, and the motives that brought them to the island.

In the mean time, the other boys transferred the bark to the capacious cave; the tent was also stowed there, with every other trace of their habitation; and it was arranged that, if there was likely to be any danger of detection, the two sentinels were to announce it by a sharp whistle, when the whole family would be ready to take shelter in the gloomy but secure fortress.

Concealing themselves as much as possible among the tangled mangroves, Arthur and Jack went round to the spot from whence they had previously seen the strangers, and beneath the abundance of brushwood above the cliffs they made for themselves a complete hiding-place, with loopholes for observation. They saw the men still assembled round the boat, but the sound of the hammer induced them to conclude that Peter was engaged repairing some damage in it; and, to the great vexation of Jack, he saw his own tool-chest, which he valued so highly, standing on one side, and at a little distance lay the boughs of a large mangrove tree, and the axe with which they had been felled.

Arthur suggested that Peter had brought these men to the island, hoping to find the remainder of their property, and bringing the tools to cut down a tree and make a raft to carry away the spoils; for the light canoes which were lying on the beach were only fit to contain one person, or, at the most, two in each; and that, finding the boat, Peter had thought it more convenient than a raft for the purpose.

"Do you think, Mr. Arthur," said Jack, "they will be leaving any of the canoes behind them? I should like to see how they finish them off at the ends. But surely they'll never start off in that unlucky boat; I could hardly bide to see them enter her, knowing what we know."

But Arthur was of opinion that they were not called upon to risk their own lives and the lives of their friends, by going forward to report the character of the boat. Besides, Peter, the only person who would be able to understand their language, would probably not believe them.

So they continued to watch till Peter had completed his work, and then, by the efforts of the natives, the boat was launched, the whole party celebrating the event by dancing, singing, and flinging about their arms with childish delight. Peter selected three of the men to accompany him in the boat, which, with the aid of some long poles and paddles from their canoes, they pushed off and forced over the rocks. The rest of the natives leaped into their canoes, and followed with shouts of admiration.

In deep anxiety the two young men continued to watch the boat, which they expected every moment to see disappear; but whether Peter had found out its defects and remedied them, or the water had swelled the wood and rendered it fit for service, it was impossible to say. One thing only was clear, that as long as they could observe it, till it had passed towards the south, out of their view, it continued to move slowly, but with apparent security.

Leaving their position, they crossed over to a high point at the south of the island, from whence they could perceive the little fleet—the canoes now diminished to mere specks—proceeding towards a dark object, which they judged to be a distant island.

Satisfied that the people had all departed, they descended to the beach to inspect the scene of their visit, Jack remaining for some time silent from the mortification of seeing the product of his labors appropriated so successfully by the unscrupulous Peter; and almost disappointed that he had not witnessed the boat go down, as he expected. But when they reached the strand, he recovered his spirits at the sight of a canoe which they had not been able to carry off conveniently after manning the boat. It was not useful as a prize, for it would only contain one person in comfort; but he was able, as he wished, to examine the workmanship.

"Shall we carry it off, Mr. Arthur?" he said. "A fair exchange is no robbery; and you know, sir, this is poor payment for my good boat."

"I think we had better leave it, Jack," answered Arthur. "The blacks will certainly return for it; and when they find it removed, they will be convinced that we are still concealed on the island. If we remain unsuspected, Peter will naturally conclude from the sight of the wrecked boat, that we are all drowned; and will then think no more about us. You see the simple construction of the canoe, closed at the ends by the stringy bark, which we can easily procure; or better still, we can use hempen ropes, of which we have still some; and we must strengthen the bottom by an extra layer of bark, or by thin planks."

"It's not badly put together," said Jack, with a critical air; "but it will be strange if a regular taught English carpenter cannot beat it. I'm not daunted,

Mr. Arthur, after all my vexations. And here's something that pleases me better; and, say what you will, sir, this is my own, and I'll take it."

This was a small saw, which had been left beneath the lopped branches of the mangrove; and Arthur, prudent as he was, not only agreed that Jack had a perfect right to carry away his own property; but he thought he might do it with safety; for, in the place where it was lying, it would certainly be washed away by the next tide, if it was left behind; and, charmed with their prize, they hastened home to report that the intruders had departed.

Hugh and Gerald were in a high state of indignation at the audacity of Peter in carrying off their boat; and Wilkins was furious, upbraiding Jack for his professional unskilfulness; when a fellow like Black Peter could make the boat fit to stand a voyage.

"We do not know yet how the voyage ended," said Margaret. "It may be the boat has again foundered where help could not be had."

"God send it may!" said Wilkins. Mr. Mayburn reproved the thoughtless man for the exclamation, telling him he ought rather to pray that the sinful man might be long spared, that he might have opportunity to repent.

"Him repent!" cried Wilkins; "bless you, master, ye might as lief look to Miss here turning bush-ranger! It's not in him. He were just born for nought but to die a rascal, and that he'll do, and no mistake!"

"It is a mistake, rash man!" replied Mr. Mayburn. "God sent no man into the world marked for perdition. There is ever a door open that the vilest may enter. Let us all pray that he may find that door; and if God permit me, I would gladly use my humble efforts to reclaim the wretched sinner."

"Well, all I can say is, sir," answered Wilkins, "God send ye may never have a chance. Ye're a deal ower good to be thrawn away in running efter such a rogue, and ten to one he'd twist yer neck if ye said a word to him."

Wilkins could not be convinced that there was any hope for Black Peter; and Margaret besought her father henceforth to talk to the ignorant man of his own peril, rather than of that of his worthless comrade; of whom he was not yet in a frame of mind to tolerate the mention.

The bark canoe was now begun in earnest. It was twelve feet in length, and broad enough to admit two persons seated on the bottom, for benches they did not venture to introduce. The ends were closed firmly with the stringy fibres of the tree named the "stringy bark tree," as the tough fibres of this bark seemed more suitable for the purpose than the hemp-twisted ropes found in the ship.

Ten days completed the first canoe, and hardened the gum used to coat it. Paddles and oars were added, and then the workmen fondly looked upon it as a success, and Jack was sanguine in his expectation that in fair weather it must reach the mainland safely. But it was not large enough to contain the whole party, and a second visit to the interior was necessary, and a second gum-tree was barked. At this visit, and on several occasions, the younger boys looked out on the coast for traces of the natives, but all continued so tranquil that they began to hope they should not again be disturbed.

Before they began to make the second canoe they made a trial of the first, by carefully conveying it over the reefs, and launching it beyond them. Wilkins offered to take it alone; but Jack chose to accompany him, that he might note any imperfection and correct it. It floated beautifully, was easily governed, and the workmen were full of pride and hope as they deposited their canoe in the cave, and turned to work at another.

"If we can but succeed as well with the next," said Jack, "we shall have nothing to dread but a gale, or too heavy a loading. Let us consider, Mr. Arthur; we shall be four in the first boat, and five in the second. Five will be too many for it, sir."

"And my clothes," said Margaret, "the gun, knives, and axe, with all our table utensils, besides necessary provisions. How are they to be stowed?"

All were silent; for to stow all these things besides the four passengers, would be more dangerous than even the fifth person.

"I say, Jack, my lad," said Wilkins, "ye'll have to rig up a catamaran, like them they have down yonder, to land folks over a high surf. I'se see and manage it myself, and then ye'll be shot of me. Ye ken I'se a good-to-nought; and maybe I'd be bringing down a storm on ye all, like that Jonah as master was reading on."

Though Mr. Mayburn assured Wilkins God would not pour his vengeance on them for protecting a man who had shown some hopes of amendment, the suggestion of Wilkins was fully approved. A catamaran was obviously desirable, and as soon as the second canoe was completed, they set to work, lopped the stems of the mangrove, and lashed them together to form as large a raft as they required. This they surrounded with a frame of thin wood, and the catamaran was completed to the satisfaction of the workmen, ready for the cargo to be tied to it. Gerald named it the luggage-van, and declared he would certainly take his passage on it.

When all was finished, it became an object of consideration what might be the nature of the coast they should land upon. They had read that many parts of the west coast of Australia were mere deserts, arid and barren, without food or water, and they knew not but they might be driven on such an inhospitable shore. It was therefore advisable, before they abandoned the plenty that now surrounded them, that they should collect stores for possible contingencies. The brandy cask they had found in the wreck was large; this, before they embarked, they proposed to fill with fresh water from the tank, the most important provision for the voyage. And for the rest, one fine morning the whole party set out with bags and baskets on a foraging expedition to obtain food to victual their fleet.

CHAPTER IX

When they arrived at the lake, they found the margin crowded with the nests of aquatic birds, built among the reeds, and a dozen fine ducks were soon taken. Ruth filled a large basket with eggs, and finally a quantity of fish was procured. With this ample provision they turned homewards; but passing the plot they had sowed with potatoes on their first arrival at the cove, they were astonished to see how forward the plants were; and on digging they found young potatoes, of which they carried away a small bag; but as they still had a large supply of those found in the wreck, they left the greater part for the benefit of succeeding visitors.

When they came near the height above the beach, on which they had first seen the footsteps of the natives, Hugh and Gerald went to the cliff to look over once more on the well-remembered spot, but started back immediately, for, to their deep distress, they beheld a considerable number of naked savages, painted with white chalk in a most frightful manner, dancing, singing, and throwing up their arms as if they were frantic.

The boys made a signal of silence to the rest; but Ruth, who was always, as Jenny said, in the wrong place, had followed the boys to the cliff, and, curious to know what they had seen below, she leaned forward to look down through an opening in the bush. O'Brien, alarmed lest she should be seen darted forward to seize her arm and draw her back; but startled by the action, and terrified by the scene below, she lost her balance, and, encumbered with the heavy basket, tottered over the edge, rolled down the steep cliff through the crackling, thorny brushwood, and alighted amidst the strange wild crew on the beach.

Springing up and looking round, the distracted girl uttered a succession of shrill screams, and the natives, in equal terror and amazement, gazed on the strange creature that had so suddenly descended amongst them. Her hair, which was very long, and of a fiery red color, was flying loose over her scarlet cloak, her wild eyes were starting from her head, and her pallid face was streaming with blood from the scratches she had received in her descent. For a moment the savages appeared paralyzed; then, without looking round, they fled to their canoes; and the next minute were seen paddling with all speed from the shores haunted by such a frightful spectre.

By this time, Jack, in great alarm about his sister, had descended to the beach, and was immediately followed by the rest of the young men; and the distressed, woe-begone aspect of Ruth, who continued to sob and groan even after her fears were subdued, made Gerald laugh heartily, in spite of the tragic consequences that might have ensued from the accident.

"Come along, girl," said Jack, kindly. "Thank God you are not much worse; so what have you to cry about now?"

"It's the eggs, Jack," she sobbed out. "What must I do? They're all broken, and what will Jenny say to me?"

"Never mind that," answered he; "take up your basket, and come away with me to the lake, where you can wash your face and fill your basket again, and make the best of a bad job."

Jack's practical philosophy consoled the weeping girl, who collected more eggs, and soon recovered from the distress of her adventure. The boys found that the timid natives had left behind them in their fright spears, boomerangs, and some excellent cordage, twisted of the fibres of the stringy bark tree. Wilkins would gladly have carried off these, and unwillingly relinquished them at the command of Mr. Mayburn. "What matters," said he, "standing on ceremony with them there black fellows. Why, they would niver ax your leave to snatch t' bite out of yer mouth!" which observation drew down on Wilkins a rebuke from Mr. Mayburn, and an exposition of the law of honesty, as established by God and man.

All the property of the natives was therefore left untouched, and the family returned to their own quiet nook, now more anxious than ever to leave a place to which curiosity, or the desire to recover their weapons, might at any moment bring back the late undesirable visitors.

Every one was now busily employed: a small number of potatoes were again planted, and the remainder of their store packed in sail-cloth bags. The ducks and fish were cooked; the eggs of the wild-fowl, as well as a quantity which Ruth's poultry had produced, were boiled hard, and packed with soft grass in a box. The water-cask was filled; and then all the packages and provisions were lashed securely to the raft, which they had finished by a mast and sail made from some rent remains of canvas on the masts of the wreck.

The large sail which had formed the tent cover was spread over the whole of the freightage and nailed down. Then the bottoms of the canoes were spread with fine grass for seats, and after a thanksgiving to God, who had given them the power and the means to accomplish this important undertaking, the family lay down in the balmy, dry, spring air of that delicious climate, to take their last night's rest on the friendly isle.

The first dawn of morning roused them to action. Spies were sent to the heights to ascertain that the coast was quiet; then the first canoe, containing Mr. Mayburn and Margaret, Arthur and Hugh, was launched, and carried safely over the reefs. Jack and O'Brien, with Jenny and Ruth, filled the second, and Wilkins followed, paddling the heavy raft.

"I'm not easy in my mind, Jack," said nurse, "for Master Gerald is up to any mischief; and if he sets Ruth on, we'se all be drowned."

"Keep your eyes on her, Mrs. Wilson," answered Jack; "and if she will not sit still, we'll have her tied upon Wilkins's catamaran." O'Brien's laughter at the idea of Ruth being stowed with the luggage, made the poor girl shed tears; but she was comforted with the care her chickens required, she having persisted in retaining the charge of her pets.

For an hour they labored steadily, without any rest, till a westerly breeze got up, and Wilkins, to his great relief, was able to hoist his sail; for he had previously been crying out for a helping hand. Then the catamaran floated briskly over the waves, which were, however, a little more raised by the wind than was pleasant for the slender canoes. But even the most timid took courage when the long line of low coast became plainly visible. No threatening rocks or foaming breakers appeared to create terror; and all seemed so favorable to the voyage of the unskilled mariners, that they began to be fastidious in their choice of a landing-place.

"Let us coast awhile, Arty," said Hugh, "till we come to the mouth of a river, which will insure us a fertile coast. There is no occasion for us to land on a desert."

"There would only be one danger in such a choice," replied Arthur,— "The natives may also prefer the fertile coast, and would be likely to oppose the landing of intruders. I think I should prefer to land at first on an uninhabited spot. We could then examine the country, and determine our future course. It appears to me, as we draw nearer, and can observe the low coast opposite to us, that the landing would suit our canoes. What do you say, papa?"

"I think you are right, Arthur," answered he. "I see trees above the beach; and surely I distinguish large birds on the shore, a still more encouraging prospect."

Margaret looked intently for some time in silence; then, turning to her brother, she said, "Are those figures we see really birds, Arthur?"

Arthur looked round once more towards the coast, and then, calling out to the other boats, "South! south!" he altered the direction of the canoe, and said,—

"After all, papa, we must coast a few miles, at least; for those figures are the natives, who are, as I now see, armed with spears, and will probably resist our landing, regarding us as foreign invaders. We must not begin our pilgrimage by going to war."

"Do you think Peter is with them?" asked Hugh.

"I do not suspect that he is," said Arthur. "I fancy Peter's associates were islanders; but we must avoid all intercourse with the natives as long as we can."

"How glad I am, brother," said Margaret, "that we are sailing south. How happy we should all be if we could ever reach the dear Deverells."

"My dear sister," answered Arthur, laughing, "you surely do not expect that we can voyage along the whole coast of West Australia in these shells. If we ever purpose to meet the Deverells again, we must have stout vessels for the sea, and wagons and horses for the land journey; which could only be obtained by the influence of some powerful fairy in our present desolate position."

"Nevertheless, Arthur," said his father, "if God permits us to set our feet on that continent in safety, my aim shall be to discover, if possible, the estate of that estimable young man; and to offer myself to undertake the church of his new colony. I now despair of ever reaching my destination in India, and my heart and my wishes point to Daisy Grange."

The eyes of his children sparkled as they listened to the speculations of their father; though Arthur smiled and shook his head, and Margaret sighed, as they thought on the difficulties of so prodigious an attempt.

"Never despair, Meggie," said Hugh; "we'll do it. We are all strong fellows, in sound health, and I flatter myself tolerably ingenious. I feel full of resources, and Jack is a mine of wealth. If we succeed in crossing the sea in these slender toy boats, I do not see why we should not traverse the whole continent of Australia, with our stout frames and bold hearts."

"To me," said Mr. Mayburn, "it would be the realization of a long-indulged dream to set my foot in a new and lovely world,

> 'To slowly trace the forest's shady scene,
> Where things that own not man's dominion dwell,
> And mortal foot hath ne'er or rarely been.'

Yes, my children, I also believe that, by God's help, we may penetrate the wilderness, and look on wonder hidden since the day of creation. I am content to encounter hardships. Let us go on."

"But, papa," answered Arthur, "*c'est le premier pas qui coûte*; and this first step we have yet to make—the step upon *terra firma*. Margaret thinks that must be very easy; but we poor mariners, who know 'the dangers of the seas,' have some notion of the difficulties of landing a bark canoe on an unknown coast, without rudder, lead, anchor, or any nautical appliance; and not one amongst us, as you know, papa, far advanced in the study of the grand science of navigation."

"That is wholly my fault, my boys," answered Mr. Mayburn. "I ought to have arranged that the charming science of navigation should form one of your mathematical recreations; but I never dreamed that you would be called upon to make use of a branch of knowledge so rarely cultivated in the quiet life of retirement to which we were called. But are we not some miles from those threatening savages now, Arthur?"

"Not quite far enough, sir," said Arthur. "They may have watched, and intend to follow us. We will put a dozen miles between us before we make for the shore. But I see poor Wilkins is quite worn out, and, as his sail is useless now, I must spare you to help him, Hugh, and papa will take an oar."

They approached near enough to mark the variations of the coast, now flat and sandy, then rugged, and occasionally bristling with rocks, which would have torn their little bark to shivers if they had encountered them. At last every arm was exhausted, and the opposite coast being low and untenanted, they rowed up to it with caution, looked keenly round for reefs and hidden rocks, of which they were in great dread.

"Let us run in first," shouted Wilkins from his raft. "We can bide a shock better nor ye, and likely we may help ye out of yer troubles a bit, when we've gotten this ugly craft landed."

Margaret felt some alarm for Hugh; but Arthur reminded her that Wilkins was, in fact, the only sailor amongst them; besides, rough as he was, he was too much attached to the boy to lead him into any danger. So the canoes lay to, watching the clumsy catamaran paddled into shallow water. Then they saw Wilkins wade to shore, towing in his raft with a rope, till at length, by the aid of Hugh, it was safely drawn on a low, broad, sandy beach.

Wilkins then hailed Arthur, pointed out the mode of bringing in the canoes; and wading out breast-high in the water to assist him, finally all were happily landed.

"There's an ugly sand-bank just out yonder," said Wilkins, "and I were feared ye might run atop on it. Now ye niver thought, master, these bits of cockle-shells should turn out grand sailers as they are. I say, Jack, man, ye'll try a three-decker next, I reckon."

Wilkins was in high good-humor, tired as he was, with his successful voyage; and declared Hugh was a clever little chap, and he liked him better than any other lad he had ever seen. And now Margaret saw, with a hopeful heart, that the man was really changed; his rough and lowering countenance began to look brighter; and the desperate convict was thus providentially led into the path of reformation.

"Now that we are really landed," said Mr. Mayburn, "I would ask what we are to do."

"I should answer, papa," said Hugh, "let us eat, and rest; for you have no idea how tired and hungry Wilkins and I are."

All declared the suggestion was excellent, and while the provisions were got from the catamaran, Arthur walked a little way from the beach to inspect the country, and saw before him only a wide bare plain, skirted towards the sea by a few mangroves, and apparently devoid of all inhabitants, rational or brute. This was not a promising prospect; all that could be said of it was, that it was quiet; though they were dreadfully annoyed by the mosquitos when they sat down to dinner under the shade afforded by the mangroves.

As they ate their wild duck, they seriously discussed the future. They were reluctant to set out over the plains and abandon their little fleet, lest circumstances should render it necessary to resume their voyage.

"What say you, Hugh, my boy," said Gerald, "if you and I were to take a run across these downs, and look out for a pleasant place for an encampment, out of the way of these rascally stinging beasts?"

"What say you, Arthur," asked Hugh, "will your excellency permit two of your humble servants to set out on an exploring expedition?"

"I think it would be more prudent for his excellency to command the expedition in person," said Arthur; "I dare not trust you, my thoughtless lads, and we can leave a safe protection for the garrison in our two heroes, Jack and Wilkins; therefore let us march at once. Take the gun out of its case, and give it into my charge; and you can carry the spears and throwing-sticks."

The young men had completed, while in the island, a number of spears and throwing-sticks, from the models of those left behind by the natives; they had even successfully imitated the boomerang,—that mysterious weapon of warfare, so eccentric in its movements, and so remarkable in its effect; but they had not yet attained the art of casting it. Bows and arrows had been commenced, and these Jack undertook to employ himself in completing during their absence.

Though Arthur was a prudent and safe protector for his young brothers, and Wilkins and Jack were powerful defenders to leave behind, the family did not separate without considerable anxiety. The young men crossed the plains directly from the beach, satisfied that they were in safety on that vast open waste, on which not even a growth of brushwood offered concealment for a foe. A loose, sandy soil, covered with thin, brown grass, gave to these sterile downs the appearance of a perfect desert. To crown all, they could not see in any direction the indication of water; and, thankful that they had brought a supply of this precious necessary of existence from the island that would last them for many days, Arthur still felt every moment more convinced that it would be folly to linger on this inhospitable coast, where, unfurnished with any means of hastening their progress to a more fertile region, they should be in danger of perishing with famine.

"We shall have to try the canoes again, Hugh," said he.

"It would be all very good fun," said Gerald, "if it was not such hard work. And it's little use hoisting a sail, for ten to one we shall have a contrary wind."

"I hardly think the odds are so great as that against a fair wind my boy," answered Arthur; "but at all events hard work is better than hard fare. So we must just get such a night's rest as the mosquitos will permit us, and then try a bit of coasting in the morning. We can hardly come on a more cheerless coast than this."

"What in the world is that before us, Arthur?" exclaimed Hugh. "This coast must be inhabited, for this erection is certainly the work of man's hand. It is one of the pyramids of Egypt in miniature."

"No, Hugh, man's hand has never meddled with this structure," replied Arthur. "I recognize it from description as one of the marvels of insect industry—an ant-hill. Observe the skill and ingenuity that must have been displayed to construct this huge abode for a countless nation. This firm yellow clay is now so hardened that without some tools we could scarcely overthrow it."

"I see no entrance," said Hugh, "is it possible that it is inhabited?"

"Look here, close to the ground," answered Arthur, "at this tiny speck of an aperture, from which I have just seen a diminutive insect emerge! and it has been remarked, that these creatures, the smallest of their species, erect themselves the most lofty abodes. This must be eight feet in height, and wonderful as it appears externally as the work of that minute creature, the interior, we read, is still more astonishing—a miracle of perfection in art."

"Let us open it, Arthur, and have a peep at the curious little nation," said Gerald.

"And thus destroy the labor of thousands!" answered Arthur. "No, Gerald, you would surely never wish to be so wantonly destructive. We had better remember the advice of Solomon, 'Consider its ways, and be wise.'"

"Margaret will laugh at our exploits as foragers," said Hugh. "We have certainly seen an ant-hill, but we have not even found an egg to carry home. I wish we could pick up any token of life or vegetation in this desert. Let us make a little tour, Arthur. I have my eye on our land-mark, that tall, bare, spectral mangrove."

Arthur did not object to walk a short distance towards the south, anxious to obtain a more extensive view of the coast; but they went over the bare, uninteresting soil for two hours without any satisfaction. A single dry, withered acacia spread its thin branches before them; and Arthur was glad to climb it to extend his view along the coast line. But all appeared desolation: not a hill, a rock, or a green fringe to denote vegetation or water. He descended, much disappointed, and silently and thoughtfully they directed their steps to the boats.

It was night before they reached their anxious friends, who saw in their jaded and melancholy countenances the disappointment of their hopes.

"Didn't I tell ye all along," grumbled Wilkins, "as how north were yer point, and ye'll have to make a north course, after all. I've run along this here coast long afore this, and I say again, ye'll find neither meat nor water for hundreds of miles down south."

"I must allow, Wilkins," answered Arthur, "that voyagers have ever stated that this coast from the eighteenth to the twenty-fifth degree of latitude is certainly desert; and that in the lower latitudes it is fertile and well watered; but by returning north we are flying from the aim of our hopes, and must necessarily risk encounters with the natives."

Margaret sighed as she thought of removing still further from the Deverells, and Wilkins said,—

"Never ye heed them black fellows; they're nought but a set of reet down cowards, to be fled away by that silly bit lass. We're six clever chaps again 'em, and if we bully a bit at first, we'se drive 'em afore us like sheep."

Mr. Mayburn shook his head, and Arthur had some doubts of such an easy victory; but it was expedient to keep up the spirit of the party, and he made no answer. Then, mortifying as it was to retrace their course, it was finally agreed they should sail north next morning, keeping in sight of the coast, and avoiding the landing-place where they had seen the natives the previous day. They proposed to seek the mouth of a river, if they could possibly discover one, which might form an easy mode of access to the interior.

Jack had during the day carefully examined the canoes, added a fresh coating of the gum, which he had brought with him, and lashed the timbers of the raft tight and firm. Then, after an uneasy night of vexatious contentions with the mosquitos, they breakfasted, prayed for God's blessing on their perilous enterprise, and once more committed themselves to the ocean.

Since they first landed on their little island, the weather had continued to be invariably calm and beautiful, and even the thoughtless Ruth and the rude convict seemed to be struck with the "witchery of the clear blue sky," while the more intelligent did not forget to thank their bounteous Creator, who had tempered their little trials with this blessing. Now, cheered by the bright sky and the fresh sea breeze, the young rowers plied their oars with willing hands, singing merrily as they urged their fragile barks over the light curling waves.

Hugh had joined Wilkins, as on the previous day, and, favored by a south wind they spread the sail. Wilkins, however, augured no good of this favorable breeze, declaring the south wind was always the fore-runner of a storm; but they might as well make the best of a bad job, by easing their arms a bit. But for many hours they sailed on favorably and uninterruptedly, for Margaret had taken care that each canoe should be amply provisioned for the day. When they passed that part of the coast where the natives had been assembled on the previous day, they saw that it was now untenanted; but they felt no inclination to visit a locality so frequented, so continued their voyage; and on passing a hilly shore about a mile further north, they not only saw the people collected in numbers and waving their spears, but could hear their yells as they ventured to approach within a mile of the shore.

"I say, Wilkins, my man," said Hugh. "Do you fancy our little troop could drive all that lot of fellows before us like a flock of sheep? I should hardly like to make the experiment, unless each of us was armed with a good rifle."

"That's just what we want, Master Hugh," replied Wilkins. "It were just that there gun, as I grudged that rogue Peter a vast deal more nor bags of bread and such like. If we'd had a few more guns, we might have defied every black fellow alive atween here and Perth. They've not that sense to make out what it is, as makes all that clatter and smoke; and it's just because they ken nought about it as makes 'em so soft.... But, halloo! Master Hugh, I don't half like yon sky, we'se have some weather afore long."

Hugh hailed the canoes, to announce to Arthur the meteorological observations of Wilkins; and as the man had certainly more experience than any of the party, they could not help feeling a little alarmed. Arthur looked anxiously towards the coast for a favorable landing-place, but here, only high bare cliffs ran along the shore, against which the waves dashed with a fury that warned them they must not approach near.

Gradually, the sky grew dark with clouds, the wind was heard before it was felt; and before Hugh and Wilkins could tear down their rude sail, the raft was whirled round, and hurried furiously past the canoes towards a sort of eddy which was dashing and foaming not a quarter of a mile before them. With all the speed they could make, Arthur and his father rowed forward to rescue Hugh and Wilkins, regardless, at that moment, of the fate of the raft itself.

The two men had now got the sail lowered; the raft was dashed amongst the breakers, but Arthur's canoe gained on them, and he could hear Wilkins hailing them, "Keep clear of the eddy; and send us a rope." Fortunately the mooring rope was still attached to the canoe, and Arthur endeavored, though many times ineffectually, to fling it within reach of the doomed catamaran.

At length Wilkins secured the rope, and binding it firmly round Hugh, he flung the boy clear of the tossing raft. Arthur and the half-distracted father hauled the rope gently, as long as the poor lad seemed able to contend against the waves, and when he seemed to have yielded to their violence, they drew him, senseless, to the canoe. The cares of Margaret soon restored him, and in the mean time Wilkins had plunged into the boiling waves, and though a good swimmer, he with much difficulty reached the canoe, which they saw, with distress, was now far too much laden in such a sea.

CHAPTER X

"The catamaran is lost, master," said Wilkins, as soon as he could speak. "But life afore property any day, and somehow I'se had thoughts of late as how I'se hardly fit to die.... Now then; look about ye, young man. That there eddy's a *freshet*; there's a river comes in there, and that's where as we should be, if we can make land cannily. Here, auld master, lend me them oars, and sit ye down and look after that young chap."

Arthur agreed with Wilkins; but it was a perilous undertaking to carry the canoes over the foaming breakers, the hidden rocks of that frowning coast. His own experience rendered him hopeless of ever accomplishing the task, and he was now thankful for the advice and assistance of Wilkins.

"Then we must tow them in the other canoe," said Arthur. "Remember, Wilkins, whether we be saved or lost, we must have them with us."

"Ay! ay!" answered he. "Let them fling us their tow-rope, and do you see to belay it cannily; and if we be swamped, look sharp and clutch Miss here, and make a swim with her. We're nigh shallow water now, and we may drive in, barrin' rocks."

It was only by clinging to each other, that Margaret and her father, as well as the two women in the second canoe, were able to keep their seats, as the waves tossed up, whirled, and washed over their frail barks. Sometimes they seemed to be thrown upon land, and the next wave carried them back with it.

"Now then!" cried Wilkins, holding up his oar, and signalling to Jack to follow his example. "Now, when we ground again, you, master, jump out and hold her hard for yer life."

The next moment the canoe did ground with a shock, and Wilkins plunged the oar into the sandy shore, and held his ground firmly till Arthur and Mr. Mayburn leaped out of the canoe and held the prow; he followed their example, and though still up to the waist in water, they grasped their charge, standing close to each other, and bravely withstood the returning wave. Then rapidly retreating to the shore, they easily drew after them the lightened canoe, and placed it high and dry on the beach before the next wave overtook them.

Jack and O'Brien, though they at last happily reached the same haven, had not escaped without mishap. The canoe had been capsized by the shock of grounding, and, but for the assistance of Wilkins, Ruth must have been lost. She was dragged out senseless, but still holding her basket on her arm; and her first words on her recovery were loud lamentations at the discovery that two of her fowls were drowned.

In the mean time the second canoe was whirling wildly among the breakers, and Arthur called out that, if possible, it must be saved; and all hands were soon engaged in catching the towing-rope, by which they soon succeeded in drawing the shattered bark to the beach.

"I think that is a useless labor, Arthur," said Mr. Mayburn, "for I trust that none here may ever again be compelled to tempt the dangers of the ocean in such a frail and imperfect bark. By God's mercy, our feet are once more upon the earth, the natural and ordained locality of man. Byron, the wondrous poet who apostrophized the ocean, says:—

'His steps are not upon thy paths,—thy fields
Are not a spoil for him,—thou dost arise
And shake him from thee!'

"I feel, Arthur, that I am in my proper place, and desert or fruitful, lonely or populous, I would still remain on land."

"So you shall, dear papa, if God permits it," answered Arthur; "but not on this bare and comfortless strand. We must penetrate to a more hospitable region. It was to render this journey less toilsome to you that I meditated to secure and fit up the canoes, in order to use them in ascending the river which we see pouring into the sea, and which must be our guide to the interior."

"Ay," said Wilkins, "rivers is rivers in this queer, dry country; and other folks ken that as well as us; and when ye light on a sup of water, make sure of finding a lot of them black fellows gathered round it. But they're no better nor brute beasts, and we're a match for 'em any day."

"We shall have to risk encountering them," said Arthur, "for the sake of providing ourselves with food, for I fear we are now reduced to absolute destitution."

"We have Ruth's plump chickens," said the mischievous O'Brien.

"Oh, Master Gerald!" exclaimed Ruth, weeping; "and could you have a heart to kill the poor dumb creatures as have lived wi' us so long? I would hunger sooner nor eat a bit of one of them, not if we had fried ham to it."

The volatile boy laughed heartily at Ruth's visionary fancy of chicken and ham; and Margaret assured the sorrowful girl that only the fear of starvation should compel them to slay her pets, though the two drowned chickens must certainly be cooked, and not left on the beach for the gulls.

They had landed not far north of the mouth of what they now found to be a considerable river, to the banks of which they soon made their way, and found that it ran between high cliffs, leaving a narrow pathway at the side, almost impassable, with huge fragments of rock scattered along it. But they remained fixed in their intention of following up its course, as the safest guide in their expedition. But first they must rest, and have such refreshment as they could obtain, the provisions in the canoes being washed out in the struggle to land. They sat down under an overhanging cliff, where curtains of drooping creeping plants shielded them from the sun, the boys having brought up stones for seats; and, after fervent thanks for their safety, they all felt a peace and tranquillity scarcely to be hoped for in their destitute condition.

"It was most fortunate that the rifle was with me in the canoe," said Arthur, "and safe in the case. It is no worse for the immersion. The charges I always carry in my belt in the water-proof case; so we are provided for defence. But the raft and its precious contents, Margaret!"

"Have trust in God, my son," said Mr. Mayburn. "Look up at that magnificent snow-white bird, one of the eagle tribe, which is even now soaring over our heads. Why should we doubt? He who feeds the fowls of the air will not forget his children on earth."

"Here are lots of oysters, papa," said Hugh, "and Gerald has run after a large crab. There will certainly be turtles on the beach, and birds and eggs in the cliffs, and then we have water in the river."

"But there's not a kettle, nor a toasting-fork," said Ruth dejectedly.

"I'll provide you with both," answered the boy. Then from the roots of a mangrove, which spread below the cliffs, he tore down an enormous mussel, the shells of which were at least six inches in length, and, drawing an arrow from his belt, he gave both to the girl, saying, "Here, Ruth, are your kettles and toasting-fork."

A plentiful, but strangely cooked, repast was soon prepared, consisting of the limbs of the drowned chickens, toasted or broiled over a fire of drift-wood, and served on oyster shells. Knives they had fortunately preserved, but nothing more, and they could not help feeling the want of the common necessaries of social life.

After dinner the young men cleared the canoes from the accumulated weed and water, drew them under the shelter of the cliff, spread their boat-cloaks in them, and persuaded Margaret and their father to rest, while they held council what course to pursue next; but they found themselves so overcome with fatigue and anxiety, that at the first approach of darkness they all sought rest under the canopy of heaven before they should commence their labors.

"Are all assembled?" called Gerald, at the first gleam of daylight. "Hugh and I have already been at the beach, and collected a hat-full of turtles' eggs and some wood for a fire. And now, Arthur, we are off on another excursion; we want to climb the cliffs, to see what sort of country we have been thrown upon."

"Then you must accept me for a third in your enterprise," answered Arthur, "for papa would not approve of two such wild fellows setting out alone. Now, nurse, Hugh has made a fire to roast us some eggs, and with a shell of cold water from that jar we saved in the canoe, we have our breakfast complete."

"If you could but light on a few leaves of tea, Mr. Arthur," said Jenny, "I could manage without milk and sugar; but I shall miss my drop of tea."

Arthur could give Jenny no hopes of any tea-leaves, or even of any substitute for that agreeable shrub, but he was sanguine about procuring eggs, and even birds, for dinner. Then promising to return in an hour or two, and taking the gun with them, each of the hardy boys cut down a strong stick, and then marched off along the narrow pathway at the foot of the high cliffs which enclosed the guiding river. After walking some distance, the shelving rocks, covered with rich tropical creeping shrubs, appeared accessible, and they climbed to the summit, shaking down upon them, as they forced their way through the bushes, multitudes of stinging green ants. Then they walked first to the edge of the cliffs that overhung the sea, and looked round to observe their position.

It was plain that they were now upon the mainland, and that they had been driven into a wide bay, with headlands running out on each side, while the entrance was barred by coral reefs which it seemed miraculous that they should have escaped. Beyond the reefs they distinguished shadowy dots, which they concluded were small islets, probably similar to that which had sheltered them so long, and which they now congratulated themselves they had exchanged for a wider field and more promising prospect of reaching a permanent resting-place.

"How I wish papa was here," exclaimed Hugh. "Do look at those curious birds, and tell me what they are, Arthur. Oh, now I know they must be cockatoos, from their odd cry. Would it be right to kill them?"

"I shall have a shy at one," said Gerald, who had luckily brought his bow slung on his back; and he directly brought down with an arrow a fine large bird about eighteen inches in length, with snowy plumage and a bright orange crest.

"What will Margaret say?" exclaimed Hugh. "But it is a handsome creature, and papa will be delighted to preserve it."

"It must help to preserve us," replied Arthur, "for we are in true need. We must try to find some nests in the cliffs, and at least procure eggs to increase our rations; for a cockatoo, which has a large amount of feather upon it, will be but a small dinner for nine hungry people."

They examined the crevices of the rocks, and found many nests of gulls and cockatoos, containing eggs and even tolerable-sized young birds, of which they brought away half a dozen, and filled their pockets with eggs, and then turned from the coast to take a glance inland. The view before them was wild, and scattered over with rocks, but seemed well wooded; and from the curious mingled cries from the bushes, they judged that the feathered tribes were abundant.

Then they commenced their perplexing descent through the tangled bushes, shaking off, as they proceeded, the tormenting ants, which ran over them in countless numbers, each little creature seeming determined to make its presence felt.

"After our observations," said Arthur, "I am still of opinion that, if the canoes can be repaired, we must try to make them useful in ascending the river, the banks of which promise to afford us abundant food; while the waters supply us with their precious refreshment. We may encounter the natives, certainly; but we shall be able to escape from them more easily in the canoes, than if we were dragging slowly on by land. We must begin immediately to fit them for the voyage."

"I saw a fine gum-tree above," said Hugh, "that will supply us with materials for mending or making. We must bring Jack here; but oh! Arty, I quite forgot—his tools would be all swept away with that unlucky catamaran."

"It is a most unfortunate loss," replied Arthur; "but we must not despair. If we have not the best means, we must take the next best; we must consider and contrive, and not care for hard work."

They returned with their booty, and found Jack standing with a pensive and disturbed countenance over the canoes; while Wilkins and Margaret, the tide being now low, had wandered down to the sea; where Gerald quickly followed them, and found that their object was to watch, in hopes that any part of the cargo of the catamaran might be thrown on the shore. Their first prize was a locker filled with potatoes, which Jack had fortunately nailed up to prevent the water coming in, and thus the contents were quite uninjured. But they found a greater treasure still, in the estimation of Margaret; a portmanteau of linen, which the thief Peter had either overlooked or despised, and which had been one of the greatest comforts left them in their bereaved condition. They were fortunately all wearing good stout boots, and their outer clothing, in that charming climate, was of minor importance.

The waifs were speedily removed from the beach to the encampment, where they found Jenny and Ruth in great distress.

"This is worse than all, Miss Marget," said nurse. "With that bright bonnie river running in sight of us, we have not a sup of water fit for a Christian to drink. It's as salt as pickle; enough to poison one, and can sarve for nothing that I can think on, but just to boil fish in."

"I had not considered, Arthur," said Mr. Mayburn, "till nurse made her experiment, that the tide naturally rises up the river, probably for many miles, thus cutting us off from one of the most important necessaries of life. Now, perilous as it may be to leave the coast, it is imperative on us to move, or we must perish."

Arthur reflected for a few minutes, and then said, "Let us have some eggs, Meggie; then Jack will accompany us, and we will set out to trace the river up the ravine; and I cannot but think we shall certainly meet with tributary streams from the hills, of perfectly fresh water."

"But how shall we bring back the supplies to the camp?" asked Hugh. "We have no vessels except mussel-shells, or our cups."

"Oh, warra!" exclaimed Gerald, "if the sea would only be civil enough to give us back our water-cask! Could we not go out to the reefs, Arthur, and look for it?"

"It was too heavy to be easily thrown on shore," answered Arthur. "It is most likely fixed in some sand-bank, whence it will require a storm to move it. We must each choose one of the largest of the mussels we saw this morning clinging to the banks, and bring them in filled with fresh water—provided we meet with the water—carrying it as steadily as we are able. If we only had the canoes in working condition, we would move at once above the influence of the tide. Can we possibly repair them, Jack? We can procure bark and gum."

Jack turned out the contents of his pockets—neatly tied knots of small cords, a clasp knife, a hammer, and about a pint of nails.

"I always have a hammer and a few nails about me, you see, Mr. Arthur," said he, "and if I had but an axe and a saw, I'd not fear any work. But it's a sin to be drowned; something will be sure to turn up; so with God's help we'll manage these bits of boats, and then, thank God, Master O'Brien saved his bow."

"And here you see the remains of mine, Jack," said Hugh. "I have picked it up on the beach. You must try and fit me out again, and then neither storm nor savage shall tear it from me. Only think, papa, if I had had my bow, we might have brought down a splendid white-headed hawk!"

"Would that you had succeeded, my boy," answered his father. "A white-headed hawk would indeed have been a gem in my collection, an anomaly in the known feathered race. But, indeed, every living creature in these regions is an anomaly to all naturalists. This cockatoo is obviously of an antipodean race. Its form, habits, and peculiar notes, mark it to be of a distinct and modern family, having even little relation to the *psittacidæ* of the ancient race. I am pleased with this remarkable bird, my dear boys, and feel no inclination to have it cooked and eaten like a common barn-door fowl."

"For my part," said Margaret, "I should feel less remorse in devouring this stranger than one of our old familiar friends, Ruth's beloved pets."

There was a common outcry against this household homicide, or gallicide, as Hugh called it; but there were young birds and eggs sufficient for the day's provision; so the cockatoo was reprieved, and Mr. Mayburn carefully preserved the bird in all the glories of its white plumage and yellow crest, so curiously movable at the will of the bird.

Once more the young men set out for the very important object of discovering fresh water; and the tide being down, they walked up the margin of the river with less difficulty than in the morning, but it was not till after they had gone two or three miles beneath the thickly covered cliffs, which were perfectly alive with multitudes of strange birds, that they came to a narrow ravine, opening at the north, from which a low cascade poured a clear but slender rill into the river.

They at once decided to ascend this branch stream. Its narrow bed was guarded by lofty rocks, which hid from their eyes every prospect but that of the clear blue sky above them, and their voices sounded hollow as if from below the ground; but, to their great satisfaction, the water was fresh, clear, and cool, and no sparkling champagne was ever enjoyed more truly than the draughts they quaffed from the shells of the fresh-water mussels which were abundantly clustered on the banks and strewed around.

"Don't you feel, Gerald," said Hugh, "as if we were passing through some gloomy glen to arrive at a grand old Moorish castle—full of enchantments of course?"

"That's a capital idea, Hugh," answered he. "Then there will be a beautiful princess shut up in the steel tower, with a hideous black enchanter keeping guard over her, and a fiery red dragon at the gate, and we have to conquer him with one rifle and half a dozen cartridges, that we may release the princess."

"Why, you Irish blunderer," replied Hugh, "whoever heard that either dragon or enchanter could be overcome by powder and shot? If you have not fairy patronage, you must have valor and prudence, and resolution; and there's Arthur, though he looks so meek and quiet, would be the conquering hero."

"We will leave the siege of the enchanted castle for a more convenient opportunity," said Arthur, "and be content to carry home such valuable trophies of conquest as a few shells of fresh water. But why has Hugh climbed that almost perpendicular cliff?"

"He fancied he saw a palm-tree on the height," answered Gerald; "but if it really be a palm, I must say it is an ugly tree; and, for my part, I would much rather have found an apple-tree, only, as I suppose September is spring in this antipodean world, the apples could not be ready."

"Moreover, apples are not indigenous in Australia," said Arthur; "nor shall we, I fear, meet with any equivalent fruit. Some of the palms are really useful, but I cannot think what species of palm that can be."

A voice was heard from above, commanding them to clear the way, and a huge gourd was hurled down, rolling to the very edge of the stream. It was plainly not fresh plucked, but must have lain long on the ground; and when Hugh descended, disappointed that he had not been able to find any fruit on the tree, Arthur explained that the gourds that were known were not generally edible, but most useful as vessels for holding water. Then Jack cut a hole in the shell, which they cleansed from all the decayed matter, and washed frequently to remove the bitter taste of the contents. The gourd was slung by a cord, which Arthur himself placed over his shoulders, and filled with the fresh water for their friends.

Jack having found the *Eucalyptus* or gum-tree that he required, they stripped it of the bark, and, having filled a mussel-shell with the fresh oozing gum, they returned to the encampment, well pleased with their successful, though very tedious expedition; for the flowing tide made their return along the banks most difficult. In fact, Arthur was of opinion that if they waited for a spring tide, the river would entirely flood the ravine, and render their progress impossible except by boat.

"I was not aware," said Mr. Mayburn, "that the wide-spreading but fastidious genus *Cucurbita* extended to these strange regions; yet this gourd surely belongs to it I am curious to see the tree, to ascertain if it is of any known species."

"At all events," said Margaret, "it will be very useful to us. Its contents are truly precious, and we are most grateful to our persevering and active purveyors. And we welcome them heartily to their dinner of broiled ducklings, or whatever else these delicate little birds may be named, with one potatoe for each person, which has been boiled with salt water in a mussel-shell."

The potatoes were pronounced to be improved by their saline immersion, and the ducklings had no fault except youth and leanness. But oysters were plentiful, and the report of the explorers announced abundance in the regions up the river; so that it was with thankful hearts the family sought repose after their labors, to fit them for the renewed toil of the next day.

Jack commenced his work at daylight. He fixed large patches of bark with gum over the weak or damaged part of the canoes, and left them to harden in the sun. Then, with immense labor, they cut down with their knives some boughs for poles to propel the vessels. A single oar had been thrown ashore by the last tide, and some broken spars, from which a pair of short oars were rudely formed. Hugh and Gerald had been employed in the mean time in the search for turtles' eggs, and had been fortunate enough to meet with a quantity, as well as with a small turtle. None of the party had much taste for the rich food, but nothing eatable was to be despised in their situation; so the turtle was sacrificed, and another kettle provided for the cooks.

"The gum seems already hardened on the boats," said Arthur, "and I do not see, papa, that we have any temptation to remain on this mosquito-haunted coast longer than necessary. In another hour the tide will be flowing up the river, and will assist our voyage greatly. Shall we then at once set out on our important expedition?"

"I see the necessity of it, my son," answered Mr. Mayburn, "and am satisfied. Let us implore a blessing on our undertaking, and then go forth, confiding in the protection of the Most High."

Wilkins attended the family devotions with decorum now; but what effect was produced in his heart was yet to be developed. Hugh and Margaret, to whom he listened more patiently than to the rest, were satisfied that some change was taking place in the sinful man, and earnestly believed that he would, by God's grace, be turned to the truth.

CHAPTER XI

After the fervent heat of noon had somewhat subsided, the party arranged themselves in the two canoes, and, aided by the tide, swept up the river, which now extended to the cliffs on both sides, and effectually cut off any passage by land. Occasionally the fallen masses of the sandstone rocks, which lay shelving or sloping to the water, were covered with a rich growth of low entangled shrubs, now bursting into flowers of many a brilliant hue; amongst which numbers of pert, noisy, little green or variegated parrots hopped about, chattering over these strange disturbers of their wonted tranquillity.

"Charming! charming!" exclaimed Mr. Mayburn. "This is the sublime solitude of which I have dreamed all my life. How glorious it would be

'To hold with Heaven communion meet,
Meet for a spirit bound to Heaven,—
And, in this wilderness beneath,
Pure zephyrs from above to breathe.'

What a completion of all my hopes it would be, my children, if you could find some quiet spot where we might land, and be content to pass our lives upon it."

This desire of Mr. Mayburn was received by his children with some consternation, while Ruth, though she but vaguely understood the proposal, looked round at the prison-like rocky walls, the sombre twilight, and the dashing waters, and began to cry. Even Wilkins, who heard all that was said in Mr. Mayburn's canoe, cried out, "Nay, nay, master, that would upset all; I'se not flinch to sail wi' ye, or to tramp wi' ye; but to bide here for good, among oysters and poll-parrots, is what I can't stand. It would soon set me off bush-ranging."

"We must move onward, papa," said Arthur, "but doubtless we shall find, as we proceed, scenes that will interest you even more than this. We may even encounter peaceful tribes; and though our ignorance of their language will prevent our holding any beneficial intercourse with them, we may at all events give them an example of kindness and forbearance."

"And remember, papa," said Margaret, "we have a definite aim in our travels. We must look forward to the pleasure of joining our friends, the Deverells."

"But, Margaret," replied he, "how can you hope that we shall ever be able to traverse the vast space that must separate us? How can you and I penetrate forests, climb mountains, or cross mighty rivers?"

"Few of them last to signify, master," said Wilkins, "by yer leave; and better for us if we had more. I kenned some of our chaps down yonder as tired of slavery, and what would serve 'em but be off to Chinee, which they heared say lay to t' north; and reet glad were they to sneak back to hard work and full rations. Why, they'd gone miles and miles over dry sand, wi' niver a tree to shelter 'em or a sup of water to drink. Where rivers ought to have been, there were just dry mud and wet mud, and that were all. We'se want no boats in them there rivers."

"Pray, dear papa," said Arthur, "do not look so much alarmed at Wilkins's exaggerated reports. I have read the travels of scientific and experienced explorers, who certainly agree that large portions of the coast are desert, but give strong reasons for hope that the interior may be fruitful and well-watered. To these fertile regions, I am of opinion, we should endeavor to penetrate; for we have not means nor nautical skill to attempt a sea-voyage, even to the inhabited islands of the Indian Ocean. But it is for you to decide, papa."

"I leave it to you, my boy," answered his father. "I rely on your energy and judgment, under Heaven."

"Are we to turn up our watering-river?" called Hugh, from the forward boat.

"Here is a niche in the rocks," answered Arthur, "secure from the tide, where we will rest to-night, as we shall have our fresh water near at hand."

The nook was as convenient as any roofless place could be for a night abode; and even Margaret had now become accustomed to this wild life, and rested her head on a pillow of rock, in the open air, with the peace and comfort of a tranquil and pious spirit.

Early in the morning the boys went up the fresh-water rivulet to enjoy the luxury of a bath; and such was the profusion of fish that filled the clear water, that they succeeded without difficulty in spearing two of the large species of river-cod that they had found in the island lake; and as these weighed ten or twelve pounds each, they returned very triumphant with their spoil.

"I know it has been familiarly named the river-cod," said Hugh; "but you know, papa, the cod is strictly a sea-fish; besides, this ugly fellow, if he were not so large, is not unlike a perch."

"It is like the productions of Australia," said Mr. Mayburn; "unclassed and strange. It seems to blend the distinctive features of the cod and the perch,—the salt-water and fresh-water tribes."

"But it's safe to eat?" asked Jenny, anxiously.

"We have already tried it with impunity, nurse," answered Arthur; "all travellers praise it as delicate and nutritious, and, from its abundance in the rivers, it must be a great boon to the natives."

The fish was boiled in the salt-water. But before night they had rowed beyond the influence of the tide; and had now to labor hard to ascend the river, the high banks of which continued to be shaded by mangroves, which were weighed down with clusters of oysters and fresh-water mussels, looking like some strange fruits of this new country.

There was something so sublime and awe-inspiring in the novelty of the scenery, that the whole party long contemplated it in silence, till an exclamation from Ruth, about the "bonnie ducks," roused them to observe the flocks of wild-fowl; and Jenny thanked God that there could be no famine here; while Mr. Mayburn noted with admiration the varieties of water-fowl, beautiful and unknown, which sailed over the river or clamored noisily among the mangroves.

The labor of ascending the river in the heat of the day soon fatigued all the rowers, and they were thankful to seek refuge and rest in a narrow ravine which ran out north, and which, after the rains, would be a rivulet. At present, all that proved its existence were a few narrow channels, with here and there a pool of clear water. The rapidly springing tropical vegetation had already spread and matted itself in the very bed of the river, forming a picturesque jungle, amidst the dark foliage of which the tiny rills sparkled like diamonds. On each side towered lofty cliffs, hung gracefully with luxuriant creepers, and a thick belt of tall gum-trees and wild nutmeg-trees, covered with greedy, noisy parrots, ran along the base. Every thing was new and charming; and having drawn the canoes up in safety beneath the roots of a mangrove, they wandered slowly up the ravine, to find, if possible, a grassy spot on which to rest and eat their dinner. As they walked along, they found on each side openings in the cliffs, smaller ravines or river-beds; all similar in rich vegetation, and all equally lonely. It was a perfect labyrinth of nature; a scene of enchantment that filled the minds of the educated with admiration and holy thoughts, but shook the ignorant with all the tremor of supernatural terrors.

"I wonder much," said Margaret, "that we should find these beautiful scenes unpeopled."

"Ye'll see people soon enough, Miss," said Wilkins. "What would they do here? Queer fellows as they be, they cannot perch atop of trees like them howling poll-parrots, nor lie under water like oysters. Wait till we come on a bit of bare common, and ye'll see folks enough."

"Wilkins is right enough, Margaret," said Arthur, "this lovely spot, happily for the free inhabitants of the air and the water, is unfit for the dwelling of man. I do not think it would be prudent to wander far among these bewildering ravines, our safest guide will be the broad river; and as we cannot meet with a convenient dining-room here, I propose that we should return to eat our dinner under the mangroves, in defiance of the troublesome inhabitants around us."

But Jenny contrived to smoke away the mosquitos with her cooking-fire, though the green ants still contrived to annoy her by falling as garnish on the beautiful fish which she served on a turtle's shell. The hungry group only laughed at the petty vexation, as they gathered round the feast with oyster-shell plates and mussel-shell cups, to eat heartily, though they wanted forks, spoons, and, as Jenny declared, all Christian comforts.

With renewed vigor they resumed their oars, and pursued their voyage on the pleasant highway, which the young and ardent believed would forward them towards the distant home they hoped to reach. And when absolute fatigue compelled them to desist, they found a convenient landing-place for the canoes on a broad patch of bare sand. They drew them on shore, and, to stretch their cramped legs, walked forward till they reached a spot where a slip of the rocks had formed a gradual ascent.

Though encumbered with trees and brushwood, they were all desirous to attempt this ascent to search for nests and eggs, and, above all, to attain, if possible, the heights above, that they might survey the country through which they were passing. They found innumerable nests of ducks, geese, and swans, and of a large bird which distracted Mr. Mayburn by its resemblance to the pelican. They found also some well-grown young birds, but contented themselves with carrying off a couple of fine cygnets.

"Hark, Arthur!" said Hugh; "what a strange cry. It must be the note of some new bird. Let us follow the sound, that we may obtain it, if possible, for papa."

"Bird, indeed!" exclaimed Wilkins; "fiddlestick! Ye'll bide where ye are, Master Hugh. Ye little ken what sort on a bird that is. Ye'd better keep quiet, for them sort of birds is awkward customers. I reckon I ken that 'Coo-ee! Coo-ee!' better nor either ye or t' auld master. It's nought else but them black fellows hailing one another."

"I fear it is but too true, Hugh," said Arthur. "I have heard of the curious cry of the natives."

"Let us flee," said Mr. Mayburn, turning hastily back. "Let us not seek scenes of discord and bloodshed."

"Couldn't I steal among the trees and get a peep at them?" said O'Brien. "The wood is so thick, they would never see me, and then I could let you know what we had to fear."

"I wouldn't have ye to be over sure," said Wilkins, "that there's not half a hundred blackies skulking underneath this here scrub as we're trailing through. They're cute rogues, and like enough, they've been tracking us all along. We'se be better looking after our boats, nor after them. We'se see plenty on 'em afore long."

It was plainly prudent to retreat, wherever the unseen enemy might be; and having secured their boats beneath a spreading mangrove, they roasted and ate some eggs, and then discussed calmly the prospect of meeting the natives, which now seemed inevitable.

"I have finished another bow," said Jack; "we have arrows and spears, and a throwing-stick. And then Mr. Arthur has his rifle."

"That's worth all t' rest put together," replied Wilkins. "They can beat us out and out with spears, and them queer crookt boomerangs; but give 'em a shot, and they'll fly off like sparrows. We'll have to mind, for, ye see, they'll never come on us boldly like men, but they'll sneak and cower, and spy, to see what we're made on. And I'd like to see t' auld master there keep up his heart; for if they see a fellow among us show a white feather, we're all done."

"But I should never think of carrying a white feather, Wilkins," said Mr. Mayburn. "I confess that I have harbored the thought of holding out to them a green branch, which, I have understood, ever signifies a flag of truce among savage nations."

"A fig for yer flags!" cried Wilkins contemptuously. "Show 'em a stout heart and a long rifle, and they'll understand 'em better nor a green flag. There goes the *Coo-ee* again! Will you put out that fire, lass. Is there any sense in sending up a smoke to let 'em see where we are?"

Ruth extinguished the fire, trembling with fright, and then crept close to Margaret and Jenny. As it was now quite dark, the women, as usual, lay down in the canoes, and the men watched and rested alternately till daylight dispelled the fear of a nocturnal attack. Then, not liking their neighborhood, they launched the canoes again, resolving to breakfast on a more secure spot; and after proceeding many miles up the river, they disembarked on a flat rock that ran out from the cliffs, where they cooked eggs for their breakfast, and the cygnets to take with them for the next meal.

But on embarking again, they found, with some uneasiness, that the navigation of the river was becoming difficult. The breadth of the bed gradually contracted; the rocks on each side overhung the water, into which large blocks had fallen from above, among which the stream rushed in strong eddies, or poured over the masses in cascades; thus rendering their progress perilous, if not impossible.

Suddenly, before they had observed any premonitory signs, a terrific storm of thunder and lightning burst upon them, accompanied by a violent wind and a deluge of rain. The peals of thunder, repeated again and again among the towering cliffs, were tremendous. Ruth shrieked with terror, and Margaret, with all her firmness, trembled to hear the voice of the tempest.

The little canoes, whirled round and dashed against the rocks, seemed doomed to inevitable destruction. Wilkins, in this fearful emergency, succeeded in securing a rope to one canoe, then leaping out upon a shelving rock, he held it till, with Hugh's assistance, the three women were snatched out, one after another, to the rock, where they clung to the trees to keep themselves from being swept away by the wind; but they tried in vain to save the canoe, as Wilkins had relinquished the rope to assist the women, and they were mortified to see it hurried down the impetuous river beyond all hopes of recovery.

The river was already raised by the pouring rain, but Wilkins boldly plunged in with an oar, which he extended to the men in the second canoe, and assisted them to reach the shore; but their boat, which had been previously damaged, was whirled against a rock, and went to pieces.

"Thank God no lives are lost," murmured Mr. Mayburn, as, exhausted and drenched with rain, he crouched under the trees, the light foliage of which afforded very insufficient shelter from the torrents of rain which descended on them; and for some time they were so stunned with their fears and their desolate condition, that they could not command their thoughts sufficiently to consider where they should turn to search for a better protection.

At length Arthur pointed out that a little higher up the river a slab of rock ran out and formed a sort of canopy over the narrow hem of beach beneath. Thither, therefore, the distressed party removed, and they found even a more convenient shelter than they had hoped; for the hollow beneath the slab was raised about four feet from the ground, and extended backwards into the sandstone rock, forming a cavern impervious to wind and rain. Their entrance dislodged hundreds of bats, of strange and frightful forms, and Mr. Mayburn half forgot his fears and miseries while he looked with admiration on a huge, imp-like creature, which he asserted must be the animal distinguished by travellers as the "flying fox."

After these hideous inhabitants were dispersed, Margaret and the two distressed women gladly took possession of this gloomy retreat, which was dry and secure. Piles of dead wood lay scattered round it, which enabled them to make a fire and dry their dripping garments. To their great joy, they had been able to preserve their bows, spears, and rifle, and Ruth had grasped firmly her precious basket of chickens. At the moment when the danger was imminent, Wilkins had had presence of mind to throw on shore the locker of potatoes, and also the portmanteau, from which they all were now glad to procure changes of clothes. The cooked provisions were lost; but they roasted some potatoes, and enjoyed their simple repast, while the thunder rolled loudly over their heads, and the rain poured like a deluge into the swollen river.

"We can go no farther to-day," said Hugh, looking out with a melancholy air. "What can we do, Gerald?"

Jack was already at work in a retired nook, making arrows from the bamboos which were plentifully scattered round; and, roused by his example, the boys joined him to sharpen spears and shape bows, which were to be completed when they met with gum to cement them, and stringy bark to form the bowstrings. Arthur cleaned his valuable rifle, Margaret wove some reeds into a basket for eggs, Mr. Mayburn lectured; Wilkins alone seemed weary and out of his element, his good properties only came out when roused to action by difficulties, and as Margaret watched him lazily rolling a piece of bark for a cigar, and then lying down to smoke it, she longed for some settled habitation, that this unfortunate man, now but half reclaimed, might have useful occupation and acquire regular habits.

But even the most industrious of the party could not but find that wild, stormy day long and tedious in this damp and dismal shelter. Nor was it without alarm that they saw the river gradually rise, till the level was within a foot of the floor of their retreat; and if it should rise high enough to overflow the cave, they were aware there could be no possibility of escape, for the waters already dashed against the cliffs on each side of them. They watched anxiously. At length, with thankfulness, they saw the rain cease;

and before darkness shut out observation, the water had fallen a few inches. Then, free from their usual nightly torment of the bush-haunting mosquitos, they enjoyed a calm night's rest in the cool cavern.

Morning brought new cares. The casual storm had passed away, and it was too early for the usual tropical rainy season; but, alas! they had no means of voyaging onward, and the waters blockaded them. There was no path along the beach. They waited another day, in terror of famine or another storm. A very slight decrease of the waters was seen next morning. The cliffs were too high and precipitate for even the boldest to climb, the river too deep and impetuous to be crossed except in a boat, and the narrow hem of sand now left at the edge was barely sufficient for the passage of one person; and even it seemed to them that in some places the rocks ran out so far that all progress must be cut off.

They might, perhaps, with great risk, have made their way along the beach back to the sloping ascent to the cliffs which they had visited two days before, and thus gain the heights; but that would probably bring them into contact with the wild natives from whom they had fled in such haste. Besides, they were unwilling to leave the banks of the river, which insured them fresh water, while, at the same time, it prevented them from being bewildered in a strange and perplexing country. Arthur asked his father to decide on what they should do in this dilemma.

"I leave all to you, Arthur," answered he, "as usual. I am distracted with sinful doubts and fears. We cannot, I am aware, continue to live in a cave, as men were wont to do in the early and barbarous ages; and the prospect of perilous wanderings in an unknown wilderness shakes my weak nerves. But I will trust in Him, my children, and pray for this blessed boon; may

'Israel's mystic guide,
The pillared cloud, our steps decide!'"

"Well, then, make up your mind, General Arthur," said Hugh. "Call up the forces and arrange the march. Gerald, my boy, you can make no objection to carry the *pratees*, I'm certain."

"We must each take a share in the toil of carrying off our slender possessions," said Margaret. "Let Arthur divide and portion this duty."

"Then, Margaret," said Arthur, "I determine that Nurse and you should unpack that portmanteau and tie up the contents in bundles, for the better convenience of division."

"Never ye fash to open it out, Miss," said Wilkins. "I reckon I'se qualified to take that leather box on my back without breaking 't."

But Arthur would not suffer the good-natured fellow to be overloaded; and Margaret lightened the trunk by filling some pillow-covers with part of the contents, and these were suspended across the shoulders of Arthur, Hugh, and Jack. Two of these useful bags were also filled with potatoes, to be carried by Mr. Mayburn and Gerald. Ruth would not leave her basket of poultry, and Margaret and Jenny collected the shells and small articles remaining. The locker was unwillingly left behind, as too heavy for carriage; and then, each carrying, in addition to his burden, some weapon, they set out in single file, headed by Arthur, Wilkins following close behind him, along the narrow sandy path, which was encumbered by masses of sandstone fallen from the rocks; and occasionally rendered still more difficult by the roots of a mangrove, twisted with creepers, spreading even into the river, or a drooping acacia, or casuarina, which it was necessary laboriously to cut away, or to tear down, before they could force a passage.

CHAPTER XII

The cliffs which rose above their path were about three hundred feet in height; these were almost perpendicular, and even, in some places, overhung the river; which had again spread out to about a mile in width, while rocky masses in the midst, covered with vegetation, formed innumerable little islets, among which, even if they had saved their canoes, they would have found it perilous to navigate.

"Hugh! Hugh!" cried Gerald, who was at the end of the long line. "I see our canoe; if you will join me, we will swim to it, and bring it in."

All eyes were directed to the dark floating object he had pointed put, when suddenly Ruth screamed out, "They're alive! Master Hugh, there's a lot on 'em. They'll eat us all up."

"I perceive now indeed," said Mr. Mayburn, in much agitation, "what these huge masses are. Observe, Margaret, on that island where the tall mangrove is so conspicuous, those dark moving forms; they are alligators stretched in the sun, while some of the dangerous creatures are floating on the river. See, my children, how providentially we have been snatched from peril. One of these monsters might have capsized our little boat, and we should have been abandoned to be devoured by these frightful creatures."

At these words, Ruth shrieked out, and endeavored in her distraction to force her way past the rest; but was held back by Jack, who followed her in the line, and who tried to convince her of the folly of her fears. Nevertheless, they all felt more comfortable, when they lost sight of the islets and their hideous inhabitants.

Again the river narrowed, and now they became alarmed as a strange rumbling noise gradually increased before them. They paused for consideration; this was totally unlike the usual sounds of the wilderness, where the varied notes of the birds, and the continued humming of the insects, alone disturbed the silence.

"It resembles the roaring of waters," said Arthur. "I trust that now, when the river has obviously fallen, we need not fear that another flood should overtake us. But follow me quickly—let us lose no time in endeavoring to reach the security of a wider strand."

As they proceeded, the roaring and rumbling grew louder and louder; they knew it was the voice of a torrent, and it was with beating hearts they wound round a bend in the course of the greatly narrowed river, and saw at a short distance before them a majestic cataract, pouring its foaming waters into the river, which bounded and dashed onward like a troubled sea, even to the spot where the wanderers stood, transfixed with wonder and admiration at the spectacle.

"This is indeed the majesty of nature!" exclaimed Mr. Mayburn. "How feeble seem all the labors of man, when compared with this stupendous work of God!

> 'How profound
> The gulf! and how the giant element
> From rock to rock leaps with delirious bound,
> Crushing the cliffs!'"

"Ay! Ay! it's a grand thing to see, master," said Wilkins; "but how are we to get out on our fix? We're not made wi' wings, like them big fellows, clamoring and diving at t' top yonder."

A row of large birds were perched on fragments of rock at the very summit of the fall, plunging their heads into the rushing waters, and seeming to rejoice in the grand commotion.

"They look like pelicans, papa," said Hugh; "I can see the red pouch under their throat."

"The bird is one of the family, I apprehend, my son," answered Mr. Mayburn. "It is commonly called the frigate pelican, and is peculiar to the tropics, fishing in rivers as well as in the sea. Its wings and tail are immensely long, but the body, if stripped of the feathers, is much smaller than you would expect to find it. But observe now, Hugh, a nobler bird. See, far above us soars a superb black eagle, which seems to look down with equal scorn on the noisy birds, the dashing waters, and the helpless men so far below it."

As they slowly drew near, they calculated that the height of the cataract must be a hundred and fifty feet at least, and saw that the waters poured over horizontal strata of the sandstone rocks, each layer projecting beyond the one above, and forming a series of steps, which rose from four to eight feet in height. The water did not descend in a volume, but in courses, which left parts of the rocks uncovered, and on these parts moss and even grass had sprung up.

Amidst the admiration and enjoyment which all felt in the contemplation of this novel spectacle, an unpleasant conviction crossed the minds of even the most enthusiastic, that they were indeed, as Wilkins had remarked, "in a fix." It was impossible to proceed unless they could ascend the formidable brush-covered cliffs, where the weight of a man clinging to the bushes might bring down an avalanche of the crumbling sandstone rock to bury him in its fall; or, still more perilous, that they should attempt to ascend what Gerald called "the Giant's Staircase" — the mighty cataract itself.

The voice of the torrent drowned the weaker voice of man; Arthur could not understand that Gerald was calling out to Hugh to follow him; and before he could proclaim any interdiction, the two light-footed, active boys, by clinging to the firmly-rooted grass in the crevices, had gained a resting-place on the first step of the rocks at the extreme edge of the fall, and were calling on the rest to follow them.

At this extremity about four feet of the rocks remained dry from the summit to the base, and certainly this must be the ladder they must mount if they hoped to escape; but how difficult, how perilous, was the attempt! Jack surveyed the ground attentively, then producing from his pocket a large roll of cord, he tied one end to a mangrove-tree on the beach, and unrolling it as he went up, followed the boys, holding the line tight to support Mr. Mayburn and Margaret, Jenny and Ruth, who, assisted by Arthur and Wilkins, were one after another raised to the first resting-place. Arthur soon joined them; but Wilkins remained to see the whole ascent completed before he would leave the strand.

Distracted by the noise of the torrent, the dashing of the spray, and the terror lest the slippery stone or the supporting clump of grass should fail them, it was a fearful struggle for the timid women, and for Mr. Mayburn, quite as timid and much less light than they, to be raised from step to step, assisted always by Arthur below and Jack above; but finally they were placed in safety on the heights of the cataract. Then Jack waved his handkerchief, for his voice would have been inaudible, as a signal for Wilkins to follow; and he, more accustomed than they to climbing, loosed and leisurely wound up the cord, as he sprang from rock to rock, till he joined the grateful and happy family.

The first sentiment of all was thankfulness to God, poured forth in earnest prayer. Their next feeling was curiosity to look upon a new, open country, after being so long imprisoned in the gloomy ravine below. They saw that the river was no longer a broad, navigable stream, but was flowing through many narrow channels from the east and south-east, which united above the cataract. An open and lovely glade lay before them, thinly wooded, and covered with tall grass, and flowers of the most brilliant dyes. Birds of rare beauty and strange notes hovered about the rivulets, and the air was darkened with insects; but they saw no trace yet of man. Far away to the south-east lay a gray line of mountains, towards which the wishes of all the anxious travellers turned.

"That range of mountains must be our first aim, papa," said Arthur. "Thank God, we seem yet to be in a land of plenty; nor need we have any fear of destitution so long as we continue in a well-watered district. If you are now able to proceed, Margaret, we must endeavor to bivouac on some spot less exposed to the rays of the sun and the observation of the natives than this. Let us follow the nearest channel of the river; if we wish to diverge further south, it will not be difficult to cross it."

A sharp twang startled Mr. Mayburn, and a beautiful bird fell at his feet.

"Just as I wished it, sir," said Gerald. "I meant the bird to be laid at your feet. Wasn't it a capital shot, Hugh?"

"Lucky, at any rate, Gerald," answered Hugh. "Well, papa, what bird is it?"

"It is perfectly new to me, Hugh," answered his father, "as, indeed, all the strange creation around me seems to be. The toes, like those of the *Scansores*, are placed two forward, and two backward, to facilitate the running up trees, and in form it so much resembles our cuckoo, that doubtless it is the bird we have read of as the Pheasant-cuckoo. See, there are more running among the grass, like pheasants—and hark how they *whirr* as they take to flight, now that they have been startled by that mischievous boy."

The pheasants were tempting game, and several brace were bagged before Margaret could restrain the ardent sportsmen, and remonstrate on the wanton cruelty of destroying more than their necessities required. Then, bending their course to a low hill, on which stood a wild nutmeg-tree, they saw that it was covered with beautiful white pigeons. On this spot a fire was made, and the pheasants prepared for cooking, and then spitted on slender peeled bamboos, which were set up with one end in the ground, round the fire. Gerald would gladly have added to the feast by shooting some of the confiding pigeons, which continued to feed on the green fruits of the nutmeg-tree, without any fear of their dangerous neighbors; but even Nurse reproved the boy for his destructive inclinations, declaring it would be very unlucky to shoot a white pigeon.

Though they hoped this resting-place would have proved pleasant, they soon found it would be impossible to remain near the water, so intensely vexatious was the plague of flies. Thick clouds of these teasing creatures buzzed round, settling in black bunches on the meat; filling eyes, nose and mouth, and irritating the skin with their continual attempts to pierce it with their thin, tiny proboscis.

The boys declared the flies were ten times worse than the mosquitos; and to escape these Lilliputian foes, Arthur decided that they should cross some of the narrow rills, which now ran wide apart, and deviate towards the south, where a rising ground promised to introduce them to new scenery.

When they reached the hills, they found them steeper than they expected; but on ascending to the height, they were gratified to see before them a beautiful country. Lofty trees adorned the plain, and high grass rose even to their shoulders, as they passed through it. On several spots, vast fragments of the sandstone-rock, grown over with beautiful flowering creepers, lay in picturesque confusion; and the Eucalyptus, with its spicy flowers, the Pandanus, loaded with fragrant blossoms, and the Cabbage-palm, were also encircled by the parasitic plants which add such a grace to tropical scenery. Wearied with forcing their way through the tall, sharp, wiry grass, they stopped before a high, broken rock which overhung and flung a shade over the spot they had selected for their resting-place. Then the boys cleared the ground, by laboriously cutting down the long grass, which they spread to form beds, a luxury to which they were unaccustomed.

"We'd better have fired it," said Wilkins. "Our bush-ranging chaps always sets it in a low; it saves trouble."

"I should be grieved to destroy the luxuriant vegetation that God has spread over these plains," said Mr. Mayburn. "Besides we could not calculate where such a conflagration might end."

"Little matter where it ended," answered the man. "There's lots of this stuff, such as it is; but Ruth, lass, ye've gotten hold on a better sample."

Ruth usually released her unfortunate chickens at each resting-place, that they might have air, and seek food, and she had herself been running about for grubs, seeds, or any thing they could eat, and she now returned with a perfect sheaf of some kind of bearded grain, suspended on the ear by slender filaments like the oat, but still unripe.

"This surely should be an edible grain," said Mr. Mayburn, "and will probably be ripe as early as November, in a climate which produces two harvests. How richly laden is each ear, and the straw cannot be less than six feet in length. I conclude it is an *Anthistiria*. Feed your fowls, Ruth; the food is suitable, and happily abundant. Had we but a mill to grind it, we might hope in due season to enjoy once more the blessing of bread."

"There's not likely to be any mills handy hereabout," said Wilkins; "but when folks is put to it, it's queer what shifts they can make. Just hand us over a handful of that there corn, my lass."

Wilkins soon found two flat stones suited to his purpose, spread the shelled grains on the larger stone and bruised the soft corn into a paste, which he handed over to Jenny, saying, "Here's yer dough, mother! now see and bake us a damper, bush fashion; it's poor clammy stuff yet a bit, but a bad loaf's better nor no bread."

Then Wilkins showed Jenny that slovenly mode of bread-making, common even among the civilized colonists of Australia, the product of which is a sort of pancake baked in the ashes. But this substitute for the staff of life was thankfully received by those who had been so long deprived of the genuine blessing; but the green paste was stringy and dry, and Jenny proposed to blend a boiled potato with the next damper, to make it more like bread.

"Nevertheless," said Arthur, "if we only boil it as a green vegetable, this acquisition will be an agreeable addition to our roast birds. Suppose we each reap a bundle of the ears to carry onwards: at all events the grains will feed the fowls."

The boys soon cut down a quantity of the heads of the corn, and early next morning they rubbed out the grains, with which they filled several bags, Ruth herself collecting a store for the poultry. Then, resolving to wait till the heat of the day was over before they marched on their journey, Margaret employed herself in making useful bags of grass, while the young men sauntered about, observing the novelties around them, and procuring from one of the clear rivulets a large provision of fish for the day's consumption.

"And see, Margaret," said Gerald, "would you not have been proud, in England, of such a magnificent bouquet as this," presenting to her a brilliant assemblage of flowers.

"Now, papa, come to our assistance," said Margaret, "and name these 'illustrious strangers.' Surely I scent among them our own delicious Jasmine."

"It certainly resembles the jasmine, as well in form, as in perfume," answered Mr. Mayburn. "Yet, like all Australian productions, it differs essentially from the species it resembles. We will, however, name it jasmine. This golden flower of the ranunculus race, might represent the butter-cup of our meadows, yet it certainly is not the butter-cup. And this might be a rose, with its slender stem, and pale-pink wax-like petals—is it not a *Boronea*,

Arthur? This crimson flower resembles the sweet-pea, of which it has the scent, and the papillonaceous form. But it is vain to attempt to class, at once, a strange and marvellous new Flora. Well might Dr. Solander honor the first spot discovered of this lovely country with the name of Botany Bay, thus prophetically anticipating the rich harvests naturalists should reap in its wealth of plants. This is truly a tour of pleasure, my children, and I care not how long I linger on the flowery road."

"If it were not for the flies and mosquitos, papa," added Hugh, rubbing his tortured nose, which being rather prominent, was a favorite resort of the insects.

"What an advantage it is, in this country, to have a snub nose!" said Gerald. "Oh! my boy, it is my turn to laugh now. But I say, Arthur! Wilkins! What is yon fellow? See, papa, what a splendid spectacle!"

Not twenty yards from where they stood, and on part of the ground they had cleared from the tall grass, they saw, with admiration mingled with fear, an immense bright yellow and brown serpent slowly winding among the low stubble. No one seemed to know exactly how to act on seeing this strange visitor, except Gerald, who sprung forward, armed with a stout stick; but Arthur forcibly held him back, and Wilkins said, —

"Let him be! let him be! ye'd best not mell on him. I ken his sneaking ways; he never bites; but he squeezes like a millstone. Now then; he's after his own business. See what he's at."

An elegant brownish-grey animal, which, though they now saw for the first time, they recognized at once, bounded from the grass; and while the boys were crying out in ecstacy, "The kangaroo! the kangaroo!" they saw the wily serpent raise itself, and envelope the terrified animal in its coils; and they knew well the doom of the poor kangaroo, for the embrace of its foe was certain death.

"Now come on, all on ye; we're safe enough now," cried Wilkins; and all the young men, armed with sticks, and undeterred by the shrieks of the women, ran up to the animals, and attacked the serpent by striking the head with repeated blows. When, roused to defence, it began to uncoil itself from its victim, knives were produced; and with many wounds, they succeeded at length in putting an end to a creature at the very sight of which man instinctively shudders.

"Be sartin he's dead," said Wilkins. "I'd niver trust them fellows; I've seen one on 'em march off two ways when he's been cut in two pieces. They do say they niver die outright. But blacky has a way to settle and keep him quiet: he just eats him."

To eat a serpent was an exploit at which the civilized stomach revolted; and the creature was abandoned to take its chance of reviving to commit more destruction in the world, after Mr. Mayburn had examined it with as much interest as he could feel for a creature so abhorred. It was about twelve feet long, and certainly one of the Boa family, but resembling more the boa of Africa and Asia, than that of America. Mr. Mayburn earnestly desired to preserve the skin; but any additional incumbrance in the long pilgrimage that lay before them was not to be thought of, and he reluctantly relinquished the idea.

"I'd scorn to mell wi' such a foul beast," said Wilkins, "for t' sake of his bonnie skin; but by yer leave, I'se uncoil him, 'cause, ye see, a bit of kangaroo meat will suit us as well as he. It's canny fair meat, specially about t' broad stern."

The kangaroo, which was but a young one, not standing more than four feet in height, was extricated from the murderous grasp of the boa; but was almost flattened by the powerful pressure. The boys gathered round the strange animal with great curiosity, lost in admiration of its graceful form, powerful hind legs, and pretty small head. The long ears, divided upper lip, like that of the hare, long tapering tail, and remarkable pouch, in which a very young animal was found, were all remarked before it was skinned and turned over to the cooks. The skin was then washed, and spread to dry, to be converted into boots when those useful articles of clothing should be needed.

Before they set out, part of the kangaroo flesh was roasted, or rather broiled, to be in readiness for supper, and the rest of the meat carried off by the willing Wilkins. Then, delighted with the novelties of the day, they went on in the same direction as before, walking cheerfully along, uninterrupted by any alarm, through the wild and charming scenery, where bright skies, and birds and flowers, might have given a fanciful mind the idea of an Arcadia.

The sudden darkness of the tropics compelled them to rest at the foot of some steep hills covered with brushwood, and opening on more forest-like scenery than any they had yet passed. Tiny rills trickled down the crevices in the hills, and the rich emerald green of the turf proclaimed a moist soil, and assured them they were yet far from the dreaded deserts.

Their night's rest was again painfully disturbed, for, though at a great distance, the peculiar *coo-ee* of the natives was several times distinctly heard; nor would Mr. Mayburn and Margaret venture to sleep till a watch was arranged, of two persons, who were instructed to converse loudly the whole time; for, according to the report of Wilkins, the natives would never venture to attack a party who were prepared to receive them.

"They'll be tracking us all along, Master Arthur," said Wilkins, as he and Arthur kept watch together. "That's their way. Then they think to run down on us unawares, to pick, and steal, and murder, and eat us up into t' bargain, if they get a chance."

"Surely not, Wilkins," answered Arthur. "I know that the New Zealanders were, in their original wild state, cannibals; but I never heard such an abominable character given of the Australian aborigines."

"If ye have to rove long about t' bush," answered the man, "ye'll come on many a picked bone that niver was that of a kangaroo or a 'possum. Why, they'll not mind telling ye as how man's flesh is twice as tender as 'possum's. There's no dealing wi' 'em, master. They're just a mean lot. It were a bad job our losing them guns."

"It was a loss, Wilkins," said Arthur; "but I should not feel that I had the same right to shoot a native that I had to shoot a kangaroo."

"There's nought to choose atween 'em," replied Wilkins, "but just this—we can make a good meal of a kangaroo, and a Christian must be sore set afore he could stomach a black fellow."

"But even a black man has a soul, Wilkins," said Arthur.

"I question if these dogs have much of that," answered he; "and if they have oughts of soul, it's all given to him that's bad. Lord help us, Mr. Arthur, they're all, as one may say, lost; like them creatures as old master reads on, full of devils."

"And yet those unhappy men, so possessed, you remember, Wilkins," answered Arthur, "were not lost beyond redemption. Our blessed Lord not only banished the evil spirits, but forgave the men their sins. So might these ignorant natives, if they were taught and received God's holy word, yet be saved."

"I'se not set on gainsaying ye, Mr. Arthur, in that," said the man, "for I were nigh as bad as them mysel'; and is yet, for what I ken, if I'd a chance to fall back. I'd like not, if I could help it; now when I ken reet fra' wrong; and pray God keep me fra' Black Peter and his crew."

"Hark Wilkins! did you hear a rustling?" asked Arthur.

"Nay, but I tell you what I heared," replied he. "I heared them cockatoos flacker and cry out, on yon trees; and depend on't they hear a strange foot."

"Then they are better watchmen than we are," said Arthur. "What shall we do, Wilkins?"

"Just ye tell your folks not to be fleyed at nought," said he, "and we'll set them rogues off in no time."

Arthur warned Margaret and his father not to be alarmed at any noise they might hear, and the other young men, roused at the report of an assault, were soon in the ranks. Then, at a signal agreed, they raised their voices in a simultaneous halloo! that rang against the rocky hills. A loud rustling succeeded, and a dozen dark figures, visible in the moonlight, emerged from the bushes, and fled swiftly across the plain.

"Saved!" cried Hugh: "for this time at least. But, I say, Arthur, we must not sleep in the bush every night, or they'll catch us at last. I saw several fine roomy caves in the rocks as we came along. We must take possession of the next we fall in with, and then we shall only have the entrance to guard."

"They held spears in their hands, I saw," said Gerald; "I wonder why they did not send a few among us?"

"They're ower sly for that, Master Gerald," said Wilkins. "They'd like to come on us all asleep, and butcher us. Now they'll dog us, day after day; but if we hold on steady-like, we'se wear 'em out at last."

"If we could but put a good broad river between us," said Jack, "we might feel safe. Did you see that stringy bark tree just at hand, Mr. Arthur? I marked it in my mind, and if Master Hugh, and you, and Master O'Brien will help me, we will twist some long ropes, on our road to-morrow, and then, I fancy, if we came to a river we could not ford, we might contrive a ferry-boat."

CHAPTER XIII

Mr. Mayburn was uneasy till they set out next morning; for the thick bush-covered hill was a convenient spot for concealment. They left their sleeping-place, therefore, at the earliest dawn, and continued their progress, while the young men found several trees of the stringy bark; the strips of the bark, measuring twenty or thirty feet, were hanging from the trunk raggedly, but very conveniently for the purpose of the workmen, who collected a quantity of the rolls of bark, and carried it on their shoulders, till a singular isolated column of rock attracted them to examine it; and as it afforded a little shade, and stood in an open glade, where they need not fear hidden enemies, they rested at the foot of it, and eat their breakfast of kangaroo steaks. Then Jack, fixing short poles into the ground to tie the bark to, soon set all the youths to work to twist strong ropes of considerable length. They spent some hours in this labor, and completed so heavy a burden of ropes, that when they set out again they looked anxiously for an opportunity of relieving themselves by putting the ropes to profitable use. They directed their steps towards a rocky range before them, which held out a prospect of protection for the night; and bending under the weight of their burden, they were glad to reach the straggling, mountainous, sandstone rocks which, running east and west, interrupted their direct course.

It was always easy in these ranges to find caves or hollow grottos, convenient for a retreat, and the bright moon showed them a low opening, which admitted them into a spacious and lofty cave. It was large enough to have contained fifty persons, dry and clean—for the floor was of fine sand; and when they had lighted a fire, they discovered that they were not the first who had inhabited the cave, for the walls were covered with rude, colored paintings of men and animals—the men and animals of Australia. With great amusement and astonishment the boys looked on the kangaroo, the opossum, many curious lizards, and heads of men, colossal in size, and imperfect in execution, somewhat resembling the ambitious child's first attempts at high art.

"I think I couldn't draw so good a kangaroo as that myself," said Gerald; "but I could make something more like the head of a man. Do look, Margaret; that fellow has crimson hair and a green nose."

"They have not, certainly," said Mr. Mayburn, "attained perfection in the art of coloring; nevertheless, the uninstructed men who could accomplish these drawings cannot be so deficient in abilities as we have been taught to believe these aborigines are. I wish we could, with safety to ourselves, hold intercourse with a small number of them. Could it not be attempted, Arthur?"

"If they would approach us openly, we would endeavor to meet them amicably, my dear father," answered Arthur; "but when they steal on us treacherously, we must conclude their intentions are hostile. Even now we must prepare for defence; and though we might keep watch at the opening, I think we had better build it up."

They soon secured the entrance with slabs of stone, and then eat their supper, and slept with less uneasiness than usual.

"Who has moved them stones?" asked Wilkins, sharply, as, roused by the light streaming in, he sprung from the nook he had chosen for his lair.

"It's that fidgety lass," answered Jenny. "She's been scuttling about this hour, feeding her poultry, and setting things to rights as if we were living in a parlor; and then she roused me up to help her to make a bit of way to get out to fetch water. You see, Wilkins, she's a hard-working lass, but it's her way to make a fuss."

"A fuss, indeed!" replied he, indignantly; "and a nice fuss she would have made if she'd let a hundred black fellows in on us. Halloo, Jack! it would be as well if we were off to see after that unlucky sister of thine."

The rest of the family were soon aware of Ruth's errrantry, but they did not expect she would be far from the cave, as the water was spread in pools and rills, abundantly, at the foot of the rocks. The next minute, however, they were startled by a succession of shrieks, and snatching up their weapons, the young men rushed out, and then saw, to their great vexation, Ruth running wildly towards them, pursued by six of the natives, in their usual unclothed state; and it was plain their swift steps would soon overtake the affrighted girl, unless they were promptly checked.

"Shout as loud as ye like," cried Wilkins, "but mind not to send a single arrow without hitting, or they'll not care a dump for us. See and aim to do some damage—d'ye hear?"

The natives were yelling and waving their spears, and their opponents answered by hallooing and brandishing their glittering knives, at the sight of which the savages stopped suddenly, and looked anxiously round, as if expecting reinforcement; then discharging a volley of spears, they turned round and rapidly fled out of sight.

Ruth was left lying prostrate on the ground, and when Jack got up to her, he found a spear had struck her on the shoulder, but fortunately stuck in her wide cloak, without injuring her, though her terror and distress were great.

"They'll eat me up," she cried out. "They'll eat us all, Jack; and, oh, what will Jenny say? they've gotten my water-can!"

In her great fear, the poor girl had thrown away the useful gourd-bottle—a serious loss; and Gerald was intrusted to convey her back to the cave, while the rest went forward to the pools, in hopes of recovering the gourd and procuring water. The vessel was, happily, found, and filled with water, and the youths returned to the cave, where they found great alarm prevailing.

"Had we not better flee without delay?" asked Mr. Mayburn.

Arthur looked significantly at Wilkins, and the man said,—"Ay, ay, Mr. Arthur! ye have a head; ye can see a bit afore ye. Why, master, a bonnie figure we should cut running ower yon bare grounds—men folks and women folks, all like a pack of scared rabbits, wi' a pack of a hundred or so of these naked black dogs at our heels."

"But, my good man, if we stay here we shall be slain," said Mr. Mayburn, in great agitation.

"No, no, dear papa," answered Arthur. "I conclude that Wilkins's plan is, that we should remain here, and hold our impregnable castle till the foe grows tired of the hopeless siege."

"That's the best thing," said Wilkins; "they're a set of stiff hands, and we'se be put to it to tire 'em out; but we'll try what we can do. And, I say, master, we must give a look round for stores; we'll never let 'em starve us out. It takes good rations to get up one's heart."

"And if we have to be shut up some time," said Margaret, much distressed, "we must have, especially, a supply of water."

"In course, Miss," answered Wilkins; "that's a thing we cannot want, barring we had beer, which isn't to be had, more's the pity. Let's see; if we'd a bit of a tub or barrel, we'd easy fill't now, afore they're back on us. Nay, nay, Jenny, woman; let that meat be just now, and bring us all your shells, or aught that'll hold water."

The gourd was emptied into the large turtle-shell, and Wilkins took it back to be refilled at the pools, the rest following with the largest of the mussel-shells; and as they went on, they carefully looked out for any available article of food that could be easily attained before the return of the enemy. The air was thronged with birds, and every tree was an aviary. They might soon have brought down a quantity with their arrows, but Arthur urged on them the necessity of first obtaining the water. After they had filled all their water-vessels, they found they should only have a supply for two days, even if carefully husbanded. Thankful even for this boon, they had yet time to shoot a dozen pheasants, before the *coo-ee* of the natives, gradually getting nearer, made it necessary that they should seek the cave, and make ready their defences.

Their first care was to fortify strongly the opening which formed their entrance, and which they hoped was the only weak point. But as it was evident, from the paintings, that this cave was well known to the natives, it was expedient to search it thoroughly, lest there should be other outlets. Many branches ran from the main cave, but all seemed equally impregnable; and the only openings were small gaps far above the ground, from which the decomposed sandstone had fallen, and lay scattered in fragments over the ground. There were traces of fires, showing that the cave had been previously inhabited, but no remains of fuel; and a few withered sticks that they had brought in the preceding day were all the provision they had made for cooking their food.

"After all our wild and savage life," said Hugh, "we are not yet come down to eat uncooked meat, I really think; and by your leave, Captain Arthur, we will make a sally to pick up sticks."

"Look through this cranny, Hugh, and tell me if you think this is a time for throwing open our gates," said Arthur.

"I give in! I give in!" answered the boy. "Look out, Gerald; see what a swarm of dark wretches, all in earnest too, for they have sheaves of spears in the left hand, while the right hand is raised to do battle. Keep back, Ruth! you simpleton. You have certainly seen enough of these ugly monsters."

"Oh Miss Marget!" shrieked the girl, "they'll come in and eat us. Stone walls is nought to 'em. They're not Christian folks, they're spurrits! they 're skellingtons; I ken 'em by their bones. Oh! send them back to their graves, master!"

Within thirty yards of the rock, and immediately before it, were gathered crowds of fierce savages; their dark skins marked with a white substance like pipe-clay, in fantastic figures; most of them were painted to represent skeletons. And while, with wild and demoniac yells, they were leaping and whirling round with graceful agility, they poised their spears, ready to cast them as soon as a victim appeared in sight. There was a painful expression of surprise and vexation on every face; and Jack, usually so indulgent to his sister's foibles, could not help saying:

"Oh, Ruth, lass! this is thy doing."

"Why, Jack, honey!" sobbed she, "what could I think, when I seed that big grinning black face glouring at me fra' t' middle on a bush, and none nigh hand me: and oh! honey, I'd setten out afore I said my prayers. What could I do but just skirl and run? and I did it."

"That you did, Ruth, and no mistake," said O'Brien. "But, after all, it's better to have our enemies before our face than at our back. Will I send an arrow among them, Arty?"

"Certainly not, Gerald," answered Arthur; "we may need all our arrows, and we had better not be the first to commence an aggression. If we had had plenty of powder and shot, I have no doubt we might have dispersed them without bloodshed; but I am loth to waste a single cartridge of our small store. What are they about now, Hugh?"

One tall savage had mounted a mass of rock about thirty yards from them; and now, with wonderful dexterity, he sent a spear whirling through the air directly through a small gap in the rock, about twenty feet from the ground. Most fortunately, Arthur had ordered the whole party to gather close to the entrance, and the weapon passed on one side of them, and falling upon a shell of water tilted it over.

"Good-for-nothing rascals!" cried Jenny. "See what a mischief they've done."

"Be thankful, nurse," said Arthur, "that we saw the intention of the fellow, and were able to escape the spear. We now know our weak points, and may keep out of harm's way."

But Gerald, who thought the first aggression was committed, no longer scrupled to draw his bow, and sent an arrow, which he had barbed with skill, into the shoulder of the warrior on the rock, with such force, that he was hurled to the ground. In an instant all his companions crowded around him; he was raised from the ground, and the whole party disappeared in the bush, with every symptom of terror.

Wilkins was in an ecstasy of delight. He patted Gerald roughly on the back, saying, "That's the thing, my brave lad; ye're of the right sort; ye've let the rogues see what we can do. But if ye'd missed him we'd every soul been done. They'd have reckoned nought on us."

"It was a rash act, Gerald," said Mr. Mayburn; "but I hope the poor man is not seriously injured."

Wilkins made a grimace as he said, "Them there arrows is made o' purpose to injer, master. They're a bit sharpish to bide when they bang in among a fellow's bones, and no doctor at hand to hack 'em out."

"Didn't I tell you, Master Gerald," said Ruth, "that it were a sin and a shame to make them things as would rive folks' flesh?"

"You are the girl that said that," answered Gerald, wild with his exploit; "and weren't you right, Ruth, *astore*! I meant them to *rive*; and see how the cowards have scampered off from them. Couldn't we go out now, Arthur? You know we want firewood."

"Do not be impatient, Gerald," replied Arthur, "we have fuel sufficient for one day, and we do not know how far our foes may have fled."

"Depend on't, Mr. Arthur," said Wilkins, "there's not a bush or a rock we see but has its man. We'll have to make shift to live on what we have for a bit. They'll soon be trying another dodge."

But though the usual *coo-ee* rang through the distant woods, mingled with the soft low wailing of the voices of women, the people were not seen again during a day which seemed unusually long to the anxious prisoners. The women cooked the pheasants with the last firewood, while Margaret filled a pillow-cover with the feathers for her father's head; but they had all become so accustomed to the hard earth, or at best to a bed of wiry grass, that even Mr. Mayburn regarded this pillow as a useless luxury, and an undesirable addition to the baggage, which rendered their journey so tedious.

"I will undertake to carry the light pillow," said Margaret, "and I trust we may again meet with a river to lighten the toil of our pilgrimage."

"If we found a wagon drawn by oxen, like them Mr. Deverell bought," said Jenny, "it would be fitter for my master and you, Miss Marget."

"And a few good horses for the rest of us, nurse," said Hugh; "but say what you will, papa, of the beauty and excellence of this new country, it is a great vexation that there are no beasts of burden. Neither elephant nor camel; not even a llama or a quagga which may be reduced to servitude. No four-footed creature have we yet seen but the kangaroo; and one never read, even in the Fairy Tales, of a man hopping along, mounted on a kangaroo."

"Nothing for it but trudging, Hugh," said Gerald, "unless we could meet with an ostrich to tame."

"I fear," replied Mr. Mayburn, "that the emu, which is the ostrich of Australia, is not formed for carrying burdens, nor tractable enough to submit to the dominion of man. I am anxious to see the bird, though I fear we may obtain no advantage from meeting with it."

In rambling among the caves to fill up the tedious hours, the boys discovered, in a distant branch cavern, a heap of dry wood which had fallen through an opening in the rock, at least fifty feet above them. If this opening were even known to the natives, it could not avail them as a means of descent to the cave, and, much to the mortification of the adventurous boys, it was totally inaccessible from the interior.

"But we can comfort nurse's heart," said Hugh, "by the report that we have found fuel enough for an English winter. And see, Gerald, some of these strong straight sticks will make us a sheaf of arrows, and we can barb them with the fish-bones we preserved. Here's our work for the day."

It was a comfort to Margaret to have the two most restless of the party quietly employed; though Mr. Mayburn objected to the barbing of the arrows, so unnecessary for destroying birds, so cruel if meant for the savages. Wilkins sat down to make a pair of shoes of the skin of the kangaroo, and Jack made more ropes with the remains of the stringy bark. And thus the day of anxiety passed without more alarm.

Another morning dawned through the chinks of the rocky walls, and for some time all was so still, that they began to hope the natives had withdrawn; but before the middle of the day the whole troop presented themselves so suddenly, that they were close to the rocks, and thus, secure from the arrows of the besieged, before they could prevent their approach.

They had come armed with heavy clubs, with which they began violently to batter the walled entrance. This was a formidable mode of attack, and the only mode of defence was to accumulate more stones to strengthen the barrier. Still the men persevered, fresh parties relieving those who were tired; but the defence seemed already shaking; while Margaret, always resolute in difficulties, had herself almost lost the power of consoling her more timid father. Wilkins seemed watching for an opportunity, placed before a narrow crevice in the rock, which was shaded outside by brush, and suddenly they saw him plunge his long knife through the opening against which he had seen one of the natives leaning.

The knife entered the back of the man, who uttered a groan, and fell. He was immediately surrounded by the rest, who examined the wound, and then gazed round, apparently unable to comprehend the nature of this attack from an invisible enemy. Some of the men fled at once, many of them pierced by the arrows the young men sent after them, while others remained to bear away, with care and tenderness, the bleeding body of their companion, who appeared to be mortally wounded. These humane men were respected, even by their opponents, and permitted to retire unmolested; and for the remainder of the day, except for the sounds of mourning from the native women, which, however, gradually became more faint and distant, all continued still and peaceful.

The next morning broke on the besieged party with the melancholy conviction that their fortress was no longer tenable. The spring was already advanced, the air had become hot and parching, and the water was exhausted.

"We must endeavor, under any circumstances," said Arthur, "to procure water, or we must die. I propose that three of us should set out to the nearest pool for a supply, leaving the rest to guard the entrance; and if we are successful, to re-admit us. If the savages should attack and overcome us, then it will be the duty of those left here to close the barrier, leaving us to our fate, and to use every exertion in their power to protect and save the feeble."

Sad as was this necessity, it was imperative, and now the question was, who were to have the honor of joining the "Forlorn Hope," as Hugh termed the expedition. Arthur decided that the party should consist of Hugh, Wilkins, and himself. Jack was too useful to be risked, Gerald too rash to be trusted.

Arthur would not even take with him the valuable rifle, their prime reliance, but left it in the charge of Jack. Then, with bows and arrows slung over their backs, and such water-vessels as they could command in their hands, they cautiously went out, leaving orders to the garrison, that each man should stand before his slab of stone, to be ready to replace it before the opening, if necessary.

They reached the pool without interruption, satisfied their own thirst, filled the vessels, and then, with joy and triumph, turned homewards. But before they had proceeded many yards, a loud "*Coo-ee,*" not far from them, proved they had not escaped notice. The cry was echoed from many distant spots, and the water-carriers redoubled their speed, till a spear, whizzing close to the ear of Wilkins, induced Arthur to call a halt. They faced round, set down their water-buckets, and handled their bows. They saw that they were pursued by about a dozen men, who were thirty or forty yards behind them, amongst whom they discharged arrows, two or three times in rapid succession, with some effect, it would seem, from the confusion and irresolution which they observed had taken place among the natives; of which they took advantage, and snatching up their valuable burdens, they reached the cave before the savages rallied, and, being joined by a reinforcement, were quickly following them.

"Up with the defences," cried Arthur, breathlessly. "And now, thank God! we shall be able to hold out two or three days longer."

"Then we shall have to live on potatoes and these few green oats," said Jenny, "for we have only six pheasants left, and they spoil fast in this hot place. But, to be sure, there's them greedy hens, that can eat as much as a man, and are no good, unless we eat them."

"Oh no, Jenny, please don't!" cried Ruth. "See, here's six eggs they've laid; isn't that some good? poor bit things! Oh, Miss Marget, dinnot let 'em be killed!"

Margaret willingly granted the fowls their lives, the eggs being considered equivalent to the oats the animals consumed; and she begged Jenny to have more trust in God, who had till now continued to supply their "daily bread."

CHAPTER XIV

After they had dined with strict economy, and ascertained that their savage foes had for the present withdrawn into the bush, they resumed their usual occupations. Hugh and Gerald, impatient under their confinement, chose to ramble through the mazy windings of the various hollows which existed in the sandstone rock, searching for a long time in vain for novelty or adventure; at length they wound along a branch passage, which terminated, to their astonishment, in a wall, hung, like a bower, with garlands of flowery creeping plants, from which the notes of various birds greeted the ears of the delighted boys.

"Sure enough, Hugh, this is Fairy Bower," said Gerald.

"It is open to the day," said Hugh, "and we must find out what lies beyond it."

A slab of rock, which had fallen inwards, lay close to the wall; it was six feet in height, but by making a staircase of other fragments which were lying round, they mounted the fallen slab, and putting aside the leafy curtains which hid the opening, they looked out on a complete wilderness of rocky masses and green thickets, which appeared at once impervious and interminable. The temptation to be once more under the open sky could not be resisted, and without much difficulty the boys descended among the matted bushes.

"We will follow out the adventure," said Gerald, "till we reach the Enchanted Castle. Had we not better cut some spears as we make our way, that we may be prepared to slay the dragons?"

"We had better have had one of Jack's balls of cord," replied Hugh, "that we might have tied one end here before we set out, or we shall never be able to find our way back through such a labyrinth."

"Couldn't we drop pebbles, as Hop-o'-my-Thumb did?" asked Gerald.

"Where are we to get the pebbles?" answered Hugh, "and how could we find them again, man, among this brush? But what is this white, chalky-looking material by the pool? I cannot help thinking it must be the clay which the savages use for painting their bodies. Let us get some; I have a use for it."

They collected some of this moist pipe-clay on a large leaf, and climbing again to the opening, they cut away a portion of the creepers to uncover the rock, upon which they marked, as high as they could reach, a large white cross.

"We cannot miss that holy and propitious sign," said Hugh, "so let us venture forward, Gerald. It is such a charming novelty to be able to walk fearlessly in the open air. You observe we are now facing the south; so if we can discover an outlet from this thicket, we shall be on the direct track to continue our journey."

It was not easy, however, to preserve any direct course through the tangled brake, which was occasionally broken by patches of fine grass and rills of water, and diversified by tall trees; the various kinds of Eucalyptus, the wild nutmeg with its spicy odor, and the acacia covered with golden blossoms, the whole being mingled with masses of rock fallen from the regular range, broken into fragments and scattered far and wide; some grown over with the vegetation of years, and others freshly rent from the soft decaying mountains.

Threading their way through this lovely wilderness, not forgetting to look back frequently at their guiding signal, the boys now hailed with pleasure and admiration the sight of thousands of birds springing from their nests, while each, in its own peculiar language, seemed to deprecate the intrusion of the presumptuous strangers.

"Won't we carry back birds and eggs enough to victual the fortress for a week!" said Gerald.

"No need for that, Gerald," answered Hugh, "when we have the preserve in our own private grounds. We can just bag a brace or two, to prove the truth to our people. But, now, my boy, we must try to find the end of this wonderful maze—who knows but what it may lead to liberty?"

"It is a rough road anyhow," said Gerald. But they struggled through thick bushes, leaped over rocks, or waded through pools or rills for more than an hour, and then, fearful of alarming their friends, they proposed to return. But just as they had made this resolve, Hugh declared that he heard the sound of rolling water, and they continued their toilsome exertions till they reached at length the side of a rapid river, which poured through a narrow gorge in the mountains, and flowed towards the west. The river seemed about fifty yards across, and too deep to be forded; the banks were overgrown with tall bamboos mingled with fine rushes; but beyond the south banks, the country appeared more open.

"If we could only cross this river," said Hugh, "we should completely escape from those cowardly blacks, who have, I believe, no canoes. We will bring Jack here; he can find bark in abundance for his use, and if we help him, I have no doubt he can make a canoe that will carry us across. At any rate, let us take him a piece of the bark to tempt him to come."

They soon stripped from the stem a piece of flexible bark, and, with some of the fibres of the stringy bark, they tied this into a bag, which they filled, as they returned, with eggs and four brace of good-sized young pheasants. They kept in the track they had made in coming, and having the white cross before them as a guide, they had much less difficulty in their homeward course than they expected, and in very great spirits presented themselves before their greatly anxious friends.

"We have been out on a sporting expedition," said Gerald, flinging down the birds. "What do you think of our game-bag, General Arthur?"

"I must think that you have been very rash and imprudent," answered Arthur. "I conclude, boys, that you have found some other outlet from the cave; but how could you risk discovery for the sake of these birds?"

"We have discovered an outlet," replied Hugh; "but I think even Margaret and my father will agree that there was no risk, when they see the place. Now you must all listen to our wonderful adventure."

They did listen with great pleasure and thankfulness. The earnest desire of every heart was to escape from the constant dogged and depressing pursuit of their savage and artful foes, and the account of the unsuspected path to the river filled them with the hopes which they had nearly abandoned.

"Can we not set out now?" asked Mr. Mayburn eagerly. "Certainly not, my father," answered Arthur. "It will first be necessary that we have some means arranged for crossing the river; besides, the day is too far advanced for us to make such an important movement before night; and we must try to divert the suspicions of the savages from our flight, by letting them believe we still intend to hold the fortress."

"If you're not knocked up, Master Hugh," said Jack, "I should like well to see with my own eyes what there is to do, and whether I can do it or not. Would you mind guiding me; and Wilkins, may be, will go with us, to help me to carry down my ropes?"

Wilkins was always ready and willing; he shouldered a coil of rope, and the two unwearied boys, followed by him and Jack, set out to show their marvellous discovery to the two practical men, who looked round at the charming wilderness with an eye to the usefulness rather than to the beauty of all they saw.

"Birds is poor feeding, and eggs is worse," said Wilkins; "but if we iver get free fra' them dowly stone walls, we'se see if we can't get a shot at them kangaroos. Ay, ay! Master Hugh, any sky over head's better nor a jail; not but I've been shut in worse prisons nor yon, God forgive me; but ye see I were reet sarved then. But it is aggravatin, I say, to bar oneself up wi' one's own will like."

"See here, Wilkins," exclaimed Jack; "what a grand stock of all kinds of wood, if we had but a few good tools. I noticed that a black fellow that was fighting yesterday had a capital axe in his hand; it seemed to be made of a sort of flint stone, and I only wish we could meet with a piece fit for such a job."

"It's not a time to be felling trees," replied Wilkins, "when we've a troop of black rogues at our heels. Now come, we're here, it seems, at t' river they telled on, and a canny river it is; if we can manage to put it atween us and them, we'se have a clear coast, I reckon; for they always keep at their own side."

"Then help me to bark this tree," said Jack; "and if we cannot manage a canoe, we'll try a ferry-boat."

The tree was barked in one long sheet, the ends were tied up with cords, and this was Jack's extempore canoe. But as soon as it was hastily completed, they were compelled to speed homeward to prevent themselves being bewildered in the darkness; and even now, but for the visible white cross, they would have been unable to distinguish the entrance. "Now, Nurse, darling," cried Gerald, dancing round Jenny, "pack up your pots and pans and bundles, and you, Ruth, call up your precious chicks, and make ready. Then, at daybreak, when you hear me whistle the *réveille*, fall into your ranks, to march."

"We do not know how far the ground beyond the wilderness may be exposed," said Arthur, "and we had better look out before we leave in the morning, to observe if all continues still."

"That's all just as it ought, Mr. Arthur," said Wilkins; "ye're a sharp chap at a drill. And we'd as well puzzle 'em a bit, and rattle out a few arrows just afore we start, to make 'em believe we mean to haud our own."

In the morning, when all was ready for setting out, and they had laid the foundation of a good breakfast, the scream of Ruth, who had climbed to an aperture to obtain a look-out, announced that the objects of her antipathy were in sight. All flocked to the crevices to ascertain what they had to fear, and observed that a number of the natives were laden with bundles of dry wood, which they had piled before the rock, and made up a fire, having apparently chosen to establish themselves there, and keep a perpetual watch, and yet keep too close to the rock to be in danger from the arrows of the besieged. This was vexatious, and Wilkins said,—"Ye're tied to waste a shot on 'em, or here they'll sit and watch and listen, and sure enough they'll make out we're away, if they hear nought stirring inside, and they'll be off to stop us. Look at yon fellow, painted red, quavering about, and banging t' stones wi' his axe. That's t' chap as sent his spear close to my ears, and I owe him yet for that job. Just let me have a chance, Mr. Arthur. I ken ye're all soft-hearted, so I'se not kill him outright."

Arthur was very reluctant to waste one cartridge or spill one drop of blood; but the fierce gestures of the powerful savage, and his violent blows against the walled entrance, rendered him a dangerous antagonist; and on the promise of Wilkins that he would not mortally wound the man, Arthur resigned the loaded rifle to one he knew to be well skilled in fire-arms.

Wilkins carefully selected his position and his time, and when the savage raised his arm for the stroke, he fired into his shoulder. With a horrible yell, the man threw down the axe, and fell upon his face. In a moment the whole troop, with cries of terror, were flying towards the woods; two only remaining, who hastily lifted and carried away the wounded man, with loud wailings.

"There! we'se be clear on 'em for one bit," said Wilkins. "Now's our time to be off."

"But I should like much to have the axe," said Jack. "Surely, Mr. Arthur, there could be no harm in our taking the axe."

"And sure we will take it," exclaimed Gerald. "All fair, you know, general; the spoils of battle. The axe we may consider as prize-money."

"What does papa say? I leave the affairs of justice to him," said Arthur, smiling.

"Then, I think," said Mr. Mayburn, deliberately—"Margaret, tell me if I am right—I think we, as Christians, should set a bad example to heathens, if we carried off their property."

Jack sighed, as he looked wistfully at the axe through an opening in the rock, and said,—"It is tied to the handle with the stringy-bark, and then it seems fixed with gum. I'm sure I could manage it, Mr. Arthur, if we could only meet with the right stone; but this soft sandy rock is good for nothing."

But now no more time was to be wasted. All marched along, more or less laden, headed by the two proud pioneers, and with their various packages were safely got through the opening, and, to their great joy, once more tasted the blessing of fresh air. The pleasure of Mr. Mayburn, among the variety of strange birds, was unbounded; and he was with difficulty prevailed on to move forwards, by the promise that, under more favorable circumstances, they would all assist him in obtaining specimens of the curious new species. But now expedition was prudent, and even imperative, and over the twice-trodden track they moved silently and speedily till they reached the river.

There lay the frail bark Jack had contrived for crossing the river, and to each end of which he now attached one of his long coils of cord. Then, taking up two pieces of bark he had prepared for paddles, he called out,—"Now, Master Hugh, just take hold of the coil at the prow; step in, and we'll try her. Mr. Arthur and Wilkins must run out the stern-rope, and when we're over, Miss need have no fear."

Hugh, pleased to be selected for the first enterprise, leaped upon the slender canoe, and assisted Jack to paddle it across the rapid river; and when they safely reached the reedy bank, they unrolled their rope and secured the end, allowing the bark to be drawn back for Margaret, who was the first single passenger. She accomplished her short voyage happily, and, one at a time, the party were ferried over, bringing their packages with them. Then the ropes were cut away to be preserved, and the light boat was suffered to drift down the stream; while the thankful, emancipated prisoners forced their way through the jungle of reeds and canes, and saw before them a bright-green luxuriant plain, spreading as far as the eye could reach.

"Musha!" cried the Irish O'Brien, laughing joyfully. "Sure I have come on my own dear native bogs! the emerald plains of old Hibernia. No want of water now, my boys! Don't I hear it trickling beneath that bright turf, and won't we soak our boots well, my dears?"

"They're bogs, sure enough," said Wilkins, "and there's nought for it but making a run. Slow and sure would be all wrong here, Mr. Arthur, where, if ye don't skip, ye must sink. Here, give me hold of yer hand, old woman, and lope on wi' me."

Jenny, to whom this invitation was addressed, was not accustomed to *lope*; but, half dragged and half lifted by Wilkins, she followed the rest, who were plunging, wading, running, or leaping, from one dry spot to another, over the luxuriant reedy marsh. The ground was thronged with thousands of wild fowls, especially with numbers of a graceful, bright-colored bird of the crane species, very attractive to Mr. Mayburn. Clouds of troublesome insects filled the air; but life and liberty were in view, and small annoyances were disregarded; and, in the strength of their substantial breakfast, the travellers pursued their toilsome course across the marshy ground, till towards the end of the day, completely worn out, they cast themselves down to rest on the side of a firm hillock, beneath the shade of a lofty spreading tree, which had the rare quality, in Australia, of a thick foliage of large leaves, and seemed to be a species of chestnut.

Then the boys were put in requisition, and wild ducks procured for supper; and, after this needful refreshment, they united in thanks to God for their escape, and for the plenty that surrounded them, in a region where the air was pure and healthy, and the animals innocuous; and this night they slept in the open air, fearless of disturbance.

Next morning they proceeded on their way, after the boys had cut a strong staff for each traveller; likening themselves to a party of pilgrims with their long crooks. Still the same luxuriant vegetation lay before them, and still they continued the same arduous toiling over the soft yielding soil, in which every footstep was buried; but their stout staves and cheerful spirits carried them on for hours.

They continually saw the kangaroo bounding over the ground, and the active opossum running up the tall gum-tree, or the pandanus, and were sorely tempted to pursue them.

"But only reflect, boys," said Arthur, "on the imprudence of attempting to chase or shoot these animals now. It would be impossible for us to carry more than our usual burdens over this heavy ground. Wait till we arrive at our resting-place; and in the profusion of food around us, I trust we shall not want. But observe, papa, we no longer see the range of sandstone hills lying to the east: we are certainly entering a new region. That ridge before us will probably lead us from these tedious marshes. We must try to toil up the ascent before we rest."

It was really a toil, in the heated atmosphere, to climb the bush-encumbered hills; but on reaching the summit, they were repaid by looking down on a lovely valley.

It was on a lower level than that they had left, dotted over with green hills, and adorned with a forest-like scattering of majestic trees, beneath which the grass was as rich as that of a cultivated meadow, and enamelled with brilliant flowers; while the scented jasmine blossoms clung round the taller trees, and filled the air with perfume. Parrots of every bright color played in the sunbeams, chattering in the most distracting manner; while at intervals the discordance of their harsh cries was broken by the clear, bell-like notes of a musical warbler. Numerous silver streams might be seen at a distance, threading the plains, all on their way, Arthur observed, to swell some large river.

"Which we shall have to cross, most likely," said Hugh; "so, Jack, we must look about for materials for canoes again."

"I am almost afraid to suggest it," said Mr. Mayburn; "but why should we leave this lovely, tranquil valley? Why should we not erect a simple hut, and dwell here in peace, abundance, and contentment, without toil and without care? What say you, Margaret?"

"Would it not be an idle and useless existence, papa?" answered she.

"With not even wild beasts to hunt," added Gerald.

"No books to read, or horses to ride," said Hugh, sadly.

"Ay, it would be dowly enough a bit at first," said Wilkins, "and then them rogues would somehow make us out, and lead us a bonnie life."

"And it isn't fit, master," said nurse, indignantly, "that decent women, let alone Miss Margaret, should live their lives among heathens without a rag to their backs. Here's poor Ruth breaking her heart to think of them savages."

"I believe, papa," said Arthur, laughing, "the votes are against your resolution. For my own part, I cannot believe this rich and well-watered spot should be neglected by the natives. Depend on it, there are tribes not far distant, that might annoy us if we were stationary, though I trust we may not meet with many so ferocious as our last acquaintances."

"I am wrong, my son," replied Mr. Mayburn. "I know my own weakness of judgment, and you see I have grace to acknowledge my blunder."

"We will descend into the valley now," said Arthur, "and have a pleasant rest among this rich scenery. I hope that in a few days more we may reach some important river, which, if we can cross, we may at all events be satisfied that we have left our old enemies behind us, though we cannot tell what new ones we may encounter."

After many days' pleasant travelling over the well-watered and plentiful plains, they passed over a succession of green ridges, from the highest of which they had a view of a large river, certainly too wide to be crossed by Jack's bark ferry-boat; and now speculations were awakened of boats, canoes, and easy voyaging.

"I'm sure you could make a bark canoe, Jack," said Hugh, "that might be paddled well enough on a fair open river like that. Let us push forward and reconnoitre our chances of changing trudging for voyaging."

"I'd have ye look about ye," said Wilkins, "and mind yer steps. Yon's just t' place for 'em to gather. There'll be fish, and slugs, and snakes, and all that sort of varmint. Why, bless ye, Jenny, woman, ye needn't make such a face; I've seen 'em gobbling for hours at worms and grubs, and then they'll suck lots of stuff out of them gum-trees. But I say, what's yon black bit?"

The "black bit" was a circle where a fire had been made not long before; near the scorched spot lay half-finished spears, headed with sharp hard stones, of which some large slabs were piled near the place, and a finished axe made from the same flint-like stone.

"I will not take their axe, Mr. Arthur," said Jack, "because they have manufactured it, and of course it is property like; but stones are nothing but stones all the world over, and free to anybody. So if you'll wait I'll sit down now and try to make an axe the model of that, and it will be a shame if I cannot improve on it."

He was not denied the trial, and the result was, that Jack's axe was a capital tool. Hugh had cut a handle from one tree, while Gerald collected the gum oozing from another into a mussel-shell, and Jack selected the stone, and sharpened the edge on a block of sandstone, for the blade. Then cutting a cleft in the handle, he inserted and tied the blade first, covering the joining with gum, and finally placing it in the sun to dry. This success induced him to make a second axe, while the whole party sat down to watch the interesting work.

But the uneasiness of Mr. Mayburn compelled them at length to leave a spot which was evidently a haunt of the natives. They continued to walk towards the river over rich undulating ground covered with soft grass and the wild oats, the spring crop of which was here nearly ripe, and was eagerly reaped to increase the provision store. Then they came on a swampy soil, which had been apparently overflowed by the river after the rains, and which was grown over by a perfect forest of mangroves, thickly peopled by mosquitos. It was with difficulty they could force their way through the trees to the river, which they judged to be about three hundred yards across, flowing towards the west, and certainly too deep to be forded. High cliffs shut out all view of the country on the opposite bank; and, much as it would have been desirable, Arthur feared they would not be able to cross it except in canoes.

"I think it would be still better to sail up it," said Hugh.

"We have no canoes ready for such a purpose," answered Arthur, "nor can we yet begin to make one till our axes are sufficiently hardened to use with safety. I propose that we should draw back beyond the marshy ground, and follow up the course of the stream for one day at least. We can all be at work collecting materials for boats."

Any thing that gave them employment was acceptable to the boys, and they scampered from one tree to another to examine the quality or try to discover the species. The names they did not know, but were content to distinguish the varieties as palm, oak, ash, cedar, or box, as they fancied they resembled those well-known trees. There were also the various gum-trees, the cabbage-palm, and a new and interesting object to Mr. Mayburn, which he recognized from description, — the grass-tree, *Xanthorrhœa arborea*, the rough stem of which was ten feet in height and about two feet in circumference, and which terminated in a palm-tree form, with a cluster of long grass-like foliage drooping gracefully; while from the midst of the cluster sprang a single stamen of ten feet in height.

Mingled with the loftier trees was a sort of shrub, called by Wilkins the *Tea Shrub*, the leaves of which, he told them, were used in the colony as tea "by them as liked such wishwash;" and as Jenny and Ruth declared that they especially did like this "wishwash," they gathered a quantity of the leaves to make the experiment of its virtues.

"It certainly belongs to a family of plants," said Mr. Mayburn, "which are all-important to the comfort and health of man; and though I do not know the species, I should judge that an infusion of these leaves would produce a wholesome, and probably an agreeable, beverage. The delicate white flowers are not unlike those of the tea-plant, certainly. But pray, nurse, do not load yourself with too great a burden of the leaves, for the shrub seems abundant, and we have already too much to carry in this burning climate."

CHAPTER XV

"When are we to dine—or sup, rather—commander?" said Hugh; "I am so famished, that I could eat one of those noisy cockatoos half-cooked, and Margaret looks very pale and weary."

"We must try to reach one of those green hills before us," said Arthur; "we shall there be pretty certain to meet with some cave or hollow, where we can at least, stow our luggage; and then our cares and our sleep will be lighter; and as we go along, we will plunder some nests, that Margaret may have eggs for her supper."

They took as many eggs and young birds as they required, and went on till they found, among the hills, a hollow, capacious enough for a night's lodging, and here they made a fire to cook the birds and to boil the tea in a large mussel-shell. Ruth bemoaned again her awkwardness in breaking the tea-cups; for now they had to sip the infusion of leaves from cockle-shells. Wilkins declined the luxury; but the rest enjoyed it, and declared that it not only had the flavor of tea, but even of tea with sugar, which was an inestimable advantage.

"The plant is certainly saccharine," pronounced Mr. Mayburn.

"If it had only been lacteal too," said Hugh, "we might have had a perfect cup of tea; but, papa, don't you think it has a little of the aroma of the camomile tea with which nurse used to vex us after the Christmas feasts?"

"It is certainly not the genuine tea," answered Mr. Mayburn, "the peculiar *Théa* of China; but, doubtless, custom, would reconcile us to its peculiar flavor. We are surrounded with blessings, my children; and, above all, have reason to be thankful for this sweet tranquillity."

But, just as he spoke, a distant *coo-ee* from the woods proclaimed that they were not out of the reach of the usual cares of life; and they hastily extinguished the fire and retired into the rocky shelter, trusting that the darkness would prevent any discovery.

As soon as the daylight permitted him, Jack commenced to make the canoes, which the dangerous vicinity of the natives rendered immediately necessary. He roused his young masters, and Hugh and Gerald readily agreed to assist him; while Arthur made his way through the marsh to the side of the river, to select a convenient place for crossing it.

But he could see no possibility of landing on the opposite side, which was guarded by perpendicular cliffs; and with much uneasiness he proceeded up the river in hopes of seeing an opening, to which they might venture to cross. But after walking some distance, he thought it best to return to the family, to propose that they should take a hasty breakfast, and then move at once higher up the river, with watchfulness and caution, till they found the south banks more favorable for their attempt. There was no time to prepare tea, to the disappointment of the women: cold pheasant and cockatoo formed the breakfast. Then every one shouldered his burden, and the half-finished canoe was carried off, to be completed under more favorable circumstances.

They had walked without interruption for about two miles, when Margaret observed to her brother Arthur, that an opening in the mangrove belt, that ran along the banks of the river, would allow them to pass through, and afford them a safer and more advantageous track than their present exposed road. They could then select at once a shallow ford, or a flat strand, on the opposite banks, to facilitate their crossing.

"Let us hasten over the swamp," said she, "and secure this important advantage. Dear papa is in continual alarm on these open plains, and I am quite losing my usual courage."

But as they drew near the opening to the water, Arthur, always thoughtful, felt a distrust of this singular interruption of the close entangled belt of the river. "See here, Margaret," said he. "Beneath the roots of this mangrove you have a perfect leafy arbor, with walls of brilliant and fragrant creepers. In this pleasant bower I propose that we should leave you and your maidens, my father, and all our property, while I lead my brave little band forward to reconnoitre before we proceed farther."

The tears stood in the eyes of the affectionate sister as she submitted to this prudent arrangement, and saw her dearly-loved brothers and their faithful attendants prepare to set out on this service of danger.

"You can keep Ruth tied to one of these root columns," said Gerald, "and gag her if she opens her mouth for a scream." Then making a grimace at the trembling girl, the laughing youth followed his friends.

"Gerald is not in earnest, my poor girl," said Mr. Mayburn; "but it is nevertheless important—nay, it is even imperative—that you should preserve absolute silence and immobility."

"That is, Ruth," said Margaret, interpreting the order, "you must sit quite still and hold your tongue, whatever may happen."

The little band marched on till they came to the opening of the road, and they now saw that the trees had been burned down, and the space purposely cleared. This was a startling sight, and before they could determine whether they should retreat or go forward, two natives appeared, approaching from the river-side, who no sooner set eyes on the formidable strangers, than they turned back hastily, and fled out of sight.

"Let us be prepared for defence," said Arthur; "but, if possible, we will meet them amicably. We will stand abreast in a line, and look as bold as we can."

Loud yells were now heard, and soon a number of men confronted the small band, armed, as usual, with spears and throwing-sticks. They were apparently much excited, though not painted for war. Arthur held out a green bough, and made friendly signs to them, continuing slowly to approach with his companions. For a minute or two the savages seemed struck dumb and motionless with astonishment; then at once, they resumed their yells, leaping and whirling their spears in a threatening manner.

Still undeterred in their wish for peace, the bold youths walked forward till a spear flew amongst them and wounded Wilkins in the shoulder; who then rushed forward, uttering a loud execration, and, with a huge club he carried, struck the man who had thrown the spear senseless to the ground. With frightful cries the natives flung more spears, while two of them seized Wilkins; but he shook them off, as if they had been infants, and a volley of arrows from his friends directed the attention of the assailants from him; for every arrow had done execution. Wilkins then drew back into the ranks and cried out, "The rifle, sir! the rifle I say, or we're all dead men!"

There could indeed be no hesitation now, and Arthur fired one of his barrels, intending the charge to pass over the heads of the enemy; but one tall savage, who was leaping at the moment, received the shot in his cheek and head, and fell back into the arms of his companions, who bore him off with dismal lamentations, and the rest followed hastily, carrying away the senseless body of the man struck down by Wilkins.

They saw the savages force their way among the mangroves higher up the river, and flee to the hills at the north; and, confident that they were at present in safety, Arthur anxiously reviewed his forces. Wilkins looked very pale, and the spear was still sticking in his shoulder. Hugh was stretching out a bloody hand, grazed somewhat severely, while Gerald was waving triumphantly a large sombrero hat, woven of rushes by Margaret, and which now bore the noble crest of a spear which had pierced, and carried it from his head, without injuring him.

"Sure, and won't the Lady Margaret bestow her glove on me," cried the wild boy, "when she sees the honors I have brought away upon my knightly helmet?"

"It's been a close shave, young fellow," grumbled Wilkins, as he succeeded with a groan, in drawing out the spear, which was followed by such a flow of blood, that Arthur thought it expedient to send the two boys with him to Margaret, that his wound might be dressed; while Jack and he hastily surveyed the field for which the party had fought and bled.

A wide cleared space, sloping gradually to the river, was covered with various articles hastily abandoned. Clubs, boomerangs, heaps of wild oats, with shells of the fresh-water mussel, and bones of fish. Large sheets of bark were placed round the spot, lined with grass, and apparently used as beds. On these Jack cast a longing eye and said, "Bark is cheap enough for them that have arms and knives, Mr. Arthur, and these come quite convenient for our boats just now; and no harm at all, I think."

"Well, Jack," answered Arthur, "I think my father's scruples would not oppose such an appropriation. But can we cross at once? There seems a tolerable landing-place nearly opposite."

"We must get the canoes ready for launching as fast as we can," replied Jack; "for we cannot do better than cross, to get out of the way of those fellows, who will be sure to come back for their things. I'll just borrow this handy axe a bit: we can leave it behind us when we go."

Jack did not lose time; two of the bark beds were nearly transformed into canoes by the time that Arthur had gone to the mangrove bower and brought up all the party, with the unfinished canoe and the luggage.

Wilkins had his arm in a sling; but, though he certainly was suffering much, he made light of his wound, and Hugh had his hand bound up.

"This is a bad job, Mr. Arthur, for two to be laid off work when we're so sharp set," said Wilkins. "I say, master, ye'll be forced to lend a hand," addressing Mr. Mayburn.

"My good man," replied he, "I am willing to undertake any labor suited to my capacity; but I fear that I am but an indifferent mechanic."

Hugh and Gerald laughed heartily at the idea of papa with a hammer or an axe in his hand.

"Nay, nay, master," continued Wilkins, "ye'll turn out a poor hand wi' yer tools, I reckon; but we'll learn ye to paddle these floats. I'se be fit for a bit work, 'cause, ye see, I've gettin my right arm; but that poor lad's quite laid off wi' his right hand torn. Gather up some of them bits of bark to make paddles, Master Gerald."

"But no spears or weapons, Gerald," added Mr. Mayburn. "We must not carry off the property of these men, however inimical they are to us."

"Why, begging yer pardon, master," replied Wilkins; "there's them there spears as was stuck into us, we'se *surelie* keep. Ye couldn't expect on us to send them things as rove our flesh off our bones back to ' em wi' our compliments and we were obliged to ' em."

"That would certainly be an excess of honesty," said Arthur; "and I think with you, Wilkins, that we are entitled to the three spears that injured us. For oars and paddles we have abundance of materials; I only grieve that we have so few hands; but those are able and willing to work; so let us hasten to get ready for the water."

Two hours elapsed, however, before the three sound workmen were able to get all ready for the launch. In the mean time Wilkins and Hugh had searched for the nests of the water-fowl, and taken a supply of young birds, which the women had roasted for present and future provisions.

Finally, three bark canoes were launched, each containing three persons, and the river was crossed in safety. Finding they could manage their little barks satisfactorily, they then agreed to row up the river as long as it was practicable, which would, at all events, be less laborious than walking with heavy burdens.

Without any alarms, except from seeing the smoke of distant fires on the shore they had left, they had passed through beautiful and diversified scenery for many miles, before the rapid close of the day warned them to land; and under an overhanging cliff on the south bank of the river, they drew their canoes on shore, and encamped for the night.

Satisfied with their pleasant and expeditious mode of travelling, they resumed their route next morning, and with the necessary interruptions of landing for supplies of the plentiful food that surrounded them, and for needful rest, they continued for many days to voyage on the same broad river; and though they occasionally saw smoke rising on the north side, they never met with any of the natives.

But at length this desirable tranquillity was disturbed; for one day they were alarmed by sounds which they recognized as the angry yells of the savages in their fury, and they knew some fearful contention was taking place. The sounds proceeded from the south shore, and the river being at least two hundred yards broad at this part, they rowed to the north bank, in order to place a wide barrier between themselves and the contending savages.

Loud and louder grew the yells and cries when they drew near the scene of action, and curiosity induced them to rest on their oars, though they could not see the combat; but gradually the sounds died away, and it was plain the contending parties had shifted their field of battle.

After all had been quiet for some time, the boys begged earnestly that they might be allowed to land and view the scene from whence these discordant cries arose; and, at last, leaving Jack, Hugh, and Mr. Mayburn in charge of the canoes, Arthur with Gerald and Wilkins stepped on shore, and making their way through the jungle, came on a widely-spread, woody country, and saw, at no great distance, the scattered spears and clubs, which indicated that they were really upon the field of battle.

Cautiously drawing near, they were shocked to meet with the bodies of native men, transfixed by spears or destroyed by clubs. They gazed with deep distress upon this sad sight, and were preparing to return, when they were startled by hearing a low sobbing sound, followed by a shrill faint cry, and searching round among the low bushes, they found a native woman mourning over the body of one of the slain, while clinging to her was a child about four years old. They approached hastily; but no sooner did the woman see them, than she caught up her child, and would have fled, but Wilkins caught her arm, and pointing to the dead body, spoke a few words to her in a jargon he had acquired during his residence in the colony, which she seemed to understand, for she replied by some words in a low, musical voice.

"It's the poor fellow's *jin*, ye see," said he.

"His *jin*!" said Gerald, laughing. "What is a *jin*, Wilkins?"

"Why, all one as we should say his wife," replied Wilkins; "and there's nought to laugh at, Master Gerald, for she seems, poor body! like to die hersel'. I'se a bad hand at talking in their way; ye see its mair like a bird chirruping nor our folks rough talk. My big tongue cannot frame to sing out like a blackbird. Now there was Peter — —"

The woman uttered a scream of terror as Wilkins pronounced the name, and looking wildly round, she clasped the child, repeating distinctly, in accents of fear, "Peter! Peter!"

"She knows the rogue, I'll be bound!" exclaimed Wilkins, endeavoring by words and signs to obtain some information from her.

The woman pointed to the bleeding body at her feet, made a sign of stabbing, and again uttered in a vindictive tone, "Peter!" And on examining the wounds of the corpse, Wilkins pointed out to Arthur that they were not inflicted by the spear; for the man had been evidently stabbed to the heart by a sharp long-bladed weapon.

"That's been Peter's knife, I'd swear," said he, "and the sooner we take off, the better, for he's an ugly neighbor;—poor body! she may well have a scared look!"

As they turned away, the woman, it appeared, had read pity in their eyes, for she put her child into the hands of Arthur, and pointing towards the west, again murmured the name of Peter, and signified that he would return to murder her child and herself. Then lying down by the body of her husband, she closed her eyes, indicating that she must die there.

"What are we to do, Mr. Arthur?" said Wilkins, with tears on his rough cheeks; "my heart just warks for her. But ye see—maybe as how master and miss wouldn't be for havin' such an a half dementet, ondecent body amang 'em. What are we to do? Will ye just say? Sure as we're here, if we leave her, that rascal will kill her; for ye see this dead fellow, he's a big 'un, and likely he'd been again Peter, for he'd be like a head amang 'em."

"Oh, let us take both the woman and her child," said Gerald. "I will run forward to carry the child to Margaret and bring back some clothes for the unhappy mourner;" and without waiting for any sanction to his proceedings, he set off to the canoes with his prize. The alarmed woman started up, and looked anxiously after her child; but Wilkins made her understand she should also follow it, and she appeared satisfied. It was not long before O'Brien returned, accompanied by Jenny, who brought a loose garment for the astonished woman, on whose scanty toilet the neat old woman looked with unqualified disapprobation, as she assisted in arraying her more consistently with civilized customs; or, as she termed it, "made her decent."

Somewhat uncertain of the prudence of making this addition to their party, Arthur led the way to the boats, determined to consult his father and Margaret before the matter was determined. When the poor widow saw her child, dressed in a temporary costume of silk handkerchiefs, and holding Margaret's hand, in great contentment, her eyes glistened with pleasure, and going up to Mr. Mayburn and Margaret, she threw herself down on the strand, with her face to the ground, in an attitude of submission to her protectors.

"Poor creature," said Mr. Mayburn; "can we not restore her to her people, Wilkins? You know something of her language—inquire her wishes."

"I can partly make out what she says, master," answered he; "but I frame badly in hitting on them singsong queer words. I take it, all her friends have been killed right away, and she wants to stay wi' us."

"She's not a fit body to be company to Miss Marget," said nurse. "You're like to see that yourself, Wilkins."

"And if I did see that, Mrs. Jenny," answered Wilkins, in a sharp tone, "and I can't say I did see 't, it's wiser heads nor yours and mine as ought to settle that. They say God made us all akin, and it's, maybe, true; but there's a strange deal of difference among us, nowadays, I consate. Now, I'd not like to say that monkey-like, dark-avised poor creater were born sister to my bonnie Susan Raine, as I ought to have wed, Mrs. Jenny, if I hadn't turned out a graceless."

"It is strange, Wilkins," said Margaret, "that there was a fine, well-behaved young woman, named Susan Raine, came over with us in the *Amoor*. She was with one of the emigrant families that Mr. Deverell brought over from England."

"It's now better nor two years sin' I got a letter wrote to her, Miss," said Wilkins, greatly moved; "but, like me, ye see, she's no scholar, and I heared nought from her, and I judged she'd wed another. Then I cared nought what came on me; and I consorted wi' Black Peter, and such chaps, and took any job of work to get away from yon gallows hole, when I found as how she'd not look at me. What like was she ye talked on, Miss?"

"She was a fair, blue-eyed woman," answered Margaret, "with yellow hair, and a bright color; and she spoke with a north-country accent."

"God forgive me all my sins, and bring me to that lass," said Wilkins, "for I'se clear on 't, it was just my Sue. Mind ye tie me up, Mr. Arthur, if that bad fellow, Black Peter, comes nigh us; I ken he'll want to nab me, and make a rogue on me again."

"You must ask God to give you strength to resist the temptations of such a wretch," said Mr. Mayburn, "and your prayers will be heard. A great and good man has said of prayer, that it is

'A stream, which from the fountain of the heart
Issuing, however feebly, nowhere flows
Without access of unexpected strength.'"

"Ay, it seems a grand hymn," answered Wilkins; "but I mind short prayers best, and I'se try, master, to stick to 'em; for ye ken I'se but a soft good-to-nought. But it may please God to make summut out on me yet; and wi' my own will, I'se niver leave ye."

The question of admitting the unfortunate woman among them was soon decided. She crouched down in the stern of one of the canoes, holding the child on her lap; and the river being fortunately very smooth, they were enabled, though much crowded, to row off with the additional weight, being anxious to leave the spot before the natives should return to collect their spears. Besides, from the woman's words and signs they comprehended that the victorious combatants would come back to take her life and that of her child.

CHAPTER XVI

But it was not till they had left the bloody field many miles behind them that the woman recovered so far from her fear and stupefaction as to be able, by signs and half-understood words, to indicate to them that she was friendless and homeless; and that Peter would kill her, the last of her family; and from the report of Wilkins, and other sources of information, Mr. Mayburn concluded that it was the custom of these northern people to live in families, or *clans*, rather than in tribes of many, one man being the head of the house, if we may so speak of those who rarely have a house; but who live, like the beasts of the field, in the open air, unless driven by the rains to take shelter in caves.

From the woman they learnt that her name was Baldabella, and that of her child was Nakinna. She was young, and her features were not unpleasant; her eyes were brilliant, and her voice soft and musical; nor was she disfigured in any way, except that through the gristle of her nose she wore a fish-bone. The only garment she wore when she was discovered, was a short cloak of the skins of opossums, sewed neatly together and pinned round her neck with a pointed bone. When they drew the canoes ashore at the close of the day, on a narrow strand, Baldabella looked with wonder on the arrangements made for the night, and the process of broiling birds and roasting eggs at the fire, and drew away when invited to partake of the strangely-cooked food. Then she plunged her fingers into the mud at the edge of the water, and soon went up to Margaret, and put into her hand some small gray reptiles resembling slugs. Margaret shrank from the feast, shaking her head; but the woman put one into her own mouth, and swallowed it living with great relish, crammed one into the mouth of the child, and then returned to hunt for more.

Jenny held up her hands to express her abhorrence; Ruth stared at the woman with terror, evidently looking on her as a kind of sorceress; and O'Brien laughed, as he said, "Well, nurse, you need not be so much disgusted; I dare say these snails taste as well as the ugly oysters which we are cannibals enough to swallow alive."

"Oysters, Master Gerald," answered nurse, reprovingly, "are eat by decent Christian people; and I see no harm in them, specially with pepper and vinegar; but these things are varmint. Our ducks in England would hardly touch them."

"A duck is not a fastidious feeder, nurse," said Margaret, "and I would not answer for its nicety in this matter. But this poor stranger prefers the food she has been accustomed to, and we have no right to scoff at her taste. If she remain with us, no doubt, in time, she will conform to our habits."

For many days longer they continued their uninterrupted voyage up the river, the widow becoming daily more at home with her protectors. Margaret clothed her in one of her old dresses, with which she was much delighted, and in other respects she began to adopt the customs of her strange protectors. She voluntarily discarded her nose ornament; she bathed herself and her child daily; she at length ate the same food, and imitated the manners of her friends.

Margaret made light dresses for the little Nakinna, who rapidly caught the English names for the objects around her, and from her the mother learnt many words. But it was with deep concern that Mr. Mayburn saw the perfect indifference with which Baldabella regarded the religious worship of the family. She looked at first much astonished to see men and women kneel down, and to hear the solemn prayers pronounced by Mr. Mayburn; but she soon turned carelessly away to dig for worms, or to collect sticks for the fire.

Not so the little Nakinna; for, after observing the devotions two or three times, she walked up to Margaret, knelt down by her, lifted up her little hands, and seemed to listen with interest, though she could not yet understand. This act of docility and obedience was very gratifying to her kind instructress, who anxiously wished for the time when a mutual understanding might render it possible to communicate to these heathens a knowledge of the truth.

"Can it be possible, Wilkins," said Mr. Mayburn, "that these wretched natives are so lost as not even to acknowledge a Supreme Being! not even to 'see God in clouds, and hear Him in the wind!' not to feel that there must be a spiritual Ruler of the universe?"

"Why, to my fancy, master," answered Wilkins, "t' men folks isn't altogether dull chaps; but them poor jins just get all their sense knocked out on their heads. Poor bodies! they're no better off nor dogs nor asses. They work fra' morn to night, and hug heavy loads, and get kicks and short allowance for their pains."

There was a crushed, subdued look about the woman that rendered Wilkins's assertion not improbable; but Margaret hoped that, by kind treatment, the dormant intellect of the native might be developed.

At length the river became more difficult of navigation, the stream more rapid, and encumbered with fallen rocks, while rapids and falls compelled them to land continually among thick jungles, or on the narrow strand below precipitous cliffs. A mountain range was now visible before them, and they concluded that they must soon reach the source of the friendly river, when they should have to abandon the canoes for a less safe and convenient mode of travelling.

"We cannot stand walking again," said Gerald. "Couldn't we carry the canoes forward awhile? and perhaps we might have the luck to fall in with another river. What a grand thing it would be if we could find one flowing to the east or the south, that we might run easily down the stream without any hard work."

"That is not very probable, Gerald," said Arthur, "when we are yet so far from the central part—what we may strictly term the interior of the country. But we will certainly spare ourselves the labor of carrying away our canoes when we leave the water; for there can be no difficulty, in such a richly-wooded region, in procuring materials for making canoes, if we should need them. The noise of the waters seems to grow louder, and I fear we are again approaching some great cataract, which will probably, like the last we encountered, terminate all hopes of boating. I propose that we should at once make for yonder niche in the cliffs, and unlade the canoes. Wilkins and I will then row up as high as we can in a lightened canoe, to endeavor to find out a mode of ascending from this deep gully."

"If we are to land," said Gerald, "it will be easy enough to climb these wooded heights."

"Easy for you, my boy," said Arthur, "especially if you had no encumbrances; but think of papa, and Margaret, Baldabella and her child, and all the bags and bundles which constitute our wealth. We must endeavor to discover an easier road, and in the mean time we will disembark at this convenient spot."

Mr. Mayburn and Margaret remonstrated with Arthur for exposing himself and Wilkins to more danger than the rest, but were at length persuaded that the expedition could be executed with more safety and success by a small party; and two of the canoes, with all the stowage, were therefore landed in a shady nook, while the two men rowed on in the third boat. Margaret and her father waited uneasily, but the two boys amused themselves by penetrating into the woods, to seek birds; Jack cut down branches of trees, and formed them into spears, arrows, or forks; Jenny and Ruth cooked some birds, and Baldabella, armed with a spear, waded into a shallow creek of the river near them, and speared two large fish, of the species they called the fresh-water cod. Still everybody thought the hours went slowly, and were truly glad to see the light canoe gliding swiftly down the stream with Arthur and Wilkins, who drew it ashore; then Arthur said, —

"If possible, we must make our way along the banks, for the river is even now dangerous of ascent, and at no great distance our voyage would be entirely arrested by a cataract, similar to that we encountered soon after our reaching the mainland. Wilkins and I, after mooring our canoe to the mangroves, climbed to the heights, and found we were then only at the base of successive ranges of hills, which terminated in high-peaked mountains, apparently inaccessible. From these hills flowed many rivulets, which unite at the grand cataract and form this river."

To make further progress in their journey, it was therefore necessary that they should reach the country above the high rocky banks of the river, and Arthur said that on their return they had noticed one place where it might be possible for the whole party to ascend; though the path must necessarily be one of difficulty.

They dined on roast birds and broiled fish, and then began an active preparation for walking. Every thing that was worth transporting was reduced to as small a compass, and made as portable as possible; the canoes were reluctantly abandoned, and then the long train, headed, as usual, by Arthur, set out; Baldabella quietly taking her place in the line, bearing her child on her shoulder, and resting on her long fish-spear.

"I could fancy we were the Israelites, wandering in the wilderness," said Gerald.

"You will please to recollect, Gerald," said Hugh, "that the Israelites exceeded us in number in a *trifling* degree, extending to hundreds of thousands, we are told; and then, though Arthur is doubtless a clever fellow, he cannot be such a guide as the wise and gifted Moses."

"The Israelites had a more infallible Guide," said Mr. Mayburn, "than even their great leader Moses, until by discontent and disobedience, they rejected the Holy One. Let us take warning, my children, lest we should, in like manner, forget the certain protection which our Heavenly Father extends to all his faithful people."

They slowly wound along the narrow strand, sometimes sunk in mud, sometimes climbing over mounds of pebbles or piles of drift-wood, anxiously examining the thick matted woods which covered the precipitous cliffs, and even occasionally intercepted their path. For some time they despaired of finding any spot favorable for the purpose of reaching the level ground; till Arthur pointed out the place which he had previously noticed, where the banks had given way, and a great fall of rocks had formed a sort of sloping staircase, less encumbered with the brushwood, and less abrupt than they had expected.

"If we ever succeed in reaching the height," said Arthur, "this must be our path. The strong must lead the way, and aid in drawing up the feeble. These drooping creepers will be convenient to cling to, that we may not lose the ground we have made. Give me your hand, Meggie."

With many a slip downwards, a scream, and a rending of garments, the women were dragged up through the almost perpendicular wood. Baldabella alone, erect and firm in foot, despised assistance. She disencumbered herself of all loose drapery, and clasping her child, she stepped among, under, or over the bushes, with speed and safety; and long before the men had reached the height, she had quietly resumed the garb of her sex, and was seated to wait for the arrival of the less-practised climbers. They were scarcely all assembled, weary and tattered, at the head of the cliff, when Ruth, who was the last, suddenly uttered a piercing shriek, and rushed down into the matted bush again, pursued by Jack, who captured and brought her back, struggling and exclaiming against his interference.

"Oh, Jack, man, let me be," cried she; "didn't thou see 't? It's an uncanny place, this. I seed it mysel', Jack; it were a little auld fairy, grinning at me, wi' a long tail."

Jack was too enlightened to have any dread of a fairy, even with a long tail; and he persisted in bringing up Ruth, pale and trembling, to the rest of the party, though she continued to cry out, "Yonder she sits! Jack, honey! keep out on her way; she'll charm thee."

As soon as the boys heard Ruth's story of the tailed fairy, they ran with great glee to the spot she pointed out, and there, perfectly calm and immovable, they beheld the old fairy, in the form of a very extraordinary lizard. It was seated on its tail, apparently undismayed by the presence of observers; and Mr. Mayburn was called to the spot to examine the new discovery. The length of the body might be five inches, but the tail was twice that length; the color yellowish brown and black. It was scaly and frightful, and its human-like face, prominent eyes, long claws, and plaited ruff, might well terrify the ignorant and superstitious.

"I recognize the creature," said Mr. Mayburn, "from the description given by more than one traveller, to be the *Chlamydosaurus Kingii*, peculiar to Australia. The frill which surrounds its head, extending even to the chest, and folded in plaits, points out the distinct species. This ruff is a curious membrane, which can be expanded, by means of slender transverse cartilages, at the will of the animal, when it is roused to anger."

"Then observe, papa," said Gerald, "how indignant it is at our impertinent remarks. See how it spreads its broad frill, and shows its sharp teeth, as if it wished to bite us. Must I knock it down?"

"Truly, Gerald," answered Mr. Mayburn, "my curiosity would overcome the feelings of humanity, and I should be tempted to desire to obtain the creature; but I see Arthur shakes his head at the suggestion. And, after all, we have no right to slaughter the unoffending animal."

Baldabella, on whose ears Mr. Mayburn's words fell in vain, looked with glittering eyes on the reptile, and raising her spear said in her new language, "Baldabella eat him." But the lizard, with an instinct of danger, ran swiftly up the tree, assisted by its hooked claws, and escaped the blow. When far above any fear of attack, it again calmly sat down, looking down on the baffled woman with a frightful sarcastic grin.

"There now!" said Ruth, "didn't I tell ye she were uncanny? She heard all 'at were said, as sure as we're here." For Ruth's conviction of its supernatural rank was not to be shaken by Mr. Mayburn's scientific demonstration.

After satisfying their curiosity in looking at the frilled lizard, Arthur called on his forces to resume their march. Before them now lay rich green hills, rising gradually above each other, and intersected by clear streams, flowing into the river they had left. These hills were the first steps to mountains which rose, high and rugged, even to the clouds. The hills, though tedious, would not be very difficult to ascend; but how to pass the mountains they could not yet judge.

The mountain-range ran, as far as the eye could reach, from north-east to south-west, and completely intercepted them in the road they desired to pursue. To pass them, if possible, must therefore be their aim; or a vast deal of time must be lost in making a circuitous course.

"We will ascend the hills, at all events," said Arthur, "and look round us. We may, perhaps, find some natural pass. We might even try a kangaroo-path, which must be found, for, see what herds of the animals are bounding along under the lofty trees on the hills."

"Oh, do let us have a kangaroo-hunt, Arthur!" exclaimed Hugh. "We are hungry, and kangaroo meat would fill us; and therefore, papa, we have a right to kill and eat."

"Let's see ye set about it," said Wilkins. "They're sharper fellows nor ye think on, them kangaroos, my lad. They're a match for most folks, barrin' ye have dogs, or follow them up till they fall tired, and that'll maybe, not be for half a day. I ken a good deal of kangaroo-hunting; but I'se not clear that them there chaps is so shy as down-country beasts; ye see, they'll niver like have clapped eyes atop on a man, and they'll not ken man's crafty ways."

"To the disgrace of human nature," said Mr. Mayburn, "what Wilkins suggests is true: wherever he is recognized by the brute creation, they instinctively

'Shun the hateful sight of man.'"

"Well, sir," said Gerald, "that is, I suppose, because the ignoble fears the noble—the coward the brave."

"And you may add, Gerald, the slave his tyrant," continued Mr. Mayburn. "It is ever thus with

'Man, proud man!
Dressed in a little brief authority.'"

"But, papa," said Hugh, "we are in need of food, and you must allow that it is more humane to destroy one kangaroo than a dozen cockatoos or pheasants."

"I agree with Hugh, papa," said Margaret. "We will, if possible, content ourselves to-day with taking one life."

Armed with spears and throwing-sticks, bows and arrows, and one boomerang which Baldabella had found, and which no one but herself could yet use, the hunters preceded Mr. Mayburn and Margaret. By the directions of the experienced Wilkins, they spread along in a line, to guard the foot of the hill; for he said the animal always took a downward course when it was alarmed, for, as its fore-feet never touch the ground in its greatest speed, it has more time in a descent to draw up the hind legs, to make the immense spring, than it could have with an ascent before it.

No sooner had the timid animals seen the strange forms of the hunters than they started off with such incredible speed, that no one unacquainted with their habits could have believed that their flight was a series of jumps, and that their fore-feet never touched the ground. In their confusion, some of the animals tried to penetrate the rank of the hunters, while some fled to the right or to the left. The spears and arrows showered amongst them, and more than one beast carried off the weapon sticking in him. But it was the boomerang of Baldabella which, after complicated and mysterious evolutions, struck and stunned a large animal, which Wilkins presently despatched with his knife.

Arthur then recalled the hunters, saying, "We will have no more slaughter. This large animal will supply us with as much meat as we can consume while it remains fresh, and it would be wanton to slay more."

The rear rank then joined them. The body of the kangaroo, suspended on a long pole, was shouldered by Wilkins and Jack, and the march was resumed. They ascended and descended several hills, till night and fatigue compelled them to rest in a little hollow, where a cooking-fire was made, and they supped with great enjoyment on venison steaks; and, like the early inhabitants of the world, before luxury and artificial wants had enervated them, they slept beneath the canopy of heaven, among the everlasting hills.

"Get up, Arthur," cried Hugh, early next morning. "Get up, and come to see our mountain-pass. Gerald discovered it, and therefore we propose to name it the 'Pass of Erin.'"

CHAPTER XVII

Arthur was soon alert, and followed the boys, who led him up the side of the next high hill and along the ridge for about three hundred yards to the south west, and then pointed out to him a narrow rent or gorge in the mountain, lying far below the hill on which they stood; but from this hill a gradual ascent, formed by fallen rocks, made a rude path to a narrow shelf or terrace which they now saw far above them, and which ran along the precipitous side of the rocky wall. Arthur shuddered as he said, "Is that narrow terrace passable, do you think, Gerald?"

"Oh, yes," answered he; "Hugh and I had a run along it before we woke you, and it is not half so bad as it looks. We shall manage very well if we go 'goose-walk;' but I think it would not be safe for two abreast. To be sure, it is rather confusing to look down into the depths below; but we must give them all a caution, and I think it would be better to blindfold Ruth."

"There is nothing for us but to try it," said Arthur. "Let us return to breakfast before we set out."

"Yes, we might as well reduce the bulk of the kangaroo," said Hugh, "for it will be awkward to carry it along our pass."

But when the plan was fully arranged, it was judged expedient to cut up the kangaroo, and only carry away sufficient for another day's consumption. Even the useful skin was reluctantly abandoned, as Arthur knew well they must have no unnecessary encumbrance. Ruth could not, however, be persuaded to leave her pet fowls, but resolutely set out with her basket on her arm.

Then, after beseeching a blessing on their perilous journey, they marched forward, and gradually ascending the hills, they reached the narrow path that skirted the mountain. This natural shelving was scattered over with loose stones, and occasionally broken away till a ledge of only about five or six feet was left for them; but the creeping plants that covered the rock enabled the timid to grasp a kind of support on one hand, as they moved cautiously along the unequal and perilous path. Below this terrace yawned a deep gully, that formed the bed of a stream, which at all seasons washed its sides. This stream was now shallow, and moved sluggishly; but rugged crags, and torn-up trees, lying in the bed, showed that raging torrents must pour into it after the rainy season.

From the interstices of the bush-covered rocks sprang the gray-leaved gum-tree, the elegant casuarina, and a bright-leaved tree resembling the box, but lofty and strong. Among these trees parrots and cockatoos chattered incessantly, and on the gum-trees hundreds of little active opossums sported with all the playfulness of monkeys; and Mr. Mayburn was so interested in watching them hang from the branches, suspended by their curved tail, to rifle the nests of the birds, or feed on the numerous insects round them, that Arthur, in alarm, stepped back to hold his father by the arm.

"I tell you what we must do, Arthur," said Gerald; "we must be linked in couples, as the travellers on the Alps are; then, if one makes a false step, there's a chance for his mate to draw him up."

"No bad plan, Gerald," answered Arthur; "but we must take care to couple with judgment. The prudent or brave must take charge of the rash or the timid. I will take papa; Jack, his unlucky sister; Hugh, Margaret, or, more correctly, Margaret must take Hugh; Wilkins will take charge of nurse; and you, the neglected proposer of this wise measure, cannot profit by it, unless you will submit to be guided by Baldabella, who seems to trip along with her lively burden unapprehensive of danger."

Hugh preferred to walk unfettered; and Arthur had no fears for the native woman, whose firm and steady step showed that she had been accustomed to such rough and scrambling paths.

Arthur, who was the first of the line, now became uneasy, as, on looking before him, he remarked that, as far as the eye could reach, there appeared to be no termination to the mountain wilderness. He could have fancied that a labyrinth of broken, precipitous, lofty, and interminable rocks shut them completely from the world. It was a bewildering prospect, and even the strong heart of Arthur almost failed him, and his head whirled at the sight of such stupendous and uncertain difficulties.

A scream from Ruth recalled him to his immediate duties, and on turning round he saw her much-valued basket of poultry bound down the precipice over the bushes, till it rested on a lower ledge, some hundreds of feet beneath them, where it flew open, and the fowls, uninjured by their involuntary flight, fluttered from their prison, and began calmly to peck about for food; while the little bantam cock proclaimed his liberty by shaking his plumes and uttering his conceited hoarse crow.

"They are settlers now, Ruth," cried Gerald, laughing; "the first colonists—regular squatters. How astonished future travellers will be when they make the curious discovery: a species of bird remarkably like *Gallus Barndoorii*. What grand names they will bestow on them! and write long papers, and puzzle ornithologists."

But the patriarch of this new species was not allowed to squat among the aborigines with impunity; his triumphant notes were answered by a crow of defiance in a less familiar tone from a splendid cock pheasant, which pounced down on the new comer with a furious peck, that the true-trained English bird, notwithstanding his foreign ancestry, could not brook. The brave little bantam retaliated boldly, and a furious combat ensued, causing even the English hens to raise their heads from their pleasant feast, and appear somewhat interested in the event; while Ruth shrieked, "He'll kill him! Jack, honey! throw a stone at him! drive him off! Chuck! chuck!"

But though Ruth's familiar cry failed to separate the combatants *à l'outrance*, the pleased hens recognized the well-known call, and responded to it by fluttering and scrambling up the mountain side, to partake of the scattered grain; and in the fulness of their feast, they were easily captured, and stowed in separate bags and pouches, till a new dwelling could be made for them.

Then the little feathered hero below, having vanquished and left his antagonist for dead, perched for a moment on the pinnacle of a shattered rock, and crowed triumphantly, as if to defy the whole race of native birds; after which demonstration, he leisurely followed his female friends up the steep, to share their feast and their captivity.

Notwithstanding the alarm and delay caused by this accident, there was something amusing about it that was not without its beneficial effects. Ruth continued to lament the loss of her basket; but Jack scolded her seriously for her foolish fears and awkwardness, which were the sole cause of the loss. He declared the fowls were absolute pests, and wholly useless in a region where birds and eggs dropped into your hands; but his remonstrances having produced tears of penitence and promises of amendment, he relented, and promised to make for her a coop, or cage, of cane, which would be easier to carry than the basket, and afford more air to the unfortunate prisoners.

After wandering for two days along their frequently dangerous, and always difficult, aerial pathway, resting only when they came to some rocky hollow, they began to pine for a less-hazardous road; and they now perceived that, with the usual caprice of Australian rivers, the stream in the narrow bed below them had disappeared, though slender rills continually fell from the mountains, but subsided into bogs, or formed pools below.

They therefore resolved, if they could safely accomplish it, to descend to the bed of the river; and endeavor to extricate themselves from the rocky maze in which they seemed hopelessly involved.

After another day's travelling, they fancied the descent appeared more practicable than it had yet been since they set out on the shelving terrace, and it was decided to make the trial. The first step would decidedly be the most difficult. About twelve feet below them another shelf of rock projected, wider than that on which they now stood; but how to reach it was a puzzling question, for the descent was perpendicular, and quite overgrown with thorny bushes.

"If you will help me, Master Hugh," said Jack, "I think we may manage it. We must just cut down the bushes into steps like for them that feel timid."

Employment was the grand need of the active boys, and to clear a passage as low as they could reach, and then step down on the bushes to work below, was a pleasant amusement. The stone axes were now found to be perfectly serviceable, and they soon cut six clearances, each two feet deep, graduating like a staircase, of which the matted brush formed the steps, which reached to the lower terrace; and down the staircase the agitated females were, one after another, assisted, and safely placed on the broad shelf.

This was a decided victory, and they now saw, to their great satisfaction, that the lower descent sloped so much, from accumulated rocks and drift-wood, that by clearing the way with the axes, they easily reached the comparative security of the muddy bed of the vanished river. They looked round on the immense walls which inclosed them with some dismay; then Gerald said,—

"Now, Meggie, we only want the great rains to come on, and then we shall have some notion of the situation of sinful man in the Deluge."

"I trust, my dear boy," said Mr. Mayburn, "that you do not allude to that fearful judgment with levity. And surely, Arthur, we are not near the time of the terrific tropical rains."

"Usually, papa, I believe the heaviest autumnal periodical rains are in February and March," said Arthur. "We are now in the midst of summer; still I must confess I have read of continued rains, even at this season; but I trust we shall be in a safer locality before such trying weather comes on. We are certainly progressing in the way we wish to go; but the immense extent of the mountain-range is extraordinary. Fortunately, we are not in a desert, we are surrounded by plenty, and as far as we have yet penetrated, ferocious animals seem unknown; and more, ferocious man rarely encountered. I only fear for your strength, dear papa, and for that of dear Meggie."

"Fear not for us, Arthur," answered Margaret; "you know I am naturally strong; and God has given renewed life and health to dear papa. His delight in these new and varied scenes of Nature makes every toil light to him. Observe him now, pausing and contemplating something at yon large pond; let us join him. Now, papa! what is the new discovery?"

"Wonderful, my children," said he. "Behold this marvellous new creature. Undoubtedly it must be the *Ornithorhyncus paradoxus*, the duck-billed Platypus, which I should have recognized, from the numerous sketches I have seen; and my warmest hopes are fulfilled in the happiness of really looking on the rare animal in its native wilds."

"Is't a duck, think ye, Miss Marget?" asked Ruth, with a kind of awe.

"Has a duck four legs, Ruth?" asked Gerald. "Has it fur on its back, and a broad finny tail? No, Ruth, this is not a strange fowl, but a strange beast."

"Nevertheless," said Mr. Mayburn, "there are irreconcilable circumstances in such a decision. This animal, if we rank it among the mammalia, belongs to no order yet named, but stands alone. Quadruped it is, certainly; web-footed, certainly; ovo-viviparous, certainly, as the eggs are hatched before birth, and the young then suckled, like the mammalia. Feeding on worms and grubs, like the duck; sleeping rolled up, like the hedgehog; playful as the monkey, and harmless as the dove;—we cannot but look with astonishment and admiration on this remarkable caprice of Nature."

"They're ugly beasts, that I'll say," was Jenny's remark, "and not half so good as a duck for such as us; but I'se warrant them poor heathens eat 'em as we would a roast goose."

Leaving the platypus, which they now saw at every pool as they proceeded, they walked on till the ravine gradually became wider, but the mountain-line still spread on each side. Soon after, the pools disappeared, and rich grass supplied their place. Wild and wonderful was now their daily journey, for before them lay immense untrodden forests, inclosed between lofty cliffs, which rose to the clouds, and the travellers felt inspired with awe as they looked round on the majesty of Nature.

Yet the softer features of loveliness were not absent; every step was on some beautiful, usually some quite new, plant, and the lofty forest trees were of species now first seen, and were garlanded round with flowering creepers of the most brilliant dyes; while the rich perfume of the jasmine, and the heliotrope-like odor of the golden-blossomed acacia filled the air. Bright *orchidæ*, unnamed and unknown, masses of ferns of unexampled beauty, were scattered round this vast conservatory of nature; and amidst all this profusion, thousands of birds whistled, chattered, warbled, and uttered the startling foreign notes which assure you that you are in a strange land.

There was the sweet-voiced bell-bird, a pretty little creature, whose notes ring with a silver sound; there was the pert pied bird, which might seem really a magpie, if it were not tailless, which has a low flute-like song, swelling like the organ; whence it is named by the colonists the organ-magpie; and as each strain of these warblers died away, the loud, hoarse, derisive notes of a curious bird, resembling none of the known species of the world, seemed to ridicule the musical performers.

"No doubt, papa," said Hugh, "this must be the 'laughing jackass,' of which we have read an account. Do you hear the regular 'Ha! ha! ha!' from which he derives his name, and which sounds so strangely when mingled with the notes of the warblers? But now he has roused all the cockatoos and parrots, who are screaming their jargon above all other sounds."

"Just listen, Hugh," said Gerald, "those jackass birds are surely blowing a penny trumpet. Did you ever hear such a noise—laughing, braying, trumpeting? you might fancy you were at a country fair. How Ruth does stare! I say, Ruth, what do you think of them?"

"Will they be Christians, Master Gerald?" asked the trembling girl.

"Hopeless heathens, Ruth," answered the wild boy; "feathered donkeys, flying punches, instinctive mocking-birds, repeating sounds which they have never heard. See, papa, there is one of the jolly fellows, perched on yon gum-tree. What a monstrous beak he has!"

"I contemplate the bird with great interest, my boy," answered Mr. Mayburn. "It has been classed with the Halcyons by naturalists, and named *Dacelo gigantea*; yet, in its social habits, and flexible and apt organs of voice, it seems rather to resemble the jay. It is somewhat remarkable that amidst the gorgeously-attired birds that surround it, this rarely-gifted bird wears a garb so simple and unadorned. You observe that it frequents the gum-tree, and its sombre plumage, assimilating so happily with the gray foliage of the tree, is at once a protection and a distinction. How rejoiced I should be, my dear boy, if we could make a complete collection of these rare creatures; but the difficulties of transporting them safely in our journey are insurmountable."

"Wait, sir," replied Gerald, "till we catch our quaggas; then Jack will make us a wagon, which we can convert into a menagerie, filled with curious animals, and drawn by our own beasts."

"The quagga is not a native of Australia, Gerald," replied Mr. Mayburn; "nor does the country, happily, produce any of the large and fierce quadrupeds. We must not dare to think of any vehicle for travelling; yet many hundred miles separate us from the useful animals of our dear friends the Deverells; and my heart fails me when I reflect on the improbability of our ever reaching them."

Margaret sighed as she said, "And I too, dear papa, cannot help many idle wishes that we were come to open plains, and more direct paths. These lovely wilds of Nature, forests and mountains, are very charming; but they seem too romantic and unreal to be satisfactory. If we were to keep a journal, and publish it hereafter, we should, I fear, be ridiculed for inventing fairy tales."

"In truth, Margaret," answered her father, "fairy tales were not originally mere inventions of the imagination. They were the offspring of the experience of observing travellers over lovely untrodden wilds like these. And what are the miraculous transformations they describe but such as might really happen—the ingenious contrivances of man when destitute of all the resources of civilized life? Has not Jack transformed a flint-stone into an axe? and have we not cups and plates which were once the abodes of the shell-fish? Difficulties originate miraculous efforts, and man is indebted to the good fairies, Necessity and Ingenuity, for many of his comforts."

"Very true, dear papa," said Arthur; "and the fairy Necessity now calls on us peremptorily to escape from these forests, where I have twice during this day heard the *coo-ee* of the natives, though at a considerable distance before us. I have been for some time anxiously examining the south side of the gorge for any outlet which may enable us to turn away from their haunts."

They had been making their way for some hours along the southern extremity of the forest, still hemmed in by the high rocks, when Gerald, creeping into a narrow cleft, declared that he had found a tunnel, and called on Hugh to assist him in exploring it. Fearful that they should bewilder themselves in the recesses of the mountains, Arthur proposed that all the party should enter the opening, which was a cavern of great height and space, where they might remain till he and his brothers penetrated further into the rocks. They lighted some dry branches for torches, and set out, satisfied that the rest would be in safety in this secure retreat.

The boys found this tunnel descend gradually: sometimes it was narrow and low, sometimes wide and encumbered with fallen fragments of rock; still, it was airy, and they were able to pass on, till they concluded they must have walked half a mile. They were then so desponding that they thought of turning back, but at length a glimmering of light satisfied them that there must be another outlet, and they took courage to proceed, till they reached a matted thicket of brushwood through which they forced their way, and then had the pleasure of seeing the sky above their heads, though they were still in a very narrow gully. It seemed to be the dry bed of a rivulet, choked up with stones and torn-up bushes. Before them rose another line of bush-covered mountains, but not so lofty or precipitous as those they had left behind.

"Is it worth while," said Hugh, "to drag the whole party through that gloomy subterranean passage, to bring them into this glen, which seems perfectly barren and lifeless? I am of opinion that we were better in our old forest."

"Wait for my decision," said Gerald, springing up the side of the opposite mountains, regardless of the rending of his light blouse, and his scratched hands; and before long he stood on the summit.

"This will do for us capitally," he cried out. "Wide plains below, but an awkward step down to them. Jack will have to cut a staircase again."

This account of the country satisfied Arthur, and they hastened back at once to relieve the anxiety of their friends, whom they found in a state of great alarm. The cries of the savages had gradually approached so near to them, that Margaret induced Wilkins and Jack to close the opening by which they had entered with a large piece of rock. Then they had heard voices close to the rocks, and Baldabella, who was now able to speak many English words, said—"Many bad black fellows! much bad! see white man foot-walk.—Black fellow come—slow, slow—catch all—eat master—eat miss—eat old Jin—eat Nakinna—all! all!"

It was with much difficulty they restrained the cries of Ruth, when she comprehended that she was in danger of being eaten; and though Mr. Mayburn doubted and disputed the existence of cannibalism in Australia, Wilkins and Jack succeeded in inducing the whole family to move on in the track of the pioneers, rather than risk the danger of discovery at the mouth of the cave.

CHAPTER XVIII

The report of the boys decided the movement of the family, and they hastened through the long tunnel to the cheerless glen. They then sought the easiest ascent, that they might escape from these widely-spread mountains, and a herd of kangaroos in the bush, disturbed by strange voices, just then appeared, and bounded up the steep wood at a place which the travellers who followed them found had been selected with a happy instinct, for it was less abrupt and less matted with brush than that which Gerald had ascended. The strong assisted the weak, and with some difficulty all were brought to the ridge, and looked down with mingled feelings of relief and alarm on the widely-spread, thinly-wooded plains so far below them.

The descent was much more tedious and laborious. Axes and ropes were put in requisition; but finally all planted their feet thankfully on the green sward, and looked round on a new region, where their progress would be less retarded, but their exposure to observation would necessarily be greater than before.

"And I see neither meat nor water," said Jenny, despondingly.

"We have still potatoes left," said Margaret; "and though we have not yet seen much animal life, I trust there is no fear of famine. I certainly see some creature moving beneath yon golden acacia."

"Huzza! papa!" cried Gerald. "There's the Emu at last! I saw one at the Zoological Gardens, and I know the fellow at once. Now, how are we to get hold of him? I fear his skin is too tough for a spear or an arrow to do much harm, and Arthur is so careful of his charges."

"I have but four left," answered Arthur, with a sigh, "and I am unwilling to waste my shot, and perhaps attract the attention of the wandering natives. We will try arrows and spears, and, if we can, the boomerang."

"Be canny, lads!" cried Wilkins, in great excitement. "Keep at his back, I tell ye; he can see half a mile afore him, but he's as deaf as a post; and if he once gets a sight on us he'll be off like Voltigeur, and he'll be a smart chap as sets eyes on him again. Stand here, we'll try a throw now; and *Jin*, woman, gie us a touch of yer boomerang."

Baldabella was as much excited as any of the party, and perfectly understood the rules of emu-hunting. They fixed themselves at a proper distance, and then, seeing that the bird, which had been feeding on some root or herbage, had raised its head, as if about to move, they flung their spears and discharged their arrows with some effect, as a spear and an arrow were left in its side; Baldabella at the same time threw her boomerang, which struck it with such force that it staggered, and uttered a deep, booming cry; but, rallying again, it began to run very swiftly, till a second flight of spears and arrows brought it to the ground.

All the party then went up to it; and O'Brien had approached, and was about to touch it, when Wilkins seized his arm, and drew him back just in time; for the animal struck out its powerful leg, and shattered the bow which the boy held in his hand.

"He would have sarved your leg as bad," said Wilkins, "if he could have hitten ye. He has a leg like a sledge hammer for a hit. We'se be forced to give him a few more spears afore it will be safe to come nigh him."

But a blow on the head stunned the huge creature; and it was then quickly dispatched and cut up. They contented themselves with carrying off the two hind quarters, which Wilkins assured them afforded the most palatable meat, and which would be ample provision for two days.

"There are some eggs, too," said Hugh, "which we might carry off for papa; but they are so tremendously large and heavy."

"The egg is, I believe, excellent food," said Arthur; "but with food we are abundantly supplied. I think we must take two, however; one for papa, the other to form into that very useful vessel, a water-bottle or bucket."

Delighted with the immense dark green egg, and the examination of the curious, fur-like plumage of the emu, Mr. Mayburn no longer regretted the forest scenery he had left, but cheerfully went forward over the green and flowery plain, till, after walking many miles, they encamped beneath a gum-tree, made a fire, and broiled some emu-steaks, which all pronounced would have been better than beef-steaks if they could have had a little salt to eat with them; but they were gradually becoming reconciled to this privation.

No one dared to murmur, amidst their blessings, because they had been a day without water; but they trusted in God to provide them with this boon, too, in his good time. The large egg was carefully cleaned out through a small opening made by Jack at one end, and then slung with cords, to make it convenient to carry next day, before they took their rest.

But the next day they had travelled for many hours, till, faint and weary, their steps were feeble and languid, when the sight of a line of casuarina-trees directed them to the bed of a river, now quite dry; and while the most exhausted sat down to rest, the young and active proceeded up the hard bed till it became mud, and a little higher, muddy pools. Into these pools they, at once, plunged their faces, and drank, and moistened their burning skin, and then each laughed at the crust of dirt left on his neighbor's face. But by persevering in walking on, they met with a pool of clearer water, from which they filled their water buckets and mussel-shells, and returned to take the refreshment to their friends, and then to conduct them to the moister region.

They continued to pursue the course of the chain of pools which must in a short time be really a river, when the periodical rains came on. The prospect of these approaching rains rendered all the thoughtful of the party anxious and uneasy; for the pleasant open air life to which they had become habituated would then be intolerable.

For two days the emu-flesh was eatable, and the pools amply supplied them with water. Then they again reached a line of low hills from which the river had its source; and through the shrubs and brushwood that covered them they forced or cut their way, and descended on a more fertile and pleasant plain.

But, to their great annoyance, they beheld before them several natives gathered round a fire, employed in making spears and arrows, which they were hardening in the fire. On one side sat two women, bruising some grain or nuts between two stones: these women wore cloaks of opossum fur; but the men were almost entirely naked, and had their bodies marked with frightful cicatrices. Though it was plain these natives must have seen the approach of the strangers, and probably now, for the first time beheld white men, they preserved a dignified composure, pursuing their labors, without any apparent notice of the intruders.

Arthur drew up the forces abreast in a long line, saying, "Walk on firmly, and imitate the indifference of the natives. I entreat you, above all, not to show the least fear."

They marched slowly forward till they were close to the savages, when the little Nakinna, attracted by the sight of a child about her own age, which was playing near the women, broke from her mother and ran up to the child. The tallest of the men then stepped from the rest and caught up the child in his arms. The distracted mother darted forward to rescue her, and was also seized and detained by two natives, while she called out piteously to her white friends to assist her.

Arthur was much vexed at this incident, which he feared would form a pretext for a quarrel; but it was impossible to abandon poor Baldabella, who seemed very repugnant to return to savage life. He therefore called Wilkins to follow him, and going up to the man who held the child, made an effort to remove her gently from his arms. The man resisted and held her firmly; then Arthur, assuming a threatening expression of countenance, uttered some words in a loud, stern tone, and at the same time pointed to his rifle.

The savage stared at him and his weapon with a countenance half of fear, half of wonder. He then pointed to the complexion of the mother and the child, and also to his own, and to Arthur's, as if he questioned the right of the white people to detain those who certainly were not of their race.

Arthur then made Baldabella comprehend that she must tell the men that if they did not release her and Nakinna, the white men would kill them all. The woman at once understood and repeated the message; and was answered by the tall savage. She shook with terror as he spoke, and turning to Arthur said, —

"Black fellow say, Peter want Baldabella. Baldabella must go. No, no! good white man! Bad Peter kill Baldabella! kill Nakinna!"

It was doubly annoying to find these troublesome natives were acquainted with the villanous bush-ranger; but it was certain Baldabella must not be left in the power of the wretch, at any cost. While he hesitated what steps to take, one of the women, roused by the cries of Nakinna, went up to the savage who held her, and spoke to him in soft, persuasive accents, at the same time attempting to take the child from him. The hardened wretch put down the child at his feet, and snatching up a club, struck the woman to the earth, senseless, if not dead.

No longer able to control his indignation, Arthur, seeing a herd of kangaroos bounding along within reach of a shot, directed the attention of the man to them, and then fired his rifle, and shot a large animal dead. Astonishment and terror overcame the usual assumed calmness of the natives, and several of them fled in confusion.

Arthur then, pointing to the kangaroo, and then to Baldabella, indicated his wish for the exchange, and the two men who still held her readily resigned their captive, and ran up to take possession of the more valuable spoil, followed by the inhuman chief; after he had, with a vindictive countenance, spurned the poor child from him with his foot. The mother caught up her child and fled to her friends, prostrated herself before Arthur, and placed his foot on her neck; then rising, she resumed her usual dignified and graceful step, and fell into the rank with the rest of the party, who lost no time in moving forward, after Margaret had seen that the unfortunate victim of the chief's cruelty was kindly attended to by the woman who was her companion.

"It were a burning shame," grumbled Wilkins, "to let them saucy niggers take off with that fine beast, and have to fast ourselves. For ye see, Master Hugh, that shot's flayed away all on 'em, and it may be long enough afore we light on 'em again."

"Have some faith, my good man," said Mr. Mayburn. "We have been fed like the prophet in the wilderness, by miracle, let us not fear, God will still provide us with food."

"At the present moment," said Arthur, "it would be imprudent to delay even to seek provisions. Our first consideration must be to move away from this part as quickly as possible, for I suspect these people will keep us in sight as long as they can."

"Ay, master," said Wilkins, "they'll need ye to shoot beasts for 'em! Depend on't they'll dog us."

This was an uncomfortable suspicion, and Margaret and Arthur talked and pondered deeply on plans and arrangements, almost regardless of the brilliant buds and blossoms that enchanted Mr. Mayburn. They walked on with regular and rapid steps over the flower-strewed ground, amidst the rich smell of the foliage and the flowers and the strange music of the woods. Kangaroos and emus were seen at some distance, but prudence forbade any delay for the chase, and they made no halt till extreme fatigue compelled them to rest on the side of a grassy hill, where the least wearied set out to search the bushes for nests. Some fine young birds supplied them with a good supper; eggs were now rarely found, but with these Ruth's fowls frequently supplied them.

"Where next?" asked Margaret. "I think, Arthur, I can distinguish a deep-green line far distant to the south-east. May we not hope it indicates the situation of another river?"

"We have ever been cheered, thank God," said Mr. Mayburn, "through all our pilgrimage, with continued benefits. We have never yet experienced the perils and privations of the desert, which has ever been supposed to exist in the interior of Australia."

"Travellers in South Australia," replied Arthur, "have certainly met with those barren regions; but in this tropical country we have, indeed, enjoyed all the plenty which nature can bestow. At present we need water; but in the morning we will, if God permits, direct our course to the green belt we have seen. If we can again resume our canoe voyaging, it will be a great relief to us; and even if the river be dried up at present, we can take the bed for our guide, and may find pools of water for our daily use. But, my dear Margaret, I am ashamed to say I feel despondent when I reflect that this is January; the autumn rains may soon come on, and we have no idea where we can shelter you and dear papa from the fury of tropical storms."

"I could soon run up a bit of a hut, with bark roofing," said Jack, briskly.

"I am quite aware of that, Jack," answered Arthur, "and have much reliance on your skill and promptness. The great difficulty seems to be the selection of a site out of the observation of the treacherous and vindictive natives; or of one whom I dread still more, that vile bush-ranger, who appears to be tracking us for some evil purpose."

"He has a spite again me, that's sartain, Mr. Arthur," said Wilkins. "Then, he'd like to put his hands on that gun; and there would be, likely, some pickings of things as would suit him, let alone money, that, like enough, ye'll have amang ye."

"But what possible use can the misguided man have for money in a wilderness among savages?" asked Mr. Mayburn, in astonishment.

"Why, not a deal of use just hereabouts," answered Wilkins; "but ye ken nought about bush-rangers, and all their rounds and changes. If Peter had cash, he'd be off to some of them far away bush publics; and there he'd have a grand tuck out, till he'd spent every rap, and be fresh to set out on a new hook. That's bush-ranging life, master."

"And a fearful life it is in this world, Wilkins," said Mr. Mayburn; "but still more fearful as a preparation for the world to come. Thank God that you are rescued from it, my poor man."

"Ay, I'se clear on't now," replied he, "thanks to ye, master; and, God be praised, there's no shame can stick to a fellow for turning round when he's got into a slough."

"Not at all, Wilkins," said his good teacher; "the best Christians have sinned and repented; and to all it is said that they must through much tribulation enter the kingdom of God."

The heart of Wilkins was enclosed in a rough husk, but the soil was not bad; the seed that was sown in it was not unfruitful, but was slowly coming to maturity.

Early in the morning the pilgrims took the road towards the green belt they had observed the previous day; and though many tedious hours intervened before they reached it, they were rewarded by discovering that the belt of trees hung over the banks of a considerable river, narrow, but deep, with high rocky banks, so far above the level of the stream on the side on which they stood, that the water which they so much required was unattainable.

This disappointment was vexatious, and they continued to pass along the edge of the cliff for some time in melancholy silence, till, at a very narrow part of the river, Jack stopped, and, pointing to a tall tree on the edge, proposed that they should cut it down, so that it should fall across the river and form a bridge. This would be an undertaking at once tedious and hazardous; but the advantage of placing the river between themselves and the inimical savages was obvious, as it was improbable that they should have the means of crossing. It was therefore agreed that they should make the experiment.

They had found abundance of the wild oats on the plain, which were now quite ripe; and Ruth was busily employed in bruising the grain to make biscuits, while Jenny roasted potatoes in the ashes, and looked down on the river with longing eyes, for the tea-shrub was abundant round them, and nurse pined for her cup of tea again. Leaving the women thus engaged, the young woodcutters commenced their operations with their stone axes, though they had failed to render them very sharp, relieving each other at intervals; for in truth the cutting down a stout tree was not a little tiresome.

But perseverance subdues great difficulties; at last the tree fell majestically, and rested securely on the opposite bank. Then the proud young workmen proceeded to lop the branches which stood in the way, levelling and smoothing the trunk as much as they were able, and running over it to prove its security; and, finally, Jack carried a rope across, attached to some of the erect boughs, to form a sort of hand-rail to satisfy the timid. With some persuasion, Mr. Mayburn was so far satisfied of the safety of the rude bridge, that he suffered himself to be led across; then Margaret and the two women were safely conducted over; Baldabella followed, looking with astonishment at their timidity, and tripping lightly along with her child upon her shoulder.

When all had crossed, the rope was withdrawn and coiled up again, and, with the aid of levers and axes, the bridge was broken and cast down, to be floated away by the stream, that the savages might not have the advantage of it in their pursuit.

The banks on which the travellers now stood were less precipitous than those they had left; they were clothed with bamboos and rushes, and in many places open down to the river, where they gladly procured the water of which they were so much in need. Then they continued to walk along a narrow muddy strand, looking with longing eyes at the smooth water, on which a canoe might have been paddled with so much less exertion than the continued labor of walking. It would soon be made, Jack declared; and, after a night's rest, all were ready to work, if the work were provided for them—the great point, as Jack said, being "to fall on the right sort of tree."

Before they had finished another weary day's walk, they had "fallen on the right tree," barked it, and, uniting their efforts, formed and gummed two canoes. These required a day to be hardened for service, during which they made paddles, cut down the oat grass to serve for lining the canoes, after they had thrashed out the ripe grain. The women baked biscuits and boiled fish, with which the river abounded, collected some tea-leaves, and finished provisioning the boats.

Next morning they were again seated in these very commodious canoes, delighted to rest after all their fatigues; for the labor of paddling on the smooth river was comparatively easy. They continued an uninterrupted voyage of many days, though they several times saw the smoke of fires rising from the brush on the north bank, and sometimes even heard the *coo-ee* of the natives, which made them apprehensive that they were not unnoticed; but they satisfied themselves that their mode of travelling defied pursuit. They rarely landed more than once a day, usually on the south bank, where they often met with some small tributary stream, abounding in fish, and the adroit spearing of Baldabella always provided them with an abundant supply, sufficient for supper and breakfast. This fish was principally the fresh-water cod, as they named it, of very large size. Every morning after breakfast, before they embarked, they walked out to look round for some favorable spot to which they might retire during the approaching rains, but in vain. Still the high cliffs continued on one side of the river; and on the side where they wished to remain they still saw spread before them marshy plains.

CHAPTER XIX

They began at last to be weary of the monotonous voyaging, and were glad, one morning, on ascending the banks, to see a change of scenery. The reedy swamps were replaced by rich grassy slopes, where tall trees and bright creeping blossoms, the fragrant golden flower of the *Acacia* and the balmy odor from various trees of the *Eucalyptus* kind, encouraged them to hope that they might find a retreat in such a pleasant region.

"Halloo!" cried Wilkins. "Just all on ye step here, and take a good look at this here tree. We're not the first white folks as has had a look round hereabout. As sure as you're there, Mr. Arthur, there's a *catch*, as they call 't, under this same tree. Look ye, I kenned it all as soon as ever I set eyes on that there criss-cross, cut wi' an honest steel blade, I'se warrant it; and says I to mysel', our own folks has been here, and we'll just try a bit at their diggings; that's wi' yer leave, Mr. Arthur."

Arthur hesitated; he certainly neither wished to commit, nor to connive at, a robbery; but he considered some information worth knowing might be found in the *cache*. He therefore sent to the canoes for shells, spades, and knives; and all the young men began to dig with as much earnestness and anxiety as if they had been the gold-diggers in the south of the country.

"If we were to find a great nugget of gold," said Gerald.

"I would rather find a good saw," said Jack.

"Or an iron kettle," suggested Margaret.

"I should like a telescope," said Hugh.

"Now, nurse, what will you have?" asked Arthur.

"Well then, Mr. Arthur, honey, if I must speak," answered nurse, "I would say a barrel of flour; but just as God pleases."

"I feel it! I feel it!" cried Gerald, flinging away his knife in his ecstasy. "It is something hard."

"Be very careful," said Arthur. "We must not damage the hidden stores. Whatever can it be? here are canisters and bags."

"It'll be tea and sugar," cried Ruth, clapping her hands with delight.

"Nay, nay, lass, what need for folks to bury tea and sugar?" said Wilkins. "Here's summut a deal better—powder and shot. And see here, Mr. Arthur, ye're a scholar; this'll be like her Majesty's ship's name on 'em."

"There is, indeed," replied Arthur, "and the date when they were placed here, which is three years ago. I fear the owners will never return to claim them now."

"All the better for us," said Wilkins. "There's nought here a bit worse, and it's all fair, ye ken, Mr. Arthur. Finders, keepers, all t' world round."

Arthur looked inquiringly at his father.

"The wisdom of the world, Wilkins," said Mr. Mayburn, "is not always the wisdom of God. But, in the case of this treasure-trove, Arthur, as the ammunition is certainly the property of her Majesty, lying useless here, I do think—Margaret, am I right?—I am of opinion that we may appropriate a part of this valuable deposit; leaving in the place a written acknowledgment of the loan. Then, if God spares us to have the opportunity, we must report our trespass to the Government."

"I think you are right, dear papa," said Margaret; "but the temptation is so great, that perhaps we are none of us in a state to give impartial judgment."

Wilkins, without listening to a word of the discussion, had taken on himself the responsibility of the offence, and was already actively engaged in moving off the bags and canisters to the boats.

"Not more than we may need, remember, Wilkins," said Margaret.

"And who's to say what we may need, miss," answered the man. "We've many a hundred mile to trot yet, and some uglier customers than t' black fellows to come on afore we've done, and that's them hang-gallows bush-rangers."

"We will compromise with our conscience," said Arthur, "by taking away half the store; and papa's portable writing-case will supply us with the means of making a brief statement and an apology."

The note was written, enclosed in a bark case, and attached to one of the bags left in the hole; the soil was then restored, and the turf carefully replaced, so that no trace of the *cache* might attract the natives.

"They'd make a bonny kettle of fish, if they did come on 't," said Wilkins; "for ten to one they'd fling t' powder on t' fire, and then there'd not be mony on 'em left to talk about it."

"We must take especial care to guard our cargo against fire," said Arthur; "and we have also another enemy to fear—the water—which might soon render our treasure useless. Therefore, the sooner we leave the boats, and 'take to the bush,' as Wilkins says, the better. This country certainly looks pleasant; but I should prefer a more woody and sheltered spot."

"If you look directly south, Arthur," said Hugh, "you will see a black spot, which, I take it, must be a thick forest. It would make a good land-mark for us, if we leave the river. What do you say? must we aim for it?"

Arthur directed his attention to Hugh's black forest, which certainly stood in the way they wished to go; and as there was no appearance of smoke, or even of former fires on the plains, there was some reason to think the district might not be frequented by the savages. These considerations decided them to abandon once more the easy canoe-voyaging, and, with the weighty addition to their burdens of the ammunition from the *cache*, they slowly set out. The plain was covered with rich high grass that would have fed thousands of cattle, but was now only tenanted by herds of graceful kangaroos and small detachments of tall stalking emus. The trees were populated with swarms of parrots, cockatoos, pheasants, and small warblers, and the air rang with their mingled notes, cheerful at least, if not harmonious.

When the dark wood became fully visible to them, Margaret observed that Baldabella seemed startled and uneasy, and frequently paused as if reluctant to proceed. But when, after an hour's walk, the sombre thick forest spread before them, half a mile across, the woman turned round to Margaret with trembling limbs, and said in a faltering voice, pointing to the forest, "Good miss, no go; bad spirit kill all people; good master, Baldabella, all die. Bad spirit very angry, say no people go here."

Margaret tried to reason with the terrified woman, who had now turned round to flee with her child; she appeared to be agitated in the highest degree, and when the child clung to Margaret, who turned to follow the rest, the distressed mother, wringing her hands, wailed in the most pathetic manner; till at length, with an air of sudden resolution, she drew herself up, with her usual dignity, and said,—

"Baldabella die, not leave good friends," and walked calmly on by the side of Margaret.

Arthur had learned previously that the natives regarded a dark wood with superstitious awe; but he now concluded that Baldabella had some acquaintance with this particular spot, and that it was an object of fear to the natives. This was a circumstance which would render it still more desirable to the travellers as a place of seclusion; and when they came up close to the gloomy forest, they did not wonder at the superstitious dread of the ignorant savages. It seemed as if neither man nor beast, nor even the light of heaven, could penetrate the mysterious spot. Lofty trees, resembling the pine, the chestnut and the cypress, as closely ranged as it was possible for nature to plant them, were so interwoven and matted together, for the height of eight or ten feet with coiled thorny shrubs and creeping plants, that they formed an impenetrable fortress that seemed to defy the impotent attacks of man.

"I wonder which of us is the favored prince who is to 'cut his bright way through,' this enchanted wood," said Gerald. "Here's an adventure, Hugh! Now for knives and axes!"

"Do not be too hasty, boys," said Arthur. "It would be prudent to make the circuit of the wood first, in order to select the most accessible point. Besides," continued he, as they walked on, "I think we must proceed with caution. We will cut a low tunnel, the entrance to which can be easily closed, if we find it possible to remain here for a short season; and thus we shall leave no trace of our presence."

"I shall be well content to remain here," said Mr. Mayburn, "amidst these noble and curious trees and shrubs. To study their varieties will sufficiently occupy and amuse me."

"And I shall be satisfied to live in a hut," said Margaret, "however rude it may be, where we can have rest and peace; where we can repair our tattered garments, and perhaps make new boots to replace these worn fragments. But I fear our abode in the forest must be gloomy and depressing."

"We can build a nest in the trees," said Gerald, "as the people did in the Swiss Family Robinson, and live in the cheerful society of parrots and cockatoos. That looks like the very fig-tree the family inhabited; let us choose it. See, it is covered with ripe figs that look very tempting. I should like to climb for some."

"The fig-tree will not fly away, Gerald," said Arthur, "and just now we must all have more important employment. We must immediately commence our tunnel, for the air is more sultry than ever, and I have fancied more than once that I have heard the distant roll of thunder. I sincerely wish we had a shelter at hand. I must call on you, my friends, to halt at once. We will try this point."

The part of the wood before which they had arrived, though quite impervious, was less thorny than any part they had yet passed, and therefore more easy to work, and they began to cut down the entangled brushwood for about four feet in height, and wide enough to admit the passage of one person only. The lopped branches were carefully collected, to be removed to the interior of the wood, when the path was completed; but their labor was long and tedious, for the forest could not be less than fifty yards in breadth. Fortunately after piercing it for twenty yards, they found the underwood less rank and entangled, and were satisfied with trampling it down to make the road smoother for the women.

This wood terminated finally in a glade of extraordinary beauty, richly clothed with grass and studded with the gorgeous flowers of the tropical regions. This glade spread before them level for some distance, then gradually sloped upwards, thickly grown with wild oats, and then with brush, to a great height, the whole forming an isolated mountain, which was apparently flat at the summit.

The young boys declared this must be the very abode of enchantment; and as the ascent was a succession of green terraces, they were all able, with some fatigue, but with little difficulty, to attain the highest ridge, when they saw, with some astonishment, that a few feet below them lay a basin or crater, covered with verdure—tall grass mingled with the usual thick brush.

After gazing on it for a few minutes, Hugh said, "What a capital place for our hut. Margaret cannot call this height gloomy, for, by mounting the ridge, we can look over the forest and survey the whole country round us. Then the flowers are so gay and pleasant, and we shall see multitudes of birds. Do look, papa, at those two superb eagles that are soaring above our heads, and that doubtless have their eyrie somewhere in this mountain."

But while they were gazing at the birds, O'Brien, who stood at some distance from them, was making ready his bow, and before they were aware of it he had skilfully sent an arrow into one of the eagles, which fell fluttering and screaming among the brushwood.

"Victory! victory!" he cried, looking round for Mr. Mayburn. "Did you see me shoot the eagle, papa?"

"I saw and admired the magnificent creatures, Gerald," answered Mr. Mayburn; "and I deeply grieved to see one fall by your hand. It was no victory, but a wanton cruelty. You have destroyed the noble bird for no useful purpose, and my heart is afflicted to observe the distress of the attached mate. See how he circles round the spot which has left him bereaved and lamenting. I am forcibly reminded of the powerful words of one of our modern classical poets, who, in describing such a tragical bereavement, writes,—

'She whom he mourns
Lies dying, with the arrow in her side,
In some far stony gorge, out of his ken,
A heap of fluttering feathers: never more
Shall the lake glass her flying over it;
Never the black and dripping precipices
Echo her stormy scream as she sails by!'"

"I thought you would have liked to possess the bird, papa," said Gerald, "and I am really sorry for the widowed mate. I feel quite uncomfortable to see the old fellow soaring round me and uttering, I have no doubt, violent abuse. But I may as well recover my game, that you may gratify your curiosity by examining an Australian eagle."

"I saw it fall just behind yon yellow-flowered shrub, which looks so like our own English furze," said Hugh.

Gerald dashed forward into the bush to search for his prize, while Margaret and her father examined with great satisfaction the rich table-land, and Jack pointed out a favorable site for a wattled, bark-roofed hut, which, he asserted, might be easily constructed in a couple of days. But while they were discussing this important affair, they were alarmed by a loud cry from Gerald, "Help, help! the enchanter has got me! Come, Arthur, by yourself, and throw me a rope!"

All were in alarm, and where to throw the rope was the question, for the boy was not to be seen. Arthur and Jack, with a pole and ropes, stepped lightly over the bushes, expecting to find Gerald plunged in a marsh. His cries directed them to a spot, where they saw only his head and one arm clinging to a bush.

"Take care what you are about," said he; "I have slipped into a hole, and perhaps there may be more like it. You had better just slide the pole along till I can catch it, and then, perhaps, I may manage to raise myself. The worst is, I hear that furious eagle, fluttering and hissing just below me, and I am every moment in fear lest she should attack me, and peck my legs to revenge her wrongs."

With the aid of the rope and the pole, and the exertions of his friends, Gerald scrambled to a safe spot in the bushes, and then they all took a survey of the cave, or grotto, that lay below; and were so much interested by it, that they resolved to explore it at once. Jack volunteered to make the first expedition, and began by attaching the rope to a stout bush to facilitate his descent, and taking with him the pole to test the security of the ground below.

The floor of the cave was not more than twelve feet below the opening, and Jack looked round to find himself in a large grotto, floored with dry white sand; the rocky sides were garlanded with creeping plants, and it was lighted by many apertures above, similar to that through which Gerald had fallen, and, like that, almost covered with brushwood. Dark branch-caves ran from this airy grotto, into which they penetrated for a few yards, to satisfy themselves that it was uninhabited; and, from the observations he made, Arthur could not but believe the whole was of volcanic origin, and, in fact, a portion of the crater of an exhausted volcano.

"We may find a capital magazine here for the powder," said Jack; "and this light part will make a kitchen for the women folks while we are building the hut Think you, Mr. Arthur, I should make them a ladder? They'll hardly like swinging down by a rope."

Arthur thought they would certainly not like such a mode of descent, and the ladder was decided on. Then he ventured to draw near the screaming eagle to endeavor to extract the arrow from his wing, but the bird made such fierce returns for his kindness, that he was compelled to retreat, and wait for a more favorable moment for the operation; and in the mean time, the youths ascended to report the discovery of the cave.

Wilkins had been employed in cutting down and bringing up the ascent a quantity of the wild oats, and Margaret and her father were found standing by a pool of clear water, which, though now somewhat shallow, would doubtless contain an abundant supply after the rain. Around this pond Mr. Mayburn had found many new and beautiful flowers, and, as soon as he was satisfied of O'Brien's safety, he hastened to point out one of his most valued acquisitions.

"Observe, my dear children," said he, "one of the most curious plants ever discovered, *Cephalotus follicularis*, one of the pitcher-plants, so named from the peculiar-form of the delicate white blossoms. You perceive that these *pitchers* on the strong footstalk contain water—in this are some drowned insects. Hence, some writers have asserted that these flowers are used by the larger insects of prey as receptacles for their food. But we must see that this accumulated moisture is to preserve the plant in its beauty during the long dry season."

"Could we not plant potatoes here?" asked Margaret. "In this genial climate we might soon raise a crop, and our stock is now very low."

"Of course we can, Meggie," said Hugh. "I understand the habits of our *solanum*. This light, dry, fresh soil will exactly suit it. Come, Gerald, let us lose no time in marking off and clearing our potato-ground, before the rains stop us. That will be more useful than shooting eagles."

The Kangaroo Hunters | 175

They were all gratified with the discovery of the cave, and anxious to see it, but were induced to wait till a ladder was made, which was to be commenced as soon as a party had returned to the wood to fill up the mouth of the tunnel. For this purpose they used part of the lopped branches, which they arranged so artfully, that no one could suspect a breach had been made. The remainder of the brushwood was to be conveyed up the mountain for firewood.

After this, Hugh and Gerald made a foray in an immense fig-tree, dispersing the feathered tenants, and carrying off a large stock of the ripe fruit. The rest returned, laden with firewood and wild oats. Then Jenny made them some tea, and cakes of bruised oats, mixed with the plentiful but insipid juice of the figs. These cakes were baked in the ashes, and much enjoyed by the ever keenly hungry boys, who named the dark hard biscuits Australian jumbles.

Before night should put an end to their labors, Jack and the young boys cut down a slender tree, resembling the pine, to make a ladder; and Margaret, with the help of Wilkins, pared off the turf, dug a large plot of ground, and planted it with potatoes. Then, worn out with a day of extreme toil, the wayfarers rested beneath a threatening sky, in the heated atmosphere which indicated an approaching storm.

A few drops of rain at daybreak roused up the whole family to prompt activity.

"It's no time to start and build to-day," said Wilkins. "Wait a bit; here's a storm ower our heads; or, if ye want work, what say ye to sinking yon bit pond a foot deeper? it holds nought, and when t' rain falls it'll overflow and half drown us, if we don't mind."

Arthur thought it was a more prudent plan to dig another pond or reservoir, rather deeper than the original one, and make a channel between the two. They should thus secure a supply of water, and prevent their potato ground from being washed away by a sudden flood.

"And, now that the ladder is finished," said Margaret, "it would be better that papa and I should descend at once into this subterranean grotto, and make it ready for our temporary abode, till you are able to build a hut; for there is certainly a prospect of rain falling to-day."

"Come along," cried Gerald, "that I may usher you into my newly-discovered dominions. Now, Ruth, we shall have you safe; you will have few opportunities of committing mischief when you are below the earth. Come and descend into the burning mountain, and take care you don't fight with my eagle."

"Oh! master, is't true—is't a burning mountain?" asked Ruth, in terror.

"It has been a volcano," answered Mr. Mayburn, "but, in all probability, exhausted, hundreds of years ago. It is now, as you see, a beautiful wilderness."

Ruth did not regard the beauty of the spot; she saw only, in her mind's eye, the red flames pouring from Mount Vesuvius, as depicted in a gaudy picture-book she had seen in her childhood.

"Oh, please, Miss Marget," she exclaimed, "stay up here! don't go down into that hole; it'll, maybe, break out again, and we'll all be burnt alive."

But Margaret remonstrated, the boys laughed and Jenny scolded; and, finally, Jack brought Ruth down to the range of subterranean apartments, where Margaret and Jenny soon planned dormitories, kitchen, and store-rooms. A large alcove was to be the chapel, and the light bowery grotto beneath the entrance was to be the drawing-room,—at least, till the heavy rains should compel them to seek more effectual shelter. Here they collected stones for seats, and rolled into the midst a large piece of rock for a table, upon which was spread the breakfast of tea and oat-cakes, at present their only provision.

Mr. Mayburn was delighted to have the opportunity of inspecting so nearly the wounded, but still fierce eagle, with its shining black plumage; and he judged it was that known as *Aquila Fucoso*. It was in vain, however, to attempt a close examination till Wilkins and Jack, after some struggling, and a few severe pecks, succeeded in holding it till Arthur extracted the arrow from the wing, and saw that nature would probably heal the wound in a few days. In the mean time the bird was starving, for it rejected with disdain the farinaceous food offered to it; and Hugh and Gerald promised, as soon as the reservoir was completed, to set out and shoot some small birds or opossums, for their hungry guest.

CHAPTER XX

The reservoir was six feet deep and ten feet in diameter, and was lined with flat stones from the interior of the cave, where large slabs were scattered round. This was not completed in one day, and on the second morning, while Wilkins and Jack finished the work, and, after digging a trench, laid down a spout of bark between the ponds, Hugh and Gerald went down to the wood below, to shoot birds. But before the end of the day the workmen were driven to shelter by the violent rain; and the two boys returned, drenched to the skin, and laden with pheasants, cockatoos, and a wild turkey, as large as an English Christmas turkey, and resembling that bird so much, that the name was considered not inappropriate. They had, thus, a handsome dinner for themselves, and abundance of food for the hungry and somewhat tamed eagle.

They were seated at their late repast when the storm began in earnest; tremendous peals of thunder rolled through the immense hollows of the mountain, and seemed to shake the very rocks from their foundation. Ruth screamed and looked round in distraction, expecting the eruption of the volcano was at hand; and even the proud eagle trembled to hear the voice of the skies. Then the rain came down in torrents, showering through the leafy coverings of numerous apertures above them, and driving them back into the gloomy security of the solid rocks; grateful for even that dismal retreat in the sudden storm.

"We need not remain in the dark, though we are in the crypt," said Hugh. "Come, Gerald, let us light some flambeaux, and fix them on the walls; then, with all these trailing garlands suspended from above, we may fancy ourselves in a ball-room."

The caverns were lighted up, and then every one found employment. Mr. Mayburn produced the head and neck of the turkey, which he contemplated with much interest.

"It certainly must be the bird described as the *Wattled Talegalla*, Arthur," said he, "and which is considered to represent the turkey in Australia; the red skin of the head, bright orange wattle, and large disproportionate feet, prove the fact; and I am gratified that you have obtained a specimen of it."

"We are all gratified, papa," said Margaret, "for it is the most useful and delicious bird we have yet found in this ornithological paradise."

The boys employed themselves in thrashing the wild oats, storing the grain in bags, and then arranging the straw for mattrasses—a perfect luxury to them, after they had for so long slept on the bare ground. They had their knives and axes, and abundant material in the boughs and spare pieces of the tree that was cut down for the ladder; and, to fill up the time, Jack presided over a school of art, where the ingenious and active employed heads and hands, and produced some articles of great use. Margaret took the opportunity to teach lessons of civilization and religion to the lively little Nakinna, and, through the child, poured the words of truth into the heart of the mother. Wilkins, who was miserable when unemployed, good-naturedly assisted Jenny and Ruth in various household matters, made a stone hearth for the fire, helped to cook, piled up the dry fuel, contrived a wattled niche for the fowls, and went out through the rain to bring in water, when needed.

Three or four days were thus passed in contented seclusion, the storm still continuing unabated; then, though the rain fell incessantly, the prisoners began to be weary, and to have a great desire to visit the world above. They engaged to bring in fresh provisions, if Jenny would provide dry clothes for them on their return from their foraging expedition; and with bows, arrows, axes, and game-bags, Wilkins, Jack, and the three boys set out, delighted to return to the light, and to the pure air of heaven, and enjoying even the cool rain.

"Do, Arthur, look at those tall birds with the crimson crest and huge wooden-looking beak," said Hugh. "One of them would be as useful as the turkey was, for a dinner dish. I suppose we must call them storks; though they are really, to us, among the anonymous creatures of this strange new world."

"Ye may find t' like of them all over," said Wilkins. "Folks down at t' colony calls 'em 'native companions;' they trust ye, poor rogues, as if ye were their brother; ye might just walk up to yon fellows, and wring their necks."

"Which I should certainly object to do, Wilkins," answered Hugh. "I could not make up my mind to wring the neck, or to feed on, 'mine own familiar friend.' We will be content to reduce the multitude of the noisy impertinent cockatoos and parrots; or suppose, Arthur, we descend to the glade below, where we can cut more wood, and shoot some opossums for our aquiline guest. The skins will make us splendid cloaks to wear this rainy season."

The Kangaroo Hunters | 179

And, careless of the wet plunge, the joyous youths descended through the brushwood, and reaching the verdant glade, they shot as many opossums as they wished; filled some bags with ripe figs, and finally, after a long chase, and many a fall on the moist slippery ground, they secured a wandering kangaroo of large size, which, in distress of weather, had by some means found its way into this enclosed retreat.

Jack had in the mean time barked a tree of the *Eucalyptus* species, and tying the cumbrous spoil with a rope, he drew it after him up the mountain. Wilkins shouldered the kangaroo, and the rest, equally laden, toiled through the bushy, moist, sloping wood, and arrived safely at the cave, to diffuse amusement and contentment among their expecting friends, and to furnish more employment for their enforced leisure time. They were all invested in dry garments; then Jack examined his prize, and said,—

"Just look at this bark, Mr. Arthur. I have seen none yet so firm and hard; it is completely an inch plank, fit for any sort of work. I could make a light wagon of it, if we had any animals to draw it; and, anyhow, I'll set about a table and some seats, directly, and then I'll try some buckets, and dishes, and such-like things. Now's the time for work, when there's no walking."

For many days the ample supply of provisions, and the amusement of occupation, reconciled the young men to the gloomy seclusion of their retreat. During this time a square piece of bark, flattened and smoothed with sharp stones, was placed on four posts, for a table; long slips similarly supported, formed stools and benches. Trenchers, dishes, buckets, and bowls, certainly somewhat rude in form, were next finished, the gum which exuded from many trees near them supplying them plentifully with an admirable cement. There is a charm to civilized minds in being surrounded with the appliances and arrangements of domestic life; and the women became reconciled, and even attached to their monotonous existence— especially when an occasional cessation of rain permitted them to live in the front portion of the cave, which was rendered pleasant and cheerful by the subdued light through the foliage.

A day of fair weather tempted the young men to leave their confinement, and not only to descend to the enclosed glade below, but to venture to break through the charmed circle of the wood, and have a scamper over the plains after the kangaroos and emus which frequented it. And on the margin of a chain of pools, newly filled by the recent rains, they once more saw the tall native companion, amid swarms of wild ducks; while, from among the wild oats whirred flocks of small beautiful birds resembling the quail, but with an elegant crest.

They filled their game-bags with birds, and a troop of kangaroos appearing in sight, they were tempted to pursue them for a considerable time. At last the animals sought refuge in a spreading thick wood, into which Wilkins and Jack, with axes and spears, followed them. The young boys in the mean time were engaged in chasing a pair of emus; till, weary and unsuccessful, they turned away in disappointment, to join the kangaroo hunters. But just at that moment they were struck with the vexatious sound of the *coo-ee* of the natives, which proceeded from the wood where the kangaroos had sheltered. This alarming cry decided them—especially as Arthur was without his rifle—to return without delay, that they might close the tunnel entrance of their abode.

Keeping as much as possible under the shelter of the trees, they quickly made their way over the plains to the Black Forest, Gerald frequently looking back; at last he said, "Jack and Wilkins are not yet in sight, shall I turn back to seek them, Arthur, or must I give them a halloo?"

"Neither, my dear fellow," answered Arthur. "However unkind it may seem, we must not risk the discovery of our retreat by attracting the natives to our heels. Wilkins and Jack must have heard the *coo-ee* as well as we; and have most likely hid themselves till the savages have passed and they can return to us safely. We must keep open, but guard, the entrance till we see them return. Now, go on, boys; take the game-bags to the cave, and then quietly bring away my rifle and cartridge-case, without saying a word about this vexatious incident. Till you return I will conceal myself behind the bushes, and watch for the return of our two absentees."

The boys hastened to the cave, to fulfil their mission; and leaving their bags, which contained some of the pretty quails, to divert the attention of Mr. Mayburn and Margaret, they returned to watch silently and anxiously, ready to close the entrance as soon as their friends returned, or if they should be alarmed by the approach of the natives. Gerald climbed a tree, that he might command the plains more effectually, and, from this elevated situation, he startled Arthur by crying out,—

"Oh, Arthur! he is killed! I know he is killed! Dear old fellow, we shall never see him more! There is only Jack."

"Who is killed? What do you see? Do speak plainly, Gerald," said Arthur, hastily.

"I see him coming by himself," answered the distracted boy. "I mean I see Jack; not Wilkins. It's quite sure they must have killed him; Jack never would have left him, if he was living."

The two boys below were now almost as much agitated as Gerald, for they plainly saw Jack hurrying across the plain alone, and when he drew near, Arthur was quite sure, from his pale and sorrowful countenance, that some heavy misfortune had occurred. He plunged into the open tunnel, and then said, "Close it directly if you please, Mr. Arthur; I am so bad, I can do nothing."

"But Wilkins! where is Wilkins, Jack?" asked Hugh.

Jack burst into tears as he said, "Oh, Master Hugh! the bad rogues have got him; and all I could think on, I couldn't help him."

"Are there any hopes? Do you think they will murder him?" asked Arthur, trembling.

"I think not, Mr. Arthur," answered Jack; "but I'll tell you all about it as soon as we've closed up this gap, and tried to keep them safe that are left."

The distressed boys hastened to restore the barrier with particular care; and then, as they slowly proceeded homeward, Jack related his melancholy adventure.

"We had got quite into the thick of the wood after that unlucky capering beast, when all at once that queer call of the black fellows rung into our ears. 'We're in for it now, and no mistake, my lad,' said Wilkins to me. 'Just you thrust yourself into that cover, and I'll listen a bit, to make out their whereabouts.' I forced myself into a thicket, matted together, for about six feet upwards, as thick as this wood round us. You had to fight for every inch of way; and I kept thinking all along that he was following me, but he was not. You know, Mr. Arthur, he is a good bit stouter than I am, and my fancy is that he had fought and rustled among the bushes till he'd been found out; for first I heard a dog growl, and then I heard his voice, speaking such words as he has never said of late—an oath, Mr. Arthur; then followed such yells! and I knew they had got him.

"Well, my first thought was to make my way out, that I might help him; but just then I got a sight of all the gang of them through the bushes. There could not be less than a hundred; and, worst of all, though he was naked, and painted like a savage, I made out at once that bad fellow, Black Peter, among them. Four men had hold of Wilkins. They had taken away his knife and spears, and Peter was taunting him, as they pulled him along. I heard him say, 'Thou wast a fool, Wilkins, to stop so long with them preaching folks; I thought thou'd a bit more spirit—thou, that aimed to take a spell at bush-ranging, like a man. But thou'll come along with us now, and thou'lt find we're a bit jollier than yon smooth, long-faced dogs.'

"Then Wilkins spoke out and said, 'I reckon my comrades were somewhat better than thine, Peter. Anyhow, we managed to keep clothes to our backs.'

"The sly rogue tried to get round poor Wilkins then, and went on, 'That's just to please those black rogues, Wilkins; but, man, we're off down south just now, to pick up stock, and cash too. Then we'll get good clothes; and as soon as we've done with them, we'll rid ourselves of these black fools, and have a grand jollification out of our money. There'll be some fun in that, man. And have these comrades of thine any cash or stuff worth lifting? I'd like that other gun they carried, and, anyhow, some powder and shot. I hav'n't a grain left—all blazed away after such game as that,'—and the good-for-nothing fellow pointed to the poor black natives, that didn't understand a word he had been saying.

"Wilkins muttered some words, very low, that I couldn't catch; but I fancy he didn't tell truth, for Peter went on to say and swear that he would soon be on our track, for we couldn't get far in these rains; and that Wilkins needn't think to join us, for he would take care and keep him in a safe place—a snuggery, he called it.

"I made up my mind that I would see what and where this snuggery was; and when the men had passed on, and were out of hearing, I cautiously tracked them to a place in the midst of the wood, which they had cleared by burning down the trees, for there lay the blackened stumps; and a crying sin it was, Mr. Arthur, to waste so much good timber. On one side there was a great rock, into which they dragged poor Wilkins, through a small opening, and I saw no more of him; but I think they meant to do him no harm, for there's little doubt Peter wants him to be useful to him. Wilkins is a shrewd fellow, moreover; and I feel sure he'll try to get away from them. But if they have him, as it were, in prison, what do you say, Mr. Arthur, shouldn't we help him?"

"Certainly, I think we are bound to do so," said Arthur. "But we must hold a council, for we shall have to act with consideration and caution if we venture to leave our fortress."

There was great distress in the family, and many tears were shed when the adventure was communicated to them; for, notwithstanding the former errors of Wilkins, and his yet unsubdued passions, he was much beloved for his kind nature and his attachment to his true friends. Mr. Mayburn himself even gave his sanction to an expedition for the purpose of attempting the rescue of Wilkins, if he did not return to them in a day or two.

But for many days after this the rain fell so incessantly that it was impossible to leave their shelter, even though all their provisions were exhausted except the valuable grain, and a scanty supply of eggs from the domestic fowls. To these they were able occasionally to add the fruit of a large tree which grew in the glade below, bearing huge pods; each pod contained several almond-shaped seeds, which were enclosed in shells. These nuts were now ripe; they tasted like filberts, and were a very agreeable and nutritious addition to their spare diet.

The wounded eagle, now quite sound, was an object of great interest to the prisoners: its nature was so fierce, that Arthur despaired of its ever becoming tamed; but it submitted to their approach when their object was to bring it food—usually the entrails of the birds, which had been reserved for it. But seeing the untamable nature of the bird, and Margaret, especially, having great compassion on its mate, it was agreed to restore it to liberty; though O'Brien declared the royal bird would doubtless, before this, have chosen another queen. One morning there was an intermission of rain; and the opportunity was taken to release the captive from the bonds which secured its legs. The leafy covering was at the same time removed from the opening above, and the glorious light allowed to stream into the cave. The sight of the sky and the sensation of freedom roused the energy of the bird, and, with a joyous fluttering of the wings, it raised itself from the ground, soared round the confined spot for a minute, then, bursting through the opening, rose proudly to a height above, and after some gyrations, as if to test its recovered powers, it sailed away beyond the sight of its hospitable protectors, of whom two—Jenny and Ruth—rejoiced greatly at the departure of a guest so voracious.

"My bonnie hens had to be pinched for that great ugly creature," said Ruth, "when now two are laying every day, and one has been sitting this fortnight; and she's sure to be lucky, Miss Marget, for I set her on thirteen eggs; two of 'em, to be sure, were not her own; Master Hugh fetched 'em in to make up a lucky cletch."

"Yes," said Hugh, "I should think it was perhaps the first time that an English hen has had the honor of hatching the eggs of the *Cuculus Phasianus*."

In due time Ruth's chickens were hatched, to the great amusement of the inmates of the cave; they were carefully tended and out of reach of danger, and seemed likely to be reared prosperously, the English family fraternizing with the Australian intruders most agreeably. A second day of fair weather determined the anxious young men to set out in search of poor Wilkins, lest the savages should have left their fastnesses in the rock, to follow their leader in his bush-ranging excursions. Day after day they had mounted high trees to scan the plain, in hopes of seeing their lost companion, or observing the departure of his captors; but no human form was seen, and Arthur felt assured that if Wilkins had effected his escape, nothing would have prevented him from making his way through the Black Forest to join them.

It was resolved to take the rifle, with sufficient ammunition to disperse the savages, and also all the weapons they possessed for, in all probability, it would be necessary to storm the fortress. Jack and the three boys were intended to be the whole force; but Baldabella so earnestly entreated that she might accompany them that they were induced to admit her into the train. She could throw a boomerang or spear better than any of them; her sympathy was excited for Wilkins, who had always been her protector; and her knowledge of the habits and the language of the people might make her very useful to them.

CHAPTER XXI

Cautiously and quietly the party wound, under the cover of the trees and bushes, across the plain, till they reached the wood that enclosed the abode of the savages. Then the peril increased. Jack led the way, and one after another they followed, step by step, through, under, or over the matted brush; and, finally, the leader placed his party in a position where they could all command a view of the rocky cave, though they stood at a short distance from each other. On the cleared ground before the cave two women were seated, bruising nuts between two stones; and several children were playing round them. The anxious young men watched for some minutes, but none of the men appeared; then Baldabella proposed to go forward to introduce herself to the women, her friends promising to rescue her if they attempted to detain her.

Disencumbering herself from the light robe she condescended to wear in civilized life, and retaining only her cloak of furs, she took her fish-spear in her hand, and penetrated to a distant part of the wood, from whence she made her appearance on the charred glade, many yards from the ambush of her friends, and with slow steps, counterfeiting great fatigue, she walked up to the women, to demand, as she had arranged with her friends, food and repose. As soon as they perceived her, the women rose and looked round anxiously, and the young men expected every moment to hear the signal call for them; but the solitary feeble form of Baldabella seemed to re-assure them. She drew near and talked for some minutes to her dark sisters; and the soft and pathetic inflections of her voice convinced the concealed party that she was appealing to that compassionate feeling which is ever so strong in the heart of woman.

The women listened, and invited the stranger to sit down by them; they fed her with the rich kernels of the nuts, and, the rain beginning to fall again, they took her with them into the cave for shelter. How anxiously the young men waited, at one moment prompted to burst out and free the captive, who seemed to have no gaoler but the women, and then resolving to leave the whole affair to the shrewd management of Baldabella. Arthur was anxiously examining the state of his rifle and ammunition, which he had carefully shielded beneath his fur cloak, when they were roused to force their way through the bush by the loud and triumphant voice of Wilkins, the low and apparently smothered *coo-ee* of the women, and, finally, by the appearance of Baldabella, rushing wildly from the cave, followed by Wilkins, excited, tattered, and emaciated. He carried a gun in his hand, and staggered up to his friends as if intoxicated.

"Take this, and load it directly," said he, giving Hugh the gun. "My hands are so cramped wi' them tough bands, that it'll be long afore I have any use on 'em. Rascals! rogues! Come on, I say; march while we can; yon screeching jins will soon bring a wasp's-nest round us."

Not caring for caution now, they hacked and burst through the thick wood, till they reached the plain; and then the *coo-ee* of the duped women rang alarmingly on their ears, and was soon answered by a faint and distant cry from the absent men. Poor Wilkins, whose legs had been bound till they were numbed, made but slow progress; and Arthur ordered O'Brien and Jack, with Baldabella, to move rapidly forward, to guard, or, if necessary, to close the pass, while Hugh and he protected the slow retreat of Wilkins.

They made no use of their arms till they saw the whole body of the savages appear outside the wood, and spears were falling round them. Then Hugh and Arthur fired their guns simultaneously into the midst of the foes, who plunged screaming into the woods. Two men lingered outside, but another volley from the second barrel, struck down one, and his companion disappeared in a moment.

"Now, Mr. Arthur," cried Wilkins, as he hurried forward, "now don't ye trust 'em. They're watching us; we'se be done if we make straight to our cutting. They're sharp-eyed chaps; we'se have to bubble 'em a bit."

Wilkins was right; and though it occupied some time, they made the circuit of the forest, before they ventured to enter; after which, they lost no time in closing up the opening with great art and care. Then the rescued prisoner was conducted to the cave, welcomed with great joy, fresh clad, and fed with pheasant, biscuit, and the unfailing tea; and his friends gathered round him to hear the tale of his hardships and trials.

"Ay, ay! this is all as it ought to be," said he; "and God be thanked I'se out on t'clutches of them unnat'ral dogs. They tied me hand and foot, all 'cause I couldn't be made to swear as how I'd turn bush-ranger, and start by robbing and murdering them as had cared for me and given me meat and claithes and good advice. That brute Peter bullied me, and kicked me when he knew I was tied fast; and he'd have put a knife into me, but likely he thought to bring me into his ways; and he were feared his blackeys might turn round on him, for they'd no ill blood again me. Then he ordered as how

I were to have nought given me to eat, and sure enough I'd been starved afore this; but them poor jins, 'whiles, popped a few bites into my mouth, and brought me a sup of water, when I were like to go mad for want on't. A hempen rope wouldn't have held me, afore I lost my strength; but them stringy bark cords are like iron.

"It were dowly wark, and mony and mony a time, master, I thought over your words, and all my bad life, and my coward's death, and God's judgment to come. And then and there I settled it in my mind, if He pleased to set me free again, I'd niver swear another oath, I'd niver tell another lie, and I'd niver miss praying for strength, when bad thoughts came into my mind. I see, Miss, ye'r crying over my black sins, and well ye may, God help me. After this, I felt a bit more cheery, and I were sure some on ye would see after me; but I niver reckoned on her to be t'first, and were quite stunned when I saw her come in with t'other jins. But I plucked up my heart; I kenned she'd mind my words, and I just said,—

"'Yer knife—cut these ropes!' and as sharp as a needle she was up to me, pulled out a knife from under her cloak, and cut me loose. But poor creaters as we are, I couldn't move arm or leg for a good bit, and her there, hauding a hand on one woman's mouth, and a hand on t' others, flayed as how they'd shrike out, till I come round a bit, and got my arms worked round from behind me, and my feet to shuffle on. Then I thanked God in my heart, and off we came, and here we are; God bless ye all. I'se niver leave ye, whiles I have life. But, Mr. Arthur, we're not safe; Peter's a cunning fish."

"There's one comfort, Wilkins," said Arthur; "they do not like to face the heavy rain, which is now very welcome; and before it ceases, we must make ready for a siege; unfortunately, we want provisions."

Ruth placed herself uneasily before her poultry hutch, and Wilkins said, "There's lots of pigeons amang yon trees; I can soon trap a lot, and fetch 'em down here alive, and we'll fit up a dove-cote, and have tame birds to eat. We'se be forced to care nought for a drop of rain, but set off and forage about inside of t' wood."

To be besieged in a subterranean cave, from whence there was no retreat, was truly an alarming prospect; and several plans of fortification and defence were projected during the continuance of the heavy rain; while, regardless of the weather, the active youths left the cave to forage for stores, and to survey the plains that divided them from their enemies.

"Do look at our potatoes, Arthur," said Hugh; "how they have sprung up the last month. In another week they will be fit to eat, and we shall have a plentiful crop of these useful roots."

Though they saw all was still on the moist plain, they did not venture beyond the wood, but easily procured birds, figs, and oats in abundance; and after Wilkins had placed his traps for pigeons, and Hugh had taken up a root of the still small potatoes, they returned to the cave, heavily laden with good things.

Day after day they brought in fruit and grain to add to the stores, and captured a number of fine pigeons, for which Jack wattled off a niche in the cave, and they were supplied with grass and brushwood for nests, and grain for food, to induce them to settle quietly. It was impossible in this climate to keep animal food eatable for more than two days; but so long as they had grain and potatoes they knew that they could live, provided they could secure a constant supply of water.

This was their most perplexing difficulty; and even amidst the rain the stony lining of the reservoir was taken up that they might bore the ground beneath it with long poles. Up to the waist in water, they bored ineffectually for an hour, the pole always striking against the solid rock. At length the pole passed through, there was an accidental opening in the rock, and the party who watched in the caves below, saw, with delight, the water trickle through into a recess some distance from the entrance. Then they all descended, to sink a well in the soft sandy floor of the cave, which they lined with slabs, and looked on with pleasure as this little reservoir gradually filled from the pool above, which the continual rains kept constantly filled with water.

It was ten days before all these labors were fully accomplished; then a dry day succeeded, and every hand was actively employed in digging up, carrying off, and storing the potatoes, which were of good size, and an abundant crop. They had made a number of bags of a flexible bark for containing stores; but now so many were filled that Margaret was afraid, if they had to set out soon, they should be unable to carry all off.

Then, after ascertaining the undisturbed solitude of the plain beyond the wood, Arthur and Wilkins set out in hopes of procuring a change of food; but no kangaroos or emus were in sight, and they feared to venture far from their place of refuge. They shot some opossums, filled one bag with the leaves of the tea-shrub, at the particular request of Jenny, and another with the leaves of a salt plant, which seemed to have sprung up after the rain, and which Arthur was glad to carry off, that he might try an experiment of which he had read.

"But, I say, Mr. Arthur," said Wilkins, "we've gone and made a bad job of it; just look ye here, we've niver thought that we were leaving a track, and here it is on this plashy bog, and no mistake. We might just as well have hung out a sign-post, to ask blacky to walk in."

Arthur was much vexed at his own carelessness, but he saw nothing could now be done but to endeavor to confuse the track as much as possible, and he arranged with Wilkins that they should separate, branch off in different directions, and finally they made a circuit opposite to each other round the wood, that the weak point might not be discovered.

"Ye see, Mr. Arthur," said Wilkins before they separated, "if Peter has an inkling that we're aback of these trees, he'd soon cut his way through, with a bit of help. But then, them fools of black fellows are as bad as our fond lass Ruth; they're flayed out of their wits of this wood, and they'll be shy of coming nigh hand it. I ken a good bit of their talk, ye see, but I'se a bad hand at framing their queer chirruping words. I heard 'em tell of bad sperrits as haunted this wood. But Black Peter's set on getting haud of t' master's money, and guns, and powder, and such like, and he's not good to put down. I seed Master Hugh's rifle as soon as they pulled me into that hole, and kept an eye on't. It were no use to them, for they'd no powder; and I said to myself, if God please to loose me, that gun goes wi' me."

They then parted to move round the dark forest, and during his walk, Arthur was alarmed to see smoke from the wood in which the cave of the savages lay; and before he reached the opening, he heard their curious and unwelcome cry, which proclaimed that the foe was near, and he feared, watching their movements, and now deeply regretted that they had left their retreat. Gladly they returned to it, and doubly secured the entrance, determining to keep an incessant watch, lest they should be surprised in their citadel.

On their return they found that Jack, assisted by Hugh and Gerald, had formed an oven, lined with slabs, on the hearth where the cooking-fire was usually made, and Jenny was preparing cakes of bruised oats, and a pigeon-pie made in a large oyster-shell, and covered with potatoes, to be baked in the new oven. The flesh of the opossum was not relished by any of the party. Jenny declared she would just as soon eat a monkey; Ruth was afraid to touch one, even before it was cooked; and Mr. Mayburn, after a long lecture to prove that the flesh must certainly be wholesome, from the habits and the vegetable diet of the class of animals to which it belonged, concluded by declining, himself, to eat of it.

"Nevertheless," he said, "I am not prejudiced by the vulgar error of confounding this little creature with the ugly opossum of America, to which it bears no resemblance, except in its marsupial formation and its playful habits. In fact, the graceful form, delicate color, and extraordinary agility of this beautiful animal, seem to rank it rather with the squirrels; and from the lateral folds of membrane, which it has the power to expand, in order to support its flying leaps through the air, it has been named by some travellers the 'flying squirrel,' though distinct from the American squirrel, and, like all the quadrupeds of the country, exclusively Australian."

The pretty delicate gray skins were carefully preserved, to be sewed together for cloaks; and the hungry boys did not disdain a stew of opossums, which they declared was quite as good as rabbit. But previous to the cookery, Arthur showed his father the new salt-shrub; and the large and peculiar form of the leaves enabled them to decide that it must be Brown's *Rhagodia Parabolica*, the leaves of which are edible. Anxious to make the experiment, the leaves were boiled for some time, strained, and the liquor filtered and evaporated several times, and at length the exposure to great heat produced some crystals of salt, to the delight of the young chemists, and still more to the content of Jenny, who treasured the precious salt, which had so long been the grand deficiency in her cookery. The leaves themselves were added to the stew, and not only communicating a salt flavor to the insipid meat, but formed a tender vegetable, tasting like spinach; and it was determined to omit no opportunity of searching for this valuable plant.

In the preparation and enjoyment of their abundant food, they did not neglect the necessary precautions for concealing their retreat. All the potato stalks were thrown into the cave, for fuel, and the ground was smoothed over as much as possible, and strewn with stones, that the traces of cultivation might haply escape observation; a watch was continually kept on the heights, and every opening that lighted the cave, with the exception of some narrow crevices, was carefully covered with a slab of stone beneath the brush, lest an accident similar to that which befell O'Brien should lead their enemies to discover the subterranean hollow.

This precaution rendered their abode gloomy, though they left the principal opening—the entrance—uncovered till any serious cause of alarm should render it prudent to enclose themselves entirely; and when a cessation of the rain permitted them, they all gladly remained in the open air, enjoying the perfume of the revived vegetation, and the joyful notes of thousands of birds which sported in the air, fluttered on the trees, or clamored noisily round the pools of water, plunging their beaks into the mud for the worms and reptiles on which they fed. These creatures supplied the family with unfailing food, and afforded Mr. Mayburn constant amusement in studying their various habits.

But a cessation of rain brought to them also a certain increase of peril. The natives were seen spreading over the plain below, hunting the kangaroo or opossum; and *Black* Peter, himself, easily distinguished, as Gerald said, because he was *white*, was observed stooping down, as Arthur suspected, to scrutinize the track, which he feared the rain had failed to obliterate. Still, occasionally heavy showers fell, and dispersed the people, who shrink from rain; and it was not till one morning, when none was actually falling, though dark clouds hid the sun, that the whole force of the savages, certainly exceeding fifty men, appeared crossing the plain; following slowly, and it seemed reluctantly, their debased chief, Black Peter.

When they had approached within a hundred yards of the forest, the natives halted at once, and Peter, after speaking some words to them, began again to examine the perplexed track, and drawing close to the trees, followed it round the whole boundary, apparently puzzled and enraged. At length he paused not far from the real entrance, and swinging round his axe above his head, he called out loudly to the people. They answered by throwing their axes on the ground, and remaining erect and motionless. The watchers above distinctly heard repeated strokes of the axe on the hard pine-trees; but they were well convinced that the efforts of one man alone could not accomplish an entrance, even for many days, and therefore felt comparatively tranquillized.

Still there was the absolute conviction that they were in a state of siege; that this man was of indomitable determination, of cruel and depraved nature, and that ultimately his obstinacy might bend even the timid savages to his will. And at this thought, fear and anxiety stole over every heart. Mr. Mayburn was persuaded to remain in the cave with Margaret and the three women, the sentinels promising to send reports of the progress of affairs to them, while, with tears and prayers they waited the result.

"Now, Mr. Arthur," said Wilkins, "just let me say my say. We've t' best on't yet: let's keep yon pass again all them rogues, and see which side tires first. We'll cut a canny hole to fire through at 'em, and load one gun after another; and as ye 're a bit soft-hearted yersel', ye maun just let me be front-rank man, and I'se pick off my chaps, reet and left, till there's not a rogue can stand again us. Folks say as how Peter's charmed; but I'se have a blaze at him, onyhow, and see if I can't stop his mischief."

"That will be capital!" cried Gerald. "And let us dig trenches, Arthur, and then won't we pepper the rascals snugly."

"But these savages are not rascals, Gerald," said Arthur; "they are only ignorant wretches, misled by a rascal. To fire on them from an ambush would be cold-blooded murder, which papa would never sanction. We have no right deliberately to destroy so many human lives."

"Ye're a real soft un, master," said Wilkins. "What's a few savages? Bless ye, t' country round about teems with 'em; they'll niver be missed!"

Nevertheless, Arthur could not be persuaded that it was expedient or excusable to destroy the surplus population of savages; and he preferred to reserve his charges for absolute defence.

CHAPTER XXII

But now they observed that Peter had returned to his party, and was talking to them with violent gesticulation; continually pointing to the wood, and waving them forward. The men drew nearer, and gathered round a thicket of low bushes, where they appeared busily engaged for a few minutes. Then the watchful sentinels saw, to their great dismay, many burning brands, one after another, flame up in the hands of the natives, who now rush boldly forward to cast them among the underwood of the forest. This was indeed a fearful sight, and no time was lost in retreating to the cave, where, after Arthur had carefully observed that no track was left to the spot, they all entered; a slab was introduced over the opening, beneath the brushwood, and now only small interstices were left to admit air and faint gleams of light to the agitated party below.

When the terrific mode of penetrating their fortress was told to Mr. Mayburn, and the reality of the obstinate siege burst upon him, stunned with horror, he remained speechless and motionless till Margaret roused him, by entreaties that he would pray for them.

"I will pray, my child," said he, "I will pray for speedy death; for death is inevitably our doom, and, alas! in its most frightful form."

"Will they burn us alive, Miss Marget?" shrieked Ruth; "and my bonnie hens, and them poor pigeons?"

"Be silent, Ruth," said Margaret. "God is great in power. It may be His will yet to save us, if we pray to Him."

"There are caves within caves here, Meggie," said Hugh. "Gerald and I know some queer corners, and we may escape beyond their discovery; and I make no doubt we may even cut our way through in some other part of the hollow, if we can only hold out long enough, and puzzle these fellows."

But the temporary depression of Mr. Mayburn had now left him; he had recovered his firmness and faith in God; and he summoned round him his agitated family, to join him in fervent prayer for help and protection in this hour of extreme need. He spoke to them long and earnestly, not denying his own weakness; and besought each to contend with his besetting sin: the strong must yield to His will; the weak must ask for fortitude; the erring must resolve to forsake his sins; and the desponding must trust wholly to Him who was mighty to save and merciful to the oppressed.

"We are now, my children," he added, "wanderers, as were his chosen people in the wilderness. Let us, then, remember the marvellous works that He hath done, His wonders, and the judgments of his mouth."

Composed and hopeful, after their religious exercise the besieged began to examine their defences and their resources. The powder had been carefully preserved in a solid rocky niche, where no stray spark could possibly reach it. The provision, though simple, was abundant—the store of potatoes alone seemed inexhaustible.

"We can surely live," said O'Brien, "like thousands of my careless, healthy countrymen, on the *pratee!* and defy famine. And, please, General Arthur, to come and see the watch-tower that Hugh and I have found out."

Arthur followed the restless boys, who carried off the ladder with them, through many a narrow winding, till they reached a very lofty hollow. Here the boys rested their ladder, and ascended as high as they could with its assistance, after which they climbed the rugged wall till a projecting ledge enabled them to stand; and when Arthur joined them, they pointed out to him some horizontal crannies between the strata of the stone, through which he looked down upon the table land of the mountain; and he perceived that this rock formed the parapet, or boundary wall of the crater.

They were thus enabled to survey their own hitherto peaceful domain, as well as the surrounding wood, from which a dense smoke was now rising. The moist and green trees had long refused to blaze, but at length, as the boys were silently and anxiously watching, they saw the red threads crawl through the black clouds; they heard the loud crackling of dried branches; and finally the broad flames rose majestically above the dark trees, and spread rapidly towards the east side of the mountain, urged by a west wind. The roaring of the flames, the noise of falling timber, the screams and discordant cries of hundreds of disturbed and affrighted birds, which continued to wheel, as if fascinated, over the flames, prevented any sound of human voices being audible; and the actors in the frightful devastation were alike unseen and unheard.

Hugh sobbed with grief as he watched numbers of his favorite birds, suffocated with the thick smoke, fall down senseless; Gerald exclaimed against the destruction of the ripe oats in the glade below, which were now blazing fiercely; and Arthur, pale and agitated, saw the fearful conflagration rapidly spreading up the side of the mountain, and dreaded the moment when, the brushwood being consumed above the cave, the slabs that covered the entrance must inevitably be detected, and they must submit to be baited in their last hold.

"Arthur, what shall we do?" exclaimed Hugh, "for the fire is running up the brush at the side of the mountain. See, now, it blazes over the edge; it has caught a heap of potato stalks that I was so careless as to leave there. Gerald, there are Margaret's favorite parterres all blazing,—the scarlet geranium, the blue convolvulus, and the sweet, home-like jasmine. How she will grieve! But, I forget, we have more to grieve for; already the sparks are falling on the bush over our grotto! What will become of Margaret and papa?"

"We must go to them," replied Arthur. "We have seen the worst that can happen; it is useless remaining here. Let us comfort them, and lead them into the deepest recesses of the mountain. We may, at least, escape the fearful effects of the conflagration."

"And then, Arthur," said Hugh, "we may surely defend them with our guns. It will be a just cause."

"It will! it will!" answered Arthur. "God send that we may not be called on to shed blood; but I believe we should be justified in doing it. Do you yet see the enemy, Gerald?"

"No, Arthur; but God is good to us," said Gerald. "The rain is falling again, and our dear Black Forest will not be entirely consumed; and perhaps we may have opportunity to escape."

The rain re-commenced suddenly, and so heavily, that in a short time the blazing conflagration was extinguished, and the progress of the invaders arrested; for, when the boys joined their trembling friends, Wilkins said,—

"Depend on 't they've crept into some hole or other; they're just downreet cowards about a drop of rain, for all their running about without a rag to their backs."

"But we cannot exist long in this state of misery," said Mr. Mayburn. "What would you advise, Arthur?"

"I should say, dear papa," answered he, "that we must defend our position as long as it is tenable, and then have all prepared, and attempt a retreat—a dangerous but inevitable measure. Jack will point out the most convenient mode of making up packages for carrying away. We must, if possible, take our potatoes, for we may meet with a sterile region."

"And the hens and chickens," added Ruth, imploringly.

"We had certainly better release them," he replied, with a smile, "and introduce a new race into the country; or else roast them and make them useful."

But Ruth so pathetically and earnestly begged to be allowed to carry her "bonnie bit chicks," that, on the promise that the young ones should be given up to be eaten, in case of need, she was permitted to encumber herself with her favorites. Jack made her a light basket for them, of a portable form; he then proceeded to pack, compress, and arrange the baggage in convenient burdens for each; while Jenny baked in the oven, which she greatly regretted having to abandon, a sufficient quantity of biscuits to fill two large bags. The boots had all been thoroughly repaired during the rains; and, as it was probable they would have to set out before the weather was settled, the skins of the opossums were sewed into cloaks, to protect them.

Thus, during one day of continuous rain, when no signs of the savages were seen, they were able to make all ready for the flight, which was now become absolutely necessary; and it was proposed that the next morning, though the clouds still threatened a continuance of rain, they should make a last substantial breakfast in their secure sanctuary, and then set out at once. The breakfast was eaten, and the burdens apportioned; but, before they ventured to emerge, the boys ran off to take a survey of the plains from their watch-tower, and hastily returned to announce the vexatious intelligence that the whole body of the savages had passed through the devastated forest, and were already ascending the side of the mountain.

"Now for the defence!" exclaimed Hugh, seizing his gun, and placing the ladder at the opening.

"Remove the ladder, Hugh," said Arthur. "Remember that papa has given all authority to me. Do nothing but what I command."

Hugh made a grimace, and touched his cap.

"You, Gerald, had better go to the watch-tower," continued Arthur. "Margaret and papa, Jenny, Ruth, Baldabella, and the child, will accompany you. We shall have sufficient force to defend the cave here."

"But Margaret can watch. Do let me have some work, Arthur," said Gerald.

"Very well, then, you shall be *aide-de-camp*, and bring me the reports of sentinel Margaret. Away! away!" said Arthur.

Margaret was placed on the ledge, to watch, and reported that Peter, followed by the unwilling savages, was already on the height. She saw the keen-eyed convict examine the ground, and take up a scorched potato-stalk, with some of the bulbs hanging to it, which had been imprudently left. He then went forward to the stone-lined reservoir, which was plainly the work of man; and pointed it out to his followers, as well as some tracks on the soft earth. The natives, however, looked sullen, did not reply, but gazed anxiously round, as if expecting some unusual appearance; and all shrunk together beneath the rocky wall in which the watchers were concealed.

When Margaret communicated her observations, Baldabella said, "Black fellow look for *Bayl-yas*—bad spirit; they not know good white man pray, send *Bayl-yas* away."

"Now, Meggie," said Gerald, springing up the ladder to her side; "I'll give them a fright, and disperse them;" and the imprudent boy uttered a deep unearthly groan. In a moment the men darted forward, and were springing down the steep, when the commanding voice of their leader recalled them; and Margaret, with much vexation, saw that he was explaining the cause of their alarm, for he pointed to the spot where she stood, in a menacing manner. He continued to speak to the men in a tone of exultation, waving his arms, till he induced them to return and accompany him in his search.

"Away, at once, foolish boy," said Margaret; "and tell Arthur all we have seen, and your imprudent act. They will not leave the spot now, till they have found our hiding-place."

Poor Gerald, completely crest-fallen, hastened to make his report and his confession; and Arthur saw plainly they should now be obliged to have recourse to arms. He ordered Hugh to wait till he should have fired off his two barrels, and then to take his place till he should have time to reload. The ammunition was put in charge of Wilkins and Jack to serve out; and cruel as was the necessity, Arthur trusted they might thus defend their position, and weary out even the malignant and stubborn convict.

There could be no doubt discovery must soon take place, as the light by degrees poured into the cave, through the small openings which the savages uncovered one after another. Still Peter saw none of these could possibly be the entrance to any concealment; but at length he stepped on the large slab; it was immediately removed, and a shout of exultation arose, as the large chasm pointed out the retreat of the persecuted family. For a moment there was a pause: even if the descent had been easy, the men were not so rash as to throw themselves into the clutches of their foes below, and spears directed against an unseen enemy would be wasted. Then Peter leaned over the opening, and called out,—

"Come on, ye cowards, and fight fairly if ye can, or else hand up them guns, wi' yer powder and cash, and then cut off, vagabonds as ye are, or I'll make this den ower hot to haud ye."

Arthur made a sign of silence, for he saw Wilkins was impatient and very much inclined to indulge in pouring out invectives against his former companion. Then a few spears and stones were flung down at random, which were easily avoided by the besieged, who had ensconced themselves in niches of the rock, and the light-hearted boys could scarcely restrain their laughter at the futile attempts. But the resolute convict was not to be baffled; he was heard speaking to his followers in their own language, and Baldabella was placed near enough to hear and interpret. When she had listened a few minutes, she turned to Arthur with a look of terror, and said,—"Bad Peter say, 'Burn all! burn white jin! black jin! Nakinna! good master! all burn!'"

The next moment confirmed the woman's report, for flaming brands thrown into the cave announced the desperate plan of the besiegers. Arthur called for water, and buckets of water were brought to quench each brand as it fell; but the suffocating smoke in that confined spot was intolerable.

"We must end this nuisance, or we shall be stifled," said Arthur; and as Peter himself, with an armful of kindled brushwood, bent over to cast it below, Arthur fired on him, and the man fell back beneath the flaming branches, which were scattered over him; then calling for the ladder, which had been brought near, the intrepid youth mounted to the opening, fired again into the midst of the assembled savages, and, rapidly descending, removed the ladder.

The yells and groans they heard from above afforded sufficient proof that the shots had taken effect, and Hugh and Gerald were sent to the watch-tower to make observations. They saw that Peter was able to stand, supported by two men, but his right arm appeared to be powerless; a wound in the shoulder was bleeding, and he was raging and stamping with agony, evidently from the burns he had received, for the savages were applying some leaves to his breast and face.

"I have never had a shot yet," said Hugh, when he returned. "It is very hard, Arthur—pray let me run up the ladder and scatter a few of the rascals."

"No, no! my dear Hugh," answered Arthur; "such a measure would be wanton and inhuman at this moment. These wretched savages are mere machines in the hands of the villain whose own cruel designs have recoiled on himself. If they had never met this man, they might perhaps have been troublesome and annoying to us, but a little experience of our superior knowledge and power would have relieved us from them. Now even, they are not detained near us from choice, for they evidently abhor and dread the place, but they stay to fulfil the duties of humanity to this wretch who has so unaccountably beguiled them."

The Kangaroo Hunters | 199

"I'll tell ye how he came round 'em, Mr. Arthur," said Wilkins. "I heared 'em say when I were chained up yonder, as how that good-to-nought were a head man, and husband to one of their jins, and he'd been speared and killed outreet by some black fellows down south, and now he were sent back to 'em wi' a white skin. Peter made 'em swallow all that rigmarole, cunning dog as he is."

"I have read," said Mr. Mayburn, "that some of these ignorant tribes have such an extraordinary superstition: believing that the souls of the departed revisit the earth in the form of white men. There is blended with this faith a strange recognition of the doctrine of immortality, and, we might hope, of regeneration; but the crimes of this wretch in that which they believe to be his second life must have startled even the untaught heathens whom he has thus deceived."

"They're off, Mr. Arthur," said Wilkins, who had ascended to the opening to look round; "there's not a soul left. I reckon they'd be right glad to quit; and that rogue Peter's not in a way to trouble us for one bit; so, what say ye, master, if we were to bolt afore they'd settled what to do? Here's t' mistress seems all ready."

"I am quite ready, Wilkins," said Margaret, "and agree with you. It appears to me, Arthur, that our best hope is, to snatch this opportunity to get the advantage of a few hours' start, that we may not be easily overtaken when that wicked man is sufficiently recovered to take the field again."

"And mind, Mr. Arthur, sharp's t' word," said Wilkins, "if we want to beat him. He let me into his schemes a bit, as how he meant to get them fellows after him down south to join a lot of bush-rangers as was to meet him. Ye see, we're not top walkers, at no time; and wi' all this stuff to hug, we'd better be trotting."

"Make ready!" cried Gerald, tying on his knapsack of bark, and putting into one pocket a canister of powder, and into the other a bag of shot; "we must trot, as Wilkins says, as well as fellows can trot carrying such burdens as ours. I say, Arty, haven't I got my share?"

"You have indeed, my boy," answered Arthur. "I fear you will not be able to get on long under such a heavy burden; but we must try, at first however, to carry as much away as we can bear. Take your bow to support you, and mount the ladder. Now, Hugh."

Hugh was similarly laden, but carried a gun instead of a bow. Ruth would not resign her fowls, and had in addition the serious weight of a large bag of potatoes. Margaret, Jenny, and Baldabella carried the bread and the remainder of the potatoes, the poor native having in addition the charge of her child. Mr. Mayburn was laden with the shells and buckets which constituted their household furniture; and Arthur, Wilkins, and Jack cleared off all the rest of the weapons and bags. The descent to the plains had been rendered easy by the conflagration, which had almost entirely destroyed the forest, and the travellers chose their path in a direction opposite to the wood which was the abode of the natives. They toiled on with swift feet and anxious hearts, scarcely conscious of their heavy burdens, for two hours; in which time they had left their desolated sanctuary far away to the north.

The ground was level and fertile, and the weather favorable; for the sun was overclouded, though no rain was falling; and relaxing their extreme speed, they still continued to walk on, till downright fatigue and hunger pointed out the necessity of rest. The best place for their encampment that they could select was in the midst of a thicket of the tea-shrub and other low brushwood. The young men with their axes cleared a spot for a fire, and niches for sleeping-places; they plucked the fresh leaves from the plants to make tea, and enjoyed their coarse biscuit, soothed by the silver tones of the bell-bird, the musical piping of the organ-magpie, and the soft cry of an invisible bird, the curious notes of which resembled those of the curlew.

Night fell on them with all the beauty of the tropical regions; the soft breeze loaded with fragrance from the luxuriant flowers revived by the recent rains, the bright stars above their heads, the brilliant fire-flies floating round them, the dying notes of the half hushed birds, the incessant hum of the restless insect tribes; all was harmony, inspiring devout and holy thoughts; and the weary travellers slept happily and trustfully till morning awoke them to resume their labors.

CHAPTER XXIII

The women had prepared breakfast, and Arthur was becoming impatient, before Jack and the two young boys appeared, dragging after them a large sheet of bark, to which they had attached ropes.

"It was Jack's thought!" exclaimed Gerald. "Is it not a capital plan?—the baggage-wagon! Off with your knapsack, Arty; Jenny, bring your pots and pans. Every thing must be tied on our sledge, and we will draw it in turns—two men to form a team."

"It will be a great relief, certainly," said Arthur, "so long as the plains continue tolerably clear and level; but, I fear, over the matted brush or the rugged mountain we shall find it useless."

"Why then, Mr. Arthur," said Jack, "it will only be taking up our loads a bit, and leaving the sledge. We can soon cut another sheet when the road gets smoother."

The sledge answered admirably, and, relieved from their burdens, they went on for several days, over well-watered and well-wooded plains, without interruption, and without delay, except when the disengaged youths lingered behind to shoot a few pheasants or cockatoos, that the bread might not be too soon exhausted. In a week after they had left the cave, they saw kangaroos again, and even the sledge was abandoned, that all might join in the chase. After a long hunt, they succeeded in killing one; and the weather being now less sultry, they were able to preserve the meat for two days. The skin was cleaned and dried, and then converted into bags for the biscuit, for showers of rain still fell occasionally, and they had been compelled to take off their cloaks to protect their valuable food.

One evening, an unwelcome return of the heavy rain induced them to look anxiously round for some shelter, and turning round a clump of tall bushes, they came suddenly on a cluster of scattered huts, formed of green boughs and open in front. Beneath these canopies several women, wearing cloaks of fur, were employed in pounding grain or nuts between two stones, while they sung some song in a low, musical tone, and in perfect harmony.

Outside the huts stood several tall men. They had a single loose garment of fur cast round them, but the bust was wholly uncovered, and marked by many raised cicatrices. They were engaged in making arrows or spears, and never raised their heads from their employment; but, with the usual dignified indifference of the savage, did not appear to notice the approach of the strangers, though probably they had never before seen the white man. Even the women continued their work and their song; and it was only when Baldabella, who had been introduced by her protectors, went forward, holding her child, to ask the women to give some good white people shelter from the rain in their huts, that the men turned to listen, and the women suspended their labor. The head of the family, pointing out an empty hut, spoke to Baldabella, and said, as she interpreted his words, "That very good for white man; for black man; plenty rain make much cold."

Glad of the refuge, while Baldabella remained to talk to the women of the tribe, the rest took possession of the slight hut, and prepared their supper of the remains of the kangaroo, of which they invited their friendly hosts to partake. The natives now assembled round them with some curiosity, tasted the seethed kangaroo, and seemed to relish it; rejected the roasted potatoes with disgust, but greedily enjoyed the biscuit, especially the jumbles, as the boys called them, which were flavored with the juice of the figs.

Then the women in return for this hospitality, brought to them some pods, which Arthur recognized to be the fruit of the *Acacia stenophylla*, the seeds, or nuts, resembling in flavor the cachou-nut. They brought also a small melon, or cucumber, now ripe and sweet, with which the plains that the travellers had crossed this day had been covered; but they had not ventured to eat it till now, when they saw how the natives enjoyed it.

"It certainly belongs to one of the most useful orders of plants considered as the food of man," said Mr. Mayburn; "and, as far as I can determine from recollection, I believe it to be the *Cucumis pubescens*. This is truly a country of rich and abundant resources; wanting but the light of civilization and religion to render it a paradise."

"Surely, papa," said Margaret, "our countrymen acted unwisely when they suffered the first steps into these lovely and untrodden wilds to be made by the vilest of criminals. Alas! alas! what must the ignorant natives think of such Christian missionaries!"

"It was an error, Margaret," answered her father, "wide in its mischief, fatal in its results; and generations must pass away before the error can be rectified. But a purer and holier influence is at work; and, in his own good time, God will assuredly enlighten the people, through the efforts of his faithful servants. Would that I were able to take my share in the great work! but, alas! I am but the barren fig-tree, and continually I hear that awful sentence ringing in my ear, 'Cut it down; why cumbereth it the ground?'"

The earnest father then called on his family to kneel in prayer, while the natives stood round in silent wonder, especially when they remarked the devout demeanor of Baldabella, and heard the little child murmuring in English the responses, in imitation of her kind teachers. After prayers the women seemed to be earnestly questioning Baldabella; and Margaret was pleased to hear the woman speak long and earnestly to the questioners, for she was convinced that Baldabella was truly a Christian in faith, so far as her simple mind could comprehend the faith.

Though they considered it prudent to keep a watch, the sleep of the family was not disturbed by any fears, for these natives seemed quiet and inoffensive; and through Baldabella they learnt that they had ever shunned the restless and destructive tribes to the north, and a still more dangerous people, whom they spoke of with terror, as the tribes of the "Great River," to the south. But, the interpreter added, they did not like the white people who came to kill the *menuah*, as they named the kangaroo; and the emu, and to carry off their weapons. But they were satisfied that these white strangers were peaceful like themselves, and they wished them well, and would show them the way through the mountains.

The weary travellers gratefully accepted this offer, for the prospect of having to ascend, without guidance, a line of mountains which cut off their progress to the south, and of being compelled to resume their heavy burdens, was alarming. Early in the morning they sought the women, to present them with some biscuit and with a pair of fowls, of which Baldabella undertook to explain the great usefulness, and the domestic habits and proper mode of feeding.

Then they once more set out, guided by the chief among the natives; and having skirted the mountains for three or four miles to the east, found a narrow gorge, through which a shallow rill ran towards the south, along the flowery margin of which they passed till they came upon another wide plain, less wooded and fertile than that which they had left, but grown over with the *Cucumis* laden with fruit. This plain was perforated with dangerous holes, which their guide told them were the dens of a large animal, very fierce, which he called the Wombat, and which the boys were filled with a great desire to encounter and vanquish.

Once on the plains, the native pointed out the direction which they were to follow, greatly to the east of south. He shook his head when they intimated their wish to proceed due south, and, according to Baldabella, declared there was "no water"—a most important objection to the route. Arthur gave the man one of the table-knives, much to the discontent of Jenny and the great delight of the receiver; and the gratified native stood watching them for some time, and then slowly returned to his people.

"Now for the wombats!" exclaimed Gerald, looking anxiously down into one of the dens of these unknown animals. But all was still and dark; and Arthur begged that there might be no delay, as, in all probability, the animals could only be drawn from their retreats by dogs, or be surprised by long watching, and time was now too precious to be spent on such an uncertain pursuit. Continuing, therefore, to follow the course of the slender rivulet, which, however, soon became but a chain of pools, they travelled for several miles, eating, as they went on, the juicy melons, as they called the *Cucumis*, till the sight of a smoke in the direction of the pools induced them reluctantly to forsake even this small supply of water, and to diverge directly to the south, till they should have passed the danger of encountering another tribe, who might prove less friendly than their late hosts.

The sudden fall of night compelled them to rest at a spot where no water was to be discovered, and, too late, they regretted that they had not brought a supply from the pools. Reluctantly they made their only meal of the day on bread; fortunately they were able to add melons; still the privation was felt; they were unsatisfied and much depressed, till calmed by the blessed influence of prayer. Then all anxiety was hushed by a sound sleep on the wide, treeless plain.

They had slept some hours, when Arthur was awaked by a startling cry, and, springing up in alarm, he seized his gun, and called hastily to Jack to follow him. The moon was shining brightly, and they were enabled to see some moving objects at no great distance, towards which they quickly directed their steps, and, on drawing near, they heard the voice of O'Brien crying out, "Arthur! Arthur! come and kill these frightful beasts! I shall be worried!"

They now saw the head of O'Brien, who, supported only by his hands, had sunk into a hole or den, and was surrounded by a troop of hideous large animals, with the form of a bear and the nose of a badger. They were actually running over the boy, and apparently very uneasy at his intrusion. Jack's spear soon despatched one of the animals; the rest fled to their dens at the sight of more invaders of their homes; and O'Brien was dragged from the hole he had accidentally taken possession of, and scolded by Arthur for his imprudence. It appeared that he had, while lying awake, seen one of the wombats roaming about in search of food, and while pursuing it with his spear he had fallen into the den, and by his cries raised the whole community of these social and harmless beasts, which, powerful and numerous as they were, had attempted no injury against the rude invader.

The wombat Jack had killed was about the size of a sheep; they divested it of its smooth thick fur skin, which was hung up to dry immediately. In the morning they had an opportunity of examining the curious, clumsy animals, which were still busily feeding. Wilkins declared their flesh to be delicate and excellent food; but, without water, no one felt any appetite for meat.

"Doubtless," said Mr. Mayburn, "this creature is the *Phascolomys ursinus*, partaking of the form of the bear and the hog; but, like the great majority of Australian animals, marsupial."

"He is an ugly fellow," said Hugh, "with his huge body and short legs; but his skin is capital; we will clean it to make a mattrass for papa, and we must have another skin for Margaret. After all, Jenny, a wombat-steak will be more juicy than this dreadful dry, husky biscuit; and I suppose we must try to eat, or we shall never have strength to get out of this desert."

The steaks were really excellent with sliced melon, if the travellers could have relished food without water; and after breakfast they set out, again eagerly watching for signs of water; but no one feeling sufficient energy to execute another wombat before they departed. They continued to struggle on over a loose sandy soil, covered with a bush resembling the heath, so dear to the northern people of Great Britain; the very sight of which cheered the thirsty wanderers in the dry desert; and they talked of the moors of home till their steps grew lighter. But the toil of dragging the light sledge over or through the bushes became hard labor; and at length Mr. Mayburn, exhausted with thirst, was so overcome that two of the young men had to support him, as they slowly moved on to escape from this desert.

"Keep up your heart, master," said the attached Wilkins; "and Jenny, woman, be getting yer cans ready; we'se have a sup of rain afore long, depend on't. Now some of ye light-heeled young uns, run on, and seek out a shelter for t' master."

The sky was dark, the thunder rumbled at a distance, and the young people looked round in happy anxiety for some shelter; but in vain,— not even a tree was to be seen; and at last they were obliged to content themselves with a little cleared spot, backed by a low brush-covered hill, and surrounded by the tea-shrub mingled with the graceful heath. There they hollowed out a sort of recess in the soft sandy hill-side, before which they hung the skin of the wombat, that Mr. Mayburn and Margaret, at least, might be sheltered. By this time the rain had begun to fall in torrents, and every vessel they had brought away was placed to catch the precious drops.

Then the boys made *forms* as they called them, beneath the brushwood, into which they crept, to escape, as far as they could, the deluge of rain. But ever and anon a hand was stretched out to obtain a draught of the long-pined-for water; and though they declared it tasted warm, they felt so refreshed that there succeeded a great appetite for wombat-steak, which could not, however, be gratified; for to attempt to make a fire was hopeless.

"What charming dormitories we have!" said Gerald. "The rain dripping through these narrow-leaved shrubs and dabbling your face all night long, will be so comfortable. I don't think a wombat's den would be such a bad thing to-night. Ruth, how do the cocks and hens like this weather?"

"I keeps 'em covered an' under my cloak, Master Gerald," answered she; "but, bonnie things, they tremmel and cower all of a heap. You see, birds and such-like, are all for sunshine."

"And sunshine enough they've had here, Ruth," replied he; "and now we must not be unthankful for the rain we wanted much. Pleasant dreams to you all, my friends!" called out the lively boy, as he dived under the bushes, to scratch himself out a den, as he said. But the rain and the thunder prevented much sleep, and at the first gleam of light, the boys issued from their comfortless dens, with some dry twigs which had formed their beds, and with which they proposed, though the rain was still falling, to make a fire to cook some meat. But before they could accomplish their plan, they were disturbed by a trampling among the bushes, and the sound of human voices.

"The savages! the savages!" whispered Hugh; "I think I can distinguish the voice of Black Peter."

"Scatter the twigs," said Arthur; "put the water-vessels underneath the bushes. Draw these skins into your form, Margaret, and crouch out of sight. Now! now! to cover, all of you!"

They had scarcely given the place the appearance of being unvisited, and drawn themselves securely under the scrub, when the voices were so close to them that they could distinguish, though they could not understand the words. Only Black Peter, who pronounced the language slowly, was sufficiently distinct for them to make out the words signifying "mountains" and "plenty of water."

The party passed close to them, but without pausing, and when the steps and voices sounded sufficiently distant, Arthur looked out, and saw the same men who had besieged them in their mountain retreat, still headed by Peter. All the men were outrageously painted white and red, though they were partially covered with opossum cloaks to shelter them from the rain. Arthur observed that they moved on towards the east, where, at a great distance, appeared a dark line, which he concluded was the mountain-range Peter had alluded to.

One after another the alarmed family appeared from their hiding-places; Baldabella was eagerly questioned about their discourse, and she replied that she had heard Peter say, "White men go to mountain, find much water. Peter go to mountain, find plenty water, plenty white fellow, plenty gun, knife. Kill white man, kill bad fellow Wilkins."

"She's reet! I'll uphold her," said Wilkins. "Depend on 't Peter's heared of some bush-rangers out ower yonder, and he'll want to join 'em. We'se have to keep clear of their track, master. Just look round ye, what chance should we have again a lot of them desp'rate rogues, wi' guns in their hands, and blood in their hearts; and when they're fairly set on, them blacks is as bad; they reckon nought of a dozen lives to get haud on a gun."

"Whither shall we flee?" cried Mr. Mayburn, in a distracted tone. "Speak, Margaret—Arthur—and you, my good man, who, steeped in evil, had yet strength given you to turn away from it, guide and save us! Alas! it is but too true; man, civilized or savage, preserves his innate and original depravity. 'There is none good; no, not one.' Men have spoken of the simple and pure life of the desert; we see what it is in truth."

"Yes, dear papa," said Margaret, "we must bid adieu to the fallacious dreams of poetry, the romance of that golden age when men were virtuous because they were ignorant. These are men to whom the temptations of the world are unknown; men who have never looked on the brilliant decorations of vice; yet they are harsh, cruel, selfish, and faithless. Is this truly human nature, papa?"

"I fear, my child, it is too truly human nature," answered Mr. Mayburn,—"fallen, degraded, unredeemed human nature. Well does a great and wise writer on the natural depravity of man picture the ignorant savage as 'a compound of pride and indolence, and selfishness, and cunning and cruelty; full of a revenge which nothing could satiate, of a ferocity which nothing could soften; strangers to the most amiable sensibilities of nature.' Then what weight of sin must rest on the souls of those who, having been taught the way of truth themselves, take advantage of the frailty of humanity to lead these heathens into the gulf of crime. Woe to those men 'who know the best, and yet the worst pursue.'"

While they watched the gradual disappearance of their enemies, the rain ceased, and Jenny summoned the party to the enjoyment of tea to their dry biscuit, before they resumed their journey, the prospect of which was still unpromising.

"We must now, defying all the threatened deserts, go on towards the south," said Arthur, "and evade, if we possibly can, our implacable and inveterate pursuers. The temptation to cross the eastern mountains is great, but I fear, Wilkins, we should hardly be safe, even in the rear of such dangerous company."

"Nay, nay! Mr. Arthur, keep out of their way," said Wilkins. "Ye heared what Baldabella said about their going to rondessvowse ower yonder wi' them roguish bush-rangers; and I see no sense in running into t' thick on 'em."

"Certainly not, Wilkins," answered Arthur. "Then we will decide on a route due south. So, forward, my brave men, and let us carefully carry away the water we have preserved, for I fear much we have not yet passed the wilderness."

CHAPTER XXIV

It was indeed on a wilderness they now entered, where low entangled brushwood spread as far as the eye could extend, unvaried by the appearance of a single tree rising above it; and as they toiled through or over this perplexing ground, carrying the bark sledge, which it was impossible to draw over the bush, they were often deceived by the sight of a line of tall reeds, the border of the bed of some river, now wholly dry, or merely muddy with the rain of the previous day. They saw no animals, except two or three emus, which swiftly fled from pursuit; and they were too eager to escape from the dry desert to waste time in the chase. For two days, successive morning suns showed them the same trackless and unwatered heaths spread before them; then the water was exhausted, and they turned away with loathing from the dry bread and potatoes.

Slowly and languidly they dragged on their weary way, still watching and hoping in vain. Another day of suffering dawned on them; and now the scorching air, the dry food, the fatigue, and the consuming thirst overcame them one after another, and before evening Mr. Mayburn said, "Let us lie down here, Arthur. God has chosen, in His wisdom, to put this termination to our efforts. Nature is exhausted; let us lie down and prepare for death."

"Not so, my dear father," answered Arthur. "God wills that we should be active, and strive to surmount difficulties, or He would not have bestowed on us the bounteous gifts of thought and action. Margaret, I know your faith and resolution; encourage my father."

"You look to me in vain, my dear brother," said Margaret. "I am unable to think or to move. Save our beloved father, and leave me beneath these bushes to die. I feel that death must be near at hand."

"I beseech you to rally your energy, my darling Meggie," said her brother, in a broken voice. "Surely, after the rain that fell yesterday, we must soon find some pools. We must not be so weak as to remain here, with our pursuers so near to us, and drought and death around us. Let us try at least to cross this muddy and deceitful gorge, and be thankful; for remember, my dear sister, if this had been now a foaming river, we should have been unable to ford it, and must have been lost in this desert."

Margaret was too weak to reply, and Arthur, lifting her with difficulty in his enfeebled arms, descended the banks, and crossed the wide bed of a river which was scarcely moist enough to leave the traces of his footsteps. Wilkins and Jack supported Mr. Mayburn across, and the rest languidly followed. They crawled slowly up the rocky banks of the opposite side, which were covered with thick scrubby bushes; and then beneath a spreading acacia, they sat down to rest a few moments, and endeavored to nerve themselves to endurance and exertion.

"Surely, Wilkins," said Arthur, "that lofty line of mountains which we can still see at the east, though so distant, ought to supply springs and streams to these plains, and there must be water at no great distance. You and I are pretty stout; can we not leave these feeble folks here, and go on to search for some relief for them?"

"Look yonder, Mr. Arthur," answered Wilkins, "just atween us and them mountains, and say if we ought to leave 'em behind us."

Arthur beheld with dismay, at about a mile's distance, a dark mass moving over the bare plain. He saw that the savages were returning, and even his firm heart failed, for here was no shelter—no hope of escape. He remained struck dumb for a minute; then he whispered to his brothers the dreadful fact, adding, "They must be nearer than they appear to be, for I surely hear them as well as see them. Certainly, some sound breaks the stillness of this solitary desert. It must be the murmur of many voices."

"It seems to me like men felling wood," said Jack.

"It is more like the blessed sound of water," said O'Brien, springing up.

Still the mass of figures, though now more defined and plainly recognized to be the savage host, approached slowly; and they could not produce the strange rumor, which momentarily grew louder, crackling, tearing, roaring, like the mighty elephant, forcing its way through the thicket. All the party now heard in trembling fear this unaccountable phenomenon, and the weeping women knelt down to pray for aid amidst accumulated distresses.

"Father," murmured the almost unconscious Margaret, "I smell water. Oh, give me some, or I die."

"It is water!" shouted O'Brien "I said it was water. It is the river coming down. Come on, Hugh, let us meet it;" and he leaped down into the bed of the stream.

"Stop the lad!" cried Wilkins, following and dragging him up the bank again. "We'se ha'e water enough, and more nor we want soon. Look ye! look ye!" and they saw a slender thread of water come crawling over the bed like a silver snake.

"Sharp! sharp! hand us a bucket!" called Wilkins; and, provided with a bucket, he descended and quickly procured a small quantity of water to relieve the worst sufferers; but before a second supply could be obtained, he was compelled to retreat in haste, and an amazing spectacle burst on the eyes of the beholders. A mighty tower of water was seen to approach, rushing, pouring, foaming; casting up from it trunks of trees, drenched garlands of creeping plants, and showers of pebbles. In an incredibly short space of time the resistless torrent had filled the deep gorge, and was splashing over the rocky banks.

Gradually the torrent subsided into a smooth, deep, and flowing river, from which the pining sufferers obtained the refreshment they had so long sought, and then, with bended knees, offered up a thanksgiving to that Great Power who had by this providential event rescued them from a painful death, and interposed an insurmountable barrier between them and their vindictive enemies, who, having now approached near enough to be aware of this unexpected obstacle, saw, with evident wrath, their prize snatched from their grasp. At the command of their implacable and well-known chief, Peter, some of the most skilful threw their spears; but the river was not less than fifty yards across, besides which, the strong east wind drifted away the weapons from their intended aim; and the invigorated and uninjured family lost no time in leaving the dangerous spot, and were soon beyond sight of the stubborn natives, and the malicious bush-ranger.

"It is plain they have no means of crossing the river," said Arthur; "but, Wilkins, what can have induced them to return from the mountains?"

"I reckon they'll have somehow missed their comrades as was to be," answered Wilkins. "Maybe they'd an inkling as how we were behind 'em and not afore 'em; and they'd niver reckon on t' water coming down; and not a soul among 'em can swim, barring Peter, and he knew better nor trust hisself among us alone. We've stopped 'em a bit now, master."

"Not we, Wilkins, but God," said Mr. Mayburn. "It was 'the Lord that brought again the waters upon them,' and saved us. To His name be the glory."

"We have still before us a long struggle through these sterile wilds," said Arthur; "but this deliverance must give us renewed courage for labor and privation. Now we may afford to eat our supper, and take our rest without fear."

The strongest of the party, before they left the river, had filled all the vessels with water, and brought them off, and very soon, almost within hearing of the noisy savages, they made a fire, and enjoyed again the luxury of tea to their potatoes, before weary nature sought repose. But as soon as it was light, they set out, after again having tea to fit them for another day of toil. The march was resumed with renewed health and spirits, but still the monotony of the matted rough desert, which rarely afforded a clear spot for them to draw the sledge, fatigued and depressed them before the day was over. And when they rested for the evening, and Jenny produced the scanty remainder of potatoes, and the still smaller portion of grain, dismay sat on every countenance, and Jack was the first to demand that Ruth's basket might be lightened, and the contents given up to satisfy the hungry and healthy appetite of the public in general.

It was found on inspection that besides three full-grown fowls, the girl was still carrying six good-sized chickens, the rest of the brood having perished, from accident or scanty food. Immediately, as a matter of expediency to save the oats, to lessen the burden they had to carry, and to feed the hungry, sentence was passed that two chickens should be executed each day, and it was hoped, before all were eaten, some region of more plenty might be attained.

With great reluctance, and floods of tears, Ruth relinquished her pets, and at the end of the three days, only the old fowls were left, and every potato, grain, and drop of water was gone. Then, indeed, they realized the misery of famine; strength and cheerfulness left them, and they tottered reluctantly forward, slowly and in mournful silence.

Sometimes an emu was seen at a distance, but none had energy or strength to chase it, and Arthur, whose mental vigor supported him, when all were sinking round him, tried in vain to rouse them from their apathy.

"Let us struggle on a little longer," he said. "Once more I see a tall line of reeds, and by God's mercy, we may not be disappointed this time. Come, Jack, you and I will make a forced march in search of succor for those who are weaker than ourselves; and if we succeed we will return to refresh and bring them forward."

With buckets slung over their shoulders, and leaning on their long spears, the two young men strained every nerve to reach the reeds like those which had so frequently disappointed them, and, cutting or forcing their way through the tall canes, they came again on the bed of a river—moist and muddy, indeed, but not a pool of water was to be seen.

"Let us ascend higher; we may find a little," said Arthur. "But, surely, Jack, here are footsteps on the soft earth. Some one has been here before us."

"Sure enough there has," replied Jack. "Men have been here; booted chaps, too; none of the savages; anyhow, not them that we reckon savages, but like enough, they'll be little better. Ay, their track runs upward; what say ye, Mr. Arthur, are we to follow it?"

"We must follow it, Jack," answered Arthur; "we must find water, or death is inevitable to us; and we are better in the rear of suspected foes than before them. And yonder are pools before us, God be thanked. Let us drink and then we will carry life back to those who are in greater need than ourselves."

The pools afforded ample supplies. The young men drank, and bathed their burning faces and heads, and then hastened back, refreshed and vigorous, bearing full buckets for the anxious party who awaited their return, and after they had drunk, and were able to converse, they were informed of the appearance of the footsteps.

"I'd like to see 'em wi' my own eyes," said Wilkins. "If it be ony of our chaps from t' colony, run-a-way fellows, I ken t' make of their boots at t' first sight. But it's a long step for 'em to have marched, poor rogues. What think ye if we stirred from here? for I'd like to tell ye what I ken about them tracks."

The whole party went forward more briskly than before, and reached the bed of the river, where Wilkins carefully examined the marks, and then said,—"Bush-rangers, as sure as ye stand there, Mr. Arthur. Here's been four on 'em; and look ye here, what call ye them tracks? I say, beasts and horses. I ken their game: they'll have druv' off a lot of stock, and they'll reckon to squat here somewhere north. But they'll find they'll have to seek out a cannier bit nor this. Like enough, master, it'll be them chaps as Black Peter was lighting on finding."

By this time the two younger boys had ascended considerably higher up the bed of the river, and reached a large pond covered with water-fowl. They were fortunate enough to shoot four ducks, and came back laden with this grateful relief to their utter destitution. They dined as soon as the birds could be cooked; and this rest, and abundant food, invigorated and cheered them to set out once more.

They would gladly have continued to travel along the bed of the river, where they might certainly have depended on a constant supply of water, as well as wild ducks; but, on consideration, it was decided that to follow the steps of lawless robbers was a dangerous experiment, and that it was advisable still to continue the southern course over the dreary desert. Their progress was, however, rendered more tolerable, by the knowledge that they carried with them water for two days, at least; and they began to perceive there was beauty, even in that wide, solitary wilderness, though it appeared unknown to all the living world.

Yet it was not altogether without living inhabitants; for, the second day, Gerald surprised them by crying out, "A turkey! a turkey!" and spears, arrows, and boomerang, were speedily sent after the luckless bird, though the sight and the cries of the strange multitude had caused it to spring from the bush where it was feeding, to the lowest branches of a tree somewhat taller than the unvaried dwarf bushes; and from thence, rather by leaps than by flight, it ascended to the high branches, where it only exposed itself more to the weapons of the inveterate sportsmen, and was speedily brought down.

It was beyond the usual size of the English turkey, to which it bore a strong resemblance, and delighted Ruth with the idea that they were coming among poultry again. The young naturalists had more opportunity of observing this specimen than the last they had killed, and they agreed that this curious bird belonged to a family peculiar to this strange country, the *Megapodidæ*, but so nearly allied to the family of *Meleagrinæ*, that it might familiarly be called the Australian turkey.

"There can be no doubt that it is, as I formerly believed," said Mr. Mayburn, "the *Talegalla* of the prince of ornithologists, Gould. The massy claw is a striking characteristic, so conformable to the habits and haunts of the bird, enabling it to run amongst the bush, or climb trees to escape its enemies, the chief of which is the *Dingo*, or native dog, which has been rather troublesome to us from its nocturnal yelping than from its appearance. Now, concluding this to be the *Talegalla*, we must endeavor to discover the remarkable nest of this bird, which, like the ostrich, leaves its eggs to be hatched by the sun. These eggs we are told are delicious; but above all, the sight of the peculiar nest would gratify my curiosity."

They had not proceeded far, when they saw, a little out of their course, a curious mound or pyramid, which they all went up to examine. It might have been the work of man's hand, so regularly and artfully the ground, for a considerable space round it, was entirely cleared of vegetation, and the decayed grass and brushwood thus removed formed the remarkable mound. The lower part seemed to have been erected some years, the decay being complete; the upper part was fresher, as if recently renewed.

"It is apparent that this pile must be the work of years," said Mr. Mayburn, "and is probably accomplished by numbers laboring in common to raise this vast hatching oven. I am reluctant to disturb a work which has cost so much labor; but I think we might partially uncover it, to observe the internal arrangement."

The boys mounted the pile, which was six feet in height, and carefully unpacked the upper layer of the hot-bed, when they soon discovered a vast number of large white oval eggs, nearly four inches in length, which were buried standing on end, with the broad end uppermost, about ten inches apart from each other. One of the eggs was partially hatched; and the young bird might be seen, covered, not with down, but with feathers.

At the sight of the feathered bird in the shell Ruth turned away with disgust from the long-desired poultry. "Nay, Master Gerald," said she, as the boy held out the egg to her; "ye'll not catch me touching an egg like that, niver sitten on as it ought to be, and t' bird chipping ready-feathered. It's unnat'ral, and they're uncanny creaters, they are."

"Why, one of these unbroken eggs would make a custard, Ruth, as good as that of an English Turkey," said Gerald.

"That's what I'se niver credit, sir," answered she. "Not a custard fit for Christians. Them black folks 'll eat aught 'at falls in their way. Oh! Miss Marget, this is a queer, awesome country!"

They did not take any of the eggs, which appeared to be in an advanced state for hatching; but they roasted the talegalla, and found it delicious meat, though it must be remembered appetite was keen and turkey a rarity.

"Now, to-morrow morning," said Arthur, "we must make for yon distant green hills; and I trust we shall find a pleasanter region. If we could but meet with one of the rivers that flow towards the south, we might try boating again, and make our journey on an easier plan. Surely we ought to have reached the division between the northern and southern waters."

"It would be a rare hit to light on a good river," said Wilkins, "for we're gettin fearfully into t' midst of a nest of bush-rangers, and we'll ha'e little chance of slipping 'em, trailing on in this way."

The morning view of the green hills was so flattering that they indulged in the luxury of tea for breakfast, though the water was nearly expended, and then proceeded hopefully over the scrub, now diversified with various species of acacia, a Stenochylus bending under its large scarlet blossoms, and a Boronia laden with lilac flowers. Cheerfully hailing the fertile regions once more, they soon reached the steep wooded ascent of the hills, where the lively notes of the birds again gave life to the solitude; while their brilliant plumage lighted up the gray foliage of the acacia and the dark gloom of the evergreens.

After an hour's laborious ascent they reached the table-land, where the fresh breeze and the balmy fragrance announced a pleasanter region. They rested, and looked round with admiration and delight on the glorious prospect below them. On the east and on the west distant ranges of mountains were visible, between which lay a rich valley studded with lofty forest trees, while here and there arose green hills crowned with rocky masses resembling towers and fortresses, or ruined castles, in picturesque beauty.

From the western range of mountains might be seen a long, dark-green line, stretching to the south-east, which they decided must be the boundary of some large river. This line they impatiently desired to reach; and, after a short rest, they continued their march over a plain rich with rare shrubs and many new and curious grasses now in seed, amongst which they hailed with pleasure their old friend the oat-grass, with which they filled the emptied bags as they passed through it. A dark and luxuriant wood formed the green line they had seen from the heights, and crossing it, they stood on the rocky banks of a rapid river which flowed to the south-east.

For a few moments they stood silently contemplating this pleasant sight, beneath a graceful *Acacia Pendula*. Then Mr. Mayburn turned to his family, with tears in his eyes, and said, "My children, let us give thanks where thanks are due. We are again rescued from famine, captivity, or death. Let us praise His name who has brought us from the dark valley of the shadow of death, to life and hope."

All kneeled down, and the little Nakinna was the first to raise her infantine voice, saying "Our Father;" and to that simple and sublime expression of heavenly trust, Mr. Mayburn added the prayers of humility, hope, and gratitude.

"To-night we must rest," said Arthur, when the prayers were concluded; "but to-morrow we must, if possible, make two canoes."

"We will bark the trees to-night, Mr. Arthur, if you please," said Jack. "The bark will dry, and I'd like all ready to start. To-morrow's never so safe as to-day."

"Jack's right," said Wilkins. "I were feeling a bit idle mysel', but there's no sense in't; so lend us hand on an axe, and I'se be none the worse for a stroke of work."

While the young men were engaged in cutting away the bark for the shells of the canoes, and the fibres of the stringy bark for tying them, and collecting the strong gum for cement, Baldabella descended to the river, and soon speared two immense fish, which seemed to be a species of mullet; and she also brought in a quantity of the fresh-water mussels, the shells of which were so useful for domestic purposes.

The broiled fish and hastily prepared oat-cake—or damper, as Wilkins called it—formed an excellent supper; and though the nights had now become cold, even in that tropical region, they slept on beds of heath, covered with opossum cloaks, without injury or disturbance.

CHAPTER XXV

At the first merry cry of the laughing jackass, which announced the dawn as regularly as the English cock-crow, the workmen rose to labor at their hopeful undertaking; and before many hours were passed the canoes were nearly finished, and the women were busy cutting down grass for seats; when Ruth, who had left them, came rushing back through the wood, with her wildest look of distraction, crying out, "They seed me! Miss Marget, they seed me!"

"Thou unlucky lass!" exclaimed Jenny. "Where hast thou been? and who's seen thee?"

"Them black men, they seed me!" answered she. "I were cutting some oats for my hens; and I heared 'em shouting out their *coo-ee*, and when I looked round I seed a lot of 'em, a long way off, and I skriked out; I couldn't help it, Miss Marget, and then they *coo-eed* again, and off I ran. But I'se feared they heared me skrike, onyhow."

Margaret, in deep dismay, communicated this unfortunate event to her brothers, and Arthur went through the wood to reconnoitre. From a hidden retreat he observed a troop of men, still at a great distance, who appeared to be stooping down to mark some track on the ground, from which he judged Ruth's cries had been unnoticed. He returned in haste to report his observations.

"They've tracked us, sure enough," said Wilkins. "Sharp's the word, lads, we may distance 'em yet, if we work hard. We'se run down t' water at a bonnie rate."

"I will watch and report their approach, while you all work at the boats," said Margaret. "Where shall I stand, Wilkins?"

"Just here, Miss," answered he, "aback of this thick bush. There's yer peep-hole; and shout when they get close up."

Margaret's first shout was a terrific one. "Arthur! Wilkins!" she cried in a frantic voice. "Oh! God help us! whither shall we flee? The wretches are firing the wood."

The savages, taking advantage of a north wind, had fired the long dry grass—a common practice with the natives. It was already fiercely blazing, and rushing towards the wood with resistless fury. The ground on which the travellers had encamped, and the spot where the young men were working, they had fortunately cleared for beds, and for seats in the boats; and now, while Jack and Arthur finished the canoes, the rest cut down the brushwood round, and flung it into the river, leaving a space of twenty or thirty yards wide quite cleared. But beyond that rose the lofty trees, that, once blazing, must shower down destruction on them.

Already the crackling of the trees announced that the conflagration was begun in the woods, and that no time must be lost, if they hoped to escape from it. Flights of white cockatoos, of bright-colored parrots, and glittering bronze pigeons, rose screaming from their desolated homes, and affrighted opossums sprang from their nests, swung on the trees, or fell senseless with the smoke on the ground. But in this time one canoe was completed and launched, with the women, all the baggage, and Mr. Mayburn and Hugh to direct it. They had been swept down the river to a considerable distance from the fire before the second canoe, imperfectly completed, whirled off with the rest of the family, who reached their friends at a point of safety, with wild looks and scorched hair.

Then they all rested a moment, to look back on the terrific and still spreading conflagration, by the red light of which they saw the frightful outline of the dark forms, among whom, though now naked, and scarcely less dark than the rest, they distinguished the muscular and ungraceful form of Peter, which strangely contrasted with the stately, slender, and agile forms of the natives.

"He's not lit on them t' other rangers yet," said Wilkins. "That's a good job, onyhow; for, ye see, they'd horses, and we'd fairly been hunted down like foxes."

Augmented by the recent rains, the river flowed in an uninterrupted course, and before the evening and the calls of hunger induced them to arrest their flight, the grateful family believed they must have progressed twenty-five or thirty miles to the south-east, with very slight exertion, through new and lovely scenes of hill, vale, rocky mountains, and rich forests.

Then, on the margin of the river, beneath the shelter of a thick wood, they landed, to thank God for their escape, and to take rest. Mussels, a sort of cray-fish, and the river-cod, formed their supper, which was cooked in fear and trembling, lest the smoke of their fire should bring on them the savages, or the flames should spread to the brushwood, a catastrophe they now regarded with horror.

Before they set out the following morning, the canoes were completely finished, and oars and paddles added: thus their progress was safe and easy, and for three days no accident arrested their course; but on the fourth day they were compelled to land, to repair a rent in one of the canoes, and were startled at their labor by the sound of the *"coo-ee"* and an alarming rustling among the trees. Without delay the canoes were carried to the water, and all embarked; nor had they proceeded twenty yards before a large opening appeared in the wooded bank, which had evidently been cleared by fire. Here they beheld the first permanent settlement of the natives they had yet met with. Many large huts stood round, formed of boughs, and thatched with bark. Several fires were burning, around which the women and children were gathered, and a number of men, armed with spears and clubs, advanced to the bank with threatening aspect, when they saw the canoes.

Loud and angry words were heard, which Baldabella interpreted to be,—"What for white men come here? Go away! go away!" And the way in which they waved their clubs and stone tomahawks was very intimidating.

"Best take no notish of their antics, Mr. Arthur," said Wilkins; and, all agreeing in the wisdom of the counsel, they rowed forward, the men still uttering defiance against the strange invaders, and apparently amazed that their threats were received with indifference. But Ruth, whom Jenny had been ineffectually endeavoring to calm, at last could no longer control her terror, and poured forth such a succession of shrieks, that the savages seemed encouraged, and immediately directed a volley of spears against the canoes.

The swift motion happily discomfited their attempt, and but one spear took effect, seriously wounding the right arm of Ruth, which she had held up to shield her face.

A few moments carried the boats beyond the reach of the weapons, and they continued their voyage, till they believed themselves safe from the pursuit of the assailants. Mr. Mayburn and Margaret bound up the wound of Ruth, which bled profusely, and was very painful, and she could not be persuaded that she should ever recover. She declared that she was killed, and she earnestly begged that she might be buried in a church-yard, till Jenny, out of patience with her cowardice, said,—

"Be quiet, ye silly wench; where think ye we're to find a church-yard among these heathens?"

"Then they'll eat me, Jenny!" she cried, in great horror.

"Be comforted, Ruth," said Margaret; "you are under the protection of a merciful God; and as long as we are spared, we will take care of you, and even bury you if it be His will that you die before us. But, believe me, Ruth, though your wound must be painful, there is no danger for your life, unless you cry and fret yourself into a fever; so pray be patient."

"I will, Miss Marget," sobbed she. "Indeed I will, if you will feed my hens, and gather corn, whiles, for 'em. Shame on them black savages as burned down all that good corn."

The fretfulness and timidity of Ruth, however, inflamed the wound greatly; and before the next day ended, they thought it prudent to disembark at some quiet spot, where she could have shelter and rest. The banks of the river had now become rocky, gradually sloping upwards to rugged and irregular mountains, amongst which they trusted to find the shelter they desired. A sloping bank offered them a landing-place, and they disembarked, and the men bearing the light canoes on their shoulders, they left the river. Jack carried Ruth, now quite unfit for exertion, in his arms, and they were soon plunged into a maze of mountains, cut apart by narrow ravines, some of which were choked with fallen stones, and through others clear streams of water poured between rocks covered with new and graceful ferns, some of which were of gigantic size.

The further they penetrated into this maze, the more they became perplexed and embarrassed. At length, O'Brien, who had forced his way through a narrow, stone-encumbered crevice, called on them to join him in a lovely little valley, of three or four hundred yards across, encompassed with precipitous, overhanging rocks, and inaccessible, except by the narrow opening through which they had entered. It was overgrown with tall grass, amongst which they saw the useful wild oats; in one corner was a deep clear pool of water, while the surrounding rocks were covered with brushwood, from which were heard the pleasing notes of the beautiful pigeon, which the naturalists judged to be *Geophaps Scripta*, and which all agreed was the most delicious bird ever placed before gormandizing man.

There were numerous caves in these rocks, and they had only to choose one dry and light for the sick woman, and then, enjoying the luxury of many apartments, the young men selected their own bed-chambers, the boats were safely stowed into one hollow, and the ammunition placed carefully in another rocky cave; and once more the family rejoiced in a temporary resting-place.

One of the caves was chosen for a kitchen, and again the active young men dug, and lined with stones, an oven, in which Jenny baked cakes of the fresh-gathered oats, a dozen pigeons were despatched, tea was made for the invalid, and all was festivity and peace. Still, Ruth's wound, which was torn by a jagged spear, showed no appearance of healing, and it was resolved to spend some days in this beautiful and untrodden solitude, to allow the poor girl to recover, and to recruit the strength of all. But it was not possible to confine the active boys to the narrow valley, and they daily found a pretext for some expedition. One day they set out to search for the *Tea shrub*, and brought home a large quantity of leaves. Another day they scaled some of the lower rocks, to obtain gum from the numerous trees from which it exuded, and brought out all the family to see a curious tree, the trunk of which, formed like a barrel, was in the thickest part not less than thirty feet in circumference.

"It is one of the *Sterculiads*," said Mr. Mayburn, "and is, I conclude, that wonder of Australia popularly known as the Bottle Tree, or, more scientifically, this peculiar species is named *Delabechea Rupestris*. It appears to be full of gum, and is, doubtless, a great blessing to the natives."

Baldabella seemed rejoiced to see the tree, which she declared was "good, very good," chewing the branches with great enjoyment; and they found there was so much mucilage in the wood, that they cut some shavings, and poured boiling water over them, when a clear, sweet jelly was formed, most agreeable to the palate, and highly relished by the whole party.

The next expedition was suggested by Baldabella, who pointed to some bees humming among the trees, and said, "Make very good dinner—very good supper; Baldabella find his nest." Margaret taught the woman the name, honey, which she concluded was the good dinner she alluded to. Then the woman caught a bee, appearing to have no fear in handling it, and catching a piece of white down which had fallen from the breast of some bird, and was floating on the air, she touched it with gum, and stuck it upon the captive bee; she now called on the rest to follow her, and leaving the valley, she stood on an elevated rock, released the bee, and kept her keen eye fixed on the white down as it sailed away, following the flight of the insect, till she saw it settle in a tree. Then she stopped, and pointing to the trunk, ordered Jack to cut it. His axe was soon at work; the bark was stripped, and the hollow laid open: they found the tree quite filled with honey, and cutting away a considerable quantity, they carried it off on pieces of bark. The bees, which were very small, either careless in the midst of plenty, or powerless to injure, did not molest the robbers. The honey was much mingled with wax, and looked and tasted like gingerbread; but, kneaded with the bitter oat-paste, it rendered the biscuits pleasanter and more palatable.

"We really seem to have all we want here, Miss Marget," said Jenny one day. "Isn't it a pity to hurry t' poor master over these weary commons and fells? We'se be sure to have winter at some end; and hadn't we better bide here a bit till it's past?"

"It is really near the beginning of winter now, nurse," said Margaret; "it is more than a year since we left England; for it is now the end of April. I felt the air a little cold during last night, though now it is mild and balmy; and the evergreen shrubs, continual successions of flowers, noisy birds, and humming insects, make it more like an English summer than the end of autumn. This is truly a charming climate."

"It's very nice, Miss Marget," answered Jenny; "but don't you think we should be better of a change of meat? One tires of pigeons always."

"Very right, Jenny," said O'Brien; "though the observation is not new. I'll tell you what we will do: we will stalk a kangaroo for you."

"No easy task, I should think, Gerald," said Arthur, "if the kangaroo be as difficult to tire out as Wilkins tells us."

"He'll lead ye a bonnie chase," said Wilkins, "that will he. Ye'll tire afore him. Ye'd better wait till Baldabella makes an end of that net she's shaping to catch 'em. She's a long time about it."

"And we may wait another week," said Gerald, "to obtain the ignoble means of snaring the poor fellow. No; I say, let us have a regular stalking-day. Arthur, what do you say?"

"I cannot have Arthur leave us for a day," said Mr. Mayburn. "I should not feel it safe for Margaret. I can rely on his judgment and discretion."

A few days after this Jack was engaged in putting the canoes in repair, and Wilkins had gone off to the river with Baldabella, to spear fish, when the two boys entreated that they might be allowed to take spears and bows — guns being prohibited, unless Arthur was of the party, — and set out after a kangaroo; for the woods and grassy hollows among the mountains abounded in game.

On the promise to Mr. Mayburn that they would not ramble far from home, they were allowed to go; while Margaret was employed in teaching little Nakinna to read, by tracing letters and words on the sand, and Mr. Mayburn and Arthur were searching the crevices of the rocks for the rare birds and the brilliant plants which, even at that late season, were to be found in profusion.

In the middle of the day Baldabella and Wilkins returned with baskets filled with large fish, and a bag of pods filled with small beans, which they had plucked in a sandy nook near the river. Each pod contained ten or twelve beans; and Baldabella's exclamations of delight showed they were considered a prize.

"I fear," said Arthur, "that these beans are too dry at this season to be useful as good vegetables, but I fancy we might roast them, and use them as a substitute for coffee, to surprise our sportsmen when they return from their expedition."

With great satisfaction, Jenny heated the oven and roasted the beans, which were not larger than those of coffee, till they became the proper deep-brown color. They were then bruised between two stones, and boiled with a little honey, and the brown liquid wanted but milk to represent indifferent coffee. The partakers of the beverage declared it to be perfect; and Wilkins was sent back to the river to procure an abundant supply, to be roasted for future occasions.

When the evening drew near, and the family, leaving their several occupations, assembled together as usual, great anxiety filled every breast, for the two hunters had not returned. They had taken no provision with them; but this was a minor consideration, for no one could starve in this region of plenty. Nor could the chase itself lead them into danger; but there remained the ever-existing terror of the treacherous and cunning natives, or still worse, of an encounter with the lawless bush-rangers. The fears of Mr. Mayburn soon amounted to deep distress, and at length Arthur and Wilkins set out to a high point of the mountains, where they could command an extensive view, hoping to see the wanderers. But before they reached the pinnacle, sudden darkness veiled the prospect, and Arthur reluctantly adopted the only means he could then use to recall the boys. He fired his rifle, and the echoes, flung from mountain to mountain, thundered like a charge of artillery; and it seemed impossible that this report should not reach the ears of the thoughtless ramblers.

After waiting a few minutes, in the vain hope of hearing some answering shout, Arthur and Wilkins retraced their steps to the caves, depressed with the ill-success of their mission. Yet such was the deep distress of the father, that his children endeavored to conceal their own sorrow, that they might console him. He mourned as lost, not only his own brave boy, but the not less dear son of his lamented friend; and long refused to be comforted. Arthur represented to him that no more could be effected till morning; but that the youths, when they had gone astray would have probably taken refuge in one of the numerous caves in the mountains, where they would be safe during the night; and he promised that at the first gleam of light, he, Wilkins, and Jack, would set out in different directions to search for them.

"And remember, dear papa," said Margaret, "this is, happily, not a country of fierce beasts; they may enter a cave boldly, secure that they shall not disturb a lion or a bear in his den. Nor need they fear the snowstorm or the hurricane. This is a pleasant land! God seems to have created it for the abode of peace. Is it not, then, fearful wickedness that civilized man, the professed Christian should scatter the seeds of evil rather than the seeds of truth among the simple inhabitants?"

"This is, truly, a calm and blessed region," answered Mr. Mayburn. "We seem to have been Heaven-directed towards it; and if my two dear boys were again safely at my side, I confess that I should feel reluctant to leave it. In this vast and lovely solitude, where man has never before planted his destroying foot, where neither storms nor wild beasts appall, and where God himself provides our food, even as He fed the Prophet in the wilderness, we seem to be brought face to face with Him. Here we see and hear Him alone in His glorious works so richly scattered around us. Such may have been Eden, before the sin of man polluted it. In this sublime solitude, consecrated to devotion and peace, would I willingly remain conversing with my God. Here would I,—

> 'Sustain'd and soothed
> By an unfaltering trust, approach my grave,
> Like one who wraps the drapery of his couch
> About him, and lies down to pleasant dreams.'"

"It is a charming vision," said Margaret. "But look round you, papa; the fresh, the restless, the aspiring spirit of youth must be exercised and disciplined by the duties and trials of life. We may not dare to rest, dear father, till we have done our work."

"You are always rational, Margaret, and I am but a selfish visionary," answered Mr. Mayburn. "Even now my idle dreams have turned away my thoughts from my heavy and real calamity—the loss of my children."

"Depend on't we'se find t' lads all right, master," said Wilkins; "and they'll tell us what a good laugh they had when they heared that grand salute we gave 'em amang these rattling hills."

CHAPTER XXVI

Sleep fled from all the sorrowful family, and they gladly saw the morning light which would enable them to set out to track the unlucky boys. The three men chose the high pinnacle from whence Arthur had fired the preceding evening for a rendezvous, and fixed a white cross of peeled rods against the dark foliage of a gum-tree, that stood tall and conspicuous on the summit, as a land-mark. From thence Arthur proceeded directly north amidst the intricacies of the mountains, while Jack went off at the right-hand, and Wilkins at the left. It was agreed that they should meet at the same spot in the evening, if the search was not successful before then. Arthur carried one of the guns; the other being left with Mr. Mayburn, that he might fire it as a signal, in case of alarm; while Arthur proposed, if he succeeded in discovering the fugitives, to recall the other two men by firing his gun.

Arthur's share of the work was certainly the most toilsome. At one moment he was climbing over some lofty rock; the next, he was searching for a pass amidst inaccessible heights; then winding through tortuous gorges, till his head became so bewildered that it was only when he observed the course of the sun, or caught sight of the happy signal of the white cross, that he was able to determine his position. Several times, from some elevation, he shouted loudly the names of the absent boys, but none answered. The day wore away, and he gladly rested for a short time beneath a fig-tree, still bearing a quantity of ripe fruit, while the ground was strewn with the decayed figs, on which flocks of bronze pigeons, yellow cockatoos, and rose-colored parrots, were busily feeding. These birds seemed to confide in Arthur's forbearance, for they continued to enjoy their feast without evincing any alarm, except by a vehement greeting, in their several notes, as if they inquired his business at their board.

The arched roots of the fig-tree afforded him an easy mode of access to the upper branches, where he filled his straw hat with the fruit, and then continued his walk, enjoying the refreshment; for the figs, though not luscious, were ripe and juicy.

"I will give one more shout," thought he; and his voice, cleared and strengthened by his refreshment, rang through the echoing mountains. He waited for five minutes; still there was no reply; but his eye caught a light smoke among the mountains. It might be the fires of the natives he thought; but even were it so, the boys might have fallen into their hands, and no time must be lost in rescuing them. He made ready his gun, and, still bearing his load of figs, he directed his course briskly towards the suspected spot. But it was most difficult to attain the place from whence the smoke seemed to proceed, and he wandered for an hour amidst intricate windings, making many unsuccessful attempts to penetrate to the spot, till at length he came to a small hollow, surrounded by dungeon-like walls, where a fire of dry wood was smouldering, but no one was near it.

"Hugh! Gerald!" he shouted; and at the sound of his voice his brother appeared, crawling feebly from a hole in the rocks.

"Hugh, my boy, are you hurt?" asked Arthur, in a hurried tone: "and where is Gerald?"

Hugh pointed to the hole from whence he had issued, and in a hoarse, weak voice, said, "Water! water!" Scarcely conscious what he did, Arthur pressed the juice of a fig into the parched mouth of the boy, who murmured, "Thank God! But, oh, Arty! can you get any water for poor Gerald?"

Putting more figs into his hand, Arthur stooped down to the low entrance, and passed into a small dark hollow, where Gerald was stretched out, almost insensible, and near him lay dead a huge kangaroo. Arthur gave the poor boy the only refreshment he had to offer, the juice of the figs; but he seemed in a much more feeble state than Hugh, and when his kind friend with difficulty got him out into the open air, he saw with consternation that his leg was bound up with a handkerchief, through which the blood was oozing.

"How did this happen, Hugh?" asked Arthur, before he ventured to examine the wound.

"It was the kangaroo," answered he; "and then, when we had killed it, we were far too ill to eat it, though we have had no food since we left home."

"I cannot tell what I must do," said Arthur. "It will be impossible to get you home to-night, feeble as you are; and papa will now be in alarm at my absence."

"But you will not leave us again, Arty," said Hugh, sobbing. "I fear dear Gerald will die. I dare not remain alone any longer."

"I must leave you for a short time," answered Arthur. "I think I shall be able to summon Wilkins and Jack to us; then they can search for water, and carry Gerald home."

Hugh burst into tears, and said, "But the bush-rangers—I cannot tell you all, Arthur, my head is so bad. There are bush-rangers; we have seen them; they will meet you, and they will come and kill us. At least, carry Gerald back to the cave."

In increased alarm, Arthur conveyed Gerald into the dismal cave, and leaving them all the remainder of the figs, he waited to hear no more, but hurried off with all speed towards the rendezvous, looking round as he went on, for some spring or pool from which he could procure water for the suffering boys. When he reached a high rock, not far from the rendezvous, he ventured to fire his gun, and was immediately answered by the shouts of the men, who, following the sound and flash of the gun, soon came up to him.

"Where are they? Oh, Mr. Arthur, have you not found them?" said Jack.

Arthur, in a few words, told the distressing story; and night being now at hand, it was agreed that Jack should return to appease the uneasiness of the family, while Wilkins should accompany Arthur back to the two anxious boys, with whom they would remain till daylight, and then bring them home. Wilkins undertook to procure water for them from a pool at a little distance, where Jack and he rested, and where they had cleaned out two large gourds they had found, and converted them into water-bottles.

These gourds were a great treasure; they carried them to the pool, filled them with fresh-water, and, after drinking themselves, hastened forward with all the vigor that remained to them after the day's fatigue, towards the spot where the boys were lying, but did not reach it till night had made it most difficult to discover it. The joy of the poor wanderers was excessive when they saw their friends arrive, bringing the refreshment they so much desired. Gerald was already somewhat revived by the figs; and after he and Hugh had drunk some water, they began to desire more substantial food; and it was not long before Wilkins had cut off, and broiled, some steaks of kangaroo venison, of which all the hungry party partook with great enjoyment. Still the boys were too much weakened and exhausted to enter into any details of their adventure that night; and when Arthur and Wilkins had collected heath for beds and covering—for the nights were now chill,—they all crept into the cave, and slept soundly till awakened by the rude, early greeting of the laughing jackass.

Then, after more kangaroo steaks, Arthur made an examination of Gerald's lacerated and bruised leg, which Hugh had previously bandaged to the best of his skill. They could now spare water to wash the wound, and the bandages were replaced by some made from Arthur's handkerchief; and Wilkins having cut down the spreading bough of a fig-tree, Gerald and the kangaroo were placed side by side upon it, and borne by Arthur and Wilkins. The procession moved slowly and silently, Hugh looking round anxiously as he preceded the litter, in dread of the terrible bush-rangers.

The rugged mountain-road tired the bearers greatly, but long before they reached the rendezvous, they saw a figure standing before the dark gum-tree, and a loud "Halloo!" brought Jack to meet and assist them. He had considerately brought with him a bucket of water; and they rested and refreshed themselves, before they completed their toilsome journey. But fatigue was forgotten when they all met again in the quiet valley; Mr. Mayburn and Margaret wept for joy, and though nurse did not fail to chide them as "bad boys," she fondled and nursed the wanderers, and produced for their comfort cockatoo-stew, flavored with wild herbs that resembled parsley and marjoram, and mixed with the beans they had got on the banks of the river.

"Keep a sentinel at the pass, Arthur," said Hugh. "We shall be watched and tracked; there will be scouts all around us. It is a miracle that we have arrived here safely."

"Oh! Master Hugh, honey, is it that good-to-nought Black Peter?" asked Jenny.

"Worse than that, I am sorry to say, nurse," answered he; "for there are dozens of Black Peters ready to snap us up. But don't look so sorrowful, Meggie, and I'll just tell you how it all happened. That big old fellow," pointing to the kangaroo, "kept us trotting after him for hours and hours, and always when we got him within reach of a spear or an arrow, he bounded off like a race-horse, and you could not say whether he hopped, or galloped, or flew. It was a beautiful sight, but very vexatious. At last we got desperate; we were tired and hungry, and we determined to have him; so we parted, that we might attack him on both sides, and force him to stand at bay. It was a capital plan, and turned out very well. We chased him into that queer little dungeon-like hollow where you found us. He flew round and round, but he guarded the entrance, and he could not escape, and at last we drove him into a corner, pierced mortally with our spears. I wanted Gerald to wait till the beast was weakened with loss of blood; but he was in a hurry to finish, so he rushed on with his drawn knife, and I followed to help him. But when the brave old fellow found he had not a chance, he faced round, and with his fore-feet—his arms, I should say—he seized me, and gave me a heavy fall. Gerald was then behind, and plunged his knife into him, on which the desperate creature struck out with his powerful hind claw, and tore and bruised poor Gerald, as you see.

"I was soon on my feet again, and then I speedily despatched the beast; but I should never like to kill another in that way; it was just like murdering one's grandfather. Then I turned to poor Gerald. Oh, Margaret! if you had seen how he bled! and how frightened I was till I got his wounds tied up! He was very thirsty, and begged me to get him some water, or he thought he must die. So off I set, keeping a sharp eye on our den, that I might find it again. I mounted a crag, and looked about me till I saw flocks of birds, all hovering over one place, a good stretch from me. 'That's my aim,' thought I, and on I dashed, over rocks and valleys, straight forward, till I saw before me a grand silver-looking lake, covered with ducks and swans; while regiments of birds, like cranes and pelicans, with other unknown species, were drawn up round it.

"I could look at nothing else but the birds for some time, I was so charmed, and I planned directly to bring papa to the place the very next day; but remembering poor Gerald's condition, I went forward, and looking round to scan the grassy plains between the mountains and the lake, I was astonished to see a number of large animals grazing, which were certainly not kangaroos, but real, downright quadrupeds, walking on their four legs. 'Here's a grand new field of natural history,' thought I. 'Yes, we must certainly take up our quarters here.' But, halloo! what did I see that moment, hobbling ungracefully up to me, but our old friend Charlie Grey!"

"Charlie Grey! Edward Deverell's favorite horse!" exclaimed Margaret. "You have been dreaming, Hugh; it could not be!"

"It could be, Meggie, for it really was he," answered Hugh. "Do you remember how we used to feed the handsome fellow with bits of bread on the voyage? It came into my mind just then, and I plucked a handful of oats, and held them out, calling 'Charlie! Charlie!' Poor, dear old fellow! he could not trot up to me as his heart wished, but he limped forward as well as his hobbles would allow him."

"Hobbles!" exclaimed Wilkins; "then he'd been nabbed by them bush-rangers."

"Sure enough he had, Wilkins," continued Hugh; "and there were five or six strong black draught-horses, besides a herd of bullocks and cows; every beast, I'll venture to say, stolen from our friend Edward Deverell. Well, I had forgot all about poor Gerald and the water, and was feeding and stroking Charlie, when I saw he had a halter on his neck; and I thought I might as well just cut the hobbles, mount him, ride off to take Gerald behind me, and away we would gallop home. But the water!—I had forgotten that we had no vessel to contain water; but, fortunately, at the edge of the lake, near a place where a fire had been kindled, I saw piles of large mussel-shells. I filled two, placed them in my hat, and slung it round my neck. Then I pulled out my knife, and stooped down to cut Charlie's bonds; but just then such yells fell on my ears that I started up, and saw on one of the heights a line of fierce looking men, attired in the conspicuous yellow dress of the convicts. Their guns were directed towards me, and there was no longer time to release and mount Charlie; in fact, I had not presence of mind to decide on doing it, but ran off as fast as my legs would carry me, just in time to escape a volley of shots from the wretches. Thankful that I had escaped unhit, I fled desperately, never looking behind me till I reached poor Gerald, whom I found very ill and restless, parched with thirst; and there was scarcely a teaspoonful of water left in the shells, from my rapid flight. I was telling him my story, when we heard a tremendous report of fire-arms, and we trembled to think the villains were pursuing me; but now I conclude it must have been your signal-shot, an idea which never occurred to me in my distracted state. I then got Gerald into that little hole, and dragged the great kangaroo after him, that nothing suspicious might be in sight if they followed me; though I hardly dared to hope that our den should escape their observation. Dear Gerald groaned and tossed about all night. How much I did grieve that I had not succeeded in bringing him the water! Nor was our condition improved next morning, for I was afraid to venture out beyond the hollow, round which I sought in vain for any fruit or juicy herb to cool our parched mouths. Gerald, in all his agony, was twice as brave as I was; and if he had been the sound one, I know he would have risked any danger to obtain help for me."

"Botheration! Hugh, my boy," said Gerald, "didn't I know all the time that it was my moans and groans that made you turn soft and sob like a girl? I couldn't help grunting out like a pig shut out of a cabin on a rainy night; and then you grunted and cried too, for company. We were a pair of pleasant, jolly fellows all day, Meggie, as you may easily suppose. Day, indeed, do I say! why, we thought it must be a week, at least! As night came on, it grew very cold, and Hugh scrambled out to gather a few sticks together to make a fire before our cave. Before he came back, I heard the crack! crack! of a gun running from rock to rock; and when I saw Hugh, I tried to speak to him; and then I know no more till I felt the cold fig-juice on my dry tongue. Won't I like figs as long as I live; and won't I have an alley of fig-trees in my garden when I locate—squat, I mean, and build a mansion, and marry."

"Mrs. O'Brien may possibly object to the *Ficus* in her garden, Gerald," said Arthur;—"it is not a comely tree in its proportions; but the question may safely rest awhile. Now, Hugh, after you heard the gun?"

"Then I threw more wood upon the fire," answered he, "that the smoke might be seen, and crept back into the cave; for I could not get over the fear that the shot might have come from the bush-rangers; and I had thus given them a signal to our hiding-place. Think of my joy when I heard the voices which I never expected to hear again!"

Jenny had wept abundantly at the tale of suffering, and she now endeavored to show her sympathy by placing before the fatigued and hungry boys another collation, consisting of bean-coffee sweetened with honey, and sweet oat-cakes; and certainly, if Mr. Mayburn had not interfered with grave sanitary admonitions, the boys were in danger of eating themselves into a fever.

"I have thought much on this unfortunate adventure," said Mr. Mayburn, when they met together the next morning. "It is a fearful reflection to know that we are in the midst of a horde of banditti, ready to intercept our least movement. What shall we do? We appear to be in safety here; but this lovely spot would become a prison to you all, if you were forbidden to move from it. Arthur, what do you say? Wilkins, my good man, do you think we are quite safe?"

"Not ower and above, I say, master," answered Wilkins; "they're just ranging hereabouts, to pick up recruits among them fools of black fellows, and to keep out of t' way of them as they've pillaged; and they're ripe for any thieving or ill-doing as falls in their way. But they'll not sattle long; they'll range off down south to turn their beasts into brandy, and we'se be better at their heels nor afore 'em."

"I think, papa, Wilkins is right," said Arthur. "We may rest a good time here without any sacrifice of comfort. We have grain and water at hand; pigeons and cockatoos in our own preserve, asking us to roast them; an excellent store of honey, coffee, and tea, as we are pleased to name the Australian representatives of these luxuries; spacious and dry lodgings, and fresh air. Certainly, with occasional forays, conducted with due prudence, we shall have abundant and excellent provision for any length of time. This monstrous kangaroo ought to supply us with meat for many days; and I think we might dry part of it in the sun, to resemble the South-American *charqui*."

"It is an admirable idea, Arthur," said Mr. Mayburn; "we shall thus avoid the sin of wasting the good gifts of Providence. I have read a description of the process; I know the meat must be cut in slices, and I should like to assist you in carrying out the plan, though, practically, I am inexperienced. The first difficulty appears to be, how to avoid the destruction of the skin in slicing it."

"Why, papa, we skinned him this morning," replied Hugh. "The skin is already cleaned and spread to dry; we shall rub it with a little fat, to render it pliable, and then we shall have a blanket or a cloak of inestimable value."

"True, my son; I had forgotten that preliminary operation," said Mr. Mayburn. "But still I cannot understand how we shall obtain the large slices;—the bones, the form of the animal, present great obstacles."

"Leave it to the experienced, papa," said Margaret. "Wilkins knows how to slice up a kangaroo."

It was capital employment and amusement for the active to cut up the huge animal into thin slices, which were spread out on the bush, and the ardent sun of the climate, even at this late season, soon dried the meat perfectly; and Margaret wove grass bags to pack it in; and thus several days passed without alarm or annoyance; and with due care and attention the wound of Gerald was perfectly healed.

CHAPTER XXVII

After a few days more had elapsed, the close confinement became irksome to all. Baldabella, accustomed to a free, roving life, pleaded her great desire to fish by moonlight; and as there was less danger for her than for the white men, this was permitted, and she returned safely with abundance of fish to increase the store of provisions. Then Hugh and Gerald, unlucky as their last expedition had been, begged humbly that they might be allowed to put their noses out beyond the bars of their cage.

"No, no! unruly boys," answered Margaret; "you have a spacious *pleasaunce* around you; be content and thankful to enjoy it."

"Then surely we may climb the woods at the side?" said Hugh. "We want to find the nests of the strange birds we hear above us. No harm can befall us in our own domain; it will be only like running up a ladder, the brush is so thick and low. Come along, Gerald, and let us inspect the wonders of our aviary."

Mr. Mayburn would really have liked himself to have a peep into the many holes and crannies of the rocks, which sent forth such multitudes of birds, and he could not object to the expedition. The agile boys made no delay, but, clinging to the bushes, sprung up the almost perpendicular side of the mountain, disturbing the domestic peace of the tender pigeons, provoking the voluble abuse of the noisy cockatoos, and finally, at the summit, regarding with awe, at a respectful distance, the eyrie of the dark eagle, which, with the fire of its fierce eyes, defied their approach.

"We will avoid any offence to *Aquila*," said Hugh. "We might come to the worse again, Gerald. But where are you mounting now?"

"Only to the peak, Hugh," answered he. "I should like to have a peep round, to find out what our neighborhood is." And the active boy soon gained the highest point, and stood there, an Australian Mercury, on the "heaven-kissing hill."

"What a wonderful sight!" he cried out. "Do come up, Hugh, to see these heights, and hollows, and windings,—a rocky chaos! It is like the beginning of a new world!" Then turning round to observe the scene at his left hand, he suddenly cried out, in a tone of alarm,—"Halloo! I'm in for it now!" and as he hastily descended from his elevated position, the report of fire-arms, multiplied as usual among the mountains, proved that the chaotic solitude was not free from the visitation of man.

"Down! down! hurry to them, Hugh!" continued Gerald, now safe from the shots. "Tell them to gather in the charqui, and the firewood, and all things scattered about. Above all, let Ruth carry off the poultry, and gag that noisy cock; the rangers are at our heels. I shall take up my abode in this darling little oven behind the bushes, and if they should mount the ramparts, I shall be able to act spy. No words about it, but be off. It is safer here than down below."

There was indeed no time for Hugh to delay, for many traces of habitation were scattered over the valley. Buckets stood at the well; linen was spread to dry; the charqui was exposed on the bushes; knives and axes were lying about, and the hens and chickens, and men and women, were all out, enjoying the open air. When Hugh dropped among them, breathless and pale, to tell his vexatious tale, they had somewhat anticipated the danger, from hearing the report of the fire-arms; and all hands were already employed to endeavor to restore to the busy valley the wild and solitary aspect of undisturbed nature. The fowls were collected into their coop, which was placed in a dark hollow; and though they did not follow Gerald's advice, and gag the tell-tale cock, they threw a large cloak over the coop, and chanticleer, duped into the belief that it was night, folded his wings, and, mounted on his perch, resigned himself to repose amidst his family.

When they had restored to the lately populous vale as natural an appearance as circumstances would allow, they all withdrew into the largest cave, and filled up the entrance, with an appearance of artful disorder, with rocky fragments, very impatient for Gerald's return to report the extent of the danger to which they were exposed, and the best mode of escaping from it. But after waiting a considerable time in their gloomy prison, weary of compelled inaction, every heart was filled with anxiety at the protracted absence of the adventurous boy. Three hours elapsed, and after listening and looking through the crevices of the rock in vain, Arthur was on the point of venturing out to ascend the cliffs himself, when Gerald's voice was heard whispering through a narrow opening, "Is it a serpent or a genie you think I am, to glide through this peep-hole? Open sesame!"

There was no time lost in admitting the welcome visitor. "Now, then!" said he; "quick! quick! the foe is at the gate. Now, my boys, do the thing nately, as we Irish say. We mustn't build it up like a wall you see, Jack."

It was not built like a wall; but by the united strength of the party, an immense mass of rock was rolled before the opening, which nearly closed it, the pendent branches from above concealing the fissures, and affording light and a means of making observations in safety.

"Now, Gerald," said Margaret, "I beseech you to tell me what is the meaning of all this alarm?"

"All my fault; my ill luck again, Meggie," answered he. "I would erect myself like a statue at the very summit of the mountains; and from thence I saw on a plain below half a dozen fellows mounted on horseback, whom I recognized, by their canary-colored garments, to be those wicked convicts. I sank down from my eminence in a moment, but not before the hawk-eyed rogues had seen me and fired. I was not hit; but I expected they would be after me if they could climb through the brush, so I crept into a snug little hollow just below the peak, arranged my leafy curtains in an elegant manner, and waited to receive my company so long that I had really dropped asleep, and was only awaked by the rough, coarse voices of men swearing and using language which I have done my best to forget altogether.

"They seemed to be in a great rage, and one wicked wretch swore dreadfully and said, 'It's the same ugly little cove as we blazed at afore. He's a spy sent out by them p'lice, and he's off to inform against us. We'll burn him alive if we lay hands on him.'

"I didn't want to be burnt alive, so I crept into a corner, and lay still as a mouse.

"'T' other chap were bigger, I say,' growled another fellow.

"'Haud yer jaw,' answered the first; 'think ye they keep a pack of young hounds like this to point free rangers? But where's he slunk?'

"'I say, Bill,' called out a third voice, 'look ye down here. It's a snug, cunning hole; will 't be t' p'lice office, think ye?'

"'How'd they get at it, man?' replied Bill. 'Dost thee think they've got wings to flee down?'

"'I'se warrant ye, we'll somehow find a road into it,' said the first voice. 'We'se try, at ony end; for we'll have to clear our way afore we set out on another spree. I'se about tired of eating flesh, now t' brandy's all swallowed; and if we could light on Black Peter, we'd be off on some grand job to set us up again.'

"'Halloo! lads! what's this?'

"Then I heard oaths, and strange screams, and blows, and something heavy flopped past my den, screaming; and wasn't I in a grand fright to think that one of these rogues had found such a ready road down to our grounds. But I soon heard the men above me again, cursing the venomous bird; and I guessed then that they had fallen in with our friend *Aquila*, and, perhaps, been worsted. I ventured cautiously to look down, and saw the poor eagle fluttering and hopping about below, half killed by the brutes no doubt; but by degrees I heard their voices dying away, and was sure they were withdrawing. Then I took courage, and slipped down my rude ladder as briskly as a lamp-lighter, and was with you, only pausing a moment to look at the poor eagle as I passed, lying crouched in a corner covered with blood, and extending a broken wing. And now, Arthur, don't you think our citadel is in danger?"

"Indeed I do, Gerald," answered Arthur. "All we can do is to keep closely hidden as long as we can, and then to fight for our dear friends who cannot fight for themselves. We have weapons,—spears, arrows, and two rifles; and we have a capital position for defending the weak. If there be no more than six men, we will defy them."

"That will be capital," said Gerald,—"a regular siege. How is the castle provisioned, Jenny?"

"Why, lucky enough, Master Gerald," answered she, "we fetched in here, because it was nighest at hand, all the dried meat, and the skin, and we filled the buckets before we brought them from the well; and that's just what we have, barring a few cakes; for one never looked for being shut up here like. There's all the oats, and the tea and coffee, and the firewood, are left in what we called our kitchen."

"We'se do," said Wilkins, "we'se soon sattle their business, I reckon," looking grimly at the edge of his knife as he sharpened it upon a stone; adding, "And how and about them guns, captain? Who's to work 'em?"

"I shall take one myself," answered Arthur; "and if I thought I could trust to your discretion, Wilkins, I would put the other into your hands."

"You may trust me for bringing down my bird," said the man; "that's what I were always up to, or I hadn't been here."

"What I mean you to understand by discretion, Wilkins," said Arthur, "is, that you are not to fire till I order you; and then to *wing*, not to bring down your bird."

"Why, what's the good of that?" remonstrated Wilkins; "it's like giving a rogue a ticket of leave, just to turn a thief into a murderer; that's what ye'll get for being soft. I ken my chaps: ye'd better make an end on 'em."

"It would be unjust and inhuman," said Mr. Mayburn. "These mistaken men may not intend to hurt any of us."

"Except to burn me alive, sir," said Gerald.

"That, I apprehend, my boy," answered Mr. Mayburn, "was but an exaggerated form of speech. But, hark! what noise do I hear?"

Sounds were heard like the rolling of stones. Arthur commanded silence, as every thing depended on their remaining watchful and still. Then voices were distinguished, and, through the green pendent branches, men were seen in the tranquil valley,—men in the felon's marked dress of grey and yellow, ferocious in aspect, coarse and blasphemous in language. Mr. Mayburn shuddered as he heard, for the first time, the oaths and defiant words of hardened infidels; and the good man kneeled down to pray that God would visit with a ray of grace these lost sinners.

"Ay! ay!" cried one, "here are the tracks of the gentry coves: and look ye, Jem, here's a woman's bit of a shoemark. What will they be acting here, I'd like to know. If we could fall on that saucy lad now, I'd just wring his neck about for him."

Gerald made up a queer face at Hugh, but they did not dare to laugh.

"Will they have oughts of cash with them?" growled another man. "What do we want with women and lads?"

"To trade with 'em, man," answered the other; "to swop 'em yonder among t' squatters for cash down. We'll thrust some of them black fellows forward to bargain for us; they're easy wrought on to do a job like that. But where can their den be? they're surely flitted."

Examining every open cave and hollow in the surrounding rocks, the men, using the most violent and abusive language, searched the little valley in vain; and the anxious prisoners began to hope that they would soon be wearied out and retire, when suddenly they were appalled by a shrill triumphant crow from the little bantam cock, which had probably discovered the deception practised on him. A momentary silence was followed by shouts and loud laughter, as the invaders rushed to the prison-house of the impatient fowls.

Wilkins muttered unspeakable words, and darted a furious glance at Ruth; and Gerald, with a deep low groan, whispered, "A traitor in the camp!" while Ruth climbed up to an opening, in great alarm, to observe the fate of her beloved pets. That was soon determined. The voice of the unlucky bird had plainly pointed out its abode; the stony prison was forced open; a crowing, a screaming, and a fluttering were heard; two of the fowls were seen to fly awkwardly to the bushes, above the reach of the marauders, and chanticleer was beheld by his distracted mistress, swung round lifeless, with his head grasped by his destroyer.

At this cruel spectacle, the simple girl could no longer control her feelings. She uttered a piercing shriek; Jenny sprang on her too late to stop the indiscretion, and dragged her from the opening, shaking her violently, and even provoked so far as to administer a little sound boxing of the ears, declaring that the girl ought to be hanged; while Wilkins, with ill-repressed fury, shook his hand at the unfortunate offender, and then said, "It's all up now! Stand to yer guns, my hearties; we'se have a tight bout on 't."

"Ay, man the walls!" cried Gerald, —

> "'Hold hard the breath, and bend up every spirit
> To his full height! On, on, ye noble English!'"

"Quieter ye are, t' better, Mr. Gerald," said Wilkins. "What say ye, Mr. Arthur, if we fix on our port-holes; and then, if we pick out our chaps, we'll soon thin 'em."

"By no means," said Mr. Mayburn. "Such a proceeding would be unfair; the men would not even see their enemies."

"An ambush is always fair in the strategy of war," said Hugh. "These men are invaders, papa, and we have a right to drive them off."

The affair soon came to a crisis; the cry of Ruth had not passed unnoticed. The men rushed up to the fortress, and with stones and clubs endeavored to force an entrance. A volley of shots and arrows drove them back, wounded, and furious in their language; but when the firing ceased, they took courage, and again advanced to renew the attempt. This time aim was taken, and two men fell dead, or desperately wounded; and they retired once more, and entered into some consultation unheard by their opponents. Then a villainous-looking fellow cried out, in a taunting manner,

"I say, ye cowardly chaps, show yer faces, and 'liver yersel's up afore yer forced to it; we'se use ye well, and keep ye till ye raise cash to pay yer ransom. Else, mark my words, if ye send any more of yer murdering shots, we'll take ye at last, and twist all yer necks while yer living."

"Mistaken man!" cried Mr. Mayburn, "why will you provoke the wrath of God by causing desolation and slaughter among his glorious works? Know you not that for all these things God will bring you to judgment?"

"Halloo!" cried the wretch; "what! ye've gotten a missioner amang ye. He'll do precious little harm."

"His only desire is to do good," said Arthur. "But you are mistaken if you think us cowards. We have brave men among us, who will not submit to any treaty with convicts. We have nothing to give you; we are shipwrecked voyagers, who have only saved our guns, and with them we will defend our lives and liberty. We do not wish to injure you if you will leave us in peace; and you have neither means nor numbers to overcome us."

"We'se see about that," answered the man. "We'se soon raise force to burn or starve ye out."

Another consultation succeeded; and finally they departed, leaving the besieged under the disagreeable impression that they had only departed to procure a reinforcement.

"What a different set of fellows Robin Hood's Free Rangers were," said Hugh. "Gerald and I have many a time longed to have lived in merry Sherwood."

"Lawlessness inevitably leads to crime," said Mr. Mayburn. "I fear the halo of chivalry and romance blinds us as to the real character of those outlaws."

"Yes, Hugh," said Arthur; "if your bold archers of Sherwood were to attempt their troublesome frolics in these days, the police would soon arrest their course, and we should see Robin Hood and his merry men placed on the treadmill."

"There's no time to talk about treadmills, Mr. Arthur," said Wilkins. "T' boats is safe; and what say ye if we be off? They'll not be back yet a bit; for they'll have to gather up them black fellows and talk 'em ower wi' lots of lies; but if we were out of this queer hole and just free-like on t' water, we'd manage to distance yon awkward scamps yet. But we ought to start off-hand."

"My good man," said Mr. Mayburn, "I feel in greater safety here than if I were wandering through the labyrinths of these mountains, where we might any moment be surprised and captured."

"We must send out a scout," said Arthur. "Who will be the safest? I object to no one but Gerald, who would inevitably rush into the camp of the enemy."

Gerald bowed to the compliment, and Wilkins said, "I've a sort of notion, Mr. Arthur, as how Baldabella would suit better nor ony of us. Ye see, these jins are used to spying work."

When Baldabella fully understood the important service required of her, she started up, ready at once to undertake it, and as soon as the heavy barrier was moved, glided through the aperture, and fled lightly on her errand. During her absence, the rest made ready all their burdens again for recommencing their pilgrimage; and the time seemed incredibly short till the woman returned with a bright countenance, saying,—"Bad men go much far; smoke for black fellows come. White man go away now; very hush; no see he be gone."

Reassured by her words, the family emerged from their stronghold. The men pulled down the stones they had piled to conceal the canoes, brought them out, and then, heavily laden, commenced their march. But at the moment of departure a loud clucking of the escaped fowls arrested the weeping Ruth, who summoned, by calls and scattered grains, the small remainder of her charge,—two fowls; which she placed once more in their coop, and with a lightened heart, disregarded this addition to her burden, and followed the procession, which was now led by Baldabella, who had discovered the shortest road through the windings of the mountains to the banks of the river. When the welcome stream was seen before them, the boats were once more launched and laden, and on the smooth but rapid river they were quickly carried from the scene of danger.

"That rogue who argued with you, Arthur," said Gerald, "was the very fellow that threatened to burn me alive, and sure enough, if we had surrendered to them, we should all have been piled up for a bonfire. Don't you think so, Wilkins?"

"Why, Master Gerald," answered he, "I'll not say that, 'cause as how they could have made nought of our dead bones. Money's what they look to: they'd sell us, plunder us, strip us of every rag we have, but, barrin' we went again 'em, and wrought 'em up, mad-like, they'd hardly trouble to burn us. But I'll not say how it might be if they turned us ower to them hungry black fellows; they'd likely enough roast and eat us, but white chaps has no stomach for meat of that sort."

"Whither can we flee to avoid these desperate cannibals?" said Mr. Mayburn. "Do you conceive, Wilkins, that the river is really the safest course?"

"Safe enough, master," answered the man, "so long as we stick to our boats, and can keep our jaws at work. But we'se want meat, and them black fellows gets thicker farther south. We'se fall in with mony an ill-looking lot on 'em as we run down; and likely enough, we'se have to rattle a shot at 'em nows and thens."

"God forbid that we should be compelled to shed more blood," said Mr. Mayburn. "I feel my heart oppressed with sorrow when I behold the sin and ignorance of these people, and, alas! I know not how to alleviate it: I can only pray for them."

"We will trust that our prayers may avail with a merciful God," said Margaret; "and if we should be permitted to reach the estate of Edward Deverell, we will all labor, papa, to diffuse instruction around us; and in His own good time, I trust, God will spread the light of His truth to the remotest corner of these yet barbarous regions. I feel already as if I saw Daisy Grange plainly before us."

"There's mony a hundred mile atween us and them ye talk on," said Wilkins, morosely; "and I'se be cast away sure enough when ye turn in among them squatters. They're all sharp enough to put their claws on an idle vagabond like me, and send him back to chains and hard commons."

"That shall never be, Wilkins," replied Hugh. "It is settled that you and I are never to part; and if Edward Deverell should refuse to receive you, we will squat by ourselves; like Robinson Crusoe and his man Friday, build a hut, and shoot kangaroos."

Arthur laughed at the plan of a separate establishment, and assured Wilkins of certain protection in that home they pined to reach; and a calm and pleasant hope now filled every heart, as hours and days passed easily while they sailed down the broad river undisturbed by cares or dread, till the failure of provisions and a great change in the scenery roused them from their pleasant dream.

"This is a melancholy and desert-like heath," said Arthur, as he looked beyond the low banks upon a wide extent grown over with the low entangled brush; "but we must make a foraging party to replenish our baskets. I can see on some marshy patches a scattering of wild oats, and we may hope to find some of the feathered gluttons that feed on them."

"And please to bring some tea-leaves, if you can find them, Mr. Arthur," said Jenny; "I get on badly without a drop of tea, such as it is."

"Now, boys," said Arthur, "get out the axes. We must clear a place among the reeds for Margaret and my father; then we will moor the canoes safely, and leave a guard to watch them, while we go off on our exploring expedition."

CHAPTER XXVIII

A nook was soon cleared, where the family landed, and the light canoes were drawn close to shore, and moored to the canes. Then the fine rushes were cut down and spread to form seats for Margaret and her father; and Arthur, with Wilkins and Jack, set out with guns and bows, leaving Hugh and O'Brien to guard the encampment. Baldabella then went off with her spear, and soon pierced several large fish; and while Mr. Mayburn took out his book, and Margaret talked to Nakinna, Jenny and Ruth made a fire to broil the fish.

Already the cooking began to smell temptingly, and the hungry little girl was dancing joyfully about the fire, watching till the repast was ready, when Baldabella suddenly threw down her spear, started forward, and laying her hand on Margaret's arm, she held up her finger in an attitude of warning, and bent forward as if listening. Then drawing a deep sigh, she whispered through her closed teeth—"Baldabella hear him, missee; black fellow come—one, two, many—eat missee—eat Nakinna—burn all!" Then snatching up her child, she gazed wildly round, and her fears were confirmed a minute after, by the fatal cry ringing through the reeds, which announced the proximity of the dreaded natives.

The boys, who were rambling about among the bamboos, searching for nests, at the vexatious sound of the *coo-ee*, left their spoil to hurry to the encampment, and entreat their father and sister to embark at once and seek safety; but Mr. Mayburn could not be persuaded to leave the absent.

"Then let us make a sally to bring them up," said Gerald; "no time should be lost; we have our bows to defend ourselves, though they carried the guns with them."

"But they must have heard the *coo-ee* as well as we did," replied Hugh, "and, depend on it, they are on the road back to us. I say, nurse, we must eat our fish cold; just pull that fire to pieces."

Ruth the unlucky, always officious, took a bucket of water and threw it over the blazing sticks; on which a dark, dense smoke rose up from them like a column, and the cries of the natives were now heard loud and triumphant.

"Oh! Ruth, Ruth!" said Hugh, "you have sent up a signal-rocket to them. Margaret and papa, do step into the canoe; there is more safety on the river than here."

"I do not see that, Hugh," answered Mr. Mayburn; "the water is so shallow here, that they could wade to us, and we must not run down the stream and leave our kind foragers."

A loud rustling and crackling among the reeds prevented more words; the boys would have sent their arrows into the thicket, but Margaret besought, and Mr. Mayburn commanded, that they should not begin aggression, and a few minutes rendered these weapons absolutely useless, for they were closely surrounded by a numerous tribe of natives, carrying spears. But the anxious voyagers soon discovered that the people were peacefully inclined, for they made no attempt to injure the strangers, but with loud cries and rapidly-uttered words, seemed to express astonishment rather than anger.

One man took Margaret's large sun-hat from her head and placed it on his own, which so much delighted the rest, that all the hats of the party were coolly and speedily appropriated, without any opposition from the rightful owners, except from Ruth, who tied her bonnet so firmly under her chin, that the rough attempts of the man to tear it from her head nearly strangled her, till Margaret stepped forward to relieve her by loosing the strings.

O'Brien, also, was so indignant when one of the savages came to claim his hat, that he flung it into the river, but the man leaped in and rescued it, and at the same time he discovered the canoes, and summoned his friends vociferously to look on these new treasures. In the mean time the fish already cooked was devoured by some of the natives, and the rest revived the fire to cook the remainder of Baldabella's spoil.

Jenny's shawl was next discovered, and appropriated by a bold marauder, who threw it, in not ungraceful drapery, over his uncovered shoulders. Another savage stripped from Ruth a large cloak which she had hastily put on to conceal the basket which contained her last two fowls, which she held on her arm. This basket was a new prize, and the fowls were regarded with much curiosity.

"Oh! tell 'em not to twine their necks about, Mistress Baldabella," cried Ruth. "Tell 'em what bonnie creaters they are, laying every day, too."

But Baldabella, shy and fearful, had slunk behind the rest, and Margaret undertook to point out to the robber the value of the fowls, by showing him the eggs and caressing the birds. The man grinned, to express that he understood the explanation, sucked the eggs, and then walked off with basket and fowls, leaving Ruth in complete despair.

Just at that moment, Arthur issued from among the reeds, and started back, overcome with amazement and dismay, at the sight of the dark crowd which thronged the little clearance. He was immediately surrounded, and before he could offer any effectual resistance, his gun and hat were taken away, as well as a bag of pigeons that was hung over his arm.

"Baldabella," said he, "ask the chief of the tribe what he wants from us. We will give him the birds, and some knives and axes; but his people must then go away, and leave us our canoes and our guns."

Baldabella reluctantly came forward, and bending her head down as she approached the chief, repeated her message in a submissive tone, and the savage replied in a long harangue which made the poor woman tremble, and which she interpreted to her friends, greatly abridged, saying:—"Black fellow say, he take all: he very angry. Good white friend all run—fast—go away! Meny, much meny, black fellows come—all very hungry—eat fish—eat bird—eat all white friend. Go fast, massa;—missee, good friend, go away!"

This was decidedly sound advice; but under the present circumstances it was no easy task for the large party to run away. Wilkins and Jack had joined them, and were immediately seized by the savages, disarmed, and held fast by their captors. The attack was too sudden to allow them any opposition, and Jack looked deeply distressed, while Wilkins was absolutely furious, till a few words from Arthur induced them to submit with quietness to have their game and their hats taken away from them.

Then the robbers paused, evidently lost in admiration of the complicated dress of their captives, which they seemed desirous to possess, but were puzzled how to separate the garments from the wearer, or probably doubtful whether they did not actually form a part of that anomalous creature, a white man. It was plain, however, that Baldabella and her child were of their own race, and the chief went up to her, and commanded her to follow him, and become one of his jins. The poor woman, in terror and indignation, refused his request, and turned to flee from him; the savage immediately seized the child, and the alarmed mother, supported by Arthur and Hugh, tried in vain to rescue the screaming girl, till the man, in a violent rage, sprung forward to the river, and flung the child into the water. But in a moment Hugh leaped in after it, and brought the half-senseless child to the distracted mother, who had plunged in after him herself.

But now the chief's attention was diverted from Baldabella to the spoils of his victims; and some of the men were sent off with baskets, portmanteaus, knives, axes, guns, and all the precious possessions of the unfortunate travellers, who momentarily expected to be murdered as well as pillaged.

When the canoes had been completely ransacked, four of the men carried them off, while the rest were collected round a skin bag which contained their valuable ammunition. One of the natives drew out a canister of gunpowder, forced it open, and filled his mouth with the powder. With ludicrous grimaces, he spat out the nauseous mixture, and raised his hand to fling the rest upon the fire. Arthur saw the motion, and calling on his friends to escape, he rushed up, hoping to arrest the arm of the ignorant man; but he was too late, and though he retreated the moment he saw the canister flying through the air, he was prostrated senseless by the fearful explosion that followed.

The very earth shook beneath their feet, and such of the natives as were not actually stunned by the shock, fled, with cries of horror, into the bush, which was already blazing in several places from the burning fragments of the fire cast in all directions. The emancipated prisoners had all, with the exception of Arthur, reached in safety the edge of the river; and though trembling and much shaken, they had not sustained any injury. Arthur was brought to them perfectly insensible; but in a few minutes, when water had been plentifully poured over him, he recovered, and except a nervous tremor that lasted many hours, and the loss of his hair, which was completely scorched off, no serious consequences succeeded his perilous accident.

But though temporarily relieved from the presence of the savages, they were still in the midst of great dangers. The dry blazing reeds rendered further progress impossible; and they gratefully thanked God that the little spot they had cleared for their landing now afforded them a secure refuge.

The wind carried the flames rapidly down the east bank of the river towards the south; and they waited in great agitation till a path should be opened for them to proceed. Their anxious silence was interrupted by the sound of a low musical wail, so expressive of sorrow that it pained every heart; and on looking round, they saw the dirge proceeded from Baldabella, who was bending over the body of the native who had perished in the explosion caused by his own ignorance, and now lay a blackened corpse on the spot from whence he had flung the canister.

The little girl was kneeling by her mother, seeming to be conscious of the solemnity of the ceremony, and raising her feeble voice, in imitation of her mother. Much affected, Mr. Mayburn drew near them, and briefly and simply explained to the tender-hearted woman the uselessness of mourning over the hapless dead, and the lesson his sudden fate afforded to the living; and he begged her to join him in the prayer that they might all live so watchfully, that the hour of death might never surprise them unprepared.

The plain truths of Christianity had fallen with good effect on the mind of the grateful and gentle woman, and Mr. Mayburn hoped earnestly that she and her child had been, by God's mercy, rescued from darkness.

"And now, let us turn away from this sad spectacle, my good woman," continued Mr. Mayburn, "and endeavor to escape from this burning wilderness, for we all have work to do in the world. Arthur, will you, with your usual prudence, decide which way we shall turn? The flames are raging before us, and these savage natives may, at any moment, beset us from behind. My judgment fails to point out any escape; but, Arthur, I will pray for God's assistance, that you may be enabled to save us all."

"We may retrace our path up the river—a discouraging journey!" said Arthur; "or we may wait till the devouring flames have cleared a road for us; but the delay is perilous. Even should we try to force our way east, into yon barren desert, destitute as we now are, we should only obtain a change of evils; and I am reluctant to leave the friendly river, where alone we can hope to obtain food and water."

Baldabella pointed across the broad river, and said, "Go quick there, find many root, many nut, no black fellow. Bad black fellow come back soon, paint all white; very angry, see brother dead; kill all white man, eat Nakinna, carry away Baldabella! God never come to black fellow."

To cross the river did certainly seem the most desirable plan; but how to effect the transit was a perplexing question. It was about a hundred yards across, but, as far as they could judge, not more than from four to five feet deep at any part; so that the young men would have no difficulty in wading across; but to the women, and even to Mr. Mayburn, such an undertaking would be very difficult, if not impossible.

Jack looked round in despair; there were no trees, and even if there had been any, he had no axe. They examined carefully the field of plunder, in hopes some tool or utensil might have been overlooked by the plunderers; but, except the spear of the fallen native, and the fishing-spear of Baldabella, nothing had been left behind. Wilkins had fortunately preserved a long knife which he wore under his blouse; and, from the mysterious form of the dresses, the pockets had escaped being rifled.

Jack looked joyfully at the knife, and said, "We might cut some of these thick tall reeds, and make a float for them, Mr. Arthur. I have a few loose nails in my pocket, and here's a stone with a hole through it; we can fix a reed handle to it, and then it will make shift for a hammer. We could easily guide them over on a float of this sort, it's my opinion."

It was at least desirable to make the experiment; so without delay the strong bamboos were cut, broken, or torn down; a range of them placed flat, close together on the ground, connected by transverse bars, which were fastened somewhat imperfectly with Jack's precious "loose nails." A quarter of an hour completed this slight frame; in which time the conflagration, which had run to some distance down the banks of the river, had left a scorched and smoking clearance, disclosing the bodies of three more victims, who had not been able to escape the rapid flames. The boys found also several nests of half-roasted water-fowls, which they snatched away at some risk from the heated ground, and brought forward for a needful repast.

"If we had but saved the ropes!" exclaimed Jack. But ropes were not attainable, nor even that excellent substitute for them, the stringy bark; and the raft was launched on the river, to be drawn or urged across by the strong arms of the men. Margaret, at her own request, was the first to venture on the frail machine, guided on one side by Jack, and on the other by Wilkins, who waded, and in some places swam, and brought their charge in safety to the opposite bank, which was covered with reeds like that which they had left.

In this way the strong men successively brought over Mr. Mayburn and the two women. Baldabella, with her child on her shoulder and her fishing-spear in her hand, plunged at once into the water, followed by Arthur, who insisted on her holding his hand through the deepest part. Finally, after a sorrowful look at the scene of their losses, and a vain search for any trifling article of their property, the two boys followed their friends. Then the disconsolate travellers, forcing their way through the reedy thicket, stood to gaze with consternation on the wild barren region that spread before them.

"God has pleased to cast us feeble and destitute into this wide wilderness," said Mr. Mayburn; "of ourselves, we can do nothing, but He is mighty to save. He rescued us from the murdering savage, from flood, and from fire, and He will not suffer us to perish from famine, if we pray and trust. Let us lift up our hands and voices in thanksgiving and submission."

The rough convict, the ignorant Baldabella, and the simple child joined earnestly in the devotions of their more enlightened friends; and refreshed and hopeful, they rose from their knees, "to walk in faith the darkling paths of earth."

"If we can but keep near the river," said Margaret, "we cannot perish for want; and, besides, it seems to lead us in the very path we wish to follow."

"Fish is better nor starving," said Wilkins; "but I reckon we'se soon tire on't, if we come on nought better. What's come to t' lass now?" addressing Ruth, who was weeping.

"I've gone and roven a hole in my boot," sobbed she, "and I don't know how ever I'se to git it mended."

The boys laughed at the small distress of Ruth; but, after all, it was no laughing matter for her. To walk over the brush-covered plain, or among the dry reeds, was a trying exertion even for the well-shod, and Margaret was dismayed when she considered how this could be accomplished when their boots should fail. "Yet why dare I doubt?" she said. "See, Ruth; Baldabella, and even little Nakinna, walk as well as we do, and they are barefooted. We must not shrink from such small trials as this."

Just then a pair of the splendid bronze pigeons, so unequalled in beauty by any of their race, winged their flight from the water above the heads of the travellers; and though they no longer had the means of obtaining these birds, as delicious in taste as they are lovely in plumage, they were satisfied to see there were animals in the waste around them.

"These thin bamboos would make capital arrows," said Hugh; "and I have no doubt we can bend one of these tall canes for a bow, if we had but the means of stringing it."

"We might, at all events, sharpen some of the canes for spears," said Arthur, "not only for defence in need, but to be useful if we should be so fortunate as to encounter a kangaroo, or meet with the burrows of the wombats."

"What has become of our raft?" asked Margaret "You had there a good stock of bamboos ready cut."

"With all my nails in them," exclaimed Jack. "What a fool I was not to remember that in time; now it will be far enough down the river."

It was too true: the raft had already been carried away by the stream out of their sight; and all deeply regretted their negligence, as they moved slowly through the entangled scrub, frequently compelled to walk actually over the low bushes. On the opposite shore of the river they could still discover the wild flames flying down before the wind, and leaving behind a black smoking surface.

When wearied with the excitement and toil of the day, they were compelled to seek rest among the comfortless reeds, they sat down and looked at each other for some time rather sorrowfully, for the pressure of hunger had fallen on all. It was Baldabella who first relieved their distress; with untired energy she went to the river with her spear, and returned very soon with a large river-cod, and an apron filled with the fresh-water mussels, now truly prized for their useful shells. A fire was soon made, the fish was spitted on a sharpened reed, and while it was roasting, Hugh, with Wilkins's invaluable knife, cut a number of short thin reeds into chopsticks, as he called them, to enable them to convey the roasted fish from the reeds on which it was dished to their mouths. Rude as the contrivance was, and laughable as were the failures made in using their new utensils, they managed to make a satisfactory supper, and were content to sleep among the reeds in the open air, though the nights now felt exceedingly cold.

For several days they continued to toil on along the reedy banks of the river, over the same cheerless bush, and subsisting on the same unvarying fish diet. Then the banks became rocky and precipitous, and the river so difficult of access that it was only at rare openings they were able to obtain water or fish. But soon after the landscape was enlivened once more by tall trees. Their path was over the grassy plains, which were even now, in the winter of the year, gay with bright flowers. More than once they remarked with thankfulness the track of the kangaroo, and the chattering of birds gave them hopes of new food, and they anxiously sought the means of obtaining them.

With what joy they recognized the stringy-bark tree, and gathered the fibres to twist into bowstrings, and with what triumph did Hugh, the first who finished the rude weapon, draw his rough string and bring down pigeons and cockatoos sufficient for an ample meal even to the half-starved, but which taxed the ingenuity of the women to cook in any way. They were finally made into what Gerald called a Meg Merrilies stew, which was cooked in a very large mussel-shell, and even without salt or vegetables was fully enjoyed by the dissatisfied fish-eaters.

Then they all sat down earnestly to make a complete stock of bows and arrows; even Baldabella worked hard in twisting the bark for strings, and when they set out to continue their journey, they felt more confidence, for they were now provided with the means of obtaining food, and of defending themselves against hostile attacks; and in another day they again met with wild oats, and, to the joy of the women, with the tea-bush. The fig-trees no longer bore fruit, but they were still covered with their usual inhabitants, flocks of brilliant pigeons, chattering cockatoos, and the satin-bird, distinguished by its flossy plumage and dazzling bright eye. Occasionally they still met with the cucumber melon, a pleasant refreshment when they were weary; and now, strong in hope, they went on their way, still keeping within sight of the river.

"Every hour must bring us nearer to some of the most remote settlements of enterprising squatters," said Margaret, as they rested beneath a fig-tree one evening; "and all our trials would be forgotten if we could once more feel the blessing of a roof over our heads and hear the language of civilized life."

"It'll be a gay bit yet afore we come on 'em, Miss," said Wilkins. "Folks is not such fools as to squat on bare commons; and there's another thing ye'll find,—we'se meet a few more of them black dogs yet, specially if we come on a bit of good land; they're up to that as well as we are. And now, as things look a bit better, I'd not wonder if they're nigh at hand."

"I agree with you, Wilkins," said Arthur. "We are now certainly in danger of encountering tribes of natives, especially as we are on the track of the kangaroos, a great temptation to them."

"I wish we could see one of the mountebank beasts," said Gerald; "wouldn't I send an arrow or a spear into him. Take notice, all of you, I intend to bag the first old fellow that shows his long nose."

A sudden spring from a thicket behind them brought a large kangaroo into the midst of the circle, and before they had recovered the surprise sufficiently to take up bows or spears, a succession of rapid bounds had carried the animal completely beyond their reach.

A burst of laughter from his friends somewhat disconcerted O'Brien, but with his usual good-humor he said, "Very well; I allow you to laugh to-night. The fellow took an unfair advantage of me; but wait till to-morrow."

CHAPTER XXIX

Next morning, when the broiled fish was ready for breakfast, Gerald and Hugh were missing. With some uneasiness the rest watched and waited for an hour, when a shout announced the approach of the wanderers, and Arthur and Jack set out to meet them, and were glad to assist them in dragging in a kangaroo.

"It is the same impudent fellow that defied me last night," said Gerald. "I tracked his curious boundings to a wood three miles from here; and then Hugh and I beat the bushes and shouted till we drove him out of cover; but he cost us lots of arrows and spears before we could dispatch him; and a weighty drag he has been for us this winter morning of June, when the sun is as hot as it is in our summer June at home. Now, Wilkins, help to skin him; we mean to have all our boots mended with his hide."

"But, Arthur, we must tell you," said Hugh, "that when we were in the wood we saw a smoke at a considerable distance to the south-west. Do you think it could possibly be from some station? Gerald wished much to go on and ascertain whence it arose, but I persuaded him to wait till we consulted you; besides, I knew you would be all uneasy if we were long absent. Have we got so near the squatters, Wilkins?"

"Not a bit of chance on 't, Master Hugh," replied he. "We're far enough from t' squatters yet. Depend on 't it's just another lot of them good-to-nought black rogues. They'll be thick enough here where there's aught to get, I'se warrant 'em."

"It is most natural and just, Wilkins," said Mr. Mayburn, "that the true proprietors of the soil should participate in its fruits. I fear it is we who are, in fact, the rogues, robbing the wretched aborigines of their game, and grudging them even a settlement in their own land."

"But we have not robbed them, papa," said Hugh. "Kangaroos and pigeons abound here enough for all; and we do not wish to hurt the poor wretches if they would not annoy us. Here is Margaret quite ready to open a school for them, if they would come and be taught."

"Margaret has done more good than any of us," said Mr. Mayburn; "she has labored incessantly to instruct Baldabella and her child, and to open to them the way of salvation. It is thus by scattered seeds that the great work of diffusing the truth is to be accomplished; and I fear, Hugh, we have been too much engrossed with the cares of this life to think seriously."

"Now, boys," said Arthur, "we had better not linger; the kangaroo is skinned, and the meat is cut up into convenient portions for carriage; let us walk on briskly till we are hungry enough to enjoy it."

Onward they moved over the extensive grassy plains, recognizing with pleasure various tall trees of the varieties of *Eucalyptus*, the Grass-tree with its long weeping branches, the Pandanus with its slender palm-like stem, and the Fig-tree with its spreading roots. Beneath one of these trees they encamped to cook kangaroo steaks, and to enjoy once more what Wilkins called "a decent, nat'ral dinner." There, with strips of skin for thread and a fish-bone for a needle, Wilkins repaired the worn and tattered boots, while Margaret and Baldabella made netted bags of the stringy bark, and Jenny and Ruth bruised the wild oats which the young men had cut down as they came along.

"The rest of the skin I mean to make into a bag," said Jack; "for we must carry with us a good stock of oats; we may, probably, again come to some spot where they are not to be found."

Mr. Mayburn looked with pleasure on the busy hands round him; and though he deeply regretted the irreparable loss of his books, wasted on the plundering savages, his composed mind soon submitted to the trial. His retentive memory supplied the place of books, and, from the rich treasures of his reading he delighted to repeat to his attentive listeners pleasant and instructive lectures. Cheered and invigorated by labor and amusing conversation, the united party forgot all their cares, offered up their devotions with calm and happy hopes, and slept among the sheltering roots of the fig-tree without fear.

Some unaccustomed sounds suddenly roused the sleepers, and they looked round to behold through the dim light of breaking day the grim visages of a numerous band of tall savages, with rough heads and beards, who were armed with spears, and who looked on their surprised captives with a sort of scornful indifference, as they beckoned them to rise and follow them. Hugh and Gerald sprung up to seize their spears and bows, but Arthur, with more prudence, ordered them to forbear making any hostile demonstration. "We are in the power of these strangers," he said; "our only hope must be in conciliation and treaty. I will try to make the best of it."

Then turning to the native who stood nearest to him, he endeavored, in the few words he had learnt from Baldabella, to make him understand their poverty and inoffensive disposition, and their desire to be permitted to proceed on their journey. The man looked round, as if to call on another to reply, and, to the astonishment of Arthur, a voice from the crowd answered in English.

"We are open to a fair reg'lar treatise, young man, Perdoose yer swag, which is the vulgar country word for what we English terminate *tin*, and then we will sign your disfranchisement."

The voice and the extraordinary phraseology were familiar to the Mayburns, and Hugh cried out, "What, Bill, is that you? How came you here? Is David Simple with you? and where is Mr. Deverell?"

The man, who had now come forward, dressed in the remnants of his formerly seedy foppery, looked annoyed at the recognition. He stared impudently at Hugh, and said, "You have mistaken your man, young master. I have no convalescence of you."

"It is in vain for you to affect ignorance of us, Bill," said Arthur; "we know you to be a ticket-of-leave man, engaged as a servant at Melbourne by Mr. Deverell. I am grieved to find you in such unsuitable company, and would advise you to join us, and guide us to your master's station, where we shall be able to reward you liberally."

"Thank you, sir," said the man, laughing scornfully; "but Mr. Deverell and I did not part good friends, and I have no innovation to visit him again. His ways is percoolar, and a gentleman as has had a deliberate eddication looks higher nor waiting on cattle; so Davy and I came to a dissolution to abrogate the place, and set out on a predestinarian excrescence."

"He means, master," said Davy, with a downcast look, interpreting his brother's difficult language; "he means as how we took to t' bush. I was bad to win round to 't; but Bill, he'd collogued with a lot of black fellows, and had 'em all in a wood hard again our boundaries; and they thranged me round, and threaped as how they'd cut my throat if I stayed after them to peach; and, graceless dog as I were, I joined 'em to drive our best stock, when we knew as how master was off for a week. It were a sore day's work, and little good do I see in living among a set of raggles like them. I warn ye, master, if ye've gotten any cash about ye, just pay 't down, and make no words about it, afore they get aggravated, for they're a bloody set, that are they."

"But, my poor mistaken man," said Mr. Mayburn, "what in the world can these savages do with money in this houseless wilderness?"

"That's our affair," answered Bill. "So open your bank, old fellow, and leave it to intelligible fellows like me to transact your gold into brandy."

"In the first place, Bill," replied Arthur, "I think it is my duty to remind you of the fatal consequences of highway robbery, and to beseech you to return to your duty, and endeavor to retrieve your error. In the next place, you cannot possibly benefit by your extortion, for we are literally and truly without money. We have letters of credit on Calcutta, and we could certainly obtain money at Melbourne, but only by our personal application at that place. We have been already stripped by one of the black tribes, of every article of property we possessed, and we are now wholly destitute. This is the exact truth. Now I suggest to you that your wisest plan would be to leave us to pursue our way unmolested; unless you or your misguided brother will accompany us to the settlement of Mr. Deverell, with whom, I think, we have sufficient influence to induce him to pardon your offence."

"Who would be the fools then?" answered the man. "No, sir, your oratorio makes no depression on me. If you haven't got money, you're worth money. You must march in the arrear of your captivators to our quarters. You shall then write a letter, which I shall dedicate to you. I never travel without my writing impediments; and one of my 'cute black fellows, as is conservant in English, shall be dispersed away to your friend Mr. Deverell, who must confiscate to me cash or stuff for your ransom; and when I see my brandy and cigars, you are disfranchised."

It was useless to attempt opposition to the mandates of the imperious and conceited bush-ranger, and the disconsolate captives reluctantly followed the man, surrounded by such a troop of natives as precluded all hopes of escape, and exposed to the insults and plunder of these savages, who wrested from them their spears and bows. Wilkins had contrived to secret his knife under his vest, and thus saved it. They had not proceeded far before they were joined by a band of women, revolting in appearance and manner, who crowded round them, rudely examined their garments, and freely possessed themselves of such as they could conveniently snatch away. Margaret looked round for Baldabella to assist her in remonstrating with these harpies, and was surprised to see that she had disappeared.

Margaret then remembered that, on the previous night, the woman had selected a thicket considerably apart from the rest, as a sleeping-place for herself and her child, and she concluded that at the first alarm of the invaders, the poor woman had escaped, her dread of her fellow-countrymen overcoming even her allegiance to her friends. After all, Margaret considered it was as well; there were two less to be anxious for, and she had no fears for the native on her own soil: she would certainly find food, and would probably wait and watch for the release of the captives.

The unpleasant march of the prisoners extended to nearly three miles; then, descending a low hill, they arrived at a lovely wooded valley, where, on the banks of a little creek, or streamlet, stood a number of rough bark huts. A herd of cattle were feeding on the grassy plain, and some horses, hobbled, to prevent them straying, were mingled with them. Naked children were rolling on the grass, shouting and laughing; women were busy bruising nuts, or making nets; and some aged men were seated in the sun with their knees raised to their heads, looking stupid and half dead.

It was the first scene of pastoral life that the travellers had beheld in Australia, and would have had a certain charm to them had they been in a position to enjoy it. But the thoughts of their captivity engrossed their minds, and they contemplated with uneasiness the fierce and threatening countenances of the lawless men who surrounded them, and who drove them forward like the cattle they had so villainously obtained, and lodged them in a large bark hut which stood at the extremity of the scattered hamlet. This rude shelter was wholly open in front, and filthily dirty inside; but they were thankful for any shelter that divided them from the coarse and abandoned robbers; and, flinging themselves on the ground, the disconsolate captives reflected silently on their perilous situation, while their captors, assembled before the rude prison, seemed earnestly discussing, as Arthur concluded, the means of making the most profit of their destitute prisoners.

After some minutes had elapsed, they were favored with a visit from the audacious and ignorant convict Bill, who addressed them with his usual pompous air, saying, —

"Gentlemen, we have dissented on dispersing one of your gang along with our embarrasser to Deverell, that he may be incensed into the right of the thing. We set you up as worth a hundred pound, hard cash, for the lot; but if we concentrate to take stuff, we shall exhort two hundred. Things is bad to sell in the bush. We expectorate a chap in a day or two as is intentionable to buy our stock, and then you must keep close quarters, for when my colloquies get their brandy they are always a bit umbrageous."

When Mr. Mayburn comprehended the meaning of this elaborate nonsense, he declared positively that he would not allow one of his children to depart on such an unjust errand, accompanied by an abandoned reprobate.

"I should like nothing better than to start off on such a trip," said Gerald. "What a surprise it would be at Daisy Grange when they saw my brown face; and wouldn't pretty Emma say, with tears in her eyes, 'Oh, Gerald! what has become of Arthur?' And grave Edward Deverell would fall into heaps of confusion, and say, 'Margaret! why is not Margaret with you?'"

Arthur laughed, but shook his head, and refused to abet any plan of subjecting the thoughtless boy to such risk.

"But might not Wilkins go?" asked Hugh.

"Not I, thank ye, Master Hugh," answered the man, hastily; "we'd like enough fall in with some of them hot-headed black pollis when we got nigh to t' station, and they're all so set up wi' their guns, that afore I could get out a word they'd sure to pick me out for a runaway, and shoot me dead; and, more nor that, I'll not say if I were let loose among them care-nought rangers, as I mightn't fall into their ways, and take to t' bush like 'em; and then, ye see, all yer good work would be flung away."

"Wilkins might be useful to you here, Master Arthur," said Jack; "but I don't see why I shouldn't go. I'm no ways feared; and I could put Mr. Deverell up to getting hold of these vagabonds and their own cattle; and then, you know, sir, I should find timber and tools enough, and I could soon knock up a bit of a wagon to bring up for Miss Margaret and the master, and the other poor things. What think you, sir, about it?"

"I must confess, papa," said Arthur, "that I feel satisfied that Jack is the right man. But can we make up our minds to part with our tried and faithful friend? I leave it to you to decide."

"My dear son," answered Mr. Mayburn, much agitated, "I cannot decide such an important question. Only consider; should his savage companion prove treacherous, our dear Jack may be sacrificed, and his blood fall on our heads. I shrink from the responsibility."

"Nevertheless, dear papa," said Margaret, weeping bitterly, "I fear we must consent. Jack will be accompanied by only one man, whose policy it will be to be careful of his life till the transaction be completed. On his return, rely on it, Edward Deverell will take care he has arms and protection. Jack is sagacious, brave, and prudent. I grieve to part with him; but I believe it may be for the benefit of all. We must resign him, and pray for God's blessing on our brave deliverer."

"And I say, Jack, my man," said Wilkins, "if ye should chance to light on a bonnie bit lass, called Susan Raine, down yonder, just ye say as how Wilkins is not altogether that graceless she counts him. He's bad enough, God knows; but he oft thinks on days of lang syne; and he's true, tell her, come what may."

It was then communicated to the vile dictator of the dark band that a messenger was ready to set out to procure the ransom from Mr. Deverell; and the next day, amidst the loud sobs of Ruth and the silent grief of the rest, Jack took leave, and set forward towards the south, accompanied by a tall, crafty-looking savage, who had evidently been accustomed to traffic with the bush-rangers, and had acquired sufficient English to serve his purpose. One of their ablest defenders was thus severed from the unfortunate captives, who hourly became more alarmed about their position. Forbidden to leave the hut, they were merely fed, like the dogs, with the disgusting remains of the untempting food of their savage captors; and but for the secret good offices of Davy, they must have perished of thirst. He brought them every night a bark bucket of water from the creek, which saved their lives.

But Mr. Mayburn and Margaret, who could not touch the decomposed fish and gnawed bones that were thrown to them, gradually sunk into a state of weakness that distracted their helpless friends. Four days elapsed after Jack's departure, and Margaret was reclining, weak and weary, yet unable to sleep, against the back wall of the hut, when about midnight, she was startled by a scratching sound outside the bark. Much alarmed, but too weak to move, she trembled, and feebly called to Jenny, who was sleeping near her. But just at that moment the low, sweet voice of Baldabella greeted her, through an opening made in the bark near the ground.

"Missee, good dear missee!" murmured the woman; "Baldabella see all, look in all *gunyoes*. Baldabella come, all sleep now; bring bread, bring fish for missee and good master."

Then through the opening Jenny received cakes of pounded oats, such as she herself had taught Baldabella to make, broiled fish, and a bark vessel filled with hot tea, a plentiful and luxurious repast. When she had given up her store, the grateful woman whispered, "Baldabella go make more bread, come again dark night. Pray God bless white friends."

The prayer of Baldabella was gratefully acknowledged and responded to by her much affected friends, who blessed the hour they were so happy as to snatch the poor widow from the death which hung over her body and soul, and to win her affections and sympathy. Invigorated by the wholesome and clean food, Mr. Mayburn and Margaret again began to hope for better days, and to plan their pleasant journey south.

For three nights Baldabella returned with her abundant and seasonable gifts; while the sordid wretch who detained them, plainly cared only for the ransom he hoped to obtain for them. But Davy continued to steal in every night with the welcome supply of fresh water, and remained to listen to their prayers and hymns, with a softened and mournful countenance.

"Ye see, sir," said the poor fellow to Arthur, "our Bill, he's up to all sorts of things; he's had a grand eddication, and knows reet fra' wrong better nor me; and he orders me, like, and I cannot say him nay; he reckons I'se but a simple chap."

"Did you ever learn your Catechism, Davy?" asked Margaret.

"They did get that into me, Miss," answered he, "and little good it's done me. I niver like to think on 't nowadays; it's just awesome, it is."

"Thou shalt not steal!" said Mr. Mayburn, emphatically.

"Please, master, not to talk on't," said the agitated young man; "it's about them beasts as ye're meaning on. But our Bill says, says he, 'It stands to reason as them as has ower mony ought to sarve them as has none.' Now what think ye of that, sir?"

"I think and know, David," said Mr. Mayburn, "that it is God's will that all men should obey His commandments, and do their duty in the station where He has placed them. You had no more right to take Mr. Deverell's cattle than these poor savages have to strip you naked and leave you to die alone in the desert, and in the eyes of God you are more guilty than they would be, for you have been taught His law. You know that God has said that the thief shall not enter the kingdom of heaven. Now, David, death is near to us all, young or old: think what will be your dreadful fate when you wake in another world, forsaken by God. Then turn to Him now, while there is yet time, and pray for repentance and pardon through the blessed Saviour, that your sins may be forgiven, and you may be brought to dwell with him forever."

"Well, master, I can tell ye if 't were to do again," answered the man, "Bill s'ould niver talk me ower to put my hands to t' job. And, after all, a poor set we've made on 't. Ye see, this is how we did it; we darked and kept quiet till t' master was off down t' country, then we marked off our beasts, and picked out our saddle-horses, and a gun a-piece. I ought to have had warning plenty about me'ling wi' a gun. Then off we set at midnight, driving our beasts and a flock of sheep, and were soon up till them black fellows as was watin' us. First we druv' our sheep till a bush public, where a sly auld hand took 'em, and gave us a lot of bad brandy and worse tobacco for 'em, and sin' that we've run and rode about t' country, up and down, hereaway and thereaway, like wild beasts. Then we're feared of t' pollis, and we're feared of all ther' black fellows, as can turn rusty when they like, and it's nought but drinking, cursing, and fighting all day long, brutes as we are. I'se fairly tired, master, and I'd fain be back among Christians; but then, I'd niver be t' fellow to peach; and, ower that, I know there's a rope round my neck, as is sartin to be tightened if I show my face at our station again."

CHAPTER XXX

Simple Davy, the whole family believed, would not prove irreclaimable, and they used every persuasion to bring the poor man to a knowledge of his faults, and to a desire to reform them; but his blind submission to his *"eddicated"* brother proved a formidable obstacle, till his heart became enlightened by the truths of religion. The cunning villain Bill was a great annoyance to the family: he continually visited them, and his absurd speeches no longer afforded them amusement, for he had now signified his intention of becoming a candidate for the hand of Margaret.

"Not that Miss would aggress," said the convict, "to live with these low *ignis fatuus* men, that we eddicated men terminate flea-beings, seeing she is not customary to their ways. But you see, Miss, I preponderate setting up a bush tavern, quite illimitable to the beat of the imperious pollis; quite a genteel hottle, where you might prorogue like a lady, and I'd not reject to adapt these lads, and give them a job at waiting; and we might revive an opening for the old governor, if you mattered having him."

Hugh and Gerald would have seized the impudent rascal and flung him out of the hut, but Arthur restrained them, and arresting his father's indignant remonstrance, he said, "Bill, my sister must never again hear such absurd and offensive language; she is too young even to think of such things, and quite unfitted by education and religion for mingling with lawless bush-rangers."

"We'll see about that, young fellow," answered Bill with a diabolical grin. "You might have permeated the young woman to speak for herself; she's old enough to be deciduous. But wait a bit till I touch your ransom, and then we'll considerate about her. She was not secluded in my bargain, and you'll find as how I'm empirical here."

The terror and distress of Margaret were very great, and but for the absence of Jack, who was always ingenious in affairs of difficulty, Arthur would have yielded to her wish, and attempted their escape, which by the aid of Baldabella in the out-works, and of David, who was much ashamed of his brother's audacious proposal, in the citadel, they did not think would be extremely difficult. The bark hut which was their prison, was situated at the extremity of the range of huts, and close to a thick wood, from which Baldabella made her nightly visits without disturbance. David had supplied the young men with some sheets of bark to partition off the back part of the hut for Margaret and her servants, and from this apartment it would be easy to cut open the bark, and escape into the wood, the savages usually sleeping on the ground before the hut.

Still, unless they were driven to extremities, they desired to defer their flight till the return of Jack, as, besides the hope that he might bring them efficient aid from Mr. Deverell, they did not wish to abandon him to the wrath of the disappointed rangers; but they explained their intention to Baldabella, and begged her to be prepared; and they hoped that they were prevailing on David to become their companion and guide.

Several days passed in the same dreary and distressing seclusion. If any of the prisoners ventured to breathe the air outside the hut, they were assailed with rude language, pelted and insulted by the rangers or the blacks. Jenny and Ruth had gone out to cut some grass to spread over the ground on which they slept, and were seized by the women, their clothes torn, their hair pulled, and the contents of their pockets discovered and torn from them.

"Ragged I am, and ragged I may be, now," said Jenny. "I wonder what good my bit housewife will do them ondecent hussies; and neither thread, needle, nor scissors have I left. And Miss Marget, my honey, there was my silver thimble that you bought me in London, and my prayer-book from Master Arthur,—God bless him!—and my spectacles that master gave me; but that's little matter, I don't need them when I've nothing left to read or sew."

Ruth sobbed out incoherently, "My bonnie purse; oh dear! oh dear! and my two shillings, and my lucky crook't sixpence, and my Sunday ribbons and cotton gloves, and my bonnie little Testament! Oh dear! where's I to get mair?"

Mr. Mayburn consoled the women, and showed them his pocket Bible, which he had still preserved, and from which he could daily read to them the words of comfort and hope; and Margaret encouraged Jenny with the prospect of one day reaching Daisy Grange, when she felt assured that the orderly and prudent Mrs. Deverell would have needles and thread to bestow on them.

One evening some very unusual sounds tempted Gerald who was always restless in his confinement, to steal out of the hut. He was absent some time, and Arthur had become very uneasy lest he should have been arrested and punished for this disobedience of orders, when, with a face full of news, he rushed back into the hut, exclaiming, "Jack is brought back! there are three or four more of those ugly convicts; and, oh, Arthur, there is Black Peter amongst them!"

This was really melancholy news, and Mr. Mayburn in deep distress looked appealingly to Arthur.

"Margaret must be taken away," he said; "I cannot have her remain among these reprobates. Then there is Wilkins, poor fellow! That wicked wretch has ever persecuted and hated him; he is not safe with us; we must care for him, and send him away. But ought we not all to depart? I feel that I am unable to judge the matter calmly; decide for us, my son."

"I shall be better able to do that, papa," answered Arthur, "when I learn what extraordinary circumstance has induced Jack to return. It is quite impossible that he can have executed his mission; and I cannot imagine that these robbers have relinquished their desire for the ransom-money. I am very anxious to see him."

The sounds of riot and discord were now heard through the hamlet; the prisoners concluded that more brandy had been brought in, and it was producing its usual delusive and fatal effects among men and women. The intoxication proceeded to madness; horrid oaths and blasphemy were the only words to be distinguished; first uttered by the white man, erroneously named a Christian, and then eagerly imitated by his heathen brother. In the midst of the confusion, Jack stole in unnoticed by the savages to his anxious friends. He was pale with fatigue, disappointment, and alarm; for he saw that the frenzy of the intoxicated wretches might at any moment lead them to murder.

"Mr. Arthur," said he, hurriedly, "I have got hold of a gun and a few charges, and David will follow me here with another, as soon as the fellows drink themselves into stupor; then we must make off without delay, or we are lost. Black Peter has determined to have his own way, and you know what his way is; and depend on it, if he had not been led off with the brandy, he would have been here to bully and threaten before now."

"Alas! alas!" said Mr. Mayburn, "how did it happen, my good lad, that you fell into the hands of that abandoned man?"

"We met him on our way, sir," answered Jack, "mounted on a handsome horse that he'd stolen from somebody's station; he was dressed like a gentleman, and three more fellows, all bush-rangers, I'll be bound, were along with him, well mounted too. They were carrying kegs of liquor and bales of tobacco to barter for the stolen cattle, which they mean to drive down the country to sell. Peter knew me as soon as he set eyes on me, and hailed me to know what had become of my comrades. Then the sulky black fellow that rode with me took on him to tell, in his lingo, what we were after. It would have made your blood run cold, master, to hear how that brute Peter cursed Bill; he said he was nought but a poor, pitiful, long-tongued fool, to swap such a prize for a hundred pounds; and he swore he would have ten times as much for the bargain, and have it for himself too. 'I've got shot of my cowardly troop, ye see,' he said to my guide; 'they didn't suit me; they ran away at the sight of blood. I'll see now if I can't put that set-up fellow, Bill, down a peg, and manage your folks a bit better, blackey.' Then he went back to his white colleagues, and said, 'You might make a penny of these two runaways; there's money on their heads; what say ye to carrying them off?'

"I cannot tell how they settled their treacherous plan; but as they had arms, they forced us to turn back with them; and Bill looked so cowed when he saw Black Peter, that I make no doubt the craftier rogue of the two will be master by to-morrow; and there will be a poor chance for us, if we do not overreach him to-night. Well, Davy, how are they getting on?" he added, as the simple fellow entered cautiously.

"They'll not be lang fit for wark," answered he. "Some's down now, and Bill and Peter had come to fighting; but them new chaps, as corned with you, parted 'em; and I seed 'em wink at Peter, and they said as how it could be settled to-morrow. But it would hardly be safe to stop for that; and if ye're ready and willing, I'se get ye off cannily afther it's dark."

"We are willing and ready, David," said Arthur, "and most thankful to have you for our guide. I will engage that Mr. Deverell will pardon and protect you, if we are fortunate enough to reach Daisy Grange; but how my father and sister are to accomplish the journey, I cannot think."

"It's all pat, sir; see to me for that," answered David. "Not a chap amang 'em was fit to hobble t' horses but me, I had it all my own way, and I brought our two, and their four, all round to t' back of this here wood, and tied 'm up ready saddled. Afore midnight, light on me to be there, and all fettled and ready. I'se get Baldabella to warn ye at t' reet minute, and then ye can make yer way out backwards, and she'll bring ye through t' wood, and we'se get a good start afore day-leet. They've no more horses fit for t' saddle, if they were fit themselves; but it will be a fair bit afore they sleep off their drunken fit."

The yells and screams of the mad drunkards grew louder and more discordant, and the trembling women clung fearfully to each other in the back apartment of the hut, where they had already cut an opening large enough to allow them to escape; but they were anxious to defer the attempt till Davy thought the moment favorable. At length they heard the oaths and curses muttered in fainter tones; and, one after another, the voices died away. Gladly the anxious captives marked the deep silence that succeeded, which was finally broken by David whispering through the opening behind the hut,—

"Come along; be sharp, and tread soft. There's a lot of chaps lying afore t' hut: ye cannot come out that way. Mind ye dinnot waken 'em. Here's Baldabella; she'll trail ye through t' bush, and I'll on afore, and make ready."

Trembling and breathless, one after another they followed Baldabella, forcing their way through the thick underwood, scarcely conscious of bruises, scratches, and rent garments, till, by the faint light of the moon through a gathering mist, they saw David holding the harnessed horses outside the tangled wood.

"Manage as ye like," said he; "there's twelve on us, reckoning t' babby, but some on ye is leet weights."

Baldabella refused to mount, and, giving her child to Wilkins, she walked on; and so light and swift was her pace, that she kept up well with the doubly-laden horses, though they proceeded as speedily as they could over the grassy plains. For six hours they continued to travel due south, silently and uninterruptedly; then the morning light cheered their spirits, they realized the fact of their freedom, and they rejoiced as they rested on a rich plain while the horses fed, and lifted up their voices in praise and thanksgiving that they were once more free in a savage land; and even poor David, with tears of penitence, united humbly with them in prayer.

All the party needed the refreshment they knew not where to seek, when Baldabella produced a netted bag of cakes and nuts, with which they were obliged to content themselves; and hoping that they might meet with water before they were again compelled to rest, they set forward with gratitude and cheerfulness. But they were somewhat disheartened as they proceeded; for though herbage and trees were plentiful, water was rarely to be met with. Hollows in the earth, which contained a muddy remnant of the well-filled pools of the rainy season, were their sole dependence—a scanty and unpleasant supply. They had long ago lost sight of the river, from which they had designedly diverged in order to mislead their pursuers, leaving it on their left hand. Fig-trees were common on the plains, but no longer bearing fruit; still, they continued to be frequented by the cockatoos and pigeons, and having made bows and arrows, they procured as many as they wished for food.

On the fourth day, Baldabella, who was before them, summoned them by the welcome cry, "*Yarrai! yarrai!*—water! water!" and they saw a narrow full streamlet, rushing to the south-east, probably to swell some large river; a consideration very tempting to the travellers, who could not venture on the direct track which David was acquainted with, lest they should be overtaken. They resolved, therefore, to continue by the water, so necessary to preserve their own strength and that of their horses; and though the approach towards a large river might place them amongst the black tribes again, they would still be on the highway which led to civilization.

They now selected their resting-places close by the refreshing stream, and without adventure, till it happened that one day they had indulged for some hours in a noonday repose under the shelter of some trees. Then the young men set out to beat the wood for birds; but Gerald soon cried out, "To horse! to horse! bold hunters. Emus are in view!" and, on skirting the wood, the whole family had a view of a flock of those huge birds, at some distance on the plain, grazing with all the tranquillity of domestic cattle.

"We are not in want of emus, Gerald," said Mr. Mayburn. "These creatures are as free to live as we are ourselves. Why will men become hunters from mere wantonness?"

"We could do cannily with one, master," said Jenny. "They're fair good eating, and ye see, sir, great strong men gets tired of these bits of birds."

Mr. Mayburn sighed at the necessity of disturbing the peace of the happy creatures, and duly impressed on Arthur his wish that only one bird should be killed. All the young men, roused at the thoughts of the chase, sprang upon their horses, and, armed with spears and bows, galloped off to the field. Crafty and swift as these birds are, they were not entirely able to elude their mounted enemies, who attacked them with spears and arrows, and at last succeeded in separating from the rest and surrounding one large bird, in which several arrows had been previously lodged. Infuriated with pain and fright, the bird ran frantically round the circle, in fruitless endeavors to escape between the horses; and Gerald, piercing it with his long spear to oppose its retreat, it turned suddenly round, and, striking out backwards with its powerful leg, inflicted such a blow on the horse he was riding, that it staggered and fell.

Alarmed at the accident, the hunters all rode up to assist Gerald; and the wounded emu profited by the opportunity, and effected a retreat to its companions, to the great vexation of the sanguine young men. They soon raised the horse and his rider. Gerald had escaped unhurt; but the horse was so bruised by the kick of the powerful creature, that Arthur saw with consternation that their journey must be delayed some time, till it recovered from the blow; if, indeed, it was not rendered entirely incapable of further service.

Mortified and dejected, the discomfited hunters returned to the encampment, where they were received by Mr. Mayburn with a lesson on humanity to animals, by Margaret with friendly raillery, and by Jenny with ill-repressed murmurs; but all were grieved at the sufferings of the poor horse.

"That beast must just lie where he is for one day, however," said Wilkins; "and I question whether that'll sarve to mend a bad job. I say, some of ye slips of lads, run up them trees, and take a look round, to see if t' coast's clear."

It was at once employment and amusement for the active boys, Hugh and Gerald, to climb two tall fig-trees that grew in front of the wood, and scan the wide scene around.

"Now, sentinels," cried Margaret from below, "please to report what you have observed."

"I can see our little rivulet," said Hugh, "winding like a silver thread over the plains to the south-east, even to the very horizon, where a gray line terminates the view. That may be the hem of the large river Arthur has planned."

"I say, Arthur, come up," cried Gerald; "I want you to look at a dark mass far away north. I could almost fancy I saw it moving."

Arthur was soon by his side, and, after examining the object pointed out, he said with a sigh, "You are right, Gerald, it does move; and I fear we are pursued at this unlucky moment, when we cannot, I fear, continue our flight. You, boys, remain to watch, while I descend to hold a council about our perilous situation."

"Hand us up the guns, then, Arthur," answered Gerald, "and see if we will not guard the pass. Not a single rogue shall advance, but we will mark him and bring him down from our watch-tower."

"That plan will not do, Gerald," said Arthur. "Your office is to watch, and, as soon as you can, to ascertain their strength."

Then the distressed youth descended to report his lamentable tidings to the tranquil party below, and great was the dismay felt by the timid.

"We might send off master and Miss Margaret," said Jack. "What think you of that, Mr. Arthur? We could hold out here a good bit, to let them have a good start down south; and then, if God helped us, we might get after them."

"Margaret, what do you say to this plan?" asked Mr. Mayburn. "There is Davy, who seems honest, could we not trust him to conduct us and our two poor women to our friends the Deverells?"

"It must not be so, dear papa," answered Margaret; "we must live or die together. Think how unhappy we should be to leave them exposed to dangers for our sakes. But could we not hide in this thick wood? It might be that the pursuers would not discover us."

"But the trail, Margaret," answered Arthur,—"the trail would betray us. Is there any mode left us to escape, do you think, Wilkins?"

"Ay, ay, Mr. Arthur, ye fancy it's best to set one rogue to cheat another," replied Wilkins. "Keep up your heart, Miss; I'se thinking we can lead 'em on a wrong scent yet."

The wood behind them spread for a considerable way along the side of the rivulet, from which it was about a hundred yards distant. The opposite banks were hemmed up to the water with a broad growth of reeds, beyond which lay a vast entangled scrub.

"We'll see if we cannot manage to send 'em ower yonder," continued Wilkins, pointing to the opposite side; "so bring t' horses here, and come along wi' ye."

By the orders of Wilkins the men mounted the five sound horses, having first led the lame one, with Margaret, Mr. Mayburn, and the women, into the intricacies of the wood, and left them, carefully arranging the bush, so that no trail could be seen. Then the horsemen, making a broad track, by riding abreast, proceeded to the shallow rivulet, crossed it, and breaking down the reeds before them, forced a pass to the scrub. Here it was unnecessary to proceed, as on the brush-covered ground it was easy to suppose the trail might be lost; they therefore returned, carefully retracing their steps to the river, and riding the horses in the water about a hundred yards down the stream, from which, at distant intervals, they brought them up singly to the wood, obliterating the trail with scrupulous care; and, finally, through several convenient openings, they introduced them into the heart of the wood, where a small grassy spot enabled them to leave the animals to graze, after carefully securing them. Here all the party assembled, to wait the event, except the three boys, who, taking guns and bows, returned to the fig-trees from whence they had first perceived the pursuers, re-ascended, and concealed themselves in the thick foliage, to watch the foe, and, if necessary, to defend the fortress.

The pursuers were now plainly visible, and the watchers discovered that the party consisted of the bush-rangers, driving before them a herd of cattle, and accompanied by a band of the natives. The procession certainly formed an imposing body, but the men were on foot, and must necessarily proceed slowly with the cattle; and if all the horses had been fit for the road, Arthur saw they might easily have escaped pursuit, and he bitterly regretted the imprudent and unprofitable chase of the emu. He now considered that the most advisable plan would be, if possible, to allow the men to pass, and then to follow them.

CHAPTER XXXI

Every moment increased the anxiety of the young sentinels, who were scarcely able to speak for agitation. At last Hugh said,—

"Isn't it a capital chance for us, Arthur, that the great drove of cattle are before the keen-eyed rangers? They will trample down our trail effectually."

This was certainly an advantage to the fugitives, especially as they remarked the cattle followed the exact track they had made. They were now able to distinguish the powerful figure of Black Peter, who was accompanied by the three strange bush-rangers whom Jack had met with him, and followed by about fifty of the natives whom they had seen with Bill the convict. These men were painted white, as if for battle, and were armed with spears and boomerangs; but Bill was not with them,—a circumstance that gave great satisfaction to Arthur, for the sake of poor David.

The whole body drew up beneath the very trees in which the young men were hidden; and whilst the cattle plunged into the river with great enjoyment, Peter was examining the trail which led to the water, and had been purposely made to mislead them. He then pointed out to his companions the broken reeds on the opposite bank, and after pouring out a volley of curses, he said,—

"They've crossed here, and not very long sin', that's clear. We're close at their heels, and we mustn't bide long dawdling here; and, Jem, see ye keep that brandy out of t' way of them black and white bugaboos, or we'se have 'em, when their blood's up, knocking out our brains, and we haven't a gun left to learn 'em manners with. Let me lay hold on my gun again, and t' first job I'll put it to will be to shoot every soul of them sneaking, preaching thieves but t' girl, and I'll set her up as a bush-ranger's jin. She's mine by right, sure enough, now that I've put an end to t' palavering of that sneaking fool Bill."

"But, Peter, man," was the answer of one of the men, "I fancy them black fellows didn't half like yer putting a knife into their leader; and down t' country folks would call it a murder."

"It saved Government a good rope," said Peter, "for that was his due. He was a bigger rogue than me, and that's saying a deal."

The fearful oaths that these abandoned men mingled with their conversation perfectly appalled the listening boys, and they felt great relief when they rose; and each drinking a cup of brandy, Peter said, —

"Now come on, and let's get our work done. Them fools will be forced to slacken their pace soon, for the beasts will never hold out over yon scrub; and when we've got our guns and horses, and made an end of the lot of thieves, we'll push on and see if we can't do a stroke of business among any new squatters."

Then the man made a speech to his black troop, in their own language, which seemed to give them pleasure, for they danced and clashed their spears, and started up to continue their route. Thankfully the watchers saw the wretches cross the river, and fall into the snare of continuing over the scrub; but they did not venture to descend for half an hour, when they had lost sight of the rangers, and concluded they must be separated by a distance which rendered them safe.

"What rascals!" exclaimed Gerald. "It was well I had not one of the guns, Arthur; I don't think I could have helped shooting Black Peter, when he boasted that he had murdered Bill. I think I had a right."

"No you hadn't, Gerald," said Hugh. "It would not have been English justice. The worst criminal has a right to a trial by jury. What do you say, Arthur?"

"We should have some trouble in summoning a jury here, Hugh," answered Arthur; "nevertheless, I should not have liked to take on myself the office of executioner. Besides, you must remember, such an act would have brought destruction on ourselves, and on all who depend on us. God will bring the villain to justice."

The boys made their way through the thick wood till they reached the little glade where their anxious friends were watching for them.

"All right!" cried Gerald; "we need not call over the roll. Now you must all be content to form the rear-guard of the bush-rangers. I suppose, Arthur, there is no need to hurry; we are not particularly desirous to overtake the rogues."

"But, my dear boys!" exclaimed Mr. Mayburn; "Arthur, do you speak. Is it safe to venture from this quiet retreat yet? Consider these lawless men might, at any moment, turn round; and it seems they would not scruple to commit murder."

"Was Bill with 'em, sir?" asked David, looking very much ashamed.

With much kindness and consideration, Arthur gently broke to the poor lad the melancholy fate of his vile brother; and David shed many tears for the unhappy convict.

"I were auld enough to have known better, sir," said he; "he couldn't have gettin' me into bad ways, if I'd thought on my prayers and turned again' him; and if I'd held out, things mightn't have turned out so bad wi' him. Them that lets themselves be 'ticed to do bad deeds, is worse nor them that 'tices 'em. God forgive me for niver speaking out like a man to poor Bill!"

Margaret spoke kindly to the sorrowful man, showing him the fearful warning sent in this sad catastrophe, and beseeching him never to forget it; but to pray continually that he might be kept strictly in the right path.

Wilkins was much shocked at the violent death of the convict; but, nevertheless, he whispered to Jenny, "He's well ta'en out of t' way; for he were a bigger scoundrel nor Peter hisself, for all his grand rigmarole talk."

As the lame horse was unfit for work yet, it was led after the rest; and Arthur, who chose to walk, selected David for his companion, and took the opportunity, while he consoled him under his heavy affliction, to direct his softened heart to good and holy aspirations. They continued their journey along the right bank of the rivulet; the country being more fertile, and the grassy plains more favorable for the horses than among the brushwood.

For three days they proceeded undisturbed, and with revived hopes. Then the scenery became still more beautiful; the ground was covered with lofty trees, on which already the young buds were forming. These trees were tenanted by thousands of lovely birds; and their cheerful notes enlivened the solitude. In the distance before them rose a pile of scattered rocky mountains, which, as they drew nearer, they saw were covered with brushwood, and might have formed a barrier to their path, but they seemed to be pierced by innumerable narrow winding gorges.

"We must proceed with great caution and watchfulness here," said Arthur; "for it is not improbable that we may have fallen unhappily upon the track of our enemies, and we must have gained ground on them, now that we are all mounted again. We must be careful to avoid an encounter among these perplexing mountains."

"We have two guns," said Gerald, "and we should have no difficulty in keeping one of these narrow passes against the whole undisciplined gang; then we could have our bowmen hid in the brushwood above, to shower down destruction on the foe. It is a grand spot for a skirmish!"

"God forbid that we should be called on to make this lovely solitude a field of blood!" said Mr. Mayburn. "How dare proud and disobedient man profane the sanctity of Nature, and desecrate her grand and marvellous works. Does not the contemplation of these mighty mountains, spreading as far as the eye can reach, broken into fantastic forms, and apparently inaccessible and impassable, startle and humiliate the presuming pride of fallen man?"

> "There is a voiceless eloquence in earth
> Telling of him who gave her wonders birth."

"Keep in the rear, papa," said Arthur; "we must reconnoitre secretly, before we venture into these mazes."

"Choose a narrow pass, Arthur," cried Gerald. "It will suit best for our manœuvres, if we come to a battle. Halloo! what wild beast can that be I hear roaring. No Australian animal that we have met with yet has such a sonorous voice."

"Oh, Jack!" cried Ruth, clinging to her brother, behind whom she was mounted. "Jack, honey, stop a bit, hear ye; yon's a bear, and I'se feared of my life; it's a bear like them 'at dances about at t' fairs!"

"A bear growls," said Hugh; "but that is decidedly a roar; it is more like the voice of the royal lion, and we shall have some sport at last. To arms! to arms!"

Jack and Ruth were some yards in advance of the rest, when suddenly from a thicket just before them, a wild bull rushed furiously upon their path, tossing his head, as if enraged that his solitude had been invaded, or probably expecting to encounter the powerful opponent which had banished him in disgrace from his own herd. He was a huge, dark-red animal, with short sharp horns and broad forehead, and his fierce and fiery eye, and loud threatening bellow, denoted him to be a dangerous antagonist.

He stopped for a moment and eyed the horse, then tore round and round, throwing up the earth with his horns, and uttering continually a deep sullen roar. Jack was turning round to avoid the unpleasant meeting, when suddenly the infuriated animal arrested his whirling course, and before Jack could extricate himself from Ruth's arms, to use his spear, the beast had rushed impetuously on the horse, and gored it frightfully. The terrified horse immediately reared, and flung both his riders off.

Jack, though considerably bruised, sprang up, dragged the senseless Ruth out of the path of the mad creature, and placed her under the bushes, and then returned with his spear ready to defend himself; but he found to his great grief his poor horse thrown down, trampled on, and gored by the frenzied animal, which continued to repeat its merciless attacks, regardless of the many wounds inflicted by Wilkins and Hugh, who had galloped up in haste to aid Jack.

At length, tired with goring the horse, the bull turned on Jack, who faced him with his uplifted spear; but before he could strike, Arthur called out to them all to draw back, and, riding up himself, he shot the beast through the head. It fell heavily, and Wilkins dismounted, drew out his knife, and went up to finish the execution; but he was too early, for the powerful animal rose again to his legs, caught the man on his strong brow, and flung him over his head to a considerable distance.

A second shot, however, despatched the bull, and then all went up to Wilkins, whom they found insensible; but, though much bruised and stunned by the fall, he was providentially unwounded by the horns of the formidable animal. The exertions of his distressed friends soon restored the poor man to his senses, and he was able to take little Nakinna, to look at the "big dingo," which astonished her so much, and even Baldabella deigned to express some interest at the sight of an animal so much larger than any she had ever beheld. Wilkins declared it was a shame to leave so much good meat lying to waste on the high road; but they were now in a land of plenty; besides, the dark coarse flesh of the bull was not of a tempting quality, and it was agreed that it might as well be abandoned.

But the question arose, "Where did this bull come from?" It was certainly not an Australian animal; and should it have wandered from any settlement, they might hope that they were not so very far from civilization; and as they discussed the probability, and continued their journey, they looked out carefully lest they should encounter any more wild cattle.

A very narrow passage, between two high wood-covered rocky walls, offered a convenient pass, and even suitable to the warlike plan of O'Brien; and Arthur taking the lead, with Gerald behind him, they ventured to leave the rest at the entrance of the pass, till they had first ascertained the safety and direction of the road.

"Arthur," said Gerald, in a suppressed voice, "I am certain that I hear a rustling in the bushes over our heads. Do stop a moment, and let me send an arrow into the bush."

"Pray forbear, my boy," answered Arthur; "if it should be another wild bull, your arrow would only irritate it; and if, as it is probable, the bush-ranger should be some harmless pigeon or parrot, let it live, we are well provided with food. Let us rather turn our thoughts to these perplexing passages, which strike out on all sides of us, and which will bewilder us till we shall never find our way back to our friends, if we go much further. Now, which of these roads shall we take? After all, Gerald, I think we had better turn back for the rest, and take our chance altogether. Which of these puzzling alleys did we come through?"

"Not that dismal hole, Arthur," answered he, laughing. "We came along here, I remember this beautiful overhanging acacia."

Just as he spoke, some stones fell from above on them; and Gerald, seizing the pendent branch of the acacia, leaped from his horse, and before Arthur could interfere was swinging and climbing up the rock.

"Gerald, you rash fellow," cried Arthur, "what has induced you to such a wild frolic? what are you about to do? Do come down."

"Not before I make out the meaning of the acacia showering down stones on my head, instead of fruit," answered Gerald; and then Arthur heard him say in a tone of astonishment, "Halloo! my friend, what will you please to be looking after?"

In utter amazement and alarm at hearing the boy address any being in that strange solitude, Arthur tied the horses to the tree, and, armed with his gun, climbed the rock so expeditiously, that he arrested Gerald's spear, as he was about to strike a tall, rough-looking man, with whom he was struggling, and who turned round as Arthur appeared, saying, "How many more on ye may there be? We can match ye all, rogues as ye are. Have ye fetched our beast back?"

"My good man," said Arthur, "it seems to me that we have been both mistaken. You take us for bush-rangers, and we thought you belonged to the same thievish community. Now, we are poor travellers, robbed by those rangers, who have, with difficulty, made our escape from the plunderers, destitute of all property."

"Ye'll surelie, not have a face to tell me that, young fellow," answered the man, "when I seed ye mysel' atop of one of our horses."

"That certainly is a suspicious circumstance," answered Arthur, laughing; "and I must tell the truth; we did borrow the horses from our jailers, that we might have the means of making our escape."

"That's likely all flam," said the man. "Howsomever, ye mun come afore our master, and make out yer story. I'se not soft enough to let ye off this like."

"We shall be very glad indeed to see your master," replied Arthur; "especially if he is of our country, and near at hand. Who is he? and where is he?"

"He's a squatter," grumbled the man, "and he's down yonder, seeking out a road to get through these in-and-out walls fit to puzzle a conjuror."

"If you will show us an easier mode of descent than that by which we reached you," said Arthur, "we will not only willingly accompany you; but we will take with us the whole of our party, and the stolen horses into the bargain."

The man looked very suspiciously at the free and easy strangers, but, anxious to recover his master's property, he led them by an easy descent to the pass, and then suffered O'Brien to go and bring up the rest of the party, retaining Arthur as a hostage. But the astonishment of the stranger was very great, when he saw the long line of the travellers filling up the narrow pass; and struck by the venerable appearance of Mr. Mayburn, who rode first, his hard features relaxed, he touched his cap with respect, and rode before the travellers, to be the first to announce to his master this wonderful encounter.

Keeping their guide in sight, they followed him through many narrow and intricate paths, gradually ascending, till they came on a wide and level grass-covered spot, still surrounded by high mountainous walls. A number of horses were feeding on the grass, and at the foot of a majestic and almost perpendicular cliff, clothed with a thick forest, were reposing a party of men, eating their repast, which was spread out upon the grass. One of the party looked round, and, with a cry of joy, the wanderers recognized their friend Edward Deverell.

"Arthur! Hugh!" he exclaimed, "my dear and reverend friend Mr. Mayburn! Margaret too! What pleasure! and what miracle can have brought us together once more in these strange and wild mountains?"

"Your man has brought us up before your worship on a charge of stealing," said Arthur, laughing; "and he certainly did not exceed his duty;

he had good grounds for apprehending us, for it seems we are actually travelling on your horses."

"I am glad they are in such good hands," answered Deverell; "but however did my shepherd meet with you?"

"Why, sir," said the man, "ye see, I heared summut like a shot, and off I set, for I was curious like to see what it might be; and I clomb and crambled about, till all at once I hears talking, and I peers through t' bushes, and there I sees one of these here young gents atop of our Sallydun, and says I to myself, 'Them's rangers, they are;' and when young master there clomb up, and defied me like, I thought it were nat'ral that they were rangers, and I laid hands on 'em."

As soon as the man had finished his narrative, repeated and joyful greetings passed between the friends, and Edward Deverell explained that his appearance at such a distance from his home originated in his desire to pursue and capture the audacious bush-rangers who had robbed him of so much property.

"I have brought with me three of my own stock-keepers to identify the cattle," he said; "the rest, as you may see from their complexion and uniform, are of that useful body, the native police."

These dark-complexioned officials were of very striking appearance; their dress was light and scanty, bristling with pistols and sabres; their feet bare, and their hair long and flowing. Their keen, glittering eyes ran over the strangers in a most professional manner, very embarrassing to Wilkins and David, who both held down their heads before the searching glances. David seemed afraid to appear before his injured master, who looked much surprised to see him attached to Mr. Mayburn's party; but discreetly deferred any investigation into the affair, till he should be informed what strange chance had brought the voyagers to India into the very heart of Australia.

"Don't you remember, Edward Deverell," said Hugh, "that Gerald and I always wished to be here, instead of broiling among the Hindoos, and being carried about in palanquins? And I believe Arthur and Margaret longed for it in their hearts, only they conceived it was papa's duty to fulfil his engagement. Yet, after all, it is not our own will, but a happy ordination of Providence, that has at length united us; and now, I suppose, we must follow your example and *squat* in Australia."

"But consider the risk, my dear Hugh," said Mr. Mayburn. "Even our experienced friend Deverell has not escaped being plundered by these savages, who are too frequently in union with unscrupulous murderers. I should live in continual dread in these wild regions."

"Why, papa," said Gerald, "there are robbers and murderers even in happy and civilized Britain."

"Doubtless there are, Gerald," said Edward Deverell. "No civilization can eradicate the black spot of our fallen nature; it is only the grace and mercy of God that can keep the evil spirit in subjection. But have no fears, my dear Mr. Mayburn; we must not alarm Margaret when we hope to persuade her to visit our lonely retreat. We have an excellent police staff; and when our servants are properly drilled, and our fences made secure, we shall be as safe as we should be in Europe. Now give the horses to the servants; sit down and eat; and then let me hear your strange adventures."

CHAPTER XXXII

Arthur was the narrator, and his long and wonderful story produced much sympathy and astonishment in his friendly hearer. At the earnest request of Margaret, the delinquent Davy was pardoned, and reinstalled in his office of stock-keeper; and Mr. Deverell promised to interest himself to obtain the emancipation of Wilkins.

"I must enlist you all to join my small force," said Edward Deverell; "for it is my intention to persevere in my attempt to recover my cattle and punish the robbers. My black allies are of opinion that the men who drove off the cattle will dispose of them to some of those unprincipled dealers who range the interior to pick up such bargains, and who can again sell them for large profits to the Macquarie gold-diggers, who make no inquiries how they were obtained. They must necessarily bring the cattle through the direct pass of these mountains, which is not quite so perplexing as that you had selected; and we are encamped here to watch for and intercept them. From your report, the party will be more numerous than we expected; but the hungry blacks who swell their train, in the hopes of receiving a share of the brandy and tobacco, are no heroes. I think, Hugh, we shall be able to give them a drubbing."

"As if there could be a doubt of it!" said Hugh, contemptuously. "We are all ready to enlist into the ranks, captain, I will engage to say—that is, with the exception of papa and the womankind; the chaplain to the regiment, and the Sisters of Charity who are to attend on the wounded."

"Most useful members of the army they will be," answered Deverell, "if we come to close quarters; for, greatly as I abhor warfare, I do not expect to settle this vexatious matter without bloodshed."

"If ye did, sir," said Wilkins, "ye'd be wrong; and, depend on't, ye'd soon have plenty more such-like customers. If a mad dog were to bite a man, and he let it run off, he'd be safe to bite other folks, and that's not fair. I say, knock him on t' head at first."

"The cases will hardly bear comparison, Wilkins," replied Mr. Mayburn; "and it has ever been a question among reasoning men whether the destitute ought to be subjected to capital punishment for seizing a share of the abundance of the prosperous."

"Robin Hood law!—rob the rich to feed the poor," cried Gerald. "Only think of papa encouraging bush-ranging!"

"My dear Mr. Mayburn, spare your compassion for these rogues," said Deverell, laughing. "These men are not destitute—they are worthless, idle vagabonds, and, according to the by-laws of squatters and settlers, they are amenable to justice. I shall certainly reclaim my own property, give the scoundrels a sound thrashing, and, if they show fight, we are prepared for actual service, and they must take the consequences."

It was long before the party were tired of conversation, and settled to take a secure night's rest; while the watchful police relieved each other, lest the rangers should pass during the night. In the morning they placed themselves in convenient posts on the mountains, where they could command all the approaches; but the day was somewhat advanced when notice was given that objects were seen approaching at a distance. Then the work of preparation actually began; along the heights of the pass were placed the rifle-rangers, as Hugh termed them, consisting of Arthur, Gerald, and himself, Mr. Deverell, and six of the police. Margaret and Mr. Mayburn, with the women, were left in perfect security in the little glen where the encampment was formed; and the rest of the party guarded the end of the pass, to secure any of the enemy who might succeed in reaching it.

"We conclude," said Mr. Deverell, "that the rangers, who doubtless are well acquainted with the pass, will drive the cattle on before them. Now we propose to secure these as they issue from this walled passage, and when they are all again in our possession, the stock-keepers must be ready to drive them off; while the rest of our troop must intercept and capture the drivers, to prevent pursuit. And now, Davy, I will test your fidelity again. Will you take up your whip and set off with our beasts to the station?"

"If ye'd not object, master," said Davy, humbly, "I'd as lief have a shot among 'em afore I set out, specially at that deep, black-hearted rogue Peter, as put an end to our Bill. I can't say, master, Bill didn't get far wrang; but Peter's out and out a worse chap, and it wasn't his place to kill a better fellow nor hisself."

"You will obey my orders, Davy," said his master, "and leave the punishment of Peter in our hands. I will take care he shall suffer for his misdeeds; and you will do your duty best by looking after your old four-footed friends. Have the rogues spared poor Lily, David? She was of a fine breed, Gerald, and I was deeply incensed at the rogues for selecting her to carry off."

"Bless ye, master, they count nought of breeds," answered Davy; "all they want is to kill plenty for beef, and to swop all they've left for spurrits and backy; Lily was to t' fore when I cut off from 'em, bonnie cretur, but she'll be hard up, if they've brought her this far. She always kenned me, master, and let me milk her; but she niver could bide them black fellows nigh hand her."

"Very good, Davy," answered Deverell. "Then your duty is to drive off Lily, and as many more beasts as you can manage, to this glen; and to remain here with Mr. Mayburn till we come up, as we hope, with our prisoners. Then we shall set out in good spirits on our long journey to Daisy Grange."

In a quarter of an hour all the arrangements were made, the brave defenders were all ready: by this time the procession was close to the mountains; the bush-rangers were driving the cattle before them, followed by Peter, with his black troop. He now appeared painted like his men with the peculiar insignia of war and defiance, his body being marked in red lines in the form of a skeleton, a decoration he had probably adopted to conciliate the natives.

The weary cattle were slowly urged into the narrow rock-bound path, one of the rangers heading them, to lead them along the right pass, the rest following them closely. The confined path rung with the lowing of the alarmed and reluctant cattle, forced onward cruelly by the spears of their drivers, whose wild and terrific oaths completed the discordant tumult. At length, when the cattle-leader emerged from the narrow part of the pass to a more open space, and had his face turned back to see that the line of animals was properly brought forward, he was easily seized, gagged, and bound by the dexterous police. Then, as the animals one after another appeared, they were driven off by the stock-keepers to the glen.

The rest of the party were prepared to capture the rangers as they followed the cattle; but the sudden cry of the leader, who had been seized, and which was easily distinguished amidst the clamor of the noisy cattle, was heard by Peter. The shrewd man at once comprehended the opposition that awaited them, and calling on his black fellows to wield their spears and follow him, he rushed on, with his men behind him, to the scene of conflict. The police on the heights allowed him and some of his black followers to proceed a little forward, and then fired a volley down into the midst of the blacks that were left behind, who, surprised and bewildered, and ever terrified at the effects of fire-arms, turned back tumultuously and fled. In vain the desperate Black Peter shouted to rally his followers, and fought desperately against the men at the end of the pass with the few supporters he had brought on. He and his troops were soon overpowered, and all captured and bound, with very little bloodshed.

"Huzza!" cried Gerald; "a glorious victory! Arthur, you must write the despatch; naming the superior force of the enemy, the cool and determined bravery of the little body of defenders, the desperate resistance of the furious bush-rangers, their complete discomfiture; and, finally, you must particularly mention the prudent, vigorous, and successful support of the young Lieutenant O'Brien, who is recommended for promotion."

"Margaret will consider us all heroes," said Hugh; "and we must hasten on as speedily as possible to allay her anxiety for us. But, Captain Deverell, whatever are we to do with these prisoners?"

"We are bound to convey or send the dangerous bush-rangers to Sydney," answered Deverell, "there to be dealt with according to law. As for the cowardly, treacherous, and ignorant natives, we must devise some punishment for them; but, if possible, we will not encumber ourselves with them, nor be obliged to feed them on our journey. For the present we must contrive to keep them in some place of security till the police return from their useless chase of the unhappy blacks who have fled."

"And who will, I hope, escape," said Arthur; "for they are but tools in the hands of these abandoned convicts, and are scarcely themselves responsible for their deeds of evil."

"See here," said Gerald; "this large cave would make a good jail, and we might build up the entrance."

"Then ye'll have to look about for a lot of caves, Master Gerald," said Wilkins, "and lodge 'em, as they say down t' country, on t' separate system, or we'se find all our birds flown to-morrow morning, I'll engage. Why, bless you, if that there Black Peter was shut up for a day wi' a new-born babby, he'd make 't a rogue for life. He'd make a parson into a bush-ranger, give him a bit of time; and my fancy is as how he's helped by that bad 'un as is his master; God save us!"

"There is no doubt, Wilkins," said Mr. Mayburn, "that the Great Spirit of Evil does readily and unfailingly stretch forth his hand to aid his wicked followers, and we should all join in your prayer, my good man. May God save us in the hour of temptation!"

Around the little hollow where the encampment was found, and where the young heroes were joyfully welcomed, were many small caves in the rocks, in which the prisoners, black and white, were separately enclosed. One of the stock-keepers had received a spear-wound in his arm; and one of the misguided natives was killed by a rifle-shot. These were all the casualties. When the police returned from the pursuit of the black fugitives, who had taken refuge in a thick wood, after many of them had been severely wounded, Mr. Deverell requested that all further pursuit should be relinquished, as the cattle were recovered and the ringleaders were now in confinement, which he knew would be a terrible punishment to them, even though it were only for one night.

Margaret and Mr. Mayburn paid every care and attention to the wounded man, and when all their duties were fulfilled, the united friends sat down, to rest on the green turf, and to talk of the hopeful future.

"Now, we are all anxious to know, Edward Deverell," said Hugh, "if you have got your house built, or if you are all dwelling in tents; and, above all, what kind of place is Daisy Grange?"

"I have got my house built, Hugh," answered he, "and Daisy Grange I will leave undescribed, only assuring you that it will be completely a paradise in my eyes when I see you all there, which I trust will be before many days are passed."

"And the daisies?" inquired Margaret.

"The daisies were at first coy and capricious in their new home," answered he, "but finally they have yielded to care and perseverance, and consented to adorn my small lawn, in sufficient numbers to justify me in retaining the dear name for my much beloved home."

"And what does Emma do in the wilderness?" asked Hugh.

"She cultivates flowers," replied Deverell, "sews on buttons, and performs other needful female occupations, plays, sings, reads, and is not ashamed to assist her mother, and Susan the dairy-maid, to make the butter and cheese."

"Is that Susan Raine?" asked Margaret, anxiously, for she saw Wilkins looking at Mr. Deverell with much agitation. "Is that the pretty, modest Susan, that was our fellow-voyager?"

"It is the same girl," answered Deverell. "Poor Susan, we are all very sorry for her; she had to endure a grievous disappointment, for she had taken the opportunity of accompanying us, as our servant, in order that she might join her betrothed, a wild fellow that had been transported for some venial offence; and when we reached Melbourne, and instituted the regular inquiry, we found the man had made his escape in an India vessel, with some vile wretches who had been working with him. I fear he is wholly unworthy of the good girl, who still mourns so deeply for him."

"He's nought but a reg'lar scoundrel," said Wilkins, impetuously, "he is; and she'd sarved him right if she'd gone and wed another; that's what she has done likely, sir?"

"That is what I certainly wished her to do," said Deverell, looking surprised at the free interference of Wilkins; "but the silly girl is still haunted by the wild hope of reclaiming the unfortunate man who was the companion of her childhood. She has refused the young herdsman who is so kindly attended by Miss Margaret; a worthy fellow, and has determined to remain unmarried for the sake of the convict who has so cruelly neglected her."

"That's like my bonnie true-hearted lass," said Wilkins, much excited. "Scamp as I were to lose her! But now please, Miss Margaret, to put in a word like for me. Tell t' master I'se nought like so bad but that there's some hopes of me, if Sue will take up wi' me; but how can I look for't?"

Margaret undertook to explain Wilkins's position to Deverell, and to plead for him to Susan; and the rough convict turned away with a tear in his eye, as the recollection of youthful and innocent days shone through the mist of evil deeds that had darkened his mature life.

Mr. Deverell was pleased with the story of Wilkins, and as he would be far removed from temptation at the settlement, and would be carefully watched by his good friends, he promised to bestow Susan on him; and now they prepared to break up the encampment, and to pursue their journey under pleasant auspices.

"But before we set out," said Mr. Deverell, "it will be necessary to come to some, arrangement about our troublesome prisoners. We must hold a court of justice, as imposing as circumstances will permit, and endeavor to alarm them, and make a salutary impression on them."

"There is a handsome rocky throne for the bench," said Hugh. "Please to ascend to the elevation, Mr. Judge Deverell, and look as grave as you possibly can; papa will sit by you in the character of Mercy, to mitigate the severity of Justice. Arthur and Gerald must take that hill, and Jack and I will remain here to represent counsel. We will not take the trouble to call a jury, because I know my lord judge has made up his mind about the sentence. Now, all you people stand round, and leave a passage for the police to bring up the prisoners. Will this do, my lord?"

"I am content, Hugh, provided you all look serious," answered Deverell. "You must make the most of our strength, and display your arms to advantage. With these ignorant natives, in their present condition, intimidation is the only mode of subjection. I hope the time is not very distant when milder measures may be used to win them to civilization. We are commencing the work by educating the children."

The glen was first cleared by sending the stock-keepers forward with the cattle, as their progress must necessarily be slow; then, one after another, the police released the trembling, crouching savages from the caves, and brought them before the judge. The poor wretches, at the sight of the array of guns and spears before them, endured all the terrors of death. Deverell, who had acquired some facility in speaking their language, made a long address to the terrified men; reproaching them with their folly and ingratitude in robbing him, who had never refused to assist them in their days of destitution, and who earnestly desired their welfare. He warned them of the danger of dealing with the bush-rangers, who always deceived them, and of frequenting the bush taverns to obtain the poisonous liquor which would in the end destroy their whole nation. He threatened them with instant death if they dared to transgress again; and then, satisfied with the fright he had given them, he relieved them from their misery by giving them leave to depart; a permission which they did not delay a moment to make use of; but sprung up the rocks, and speedily disappeared to seek the concealment of the bush.

There remained now only the four vile bush-rangers to dispose of; but these men, all escaped convicts, Mr. Deverell declined to punish, proposing to commit them to the charge of four of the mounted police, who were to conduct them, or, as these officials appropriately expressed it, to drive them to Sydney, and there deliver them into the hands of justice.

These ruffians were therefore brought from their respective dungeons, and manacled two together; their persons were searched, lest they should have any concealed arms; and their legs were then released from the fetters. Peter, who obstinately refused to submit to the incumbrance of clothing, required no search, and was coupled to one of his bush ranging friends, loudly showering curses on his conquerors.

"Do you mean us to set out fasting with these malignant scoundrels?" he yelled out. "Ye're fine Christians, to hunger folks. And ye know as well as we do these greedy black rascals will prig all our rations on t' road."

Mr. Deverell did know that the black police were scandalously harsh with their white prisoners, and he therefore ordered that these wretched criminals should sit down for half an hour, and be supplied with a plentiful breakfast of cold meat, which they began to devour ravenously, watched curiously by Ruth, who concealed herself in a thicket, that she might look in safety at these terrible bush-rangers. All the rest of the party, glad to avoid the sight of the wretches, wandered off to another little glen which opened from their encampment, except Mr. Deverell and Arthur, who had called the police to one side to give them a strict charge to be watchful and determined, but at the same time to treat their prisoners with humanity.

While they were conversing, they were startled and alarmed by a scream from Ruth, who, they believed, had left the encampment with the rest of the party, and on turning round they saw, to their great vexation, the ranger who had been linked with Peter galloping off on the horse of one of the police, which, ready for starting, had been tied to a tree near the prisoners. The police mounted the other three horses that were ready, and speedily pursued the fugitive; while Deverell and Arthur went up in haste, and found, to their extreme mortification, that the villain Peter was also missing. The remainder of the party, recalled from their ramble by the shriek of Ruth, had now joined them; and when the agitated girl was able to give an account of the occurrence, she said:—

"He reached out, and took a cloak off t' horse, and groped in t' pockets till he fetched out summut, maybe a key, for I heard a click; and then Peter jumped up and laid hands on t' horse; but t' other fellow was sharp after him, and pushed him off, and loped atop on his back hisself, and galloped off like mad, and left Peter standing. Oh master! how awful he swore and stamped about, and took off right up to me, and I shrieked out; and then he scrambled up yon wood." And Ruth pointed to the precipitous wood-covered wall of the glen.

CHAPTER XXXIII

They had not time to consider what steps to take, when Wilkins cried out, "Yon's the rogue;" and they caught a glimpse of the painted figure of the fugitive among the trees, at a height which seemed almost impossible to reach, for they all considered this precipitous rock inaccessible.

"We must not let the villain escape us," cried Jack, "or he will be sure to lead more poor wretches astray. Some of you follow me." And, without further delay, he caught hold of the branches of the lowest tree, and swung himself up, grasping the overhanging boughs, and forcing his way through the entangled bushes with toil and danger, while Ruth continued to cry out like a distracted creature.

It was strange, that in this dilemma the usual cool presence of mind of the fearless and determined ruffian seemed to forsake him. If he had sought the labyrinthine passages of the widely-spread mountain, he might easily have bewildered his pursuers; but he continually exposed himself to observation through the trees on the mountain-side.

Wilkins and one of the herdsmen of Mr. Deverell soon followed Jack, their whole mind bent on capturing this treacherous and sanguinary villain. Behind them, urged by curiosity, anxiety for her brother, and detestation of Black Peter, the excited girl Ruth, notwithstanding the efforts of her friends, plunged through the bushes to follow them, shouting wildly to her brother when she caught glimpses of the spectral figure of the convict, with the red lines painted on his body.

Onward up that tedious ascent the practised bush-ranger proceeded, not even pausing for breath; and his half-exhausted pursuers began to fear he would escape them; but, after half an hour's struggle, a light gleamed through the trees. They believed they were coming to a more open space, when, rather than allow the convict to escape, the men resolved to use their guns. The next minute they emerged from the wood, and the whole party shrunk back, astonished at the magnificent scene that lay before them. A few feet from the wood a vast abyss opened. The eye could not penetrate its depths: it appeared fathomless and dark, for on all sides it was bounded by the perpendicular cliff which descended from the verge of the forest.

For a moment only could the dizzy sight regard that terrific descent, from which only three feet of solid earth separated them; and they clung to the trees, as they looked round to search for the fugitive. To their great horror, they beheld the desperate man, making his way along the narrow hem of earth, supported by a spear he had caught up on one hand, and holding by the trees on the other, and apparently seeking for a convenient spot where he might again descend into the wood. He stopped and turned round, and observing his pursuers, who feared even to use their guns in such a perilous position, the vindictive wretch poised and flung the spear. But before it had even reached its destination, a yell of mortal terror was heard; the shelf of rock on which he stood, gave way under the impetuosity of his movement; and the doomed wretch was hurled into that vast space, beyond the reach of human eyes, his shrieks of horror growing fainter as he sank into death. While at the same time, from the tree which he had grasped, and which shook as he fell, rose a flight of black cockatoos, mocking with their loud strange cries his fearful fate.

"Lord have mercy on him!" exclaimed Jack, covering his face, and struck with awe.

"It's a judgment, man," said Wilkins. "Just see how this poor fellow is bleeding with the rogue's last will and deed."

The spear of Peter had entered the breast of the herdsman, who was bleeding profusely. Wilkins drew out the weapon, and Jack, seeing Ruth at his side, who had succeeded in reaching him in time to see the catastrophe, despatched her in haste to the encampment, to send aid for the wounded man.

Fearful of looking any longer at that dark and terrible grave of the sinful wretch, the girl tumbled down through the steep wood, and rushing up to Mr. Mayburn and Margaret, said, "He's carried off alive! Them bad spirits,—them! them!—have flown away with Black Peter;" and the distracted girl positively shrieked as she pointed to a pair of harmless black cockatoos perched on a fig-tree, which were curiously peering down on the strange creatures below; and most assuredly the coal-black plumage, lofty crest, and fan tail, striped with bars of fiery scarlet, gave to the birds an unearthly and fiend-like appearance.

"Can anybody extract sense from the exclamations of this wild girl?" asked Mr. Mayburn, much distressed. "Ascertain, Margaret, how the wretched man has escaped."

"I tell ye," continued Ruth, with decision, "I seed them black creaters, wi' my own eyes, take him up, and flee away wi' him, down into a black pit; and poor Tom Atkinson's hit wi' a spear, and ye're to clamber up t' wood to doctor him."

On the whole, the deduction drawn from Ruth's incoherent narrative was, that the presence of some of the party was needed; and Mr. Deverell and Mr. Mayburn, supplied with cold water and linen bandages, set out to climb through the wood, on the beaten track of the pursued and the pursuers; but before they had half ascended, they met with Wilkins and Jack, bearing the wounded man with difficulty through the matted and steep wood. When they were relieved by additional assistance, they soon reached the glen, and satisfied the anxiety of the perplexed family by a correct recital of the awful fate of the villanous bush-ranger.

"It's just what might have come to me, and I'd been but reet sarved," said Wilkins, "if it hadn't been for ye all. I reckon it pleased God to send ye, just o' purpose to bring round a good-to-naught chap, as not a soul else would notish, or hauld out a finger to save. Poor reprobate! Ye ken a deal of things, Miss Marget; can ye say what Peter was seeing afore him, when he yelled out, fleeing down into that black hole?"

"God be merciful to the sinner!" said Margaret. "It is not for us, Wilkins, to speak of that which God hides from us; but rather to prepare, that we may be ready for a sudden call to judgment."

It was not long before the police returned with the fugitive, whom they had overtaken and captured. He was now secured with the other two rangers, and Peter being disposed of, there was nothing to prevent the police from proceeding with their prisoners to Sydney; and the guards and captives set out on their long journey, leaving the united party very thankful for their separation from the wretched delinquents. The next morning, after praying for a blessing on their expedition, the happy friends set forward cheerfully, now safely guided by Edward Deverell, and hoping, before long, to reach the long-desired haven of peace and rest.

But many a day of toil and anxiety still succeeded: the privations of the barren and dry desert, the perils of rude mountain-passes, and the fording deep and foaming rivers, besides the subtle and vindictive pursuit of various unfriendly tribes of natives. At length they attained in safety the fertile banks of a broad and rapid river, which Mr. Deverell and his followers greeted with shouts of joy.

"My good Mr. Mayburn," said Edward Deverell, "I call on you now to offer up a thanksgiving to Him who has led us in safety through the wilderness. This river is our guide and highway; it flows on to our own much-loved home; it is the blessing and ornament, dear Margaret, of Daisy Grange."

All joined with Christian earnestness in a thanksgiving for the mercies which even the lately awakened and reformed criminals could appreciate and understand; and Edward Deverell rejoiced to see that the two convicts, Wilkins and Davy, would not be a dangerous addition to his little Christian community.

"Now, my dear friends," said Edward Deverell, "we may trust that our progress may be unimpeded. This fertile soil, watered by the river, will restore our enfeebled cattle; then we shall have milk with our flour cakes, which, prepared by the skilful hand of Jenny, disdain fellowship with the heavy 'damper' of the Australian traveller. If this abundant food does not satisfy us, the trees will give us birds, and the river fish, to diversify our diet. Ought we not to rejoice?"

"If you please, Mr. Deverell," said Jenny, "yon's a bonnie flock of geese; couldn't ye get us one for a roast?"

"We must have more than one for our large party, Jenny," said Deverell, laughing. "Come, boys, let us have a shot at Jenny's geese, and secure one specially for Mr. Mayburn's new museum."

Delighted with the prospect of sport, the boys were soon ready, and returned from the banks of the river with two pair of these large birds. Edward Deverell held out one of them to Jenny, saying, "Now, my good woman, can you tell me what this fowl is?"

"A gray goose, Mr. Deverell, sure enough," answered Jenny. Then regarding it closely, she added, "but it has a queer short neb, sir; it's like all things in this country, it's just unnat'ral."

"Nurse, it is no more a goose than you are," said Hugh; "it is *rara avis*, papa, that is,—a bird of Australia."

"I recognize it with delight," said Mr. Mayburn, "from the description of Latham and later ornithologists, who class it as a new genus; and from the curious *cere* which envelopes the base of the bill, he names it *Cereopsis*. Still it belongs to the swimming birds, though the legs are naked above the joint, and the membrane between the toes does not form the web foot. It is, therefore, less fitted for the water than the goose or swan, and is more strictly a wader, living, not on fish, but vegetable food. In fact, it is a much handsomer bird than the goose, and I would gladly preserve it, if I had the means."

"You will have means and opportunity at the Deverell station, my dear Mr. Mayburn," said Edward. "My brother Charles will supply the means, and assist you to form a museum; and Emma has domesticated a flock of these birds, which in common parlance are known as the short-billed geese; and I can assure you the flesh is most delicate, very unlike that of the common water-fowls which live on fish."

"I rejoice much, Edward Deverell," said Mr. Mayburn, "that you concur with me in admiring the works of nature,—a taste which I have endeavored to implant in my children. I remember the words of a clever writer. 'To look on the creation with an eye of interest and feeling, must be ever acceptable to the Creator. To trace out the several properties of his works, and to study with diligence and humility their laws, their uses, and operations, is an employment worthy the immortal mind of man; since it is one of those studies which we may reasonably hope will survive beyond the grave.'"

"How delighted I am that dear little Emmy is taking the first steps of study in ornithology, by setting up a poultry-yard," said Hugh. "We had many disputes about waste of time in such useless pursuits, in which I did not escape without much contumely for my bird lore. My generous retaliation shall be to improve her collection. I will get her the black swan, the talegalla, the apteryx...."

"And the emu and ornithorhynchus would look well in the poultry-yard, Hugh," said Gerald, laughing.

"That would be a great error, my dear boys," said Mr. Mayburn. "The habits of the ornithorhynchus are directly opposed to the domestic arrangements of the poultry-yard: it is not even a fowl; it is an unclassed animal, of burrowing and diving propensities, and would be a troublesome, if not a dangerous, inmate among domestic fowls."

"I will leave it to Hugh and Emma to arrange the foreigners as they may judge best," said Mr. Deverell; "but I know all our English fowls are furiously national, and would resent the introduction of strangers, even to bloodshed. Even the civil wars of the community tax the patience of Emma and her handmaid Susan greatly; and she has threatened to reduce their numbers, now become enormous."

"I can supply her with an assistant poultry-maid," said Margaret; "my poor Ruth is devotedly attached to fowls, and can manage them better than she can do any thing else in the world. Ruth, would you not like to be Mr. Deverell's poultry-woman?"

"I would like to be amang 'em, bonnie creaters!" answered Ruth, with great joy, "if you be there Miss Marget, and if they be cocks and hens; and if them black fellows will not run off wi' them."

"Our black neighbors are all tame, Ruth," answered Mr. Deverell. "We employ those who can be taught to work, clothe the women, and teach the children; and in times of scarcity or sickness, we feed and attend them. As far as their ignorant and dull nature will allow, we have reason to think that gratitude or policy would prevent them from injuring us or our property."

"But the bush-rangers," said Margaret; "are you not ever in fear of the crafty, vindictive bush-rangers?"

"During our journey," answered Mr. Deverell, "it is necessary that we should be watchful; but our black police have reduced the number of these vagabonds greatly, and our party is too formidable to be openly defied. We must necessarily pass, now and then, one of those infamous, lonely, road-side bush-taverns, as they are called, at which these villains are in the habit of congregating, that they may exchange their plunder for spirits and tobacco with the men at the station, who then forward the cattle to Sydney or to the gold-diggings. But our police-followers are well acquainted with these detestable stations, and are always prepared for any assault. Above all, dear Margaret, we have a precious charge, and think ourselves a band of brave fellows; every day diminishes our danger, for it brings us nearer to our own inhabited grounds, where the villains might venture to plunder secretly, but would certainly not dare to show themselves."

"But are your retainers spread about the estate?" said Hugh. "I thought you intended to build a town."

"I scarcely aim so high, Hugh," replied Deverell. "My stock-keepers are scattered over the cleared land in huts, to look after the cattle. I live in my castle, like a feudal lord, surrounded by my vassals, who have erected rude temporary huts. But if you will all agree to settle round me, we will really found a colony. I will make an application to purchase, instead of leasing, my immense tract of land. We will divide and cultivate it, which I never could do alone; and we will begin to build a handsome village, or perhaps two villages—one named Mayburn, and the other Deverell."

"Please, sir, have you plenty of timber?" asked Jack, roused at the prospect of work.

"You will see my woods and forests soon, Jack," answered Mr. Deverell. "Then I have inexhaustible quarries of stone in the mountains, and some good quarrymen and stonecutters on my establishment. We will have a regular English village, with a green for sports, and pleasant gardens to the cottages."

For a few days more they travelled pleasantly over the grassy turf; then they came on almost impenetrable brushwood; and as this formidable obstacle to their progress would require vigor to overcome it, they encamped to spend the night, and commence their fatigue with the morning light. But they found conversation and repose equally impossible, from the disturbance caused by the restless movements and incessant bellowing of the cattle, which struggled to escape from the pens in which their attendants had confined them. Hugh went up to them with some curiosity, to know what was the cause of this unusual excitement amongst the quiet creatures. The herdsmen were all grinning and rubbing their hands with great glee.

"Well, Patrick," said Deverell to one of the men, "what is the jest that you seem to enjoy so much?"

"It's the bastes, master," answered the man exultingly; "they know where they are, the craters! Don't they smell the smell of their own comrades, sinsible darlings! And it isn't the brush they'd mind if we were giving them lave to it. Isn't it a short cut they'd make to come at them as is of their own blood! True old Irish they are, and illegant bastes. Arrah, didn't them rogues see that when they came kidnapping? and didn't they choose them out, in regard that there were no bastes to be seen like them! Bad luck to the rappareens!"

"Can it be possible," asked Margaret, "that we are really so near to Daisy Grange that the animals scent it?"

"We are a long day's journey yet from Daisy Grange," answered Deverell; "but it is true that we are not far from the borders of my extensive estate. This formidable thorny brushwood forms, in fact, the boundary and defence on this side, neither easy nor desirable to penetrate. A very large portion of the interior of my land is not only uncultivated, but is even unknown to me. We take care, however, to have cattle-stations and hut-keepers round the boundaries, that our rights may be recognized and preserved; and doubtless these weary wanderers have been stolen from one of the border stations, and now scent with great satisfaction their old companions, and their old quiet, luxurious homes."

"Then I suppose we may conclude," said Gerald, "that if we understood the vaccine gamut, we should hear that big old red cow bellowing 'Home! sweet home!' And don't I wish we could join her, for I don't like the look of that ugly scrub we shall have to carry our horses through."

"Not altogether ugly," said Margaret; "look at this curious and interesting Banksia, with its stiff yellow robe; the white star-like blossoms of this shrub, which resembles our myrtle; and here is our old friend the tea-shrub."

"Which Jenny will have to relinquish now," said Deverell, "for the real tea of China, of which we have a goodly store. But, Jem, or some of you men over there, be pleased to fire a shot or two to chase away those intolerable noisy dingoes, which, doubtless, like the ogre, smell fresh meat, and would like to make a foray on our game."

"Let us shoot a dingo, Edward," said Hugh; "I should like to look at the fellow closely."

"It is scarcely consistent with humanity," answered Deverell, "to destroy an animal that can be of no use to us; but we have an excuse in the wolfish character of the dingo, which destroys our sheep in numbers, if not closely watched; and nothing affords my shepherds and herdsmen more gratification than to trap or shoot one of these marauders." Hugh had the gratification of shooting the *dingo*, or *warragle*, as Baldabella named it, and bringing it in for Arthur and his father to inspect. Margaret retired in disgust, the intolerable smell of the fierce-looking little animal was so offensive.

"From its destructive habits," said Mr. Mayburn, "I should have expected to see a larger animal; but of its wolfish ferocity there seems no doubt. It is remarkable that it is, unlike the land quadrupeds yet found in Australia, carnivorous, and not marsupial; thus confirming the theory that the race of dogs is to be found in every known region of the world. This dingo is a degraded representative of the noble animal, crafty, bloodthirsty, and untamable. I am satisfied with seeing this specimen, but I cannot admire the creature."

Before the first gleam of day, while the moon yet lighted up the heavens, the impatient travellers set out to cross the bush; and for more than two hours the long cavalcade wound with toil and difficulty through the tangled thorny bush. At length the lowing of other cattle than their own greeted their ears, and the fresher breeze that came over the cleared ground announced that they had passed the boundary, and were now actually entering the domain of Mr. Deverell. In a short time the mingled and familiar cries of the drovers and their charge roused the first stock-man in his hut, who rushed out in great joy to welcome the return of the expedition.

"Ay, ay, sir!" said the man, "I see they've picked out and made an end of the choicest of the stock; it's like their ways;" and he grumbled out his wishes that certain evil consequences might attend their unlawful feasts on his chosen favorites, and concluded by caressing those which had happily escaped being devoured by the robbers. He then proposed to send forward one of the shepherds to announce the good news; but the travellers, now relieved from the charge of the cattle, and having passed through the greatest difficulties of their journey, agreed to proceed forward without delay, and announce in their own persons the success of the expedition at head-quarters.

They crossed a vast tract of wild and beautiful forest ground, which was still uncleared, but at this season bright with rich flowers, and noisy with the birds that thronged the tall trees; and continued to ride forward till the heat of the noonday sun compelled them to rest two hours most reluctantly in a shady grove. Then, once more mounting, they rode forward to enter on a new region. Before them lay spread large, well-cultivated, fenced lands, stocked with sheep and cattle, and dotted here and there with the snug neat huts of the shepherds and stock-keepers; while the lowing and bleating of the animals, and the distant barking of dogs, and sound of English voices, were music to the charmed ears of the weary travellers. "His name be praised!" said Mr. Mayburn, reverently uncovering his head, "who has led us through the dry and barren wilderness to a land of plenty and peace."

The whole party were deeply affected at the first glimpse of home scenery and home sounds; but Deverell looked round with much anxiety till he caught sight of a respectable-looking man riding among the cattle at a distance, whom he hailed, and the man rode forward in haste, calling out, "Welcome home, master."

"Thanks, Harris; but tell me, is all well at the Grange?" asked Deverell.

"Charming, sir," answered he; "saw them all this morning. Old mistress quite brisk, asking after the lambs; and Miss, throng with her poultry, and telling me to look after some grain for them. And here comes Mr. Edward, sir, to answer for himself."

"Halloo! Charley," cried Edward, riding up to shake hands with his brother, "my good fellow, what have you been about, and what in the world has induced you to bring the prisoners with you?" and he looked with suspicion and annoyance at the large party of distressed and ragged followers, who had purposely turned away from him. At last Margaret looked round and smiled, and the delighted young fellow laughed with joy at seeing his old friends, and with amusement at their miserable condition.

"My dear Margaret! my good friends!" he exclaimed, "I am quite wild with surprise and pleasure. Never mind your ragged furbelows; little Emma is a capital needlewoman, and will sew up all those great rents."

"It will be a great blessing to me," said Margaret, laughing, "to see a needle again."

"A needle, Margaret!" exclaimed Charles, "we have millions of needles; Edward has a storehouse crammed with every thing that everybody can want, under every circumstance. He could supply a large English country town with goods; chests of needles, walls built up of paper, acres of that muslin stuff you wear, so suitable to the thorny bush. Ask for what you will, you can have it at Edward's grand bazaar."

"If you please, Mr. Charles," said Jack, "do you think Mr. Edward has any tools?"

"You have only to speak, Jack," answered he; "we can supply you with the appliances of the arts, from a steam-engine to a delicate lancet. I am a clever shopman, and shall be happy to do the honors of the bazaar."

"Indeed, Charles, you are a very troublesome and disorderly shopman," said his brother, "as my store-keeper declares, creating vast confusion among his neatly-arranged shelves. Allowing for some exaggeration, my dear friends, Charles has told you the fact. I found my poor people had to pay so extravagantly for the little luxuries and necessaries of life they required, either from the extortions of itinerant dealers, who are dangerous visitors to admit into a settlement, or from the expense of journeys to Sydney or Melbourne to make their purchases, that I resolved to supply them at moderate prices myself, which I am enabled to do by bringing wagon-loads of goods from Sydney, and furnishing a large storehouse which I had built for the purpose."

"But are you not afraid of the bush-rangers being attracted by your valuable storehouse?" asked Mr. Mayburn.

"I have a clever-managing store-keeper, who, with his assistant, sleeps in the place, where they have arms, two fierce dogs, and an alarm-bell loud enough to rouse the whole hamlet. Besides, our bush-rangers prefer highway robbery, or raids on the cattle, to the more dangerous attempts at house-breaking. You need fear no bush-rangers, my dear Mr. Mayburn, if you were once within the walls of my castle, where I trust to welcome you speedily. Now I wish you to look at the beautiful variety of timber trees which I have left standing as ornaments to my spacious park."

It was amongst these varied and extraordinary trees that the cavalcade were now passing. Several varieties of the *Eucalyptus* and the palm tribe, with their bare tall trunks and crested heads, were mingled with white or golden-blossomed acacias; the *Hibiscus*, peculiar to Australia; the drooping grass-tree; and one spreading fig-tree stood like a natural temple, with its pillar-like roots entwined with elegant creeping plants, with a grace beyond the reach of art. Beneath these trees the turf was resplendent with spring flowers, on which were quietly grazing flocks of white sheep, supplying the place of the aristocratic deer. As they issued from the woodland upon a grassy glade, sloping gently to the banks of the river, Charles rode forward to announce the glad tidings at Daisy Grange, which was now in sight on a pretty eminence, backed by higher hills, which stretched beyond into gray mountains. As they rode slowly forward on their worn-out horses, Mr. Mayburn was lost in admiration of the curious and happily-blended trees, and Edward Deverell said, —

"The names given by the colonists to these new and remarkable trees are puzzling and inapplicable. This tree, named by them the red cedar, is certainly not a cedar; though it is very useful, being our best timber tree, the wood resembling mahogany. The apple-tree bears no fruit, and has no claim whatever to the tantalizing name. The rose-wood, so called from its delicate perfume, is a kind of *Meliaceæ*, the fruit of which is uneatable. Then we have the cherry, *Exocarpus*, the fruit of which is useless, and peculiarly unlike the dear old cherry of England, with which, however, I trust to regale you in a few months. I can already discover the white blossoms of the tree peeping over my garden walls; and I propose that we give these tired horses to the men, and walk up the hill, that you may contemplate leisurely the imposing appearance of my baronial hall."

But however Edward Deverell might depreciate his mansion, the distressed wanderers regarded its appearance with admiration and delight as they passed over the sloping lawn, laid out with excellent taste in *parterres* of gay-colored flowers rising from the green turf, which was enamelled with the daisies of England; and saw the pretty house which offered them shelter after fifteen months of wandering.

The building, though entirely of wood, was picturesque and spacious. It was surrounded by a large garden, beyond which were raised the large storehouse; stables, and farm-buildings. Along the front of the house was a broad veranda, supported by columns, entwined with roses, honeysuckles, and the well-loved creeping flowers of England, now bursting into blossom; while the large portico was curtained with draperies of the rich flowering climbers of Australia—the convolvulus, the curious passion-flower, and other graceful unknown plants, to stimulate the curiosity of the botanists.

But it was not at this moment that all the beauties of the Grange were observed, for the hospitable doors stood open, and the agitated party were hurried into the cool and spacious hall, where Mrs. Deverell and her smiling daughter waited to welcome Edward and his unexpected companions.

CHAPTER XXXIV

The excitement of the reception was great: such screams of wonder and delight! so many tears at the thoughts of the trials and sufferings of the wanderers and so much laughter at their tattered condition! Then succeeded such haste and bustle to procure immediate aid to restore to them the comforts of which they had been so long deprived, and to spread the hospitable board with the refreshments so long untasted.

It was only by interjections and extorted answers that any details of their trials were known at first. It was necessary that they should be restored to the likeness of civilized beings; and the servants vied with their master and mistress in providing food and raiment for the needy.

"Tell me, dear Emma," said Margaret, as she brushed her dishevelled hair and arrayed herself in a clean muslin dress belonging to her friend,— "tell me if you have still, and unmarried, the pretty dairy-maid, Susan Raine, who accompanied you from England. One of our faithful attendants, though rude and unpolished, will be broken-hearted if he does not find his Susan here."

"But surely, Margaret," answered Emma, "you are not speaking of the graceless convict, Wilkins? You alarm me, for the good girl has told me her whole history; and, though she is unwilling to allow it, there is no doubt the man behaved basely in inducing her to come over from England to join him, only to find the worthless fellow had absconded."

"But let me explain his conduct to you, Emma," said Margaret; "let me tell you his story of sins and repentance and then I hope you will consent to be his mediator and friend."

Then, before they descended to join the rest, Margaret told her friend all the circumstances of Wilkins's temptation, fall, and happy reformation after having been thrown amongst them; and this was the first part of the adventures of the travellers that was related at Daisy Grange. And when the girls told Mrs. Deverell this tale of trials, she promised that Susan, who was now engaged in the dairy, should have the unexpected event properly revealed to her before she was introduced to her much-lamented friend.

The travellers scarcely recognized each other in their amended appearance, for which they had been indebted to the wardrobes of their friends; and they now proceeded to the large dining-room, where the table was spread with the plenty of an English home. Beef and mutton from the fields; fowls from the poultry-yard; pastry made by Emma; fruit and vegetables from the garden, and cream from the dairy. To these homely luxuries was added home-brewed ale from the barley grown on the settlement, which Edward Deverell said must satisfy his guests for some time, till his vines produced him grapes fit to make wine.

In the mean time Jenny and Ruth, with Baldabella and her child, had been properly cared for by the maid-servants of the establishment, who were in exuberant spirits at the novelty of visitors, and especially such wonderful and amusing visitors, who could tell them such strange tales of their travels; and even Baldabella in time got over her shyness, under the pressing hospitality of the reception; and little Nakinna was in ecstasies at the novelties she beheld and the dainties which she now first tasted. Wilkins moped in a corner in deep distress till his friend Hugh came to him, who insisted on his shaving and dressing himself neatly, and who then accompanied him to the dairy, where Susan, already acquainted with his story by Emma, was sitting weeping, but quite ready to receive and pardon the repentant man; and the mirth and festivity of the servants' hall were complete when the reunited pair joined the party.

It was late before the wanderers had recounted their adventures; and they all fully enjoyed the luxury of beds, after being so long accustomed to the open air, though the boys declared sleeping in an enclosed room was rather confining. Next morning, after a breakfast of coffee and cream, with all the other good things of the farm, they set out to see the hamlet, which was to become in time the town of Deverell. This hamlet stood about a quarter of a mile from the Grange, and consisted of a long row of wooden huts, thatched with bark, and painted green; each stood apart in a pretty garden, and each had behind it about an acre of land fenced round, where a cow, and sometimes a sheep or two, were grazing; every thing looked clean, orderly, and prosperous.

From the cottages to the river it was not more than three or four hundred yards, and before them was a green, in the midst of which was an enclosure that contained a neat stone-built church, with its low tower and bell to summon the congregation to church.

Mr. Mayburn was moved even to tears at the sight of this temple of God in the remote wilds; he seized the hand of Deverell, and said, "May Heaven bless you, my son! tell me whom you expect to fulfil the duties of this holy place."

"We have but just completed the most difficult and important work we have yet undertaken," answered Deverell. "The stone has been brought from our own quarry; but the labor of cutting and building was great and tedious. Our people are, however, pious and industrious, and they gladly worked extra hours to raise the place of worship they pined for. I have ever proposed to wait for you to be our priest, my good father; and month after month I have expected letters from you. For some of the graceless crew of the *Golden Fairy,* who escaped in the boats, reached Adelaide; and when they reported the vessel to be destroyed by fire, they asserted that you and your family had been taken up by an Indiaman. My plan was, as soon as I had heard from you where you were settled, to write to beseech you to join me. It is only during the last month that, afflicted and disappointed by your long silence, I have reluctantly turned my thoughts to the necessity of searching for another minister; and I was on the eve of setting out on a long journey to consult our worthy bishop, when the raid of the bush-rangers called me away to recover my property. Now Heaven has sent you to us, may I not, then, venture to hope that you are ours for life?"

"For life, Edward Deverell," answered Mr. Mayburn. "I am content and happy to remain with you; and I feel sure my children are determined to do the same. Teach them to be useful and happy as you are; and allow us to form part of your new colony."

"Huzza!" cried Hugh; "but you must grant us allotments to build cottages on, Governor Deverell."

"You shall hear all my plans," answered Deverell. "In the first place, you must all be our guests till dwellings are provided; the Grange is large enough for a city hotel. We will begin by building a handsome manse for our worthy pastor, with a large and convenient museum, which everybody must try to furnish with wonderful birds and eggs, and all the natural curiosities of Australia. I can spare volumes of my own to fit up the library, till we can procure all that are needed from Sydney."

"Delightful!" said Margaret. "I long to see you begin."

"Then we must have a house and workshop for our friend Jack," continued Deverell; "and constitute him head carpenter of Deverell. On your recommendation, I will venture to employ Wilkins as a stock-keeper; he shall be placed at the dairy-house, which the prudent Susan shall manage; and they shall have a good allotment, with cows and pigs of their own, to encourage them to prudence and industry. As for your female followers, Nurse Wilson, Ruth, and the native woman and child, they must remain with us, at least till the parsonage-house is completed, and Mr. Mayburn wishes to found his household."

"I propose, Edward," said Margaret, "that, if you do not object, I should teach some of the little girls of the hamlet—I see you have a number who are peeping at us from the cottages; then Nakinna will learn with them, and soon be a little English girl in all but complexion."

"That is just what I expected from you, Margaret," answered Deverell; "and Emma will be delighted to have such an associate. On this pretty spot, my brother Charles proposes to build a good house for himself, that he may be near his patients, who, I am happy to say, are few. He intends, when his house is ready, to go down to Sydney, and bring thence a wife to preside over it. He has fixed on a very charming young orphan girl, who, with her two young sisters that will accompany her, will form a most agreeable addition to our society."

"That is quite right," said Mr. Mayburn. "I rejoice to hear of his intention. And you, my dear Edward—would it not be also desirable that you should bring some lady suitable to you to this pleasant abode? If you have really resolved to pass your days here, it is your duty to marry."

"Do you think so, my very dear friend?" answered Deverell. "Then I leave the affair in your hands; you must kindly select a bride for me."

"I, my dear Edward!" exclaimed Mr. Mayburn. "I that have ever lived so much out of the world, and that am now a perfect solitary. I am actually acquainted with no young ladies in the world but your sister and my own child."

"Perhaps, papa," said Gerald archly, "Edward would be satisfied to take Margaret."

"How exceedingly absurd you can be, my dear boy," said Mr. Mayburn; then, after a few minutes' consideration, he added: "The thought never occurred to me before; it is not an absurd idea. I really do not see why such a pleasant arrangement might not be."

Margaret fled from the delicate discussion, and Edward Deverell then assured Mr. Mayburn, that not only he should be satisfied to take Margaret, but that he had never thought of any other person; as everybody but Mr. Mayburn understood long ago.

Then Margaret had to be asked if she would consent to be the mistress of that comfortable and happy household, to which she agreed, providing Mrs. Deverell and Emma would still continue to share the pleasures and duties of her home. And Edward told her all his plans for extending the population of his colony, and regulating it according to the laws of England and the commands of God. The great hall was, when needed, a hall of justice, and his people knew they were amenable to the law as much as if they lived in England.

"You should see how grave I look when I am seated on my throne of office, Margaret," said Deverell: "I must have Mr. Mayburn and Arthur on the bench in future, to give more dignity to my court. And now I must show you a domain which will be especially your own—my gardens, orchards and vineyards."

No labor or expense had been spared to enrich the gardens with all the fairest products of Australia and England. Conservatories and hot-houses were not needed in this charming climate, where the most delicate flowers and choicest fruits reached perfection in the open air. The rich blossoms of the apple, peach, apricot, and nectarine were now glowing on every side, and the trees, though so young, gave promise of abundant fruit; and the fragrance of the strawberry beds proclaimed the fruit to be ripe. Margaret was delighted with all she saw, and astonished at the thought of the labor and perseverance that must have been used.

A long avenue was shaded with the broad and luxuriant leaves of the vine, on which small bunches of grapes were already formed, a young crop, but giving promise of the rich vintage future years would bring.

"When my vines have reached maturity," said Deverell, "I shall require all the heads and the hands I can command, in order to make good wine from my own vineyard, of which, if God spare me, I have no fear. And I hope, Margaret, you are pleased with the delicate and fragrant blossoms of my orange-trees. They are yet but low shrubs; but I trust we shall live to see them tall and productive trees."

But it required many pleasant days, and many rambles about the domain, to see all that had been done, and all that it was proposed to do.

Mr. Mayburn's new dwelling was planned and immediately commenced, orchards and gardens were marked out, and a list of fruit-trees and seeds made out. Jack was in his element, superintending the cutting down of timber trees, and then manufacturing them into tables and chairs, and other useful furniture, to his heart's content.

"It's a great comfort, Mr. Arthur," said he, as his three young friends stood near him in his new workshop. "It's a great comfort to have a good chest of tools again, and that thief, Peter, no longer here to make off with them; and to be working at good jobs that we shall not have to run away and leave behind us, as we had to do when those ugly black fellows were always hanging at our heels."

"But, Jack," answered Hugh, "do you know that Mr. Deverell has a number of those black fellows employed on his estate, who not only wear clothes and live in huts, but speak English, behave quietly and honestly, and attend prayers regularly with the other work-people. Baldabella is very glad to meet with the native women, who are not *jins* here, but wives; she certainly holds herself a little above them, but she condescends to teach them decorum and the manners of society. We are all to be employed in the schools immediately, and then you will see what wonders papa and Arthur and Margaret will effect among these poor natives."

"Well, Master Hugh," answered Jack, with a certain air of incredulity, "I hope, by God's help, it may turn out as you say; but you'll not get Wilkins to believe such a thing. He hates blacks like toads, and always did. There's Susan, however, she is a quiet, good lass; but she has a good spirit, and maybe she may win her good man to think better of them. But, Mr. Arthur, now you are at your proper work among books, and Master Hugh and Master Gerald, they'll be riding about on the land, I shall not see much of you; there's no need for any of you to take up a hammer now."

"Your workshop will always be a favorite resort, depend on it, Jack," said Arthur; "but I am going to read hard for the next year, to make up for lost time. Then papa intends me to go to England, to be entered at one of the universities."

"And to return to us the Reverend Arthur Mayburn," said Gerald, "ready to help papa, and, I should say, to marry little Emma."

"But I shall always come and help you, Jack, when I have time," said Hugh; "we should all be mechanics here, in case of vicissitudes. My particular pursuit will be to study medicine with Charles Deverell, to be fitted for the second doctor when our colony shall be so much increased that two are required. Gerald is to be farmer, and hunter, and game-keeper, and ornithological assistant to papa; and then, I think, Jack, we shall form such a pleasant, cosy family circle, that we shall none of us feel any inclination 'to take to the bush.'"

"Farewell to the cowardly bush-rangers," said Gerald. "They never dare face such a band of heroes. I shall be head ranger myself; and on grand occasions I shall call you all around me for a field-day, to beat the bushes, and keep up our character of successful Kangaroo Hunters."